The Exiles

The Exiles

A NOVEL

Allison Lynn

NEW HARVEST
HOUGHTON MIFFLIN HARCOURT
BOSTON   NEW YORK
2013

This edition published by special arrangement with Amazon Publishing

Amazon and the Amazon logo are trademarks of Amazon.com, Inc. or its affiliates.

For information about permission to reproduce selections from this book,
write to Permissions, Houghton Mifflin Harcourt Publishing Company,
215 Park Avenue South, New York, New York 10003.

www.hmhbooks.com

Library of Congress Cataloging-in-Publication Data
Lynn, Allison.
The exiles : a novel / Allison Lynn.
pages cm
"New Harvest."
ISBN 978-0-544-10210-1
1. Family secrets — Rhode Island — Fiction. 2. Rhode Island — Fiction. I. Title.
PS3612.Y544E95 2013
813'.6 — dc23   2013001714

Printed in the United States of America
DOC 10 9 8 7 6 5 4 3 2 1

For Mike

How wild are our wishes, how frantic our schemes of happiness when we first enter on the world!

— THOMAS CARLYLE

IT'S 5:10 P.M. AND the bay is a hazy blue, the sky a hint of orange, the land full of promise, promise, promise. Cars creep across the bridge as if pulled by the force of that promise itself. Look, sailboats! Hark, a resort hotel. Ho there, bloated gulls line up along the bridge's side rails and point their beaks toward the traffic, guiding the way. In three days the high season will be over and Newport's ice cream vendors, trinket traders, and yachtsmen will crawl deep into their off-season dens to hibernate. Off-season: the beach's sand will turn gray and flat overnight; the historic mansions will offer tours only two days a week; boats will be pulled from the water.

Atop the bridge's crest, a Jeep Grand Cherokee — an all-American car, a New World fortress-on-wheels — begins its slow tumble toward the far shore. The Cherokee is jam-packed. File boxes, duffels of clothing, a Snickers wrapper on the floor, two deflated AeroBeds in the wayback, the remnants of a vitamin drink spilled on the dashboard, a sleeping child stashed in a car seat behind the driver. Nowhere is promise felt like inside this mobile homestead. The Jeep's high-gloss grill nearly crushes against the slow-moving Saab ahead.

Emily leans her elbow against the Cherokee's passenger-side window and watches the mast of a smooth-sailing sloop cut through the crisp harbor below. Two lightweight kayaks follow in the sloop's wake, the kayaks' narrow hulls reflecting the sunlight like viperfish. Emily knows that this day isn't so bright elsewhere. Further down the coast, where the Cherokee began today's journey, the landscape is overcast and downcast with smog and dust and oppression. Down there, autumn smells metallic and stale.

In the other direction, up the coast and deep into New England, the fall stings: They've already had a first frost this year, and it's only two weeks into October.

But *here* there are colors on the trees and a stillness to the water and land up ahead.

And this bridge! Emily loves bridges. The view from the top; the moment spent not here nor there, indebted to neither coast. It is almost four years to the day from the first time she drove over a bridge with Nate. The Third Avenue Bridge, in a taxi with scratched and foggy windows. Nate and Emily were fresh off separate red-eye flights and both reeked of airplane. Emily had grinned and shuddered and said, her voice groggy, "Man, I love bridges."

"Especially the Third Avenue," Nate replied, "cheap bastard-child of the Triborough."

They were strangers then.

Today, safe in the air-conditioned tank-of-a-Jeep, Nate breathes easily behind the wheel. He pushes his sunglasses to the top of his head, alternates his foot from brake to gas to brake, and steals a glance at Emily and at the boy in back.

In front of Nate, to the left, on the north side of the shore, painted wooden residences stand erect against the harborfront. He, too, is thinking about the Third Avenue. He'd saved twenty bucks by sharing that cab with a stranger — albeit an attractive, youngish female stranger toting world-weary luggage and a coffee — and has gained a son by her in the years since. Not a great financial trade, he smiles now. He has the kid's college tuition to pay down the line and plenty of expensive toys the tyke will want even sooner. Nate watches enough TV to know that the erector sets of his own childhood have been replaced by high-tech gaming systems and $700 snowboards. He'll deal with those issues when the time comes, if the time comes. For now, the boy himself is like a gift. Precious and beautiful, completely unexpected and easily broken.

"Hey. Hey!"

Emily's voice and a brief thud come at the same instant.

Nate slams his foot on the brake only to realize that the car is already at a standstill, given the nonexistent pace of the bridge's traffic.

"Oh my god," Emily says softly.

It takes Nate a moment to place the commotion. He follows Emily's gaze to the hood of the car, directly in front of her. A warbler, tufted gray and no larger than Nate's fist, lies still. His beak is an inch from the windshield.

Nate and Emily both take their eyes off the bird and whip their heads around to the backseat. The boy, Trevor, is safe. Oblivious, he continues to sleep.

Emily finds her voice again. "Did you see it?" she asks. "Oh my god."

"I didn't see a thing. I was looking at the shore. I was in a daze, I think – "

"It came straight for the windshield. Right at it like a bullet. Like he'd been shot out of a bird cannon. Imagine if we'd been moving." She begins to lower her window, as if she might reach out to the bird, summoning it. But, then, the warbler slowly stretches his wings, the feathers stiff, laden down with the salt air. Hesitantly, and then with more confidence, he takes flight. The bird is gone. Traffic slowly starts moving again.

Nate steers with one hand and reaches out past Emily with

the other. He touches the inside surface of the windshield, feeling the spot where the bird must have crashed. The impact hasn't even left a mark. "Did that really just happen?" he asks.

"I saw it with my own eyes," Emily says with a nervous laugh. Outside her window, the gulls, stiff on their perches, seem to be looking right at her. She is guilty; she has maimed one of their own. Nate lowers his window, too, and lets the smell of the outdoors waft through the front seat. Salt and dirt and those turning leaves. Steadily now, without stopping, the car is moving forward. They are just about to the far end of the bridge. The sky is growing pinker. It is almost day's end. It is nearly time to start over.

PART I

Friday

CHAPTER 1

Loser

NATE BEDECKER STUMBLED as he stepped out of the Jeep. He briefly, embarrassingly (though no one was looking — he'd checked with a quick sweep of his eyes) tripped over the reedy thatch of grass that bulged above the Newport curb. Three hours of driving and he'd forgotten how to use his legs. It was like old age, being thirty-eight: His muscles had no staying power anymore; the first steps he took after rising from bed each morning were a chore, his knees cracking and his ankles turning. Should he be worried? That question hovered each time his muscles strained beyond their comfort zone. He was fine, he told himself. He was normal. As proof, he had only to glance at his friends, a ready control group of hipsters and sad sacks, singletons and proud poppas, travel addicts, hedge fund honchos, and workaholic captains of industry who happened to be Nate's own age. Every single one of them was showing signs of wear. En masse, they were losing their stamina, their hair, their ability to digest dairy.

It was inevitable, these slow-motion side effects of aging.

What Nate worried about, instead, was the onset of more acute ailments. He was on the constant lookout for sudden muscle twitches and the wham-bang of a memory lapse, symptoms of a deeper physiologic flaw waiting to emerge. So far, Nate appeared to be okay. His handshake remained strong. He usually held firm footing when he walked. Today's stumble, he told himself, was simply a product of the long drive.

"Whoa boy, we're not in Kansas anymore," Emily said, walking around the car to where Nate stood. Her eyes were on the shingle (*Robert Daugherty, Esq.*) jammed into the lawn to their left. This was as close to downtown as a person could get in Newport, and yet the square, clapboard office building had a shingle hung outside. And a picket fence. Around Nate, the town loomed in various shades of elm and weathered brick.

"He's a solo operator?" Emily asked.

"He's got a secretary and an intern," Nate said, shaking out his legs. Ferguson and Neiman, the two senior partners at Nate's new office, had used Daugherty for their own house sales and recommended him unconditionally. "Ferguson and Neiman say he's the best."

Ferguson and Neiman also said, insistently, that Nate wouldn't regret this move, this complete upending of his and Emily's life from high-rise Manhattan to scenic Rhode Island, a place that Nate hadn't, ever, expected to call home. He hadn't honestly expected to leave Manhattan. Not yet, at least. New York had become a security blanket, wrapping him and Emily in tight, keeping them close to their friends, to reliable restaurants, twenty-four-hour emergency services, and a top-notch gym on their block. *Security* was the wrong word for it, though, given the price that it all cost. Their life savings and then some. Last year, rent for their apartment passed the $5,000-a-month mark, and the cramped two-bedroom didn't boast any luxuries. No washer-dryer, no fireplace, no outdoor space, no second bathroom. They were thankful simply to have an elevator in the building and a daytime doorman to help lug in the baby supplies.

It was staggering when Nate thought about it, though he tried not to: Post-tax they were paying more than $60,000 a year in rent and had no equity to show for it. Other than the Jeep, which he'd spent $300 a month to park in a bargain lot by the East River, he and Emily owned nothing except an expensive New York lifestyle in which even the simple pleasure of eating out with friends — something they'd given up finally, making pathetic excuses every time they were invited to a restaurant — could cause a significant crater in their bank accounts. For the past two years they'd been skating just above disaster, putting on a good face at parties, trying not to eye their neighbors' effortless lives with envy. "Do you know how much Okite countertops *cost?*" Emily remarked to Nate, in a stunned whisper, when they'd spent the weekend at his officemate's beach house in June. The bungalow's kitchen had two separate wine refrigerators and an induction cooktop that had been shipped in from Denmark.

"Normal people can't afford to live here anymore," Sam Tully said last winter at the Belkins' awkward, tepid Christmas party. "Unless you're making $600K a year, you're priced out of the real-estate market. You're better off living in Jersey."

The proclamation hit Nate with a thwack, as if he'd been found out. On Wall Street, there were only heroes and also-rans, and after fifteen years in M&A, Nate was clearly not one of the anointed. He was hundreds of thousands of dollars a year behind ($450K to be exact, but who was counting?) the guys in his class who were earning that $600k, the guys who would eventually make managing director. Some of them already *had.* Nate, meanwhile, was pulling in a base-level salary and negligible bonus – not quite enough to maintain a lifestyle that got more expensive by the week. The goal then, as he saw it, was to get out before he turned into a joke, a poverty-ridden hanger-on. He'd seen the older also-rans, the smart ones, leave Wall Street for in-house positions at reputable corporations or for smaller banks, in Chicago and Houston. Each year there was an international crew, too, affably unexceptional associates who transferred to Venezuela or Singapore. Word had it that anyone could make managing director in Singapore – but the title didn't mean much there. It was like grade inflation in college.

In truth, it didn't matter where you went. The aim for the middle-feeders was simply to get out of their dead-end Wall Street jobs while they still had something to offer. "Choose the path of least embarrassment," Nate's father, George Bedecker, used to tell his sons on the rare occasion that he happened to be in the room with them. "Guard your reputation and flaunt your skills," he'd tell the eight-year-old Nate. "They're your only valuable assets."

What about your family? Nate always wanted to ask. What about valuing the people you live with? On the nights when George was home, young Nate went to bed with his radio on, sports scores and play-by-plays, so that the last voice he heard before falling asleep wasn't his father's. If Nate died in his slumber, if a nuclear winter or an alien invasion or a fatal mystery virus hit the Bedecker house during the night, he'd die with the sound of a Cleveland Indians home run in his head, not his dad's misplaced aphorisms. Thirty years later, though, it was the old man's voice that resonated when Nate got the call about an opportunity in Newport. His was the advice that Nate followed when he chose to save both his reputation and his bank account by jumping ship from Manhattan and taking the position.

The job was with a young fund being run by two older, established money managers whose flagship was in Boston. They'd needed a new associate, preferably with Wall Street experience, to man their Newport satellite office. Nate was an ideal candidate. He had the experience (he was decent at his work, simply not the best in New York) and the incentive to move into a smaller pond. Halfway through the interview process he began to truly covet the job, knowing in his heart that it was his chance to leave the rat race, to lay down roots in the kind of place where he'd be ahead of the game from the start, where lawyers protected their interests with nothing but kind words and a picket fence. He and Emily would be able to live large, or at least respectably, in Rhode Island. If nothing else, they'd be able to pay off their bills every month. That was the goal, Nate realized, a modest goal yet nearly impossible to attain in New York City. So now he stood outside a Newport real-estate lawyer's office, watching his legs for spasms (none, he was *fine*) and preparing to fetch the keys for his own first home: a '60s-era faux-Victorian that sat wedged on a postage-stamp lot with a wonky plastic swing set in the backyard.

Emily stepped closer to the lawyer's squat office building, just a door down from where they had parked. "This looks like the saltbox my grandfather lived in when I was a kid," she said.

"It probably way outdates your grandfather. We're in the historic district, I think."

Nate opened the back door of the Cherokee. He leaned in, unhooked Trevor from the car seat, and hoisted the boy into the New England air. Trevor squirmed silently, compressing his body into a small ball, still waking up from his ride-long nap. When he finally opened his eyes, he quickly closed them again and held one of his small, tight fists up against his face, apparently unsure of what he was seeing. *All that grass!* Trevor had spent his entire ten-month childhood in the city and was most at ease in small, enclosed spaces. He was already detail-oriented, more captivated by the tiny than the grand, more entranced by the wisps of yarn that frayed from his baby blanket than by sweeping vistas. So while other parents dreamed about moving to the country for their children, Nate worried that this relocation would traumatize his son. The boy had just learned to navigate their apartment, crawling from the kitchen to the living room (stopping to ponder each crevice in the wood floor) without scraping his knees on the high molding. Occasionally Nate himself lay on the hardwood floor of their now-gone Manhattan home, trying to get his own glimpse of Trevor's perspective, but instead all he ever saw was his own childhood, his own skewed outlook.

"Hold on —" Emily came to Nate's side by the Jeep's back door. She fished the car keys out of his pocket and popped open the hatchback, revealing all of their goods to the Newport street. They'd densely stuffed the trunk with everything they'd need until the movers arrived in a week, squeezing their belongings into the car and the air out as if preparing their property for pickling. Emily slid Trevor's stroller — a Bugaboo they'd nicknamed Ollie, as if it were their other child — from its tight spot at the top of the pile.

"Goddamn!" Emily said as the stroller thudded loudly to the pavement. High-tech didn't mean lightweight. "This thing is going to kill us one of these days." She slammed the trunk shut. Trevor continued to squirm in Nate's arms as Emily propped Ollie open. Straightening the wheels, snapping the seat into the chassis — it was all second nature to them by now. Emily slipped the car keys back into Nate's pocket as he lowered the boy into the carriage.

• • •

Bob Daugherty stood in the door to his office.

"Just in time. Get the hell inside," he said, waving Nate, Emily, and the stroller through the entryway. He was all kinetic energy, not the calm rock he'd been the few times Nate had spoken to him previously.

"It's good to be here," Nate said. He followed Bob past the reception area, where the secretary's seat was deserted. The staff must have been sent home already for the holiday weekend.

In the inner office, Bob sat behind the desk and Nate lowered himself into a chair in front of it. The desk was ornate, constructed from traditional heavy mahogany, with worn leather accents. The walls of the office – other than the narrow sliver by the door, which was adorned with Bob's framed diplomas (Bates, UConn) – were erratic, crammed with Japanese silk screens and odd oversize watercolors of Chinese lanterns.

"Hey, Em?" Nate called to Emily, who sat in the empty reception room with Trevor. "Come in here." She and Nate were equal owners of the house, both names on the deed. They might not have a marriage license, but now they had a kid and a house to bind them. It was the real thing.

"Hey," Emily said as she slunk into the office. "Everything set?"

"Everything's fine. Glad you made it in. Holiday traffic can be a bitch in this town," Bob said. Nate relaxed.

"It feels like we spent hours on that bridge," Emily said. "We pretty much eased our way into Newport, but we're here, at least. We hit a bird."

"It's beautiful, though, that view coming in," Nate said, giving Emily a brief glance. Bob didn't need to know about the bird. The bird was fine. "We could have timed it better than Friday at five, for sure," he said.

"For sure," Bob repeated with a tight grin. He passed a folder across the desk and leaned forward, sharp elbows on mahogany. "It's all in there. Your copies of the paperwork, two sets of spanking-new keys. I'll be heading away for the weekend, immediately, to be frank, so if you have questions, ask now. Give it all a good read." On the two front corners of Bob's desk sat sprawling bonsai trees. Miniature, shrunken topiaries, like Charlie Brown Christmas trees, hopelessly stunted.

Nate slid the papers out of the envelope and palmed the keys. The papers were warm, but the keys were cold and light, as if crafted from a space-age alloy. He quickly eyed the contract (they'd already combed through it carefully) and then handed it to Emily, who gave it her own compulsory once-over. If the sellers had snuck an insidious clause into the text, Nate and Emily weren't going to catch it today.

"I think we've already got this; it looks great," Nate said. "Shit, the house is ours."

Bob nodded. "You own a home, kids. Newport's newest residents, for what it's worth. That and a quarter will get you, well, nothing."

Nate laughed, halfheartedly. Ferguson and Neiman had worked hard to sell Nate on the town, as well as the job. Though both partners lived in Newport only on the weekends, they'd lauded the local school systems (public and private), the summer boating season, the audacious diversity of the year-round residents, and each had said to Nate, separately, "You, of all people, will be impressed by Newport's architecture." They hadn't mentioned Nate's father by name, never stated outright that the thrill of possibly working with George Bedecker's son had perhaps, maybe, spurred them to interview Nate in the first place, but Nate understood. He was the son of a heavyweight. Ever since Frank Gehry completed the Guggenheim in Bilbao and

Santiago Calatrava torqued his first skyscraper, architects had become rock stars again. They unabashedly lusted after the awe that Frank Lloyd Wright had inspired more than fifty years ago, and when that awe proved elusive they each settled for popular acclaim, instead. Nate's father had been raised in Rhode Island, not far from here. Yet when he first hung out his shingle in the 1960s, he claimed Cleveland as his home base. From there (and later Chicago), he'd spent the last half century designing structures that were minimalist and industrial and dateless — though some critics argued otherwise — and functional. For a time he'd been well known for this. He'd spawned the short-lived neo-Bauhaus movement, erecting angular university libraries and stacked-box office buildings through which tens of thousands of anonymous businessmen continued to pass each day. But what had George built lately? Nate hadn't seen much.

Nate hadn't, in truth, been looking. He worked hard to keep his eyes averted from the architecture scene, but with that one line, "You, of all people, will be impressed by the architecture," George's presence entered Nate's new work life the way it entered all of his relationships, the same way that the senior Bedecker's buildings were specifically designed to cast imposing shadows over their neighboring constructs. In contrast, Nate and Emily's new house was small and compact and not showy at all. Any decent architect would dismiss it out of hand. It was *too real life*. It was *derivative*. It was *derivative of derivatives*. Nate loved it.

It was in this new home that tonight, after Nate and Emily stepped over the threshold for the first time, Nate was going to talk to her about his history. He'd promised himself that he would finally open up to her about the way he checked his body for shakes every day. He'd talk to her about how, last week, he'd briefly felt his emotions grow irrationally out of control. The movers had been in the apartment at the time, tossing his stereo components through the air. So Nate's outburst might simply have been a rational response. Or it might have been a sign that he was sick. *Sick.* He liked the word's implications of not merely physical ailment but psychological perversion as well. It felt like a joke. A laugh: that was something Nate could handle.

Nate took the contract back from Emily and returned the papers and keys to the envelope. He opened his mouth to say something insignificant, anything, to Bob. "Hey," he said, like a dimwit. "Okay."

"Ready to move in?" Emily said.

Nate nodded and stood. He said to the lawyer, "Thanks so much. That was easy."

"It's nothing," said Bob. "Really, my pleasure. It's my job. You need anything, just call. Not this weekend, of course," he grinned, and Nate noticed a packed suitcase in the corner of the office. A canvas tennis bag with the racket handle poking out of a pocket was balanced atop the luggage. "It's hell over Columbus Day around here, frankly a carnival. Tourists will be leaching out of the woodwork for the next three days. I'll be back on Tuesday when the commotion dies down."

As they left the office, Nate tried to focus on only the simple tasks in their immediate future (get to the Jeep, strap Trevor into his car seat, drive to their house) rather than their intermediate future (reaching that house). He kept his eyes on the steady tread of his running-shoe-clad feet, fixating on the sneakers' soles, on the spots where the tawny rubber splayed beneath his toes. He barely noticed his surroundings as Emily pried open the building's front door and pushed the stroller ahead of her, as they walked outside, as he helped her carry Trevor and his Ollie down the stoop and strode another fifty feet to where they'd left the car. By the time Nate looked up and refocused, he saw with a dull thud that the street outside Bob's office was empty.

"Please," he heard Emily say softly, as if afraid of her own voice. It was dead silent, a sudden ghost town in front of them. Even the trees stood motionless in the evening air. The yard surrounding their lawyer's office was littered with small elms and one full-grown maple that towered strong over the bare street. What happened to all that holiday traffic? Tourists leaching out of the woodwork? *What happened to their car?* Nate looked back up at the office building and then, with his eyes, traced the path to where they stood now. They were less than twenty yards from Bob's door.

"Please, Nate," Emily said, her voice nearly inaudible. "Tell me this is not where we parked the Jeep."

The space in front of the curb was empty, a gasp where the Cherokee had been. On the corner of the block, a few car lengths away, a standard steel mailbox rose up from the grass on the tree belt. Nate hadn't noticed a mailbox when they parked. It occurred to him that this wasn't where they'd left the Jeep after all. They'd parked on the next block or around the corner. Maybe they'd left the car in the narrow alley behind the lawyer's office. Wasn't there an alley back there? Nate couldn't remember. No, he *could* remember, his memory remained intact; this was the one thing he knew for sure and held onto. His brain was still running on all cylinders. This gape of pavement was exactly where they'd left the car. They'd parked right here and loaded Trevor into his Ollie and together they'd walked from this space to the office and back again. Except that now there was no car, not right here, not in front of Nate. Holy fuck.

"What the *hell?*" he said, barely louder than Emily. He rubbed the ignition key between his thumb and his forefinger, feeling its tangible weight, and then scanned the air by the curb one last time, willing the car to actually be there "Fuck. Are you kidding me?"

"Watch it," Emily caught her breath and nodded toward the Bugaboo. Trevor was finally at an age where he seemed to understand the things they said, including the filth that occasionally spewed from Nate's mouth when, for example, Nate found that his car had up and disappeared. The car, gone. Nate's skull felt crushed.

"Sorry, chief," he said, crouching to the stroller's height, trying to erase all trace of his profanity from Trevor's memory. *Shit,* it seemed he was always apologizing to his son. Ten months of apologies and counting. "Okay, little one?" Nate's six-foot-plus body was coiled to the ground, his voice thin. "Nothing for you to worry about." Trevor, silent, looked terrified, on the verge of tears. Sweat stuck his fine dark hair to his forehead in strips. From birth, the boy had been timid, appeared to flinch from the world around him. Even his smiles (and he did smile, all the time) had a knowing edge, a hint of doubt. Other people called this demeanor sweet, but it worried Nate. He tried to sanitize the world for his son, to ensure that the boy wouldn't have cause to retreat even further.

Nate took a deep breath and nearly gagged. The air smelled like suburban mulch.

"Didn't you lock the car?" Nate said, rising to his feet. Emily was standing on the pavement, in the space where the car had been.

"You're the one with the keys, Nathan. Did *you* lock the car?"

Nate winced at the *Nathan.* And at the fact that he *was* the one with the keys. Come to think of it, he remembered locking the doors, really, hearing the locks catch and the alarm activate. He could hear it as if it was just a few minutes ago. It *was* just a

few minutes ago. They'd been in Bob's office for less than half
an hour.

Behind them, the lawyer's office remained lit. It wasn't yet
6:00 p.m., but the sun was already dipping below the horizon,
turning the evening's air a flush blue-pink. Nate thought of their
attorney's digs in New York, the sterile steel conference room,
the hush of the carpeted hallways, the paralegals drinking coffee
out of recycled paper cups in the law library. A guy would get
there via cab or subway and there's no way he'd walk outside to
discover that his car had been stolen. Nate instinctively missed
those offices – he missed New York.

"Maybe it's an optical illusion," Nate said. *Maybe the car is
still right here.* Maybe he could will it.

Emily spread her arms in the air, deep into the space where
the car had been. "No car," she said softly. "No car at all."

There were no *cars*: Other than a scattering of parked vehicles, the entire street was empty. Just a space where they had left
the Cherokee, carefully checking the distance to the curb as
he parked, measuring, mentally, the correct distance (this was
it, he'd parked perfectly in one shot), before they unloaded the
Bugaboo and dutifully locked the doors (they *had!* Nate was
sure of it) and made their way inside to meet with the lawyer
and take possession of their house.

Emily stepped back up on the grass and stood next to Nate,
as if waiting for a bus. Her hand brushed his and he gave it a
quick squeeze, a Pavlovian response. Her face was so pale and
blank, as if this was simply too much for her to take in, and Nate
wanted to fix it, to make it all okay. But how? Their car was gone
and they were living in Newport where they had not a single
friend and it was about to be off-season and Nate couldn't even
offer her a toke from his pot stash because the pot was hidden

under the Jeep's front seat, stolen with the car, and he didn't want Emily to know that he still smoked, anyway, since he'd sworn to give it up when she was pregnant — and now, suddenly, breaking the street's eerie stillness, a deep-throated scream came from below, from deep within Trevor. Like ash from a volcano, the boy erupted.

Trevor's face turned red and tears welled in his eyes and saliva slipped in a steady stream out of his wide-open hollering mouth. "Please Trev, please," Nate pleaded. He bent down and unbuckled the Bugaboo's straps.

"Take a breather, captain," he said, picking up his son. He clutched Trevor tightly to his chest and, after only a minute, the screams slowed and then stopped. The boy was a sucker for the human touch. "Everything's okay, just a minor glitch in the plan," Nate said. Trevor looked poised to let loose again but Nate clutched him tightly, reining in the child's wiry limbs.

Nate had bought the Jeep new six years ago. It was his first car since high school, his first adult car. He'd paid extra for the custom foot rugs, leather seats, seat warmers, snow tires, and just ten months ago a new addition: the highest-end, safest car seat on the market. The Cherokee itself hadn't won any safety awards, but that hadn't bothered Nate when he picked it out, when he was barely into his thirties, before he knew Emily and before he thought he'd ever, even in old age, have a child. He'd loved the size of the machine. He called it a *car* or sometimes even a *truck*, afraid to say *SUV*, to be *that guy*. It used to be that the careful choice of the right word was all it took to make Nate feel secure.

Now the truck was gone. He looked down the street to his left, almost expecting to see its taillights pulling around the corner, making an escape. Or its headlights, sheepishly returning. It was just a vehicle, Nate told himself as Trevor held off on his intermittent banshee act and Emily stared hopelessly into the open air. It was just a car, but it was the one thing he'd bought and paid for outright, with cold hard cash, and outfitted to his specifications, detail by detail, until it performed as promised, no surprises, completely reliable and, in a pinch, family-friendly.

"Sorry. About the dig. Saying you hadn't locked the doors," Nate said to Emily, taking her hand, putting all three of them in human contact, Trevor to Nate to Emily. "This is just — " but what was left to say? "I didn't mean to lash out."

Across the street a yield sign stood tall and firm and sunny in its bold yellow affirmation. Emily squinted down the street. It was hot today, hot for October, hot for evening time, and the air waved above the pavement.

Then a car, so new that its glare hurt the eye, pulled up, drove past the space, and began to back into it. The compact hot rod had high-performance wheels and rust-proof weather stripping, features from the future. Its engine was nearly silent, emitting only the muted electric purr of a hybrid. The driver shut off the ignition and got out, locking the doors, Nate noted, before glancing at Nate and Emily and Trevor as if maybe he knew them. Then he turned and made his way down the sidewalk. When he was out of earshot, Emily motioned to the silver sedan. "You want me to hotwire it?" Her voice had its strength back and she appeared to be on the verge of smiling. "It seems we're owed a car."

"And then some," Nate said. Because honestly, he thought as he held Emily's hand tighter and pulled her close, the car was the least of their problems.

CHAPTER 2

The Tally

EVERYTHING IS IN THAT Jeep," Emily Latham said. She leaned toward the cop and strained to be heard over Trevor's cries. The boy's deep wails cut through the police station's surrounding din with the sporadic ceaselessness of a jackhammer. It was all too much: the wails, the buzz of the intercom overhead, the ringing of distant phones, the brush of Nate's arm against hers, the patient grin of the uniformed officer across the counter. The officer was strapping but soft, like a high school baseball coach who hadn't run the bases himself in at least a decade. Emily felt light, nearly high. "We'd packed all of our things in that Jeep."

Nate was quiet beside her. A month ago, his reticence would have surprised Emily. But now? She wasn't sure. Over the past month, Nate, who had always been so good with talk and so eager to take the lead, had gradually begun to go mute, to burrow deeper inside himself. He'd adopted a noiseless diffidence, as if he had shifted slightly, like a door off only one of its hinges. Finally, in the past week, he'd completely stopped looking Emily in the eye. She blamed stress. The move. The new job.

"Nate?" Emily pleaded as Trevor continued to wail. The boy arched against the Bugaboo's slick nylon chest restraints and screamed. The precinct's hard surfaces (linoleum on the floor, cement on the walls) amplified the noise. "Hey, Nate." Nate was the free one. Emily was fully engaged with the officer.

"You bet." Nate leaned down and lifted the boy from the stroller.

Everyone in the building was in a rush, sporting crisp uniforms and insistent tones of voice. When Emily had entered through the precinct's heavy glass front door, two uniformed cops sped past and shoved her out of the way, hard. A full arsenal hung from their belts and narrowly missed clocking the stroller and the helpless Trevor within it. Oh God! Emily had held her breath. At least she still had her child. She'd seen all the headlines, nearly weekly, it seemed. *Carjacking in Supermarket Parking Lot, Toddler Still Strapped in Backseat.* It was the epoch of public fear: carjackings, avalanches, suicide bombings, tsunamis, subway fires, lightening strikes, hurricanes. In the years since 9/11 (three years, enough time for the world to feel both semi-recovered and still tremendously perilous – enough time for Wall Street to be hitting record highs again, trumpeting the survival of capitalism with each day's closing bell) it seemed that history – both man-made and geological – was aiming to prove that survival was merely a matter of luck.

"Really, all of our things were in the car," Emily said to the cop behind the counter.

"We need to document your belongings specifically," the cop said, nodding.

"Sure," Emily said – while grabbing her ringing phone from her pocket. Instinctively she flipped it open.

Jeanne's number scrolled across the display. Nine times out of ten, when Emily's phone rang it was Jeanne. They were best friends the way people were best friends back in high school, gossiping on the phone at regular intervals as if e-mail still didn't exist. Even now, with Jeanne deep into her medical residency, the friendship hadn't suffered. It turned out that Jeanne's schedule as a resident was grueling but irregular, mirroring Emily's as a full-time mom. While Nate was at work, Emily and Jeanne had spent hours together over coffee and wine and tubs of hummus from the deli, talking about Nate and Emily's Newport move, their new house, their launch into small-city living.

"Hey," Emily said into the mouthpiece. Nate shot her a look. She shouldn't have answered her phone while dealing with the cops.

"I just got a call from Taryn Carver," Jeanne said, sounding breathless, enthused. "You heard about the Barbers?"

"Yeah," Emily said.

This morning Emily had gotten voice mails from three separate friends announcing that Anna and Randy Barber were missing a Matt Rufino painting, an oil-covered canvas the size of a square dinner plate. According to Tania Osbourne's message, the painting had been missing at least since the Barbers' party on Wednesday night, maybe earlier.

Each of the messages made Emily flinch. The Barbers' was the last party she and Nate had attended before leaving the city. The last time, for a while at least, they'd be in a room full of people they knew, in a neighborhood they could instinctively navigate, eating the kinds of thoroughbred meats and cheeses and feta-stuffed olives that had become so endemic to Manhattan. Jeanne hadn't been at the party – she was in upstate New York for the week, and for this weekend, too, at yoga camp. Jeanne wasn't in the Barbers' usual social loop, anyway, though

she and Anna had plenty of friends in common, through Emily
and Nate and a short-lived book club to which all three women
had once belonged.

"You heard about it upstate?" Emily said into the phone. Her
head throbbed but at least Trevor was quiet for the moment.

"Art-theft gossip travels fast. It's pretty unbelievable."

"I guess." But was anything really unbelievable anymore? Sci-
entists had discovered evidence of water on Mars. Grandmoth-
ers were giving birth to their own grandchildren. People spoke
to one another on phones that were plugged into nothing. Anna
and Randy Barber left a quarter-million-dollar painting leaning
unwatched against a wall in their study. How stupid could the
Barbers be? "It might not have been taken at the party." Emily
said. "Cath Oberling says there aren't any clues."

At the word *clues*, the officer across the counter glanced up.
She shook her head (*it's nothing!*) and he looked down again
and continued sorting through his stack of photocopied forms.

"I need to go," Emily said to Jeanne. "I'll call you later."

Emily smiled apologetically to the cop and felt a wheeze
coming on, her chest tightening. "Everything was in the car,"
she said again to the cop. Everything was in the car: The statement felt fake as soon as it was out of her mouth. Everything
wasn't in the car. Emily still had her phone, obviously, and
her purse, and the ridiculous stash of junk in that purse. Not
to mention all their goods that would be arriving in the moving truck next week. "Everything was in the car," she repeated
(again, again!), sounding more idiotic with each regurgitation.
She was surprised her words came out at all. The Barbers were
probably talking to the cops right now, too. Their stolen artwork
was worth more than the Jeep — by a factor of ten, at least. Even
when it came to their thefts, Nate and Emily didn't stack up.
Emily choked at the thought.

She needed to focus, to keep her head on straight. *Easier said*, she thought. Even on good days, when their Jeep hadn't been stolen and when all of New York hadn't called to gloat over their friends' stolen Rufino (because, truly, people seemed to be gloating, sad and shocked and gloating), Emily was prone to panic. Day-to-day living had made her head spin so often that she carried a full bottle of beta-blockers in her purse (oh! how easily she'd taken to calling her diaper bag a purse!). Jeanne had prescribed the blockers not in her office at the hospital but over a gossipy brunch during which she'd promised they were low-dose. Inderal was mild, Jeanne had said, recommended for performance anxiety and stage fright, not generalized nerves. That appealed to Emily. She hadn't wanted Xanax or any of the other usual suspects anyway. She'd seen friends grow dependent on those drugs, swapping them at parties and trading notes. All Emily had wanted was something to take the edge off her need to act the part. "You've got to quit carrying the weight of the world on your shoulders," Jeanne, her most ruthlessly honest friend, had advised. Jeanne had seen Emily through the tumult of college — they'd lived next to each other freshman year and seemed to be the only women in their dorm without eating disorders — and nearly two decades of traumas (all marked by panics, ranging from mild to severe) since. "Emily, you need to relax."

Relax. It was the catchword, the common parlance, the impossible to sustain cure-all. Relax. "Relax. At least you have your health," Emily's mother used to caution, coaxing Emily to take it easy each time she lambasted herself over her love life or a bad grade as a child. "There's no excuse for tears when you still have your health," her mother would say. She had a point. All Emily battled, on most days, was nerves, a small complaint. Everyone suffered from anxiety to some degree. In college

Emily had studied philosophy and religion, historical thinkers and writers of social commentary. She'd immersed herself in Rousseau and Kant and Hegel and spent half of a semester on Thomas Carlyle. Each of these men had been, in his lifetime, little more than a tightly wound nervous disorder with legs — and with a striking talent when it came to the written word. Emily had idolized Carlyle while she was an undergrad and almost went to grad school on a fellowship to study his work. Sure, Carlyle had flaws — he'd spoken out against democracy and treated his wife like a housekeeper — but looking back on it, Emily wondered if perhaps Carlyle was simply ahead of his time. Today, in the new millennium, democracy was coming apart at the seams and young women, even the educated and the criminally overeducated, were choosing housekeeping over career. Oh God, that thought could drive any woman to pop pills.

This evening, though, Emily hadn't touched her beta-blockers. What she'd felt on the street corner in the absence of their car wasn't her familiar panic, but rather an elevated sensation. She felt almost free, startlingly unencumbered. Because if moving to Newport was intended to be their escape from New York, why had they tried to bring so much of the city with them? Why had they so forcefully overstuffed the Jeep's cargo bay? (Why hadn't she left her purse in the car? she thought, momentarily wishing her bag and its contents were gone as well.) It was apt, wasn't it, the Jeep being stolen? It was payback. It was a sign that it was time to halt her furious attempts to claw her way to the top. If the Jeep theft turned out to be her only punishment, she'd be thrilled.

"We left the Jeep for only ten minutes. Fifteen at most," Nate told the cop. "We locked the doors."

"We did lock the doors, right?" Emily said. Nate had the keys.

It didn't matter. Locked or unlocked, the car was gone, with everything in it. Yes, they still had their goddamn health. And when it came down to it, Nate and Emily had plenty of *stuff*. The moving truck was packed with their furniture, suitcases of clothing, books, appliances, and Emily's shoes, or most of them. And Trevor wasn't in the car. Emily was thankful for that.

Their most private, and damning, financial papers were in the Jeep, though. They'd prepared for a snag in the house-closing process and had brought boxes of documents: tax returns, bank statements, pay stubs (what paltry numbers on those pay stubs!), a credit report, old credit card bills. And there *were* shoes in that car, including at least one brand-new pair of driving moccasins Emily couldn't afford. Handing over her Visa card at Tod's last month, she'd looked at the total and thought of all the diapers that this one pair of moccasins could buy, all of the future school lunches. She'd guiltily bought the shoes anyway, full price at $350 plus tax, and when packing for Newport she'd taken them out of the pile for the movers and stashed them in the Cherokee's backseat. She was sure she'd want them in the week before the movers arrived. She wanted to look good in her new life. Tonight those overpriced Tod's, along with the small duffels of clothing they'd packed to last the week (the things they couldn't bear to live without) were driving somewhere in a direction away from here.

As a rule, Emily rarely sank money into high-end shoes. What she coveted, most of the time, wasn't the footwear and handbags and overpriced artwork that she saw other women of her generation collect with astounding fervor. Emily appreciated good shoes, dreamed about them even (though she'd had nightmares after buying the Tod's — deep-in-the-night frights about financial insolvency, about landing destitute in a soot-covered rooming house). But what she wanted more than shoes and bags and all the other material possessions was the kind of financial assurance that friends like Tania Osbourne and Anna and Randy Barber took for granted. The designer shoes, the bags, the Rufinos: Their true value lay in their symbolism, their act as signifiers of that desired economic stability.

Back in the 1970s, Emily had seen her mother, a feminist academic, struggle as a single parent, having to pawn, once, even their outdated TV. Emily had worn hand-me-downs acquired not from same-sex relatives but from yard sales and kiddie consignment shops. Every day, she'd brought her lunch to school from home while her friends ate the mass-produced chow sold in the cafeteria, nuggets of pulverized potato and chicken served on smartly compartmentalized trays. She told her mother that she didn't mind any of this, that peanut butter trumped tater tots any day. But that hadn't been true.

A decade later, after her career finally cohered, Emily's mother began portraying the disintegration of her marriage as empowering. The woman seemed to have no recollection of the financial struggles she and her children had endured. "I don't wish divorce on you at all, ever," she had said to Emily and her brother after finally relocating the family to a spacious, if basic, apartment, "but power to the century we live in, replete with options." As for what options Emily's father chose for his postdivorce life, Emily never knew. When he died of heart failure, twenty years later, neither Emily, her mother, or brother attended the small memorial service in Albuquerque, where he had been living for more than a decade. He'd completely absented himself from their lives. Even his occasional gifts, mailed by FedEx, had ceased arriving years earlier. And today Emily hardly remembered the man. What she could still picture (and taste) in detail were those generic peanut butter sandwiches. Now that she had a child herself and had achieved at least the semblance (to the easily fooled observer) of solvency, Emily never wanted to chance landing her own family in that kind of situation.

The hopeful dream of stability was the reason Emily had passed up grad school; a history PhD would never have allowed her the luxury of financial peace of mind. In the end, it turned out that her career in experiential advertising hadn't afforded her this treasure, either. While working at the agency, she'd earned enough dough to support a small, frugal family in most cities, but in Manhattan her salary was eaten up, in a minute, by day-to-day living. After fourteen years in advertising and nearly a year off raising Trevor, she had no bread in the bank. Nate had none, either, nothing saved up at all. It was this fact that had pushed Emily over the edge.

"All of our financial records were in the car," Emily said to the cop, reality and defeat setting in. "They've got Nate's computer, too."

"Shit, and tax returns, two years of tax returns," Nate said, looking nervous. "Does this sound like a bad joke yet? Honestly, it's an identity thief's dream. Do you think you'll find the car? Will you go through it to see what's missing if it's found, or is that left up to us? It's private stuff, you know, those items in the car."

"It's car theft. We see this all the time, don't worry," the cop said, presenting them with a stack of forms and a pen.

"But the car, you're not going to, you know, rifle through it? It's completely packed with stuff right now. Seriously, it's private," Nate said. Emily winced. What was Nate so worried about? Did he think the cops were going to wear his underwear on their heads? Who cared if the police rifled through the stuff, as long as they got it back.

The cop leaned away briefly to answer a ringing phone, putting the caller on hold. "If we find the car, there's procedures we follow," he told Nate. "Whatever's left in it, if anything is left in it, you'll get back."

Nate paused and nodded, then reached for the forms with one arm while balancing Trevor in the other. The boy looked ready to burst again at any moment. If only Emily could see her son's skewed smile, just once.

"Trevor's Rasta CD was in the Jeep, in the CD player," Nate said to Emily without taking his eyes off the papers. The word *Rasta* made the boy look up in anticipation. The kid loved the CD's conga-beat versions of the Burl Ives classics; some days it was the only thing that could lull him into submission. "We're going to need to replace that as soon as we can."

"Or sooner," Emily said as she continued to steady herself against the counter. Finally she dug into her purse for the bag of dry Cheerios that she'd prepared this morning. Trevor needed to eat, no wonder he'd been putting up such a fuss. Emily rested the food on the counter and took hold of the boy, their boy, as Nate slowly and neatly completed the forms, diligently filling in the blanks, documenting all that had disappeared.

CHAPTER 3

Welcome to the Viking

A T THE HOTEL VIKING, no one was behind the check-in desk. Nate tapped his fingers on the counter and waited, conspicuously leaning across the slab of marble and looking for help. When no one showed up, he resorted to the *Ring for Service* button, lightly depressing its small plastic buzzer.

He couldn't help but notice the redundancy of the situation: He and Emily were looking for a hotel room in the town where they already owned a house, their first home. That home was a shell right now, though, devoid of furniture and the other comforts that would eventually make it inhabitable. Their original, pre-car-theft plan had been to stay at the house, anyway, during the days before their movers arrived. With that idea in mind, they'd stuffed the AeroBeds, a set of linens, and a few bath towels into the back of the Jeep. They'd even joked about it, gloating over the fact that they would be camping inside their own house. Nate had talked about how he and his brother Charlie had camped out in their family's front yard a few times as kids,

setting up sleeping bags on the hard ground beneath their living room's expansive, plate-glass windows. As Nate waited for
a check-in clerk to appear, he wondered what Charlie would
make of today's predicament. Charlie would have been able to
put a positive spin on it, to infuse their sudden state of carless-
ness with a sense of adventure. Bad times had never bogged
Charlie down, the way they did Nate. Of course, Charlie had
never really hit bad times.

Now Nate and Emily's AeroBeds and provisions were gone.
At the police station Nate had suggested that it might be fun to
stick to their plan and camp at their home regardless, spreading out on the hardwood floors (they'd conceived Trevor on a
floor in Manhattan, if they'd pegged the date right), but Emily
shook her head. They had a child now and had to act like adults.
They couldn't sleep on the floor, she'd explained. Trevor, for
one, wouldn't put up with it, and it was too late to buy new
beds tonight, since the stores were already closed. Even if stores
were open, Nate and Emily had just canceled all of their credit
cards and put holds on their bank accounts — all of their financial statements were in the Jeep, after all, putting them at risk for
identity theft and credit card fraud. Immediately after canceling
the accounts, it occurred to them to hit a bank machine, to stock
up on cash, though by then it was too late. So what did Nate
expect to buy new beds *with?* All they had, until the weekend
was over, was the money in their wallets.

Emily was right and there was no sense in arguing. The night
had been stressful enough already. After discovering the Jeep's
theft, Nate and Emily had headed back into Bob Daugherty's
office to call the cops and then followed the lawyer's directions
to the precinct, declining his offer of a ride, "since it's so close
and all." Emily and Nate took turns pushing Trevor the quarter mile to the station. The boy had remained shockingly quiet

during the walk, except for occasional bursts of dialogue featuring his favorite, and only, word. "Ba!" he'd say, or maybe "bap," effervescent, bubbling over, as if he were the first man to discover language, as if he were not the same exact child who just moments ago had been screaming like a crazy person. *Bababap!* Nate claimed the word was an attempt at Papa. Emily countered that it could almost as easily be *mama*. Or *barbarian*. Or *bastard*. That last one made Nate laugh, and Emily, too. Trevor, too young to even eat honey, declaring his station in life.

After filling out their forms and registering the theft (easier, in the end, than registering a car itself, Nate thought), they'd used a spare phone at the precinct to call a few inns where the cops had connections, brother-in-law owners and high school friends working as the concierge. The inns promised to be affordable, in Newport terms, but none of them had anything resembling a vacancy. "We book up on the holidays. There's nothing I can do, we've had a wait list all season for this weekend," one particularly sympathetic innkeeper told Nate. "Your only bet is a big hotel. The biggies get last-minute cancellations, even on the high-flow nights." Nate could have called his new bosses. They both owned multi-acre estates on the water nearby, spreads so large that undoubtedly they'd have unoccupied bedrooms, but Nate wanted to start his new career with a clean slate. Bob Daugherty had offered them help as well, but Nate turned him down. He didn't want to take a handout from a near stranger.

The cops drove them into town — Nate and Emily in the cruiser's backseat with Trevor between them, nestled in a police-issue baby seat — and left them on the Viking's doorstep. If any of the big four-stars had a cancellation and would be willing to take in this family without credit cards, it was the Viking. Nate was already in their customer database. He'd stayed at the hotel twice while interviewing for his job.

Finding a room here tonight, though, didn't look promising. The Viking's lobby was buzzing with guests who'd already checked in. A bellhop struggled to fit two rolling luggage carts into one elevator, shoving a soft duffel atop a bulging suit bag. The hotel was teeming. It wasn't merely Columbus Day weekend, it was also the final weekend of the season in Newport — the city's last hurrah. Still, there could be a vacancy. People canceled hotel rooms all the time, just as the innkeeper said. Nate had friends who were so accustomed to welshing on plans that they didn't even bother to void their reservations. They simply didn't show up to claim the rooms they'd booked and, on a regular basis, forfeited the one-night security deposit.

And Columbus Day wasn't really a holiday anymore. It had fallen out of favor and been replaced by Martin Luther King Day and other more appropriate celebrations, celebrations that didn't commemorate the cannibalization of a pristine continent by white men in tall ships. Lately, all across the United States, accountants and schoolteachers and other hardworking folk had seen Columbus Day excised from their days-off schedule as if the great Italian navigator never existed, as if the Europeans in North America had simply materialized from the earth in a late-breaking act of Darwinism: the great 1492 mutation in which, with one time-lapse generation, tadpoles wandered onto dry land and quickly evolved into men, women, and children with pale skin and a strange proclivity for eating their food with forks.

"Can I help you? Reservations?" A uniformed clerk appeared behind the counter, a lanky twenty-year-old with prepster hair and epaulets on his shoulders. Reservations, Nate had plenty of those.

"Actually, we don't have a room booked," Nate said.

The clerk raised his hands, palms to the air. "And you're looking for? A room?" the kid asked. Nate had the feeling that this guy was trained as a car valet, pressed into desk duty because of the holiday crowds. Either that or anyone could get a promotion in Newport these days. Nate smiled.

"The thing is, we hadn't expected to need one, or we'd have made a reservation," Nate said. "Our car was stolen tonight with all of our financial papers inside, and so we've had our credit cards canceled and holds put on our bank accounts. The police thought you might be able to help us out with a room." When the clerk still didn't respond, Nate continued, "I stayed here last month, so you should have my name in your system. I'm a loyal customer. You should have a record of me being an upstanding guy and all." Nate's tone was sweet and accommodating. If this didn't work they'd be out on the street.

"You don't have credit cards?" The kid gave Nate a once-over. He'd probably never met anyone without a credit card before. He'd probably never met anyone without an iPod and an Xbox, either. Meet Nate, Mr. Suddenly Unencumbered. His iPod had been stolen with the Jeep. He'd forgotten to mention that on the police report.

"I have a copy of our police report; you can confirm the theft for yourself. You can even make imprints of our cards. I mean, we have the plastic, it's just that they've been canceled." Nate didn't even know yet if this hotel had a room vacant. His whining might be for naught in the end. "On Monday we'll have new cards, and our bank accounts will be activated again. You can call the banks yourself to verify that we have legitimate accounts."

"On Tuesday," the clerk corrected, his voice flat. "Monday's a bank holiday."

Banks, the last great champions of white colonialism, keeping Nate from his money for one extra day. "On Tuesday," Nate agreed. "We'll need a room until then anyway."

They'd need a room until their accounts and cards were unfrozen, allowing them to purchase the few necessities that would make their empty home livable. Or maybe their car would be found tomorrow, with their belongings still miraculously jammed inside. Nate hadn't been able to get a straight answer from the cops as to whether the officers would go through the luggage if the car were found. Nate hoped not, half-wished that the car would be discovered empty. It's not as if he was an actual criminal. It was just a little illegality — one tiny dime bag of pot under the seat, his just-in-case stash. He hadn't smoked for more than a year until a month ago, when suddenly he needed a release, needed to free his mind for a time. His car stash was so small that the cops probably wouldn't care. Emily would, though.

"I'll get a manager," the kid said. He shrugged before turning away and added, "Good luck, man."

Emily approached carrying Trevor. She had a hopeful smile on her face — her shoulder-length hair tucked behind her ears, her face open, keen — and Nate understood that he wouldn't be having his soul-baring talk with her tonight as planned. He had to talk to her eventually, he knew that, but maybe his timing had been wrong all along. Even if they *had* made it to their home tonight, would it have been fair to lay so much heavy information on her right now, to bring her farther down only hours after arriving in a strange city? A city she hadn't wanted to move to in the first place? She'd be in a better emotional place in a week or a month or a year, once their life here was tangibly underway. Or perhaps he should have had this talk with her already. A month ago.

"All clean," she said, motioning to the boy's diaper. "Next one's yours. I've got my head back on, ready to roll with the punches." She really did seem ready to roll, unnaturally so.

Was she on something? Nate knew she had habits, even if she didn't admit to them. Emily lifted the boy, sat him on the marble check-in counter, and followed Nate's gaze to where the Bugaboo was parked in the corner of the lobby. "What? You think I forgot to lock Ollie, too?" she said. Then, "Sorry, bad joke."

"Don't worry about it," Nate said.

"Are they going to give us a home here? I think I could get used to this."

"No word yet. I was just thinking about your college studies, of the ancient brainiacs. There's something Darwinian about this whole escapade." He looked at Emily and Trevor, and then past them, at the small expanse of the lobby.

"Sure. But I wouldn't call the eighteenth and nineteenth centuries ancient."

It was squarely nighttime now. Over Emily's shoulder Nate saw older couples drift into the lobby. The men wore navy blazers and lightweight slacks. The women, in cinched-waist dresses and pale pantsuits, clung to the men's arms. Coming in from dinner, it looked like. A cluster of younger women, younger than Emily, ran through the lobby in stilettos and halter tops, sherbet-colored wraps draped over their shoulders like ballasts. Two men in badly pleated pants and surf T-shirts wandered out of the bar. Nate reached for the waist of Emily's low-slung corduroys. She moved closer to him.

"Excuse me," an older man got their attention from behind the counter. He was in his fifties or so, distinguished-looking, wearing a suit with a name tag instead of a uniform with cheap tassels. When homeless, this was the sort of man you could count on. Nate smiled for real. The older man continued, "Why don't you give me the name and number of one of your canceled credit cards and we'll at least have that on file for you. On

Tuesday you can give us a new number and we'll transfer the charges. You'll be checking out on Tuesday?"

"Great," Nate said. He pulled his wallet out of his pocket and slid a card to the manager.

"And you have no reservation, yes?"

"No reservation," Emily said.

If they had made a reservation, it wouldn't be for a stay here. They'd be at one of the motels they'd passed on the drive in, and they'd have booked months ahead at an early-bird Internet rate. But Nate had a track record with the Viking — and it seemed that the hotel actually had a room free. It might be the only vacancy in Newport.

"We've had two cancellations. You can take your pick," the manager said, glancing down into a recessed screen in the counter below him. "Both are upper-floor suites."

"Perfect," Nate said, not asking the price. "That sounds great. Either suite, and if you could have a crib set up, we'd appreciate it. The little guy has a thing for sleeping in cribs."

The manager grinned and took a good look at Trevor, still propped on the counter and tiredly sucking on Emily's cell phone, his eyes only half open. The boy loved technology, preferred to teethe on the nearest TV remote even when he had brightly colored toys within reach.

"Can't that thing give him cancer?" Nate asked Emily, eyeing the boy. Behind the counter, the manager typed furiously into his computer terminal.

"It's turned off. He's safe," Emily said. "You forget that kids are nearly indestructible." She fumbled through her bag while Nate accepted two card keys from the manager. When he looked back at Emily, she was pulling Trevor's sweater from her bag and tugging it over the tot's sleep-lolled head. Safety, as Nate saw it, wasn't something so easily guaranteed.

CHAPTER 4

Settling In

SECURITY? PEACE OF MIND? Was that so much to ask? Emily felt the weight of her wants as she and Nate and Trevor settled into their suite. They couldn't afford this room. They couldn't even afford the tax on it. Sure, she'd once stayed in luxe hotels frequently, for work. She'd traveled regularly to Chicago, L.A., Miami, Denver. She'd stayed in rooms stocked with complimentary champagne and pillow-top mattresses, all on the company's Amex. Those overnight trips had felt like fractures in time, as if she'd stepped through a portal into a world where she was herself, only glossier. The trips were one of the few things she truly missed about her career. Recently she'd also begun to miss the simple act of being skilled at something. Though she'd never planned to be in experiential advertising – she fell into the job after declining grad school – it turned out she was good at the work, often great. For a time, she'd even convinced herself it was worthwhile. Until it wasn't. It fell apart in a single moment.

She'd been perched on the edge of her creative director's desk, leading the team through her concept for a client's
new potato chip — a toasted, canola-oil version of their market
leader. The director's office was large but cramped, filled with
a menagerie of blow-up toys, rubber monsters, movie posters,
presidential bobbleheads, an electronic keyboard, and the req-
uisite Magic 8 Ball. Despite the distractions, the team appeared
entirely focused on Emily. Her concept involved positioning
the new chip as a niche product, rolled out slowly (first in only
the top five markets, mimicking the typical rollout of a gourmet
offering), with interactive street booths manned by actual chefs
who'd hand out samples and suggest (seriously? seriously) beer
and soda pairings. Once they'd solidified those elite markets,
they'd launch nationally with a sponsored chip-dip competition,
revealing the winners in a six-part commercial series, TV spots
with an ongoing narrative. At the same time, they'd roll out commercials for the commercials, meta-ads. The idea was cheeky,
especially for a low-market national company, a company that
sold snack foods available primarily at minimarts. The idea
mocked the current trend toward small-batch gourmet goods,
even as it lured in that exact consumer demographic. Emily's
concept was both novel and (could it be?) brilliant. Brilliant not
merely in her own eyes — she could sense that the rest of the
five-person team felt it, as well. While she spoke, they remained
hushed but jittery, as if carbonated. Other snack-food brands
had done almost nothing in the experiential realm. Nobody had
even thought small, and here was Emily thinking big. As her
team's excitement grew, Emily, too, turned giddy. She'd leaped
from a ledge with this idea, and she was flying. Nina Searle, the
creative director, leaned in toward Emily, grinning.

"We'll present it as is. Friday," she said.

"Tom Bascombe's group can produce the street booths," said Aaron Nielson, the man who made things happen. "Shit, Emily. We could fast-track it."

"Maybe not Bascombe this time," said Nina.

The room hummed. They'd nail this account. They'd make inconceivable amounts of money for the conglomerate that owned the toasted chips. They'd make money for the umbrella corporation that held the strings of their own ad agency. They'd sign other emerging food accounts. They'd soar, for a while at least. And who, in this industry, cared about the long-term anyway?

"So no Bascombe, fine. I'll get Cal Tomlin," Aaron said. "I owe Tomlin a favor. He'll love us for this. Everyone wins."

"Oh, Emily, the commercials for the commercials," Nina flipped through the account memo. "Awesome."

Oh, Emily! To use a figure of speech from Nate's playbook, Emily had hit one out of the park. *We'll present it as is!* Even Maggie Yen, the group's assistant, was caught up in the thrill, nodding in quick bursts, bouncing on the balls of her feet. *Oh, Emily!* Emily was on a high, her chest inflating with the helium of a job spectacularly done. It was inebriating (even more so than the beta-blockers she'd taken to calm her premeeting nerves, even more so than the four cups of coffee she'd drunk in gulps that morning). She wanted to remember this moment. The creative director touched her shoulder in apparent blessing. *Oh, Emily!* She was buoyant, aloft. And then — wait! what's that! — from her new vantage point, Emily understood something that she somehow hadn't fully grasped before.

It was a potato chip.

So much glorious thought, all to promote a potato chip.

Bit by bit — first her head and then her gut and then the perpetual-motion machine of her heart — Emily began to deflate.

She'd knocked herself out for a potato chip. It wasn't even her potato chip. She had neither conceived nor produced it. She had simply come up with a campaign. For a fried, processed runt of a root vegetable. A nothing. They were all nothings: the chip, the energy water she'd promoted last month, the breakfast pastries she'd guerrilla-marketed at the beginning of the year. None of these products were actually hers. And even if they had been? They were insignificant. When had she started to believe that these things mattered? She couldn't remember. It had happened without her noticing.

She'd had two dreams when she graduated from college: financial security and the chance to play some small role in making the world a better place. This job was helping her accomplish neither. On the financial front, she'd seen where the creative directors lived – apartments only marginally more spacious than her own. Their walls were hung with cheap lithographs, reproductions or pieces done by their friends. (None of these creative directors had ever seen a real Rufino in person, Emily was sure of this! They'd certainly never owned one.) Their jobs were deemed creative and cutting-edge (the experiential being a new realm in advertising), as if creativity was the payoff, making the salary moot. These directors had reached the summit yet still lived paycheck to paycheck. After they had kids, they moved so far into the boroughs that they might as well have relocated to Delaware. And slowly their intellect was dying. This job had thoroughly entertained Emily, until she saw it for what it was: a derailment. Carlyle, Schopenhauer: Sometimes she imagined them as her contemporaries. They'd be ashamed of her.

The week after presenting the chip campaign, she lost interest halfway through storyboarding a corporate video for a whole-grain cereal. Three months after that, the act of monitoring client conference calls had become unbearable. Two weeks later, she found herself pregnant. Finally, hardly a month into her maternity leave, she gave notice. She was long gone from the office by the time the potato chip campaign debuted – and received high praise from both consumers and industry analysts. Emily would go back to work, sure, but only when she found work that meant something. She thought hard about what that work might be, and she thought often of her mother's career. Her mother had never made significant money (her mother had never, in her entire life, stayed in a top-flight hotel), but she'd been granted tenure, earned respect, and she'd put the bulk of her lifetime energy into researching, publishing, teaching. Despite her shaky start, her life's work had meant something.

"Hey! There's a DVD player," Nate called to Emily from the living room of the Viking's suite. "And a library of black-and-white classics."

"There's a DVD in here, too," Emily said as Nate walked into the bedroom.

For work, Emily had once stayed in a room with an in-bathroom DVD player, nestled conveniently next to the bidet. The Viking's suite wasn't quite so high-tech, but aesthetically it was sumptuous, grand, beflowered. Expensive. It had a living room, a foyer, two couches. Emily tried to reframe the fact that there were no cheaper rooms available as good news. This was the last luxury they'd see for a long while. More important, nobody would suspect they were here. That was a bonus. Emily didn't want to be found.

"His-and-hers media systems?" Nate said.

"That sounds almost dirty," Emily said. Nate smirked.

Trevor lay sprawled across the bedspread, asleep. Next to him, Nate and Emily's cash was haphazardly piled like the take from a roadside bake sale. Emily counted $84.16 total. It was all they had until Tuesday.

"Trevor's beat," Emily said.

"Me, too. And starving." Nate picked up a menu from the nightstand. "Room service? We can do it up. It's — "

"Free dinner," Emily finished the thought. Free, meaning they could charge it to the room and it wouldn't come out of their meager stack of greenbacks. Free, meaning the shock of the bill would be delayed for a week, at the least.

"Too bad we can't charge diapers from room service," Nate said. They'd counted eight diapers in Emily's bag, enough to last them a day and a half. "They've got lobster lyonnaise, that's an apt culinary introduction to Newport for Trevor. Oh, shit." He looked at Trevor, and at the pile of money next to him, and paused. Then he continued, quietly. "I had a brand-new hundred that I left in the glove compartment. It's sitting there in the Jeep."

"For emergencies?" Emily said.

"Yeah," he grinned. And then, after a pause, "Fuck."

"What?"

"Nothing," he said. But it was definitely something. "Every time I think about the truck being stolen, it's like a slap in the face. I should have left you outside to watch it."

"To watch it? It's an old Jeep."

"An old Jeep stuffed with our shit, with a computer, an iPod, my emergency cash, our complete financial life laid out in sickening detail," Nate said. He touched his ears, as if feeling for the ghosts of his lost iPod earbuds. "We could call someone to lend us money, just enough to tide us over," Nate said. "It might be good to hear a voice from New York. They'll all get a kick out of our Cherokee theft." He paused. "It's, like, proof that all hell breaks loose the minute you step off the island of Manhattan."

The last thing Emily wanted was contact with New York. She'd been ignoring the messages on her cell — the calls from

Tania Osbourne, Cath Oberling, and finally Tricia Haynes, a compulsively social friend who'd probably been the last to leave the Barbers' party on Wednesday. Emily first met all three women during her early days in New York, when they'd traveled the young-Manhattanite cocktail circuit together, carefree, adulthood barely breached, the social playing field still level back then. Tricia's message today, like the others, was a breathless recap of what she'd heard about the Barbers' art theft. Everyone, it seemed, was talking about the painting. The news was spreading without prejudice, like radioactive contamination.

Emily and Nate had arrived late to the Barbers' apartment two evenings ago. Emily had been wary of showing up too early to the party, given that she and Nate barely knew Anna and Randy Barber — despite the dozens of dinners the four had co-attended, the relentless litany of holiday parties where they had crossed paths, discussed the dangers of mercury in sushi, critiqued the ethics of stealing wireless service. Still, Emily welcomed the invitation. The Barbers always threw a great bash and were generous with their guest list. They certainly had the funds for it.

On the phone, Anna had told Emily that Wednesday's fete would be a low-key affair, nothing elaborate. Emily saw through that lie as soon as she walked in the Barbers' door. The party was staffed with a full catering team. Two separate bars were set up, and the Barber children (apparently there were three, though Emily had never seen them) had been stowed at their grandparents' for the night. Anna was draped entirely in jersey and had gold bangles stacked up her arm, turning her almost robotic in appearance. Emily was underdressed. She was always underdressed, it seemed.

"Our clothes are packed," she told Anna at the door, hoping to justify her cashmere-tee and jeans combo.

"Don't we all," Anna said, and laughed.

"Excuse me?" Emily said. "Don't we what?" But Anna was gone.

Inside the apartment, everyone asked about Nate and Emily's Rhode Island plans — yet the minute they brought up the topic, the same people changed the subject, as if Newport might be contagious and spreading. Nate went to the kitchen for more ice, and Emily found herself wedged into a corner discussing Peter Harvey's recent airstrip acquisition. Jules Denny said she'd developed a midlife fear of flying. (Peter had laughed: *midlife, my ass!*) Tristan Volk said he'd lost his laptop in Heathrow last week, his fifth lost electronic device in four months. Emily noted how merely attending parties like the Barbers' — drinking syrupy cocktails with friends who'd acquired airstrips and second homes — had once made her feel lucky, feel as if anything might be possible in her own life, but it was getting harder and harder to feel wealthy by proximity. At this last party, she heard the voices of her former coworkers in her head, deriding the trust fund/Wall Street crowd and their easy lives. Meanwhile, Tristan wouldn't stop talking about his lost laptop, about how he might as well buy two at a time, at the rate he was misplacing them. Emily politely nodded, nodded, nodded her head. She wanted to care, she did, but she was stymied by this thought: If she and Nate had these people's mere problems, if they had Anna and Randy's spread, their collection of art and artifacts and family silver and a staff to keep it all in place, if Nate and Emily had the cash to buy even one new laptop, if they had any of this they wouldn't have to leave the city. There would have been no Newport move for all of the Barbers' guests to avoid talking about.

There was a time when Nate and Emily hadn't needed these people, hadn't jumped to accept their every invitation. When Nate and Emily were first dating, just a few months in but already implicitly exclusive, they had wanted nothing but each other. That first summer they stayed in town on weekends while everyone else fled to the Hamptons (or Rhinebeck or inherited greatcamps in the Berkshires). Manhattan felt palpably vacant on those Saturdays and Sundays, and sometimes during the weeks, as well. Restaurants sat empty and doled out prime reservations as if they were kittens in need of a home. The city was Nate and Emily's playground. They ate out nearly every night and made a habit of regularly charging meals they couldn't afford. That was excusable back then. They had no kid, no responsibilities; it would all work out in the end. New relationships were expensive, always, and Nate had paid most of the time anyway.

That summer had been dreamy, full of warm weather and ridiculous plates of food and giddy midafternoon sex and truckloads of we've-got-the-the-world-on-a-string attitude. *We had the world on a string*, Emily thought now as she eyed the nauticalprint curtains in the Viking's suite. Four years after that summer in the city, two days after the Barbers' party, she and Nate were hanging on by a thread. She'd seen the looks of pity in the eyes of Anna and Randy's guests. Poor Nate and Emily, financially evicted from Manhattan.

Nate leaned against the suite's minifridge and flipped open his phone.

"Please," she said, "don't call New York." They'd been gone from the city for less than a day. She felt dizzy and nauseous and closed her eyes briefly, trying to focus on the colorless void behind her lids. Sometimes she thought she should have kept her stupid job — the pay had been paltry, but it was something. Of course, post-tax, it would barely have covered daycare for Trevor. "Don't call the city."

"Really?" he asked, his phone still open.

"Really."

He eyed her skeptically.

"Seriously, Nate. Don't call. I mean, who are we going to contact? And to say what? 'Hey, buddy, can you wire us a thousand bucks from your upcoming bonus so we can afford our stay at the Viking?'" Emily wanted to throw up at the thought. She imagined the gossip about their Jeep theft, their lack of cash, making the rounds with the same speed as the Rufino-theft news. Even Nate, who usually lay far out of the gossip loop, had heard about the painting. Sam Tully left him a message this morning and Nate picked it up when they stopped for gas outside New London. "I don't get it," Nate had said to Emily. "Someone took Randy's Rufino." Emily had nodded, said she'd gotten the same message from a few people already. "It's not like Anna and Randy needed any more art," Emily had said to Nate.

"I don't think people wire money anymore," Nate said now. "It's done online."

"Right," Emily said, realizing, as she spoke, that a thousand bucks most likely wouldn't be enough to cover their suite for three nights anyway. Of course the thing to do with that hypothetical thousand would be to *leave* the Viking, to buy new air mattresses and a change of clothes and the essentials they'd need to move into their new house — but the suite was so nice, and they could make it until Tuesday on $84.16 if they handled it right, and it wouldn't bankrupt them (or bankrupt them more) to live in luxury so briefly.

"We look desperate already, moving here," Emily said. "Could we at least save face and not alert the masses that, two hours in, we're carless, homeless, and bankrupt?" She needed to take deeper breaths, to keep the oxygen coming into her lungs. They *were* desperate. "We've got eighty-four bucks. Add in whatever we can charge to our room, and it's more than enough for three days."

"Okay," Nate said. He sounded hurt. She'd implied that they were losers, that he was a loser for landing them in this state. Trevor rolled over and crushed a slew of one-dollar bills under his splayed legs.

"Em, you've got to stop doing this," Nate said, picking up a wadded twenty-dollar bill. She had a tendency to crumple up her cash, condensing it into small balls. Nate's bills lay flat and new, straight from the cash machine to his wallet to wherever they went next. It was like a symbol of their relationship, the kind of obvious trope that Emily would have derided as an undergrad. Technically she and Nate weren't wed, and their finances were completely, visually separate.

"Here, hand it over," Emily said, reaching for the room-service menu. Food would ground her. "I'll call down and order." She scanned the list of entrées as she walked from the bedroom to the living room, where she'd be able to talk on the phone without waking the boy. It was a miracle that he hadn't roused already. "Oh God, these people love their hollandaise," she said.

Nate groaned in assent from the bedroom. "Get wine!" he said, just loud enough to hear through the open doorway. "A bottle of wine."

"Yes, sir!" Emily said. And as she picked up the phone to dial for room service, she noticed on the small desk the slim volume of Newport's phone book. This was something else she'd loved during her corporate-travel days: the phone books in every room, each one like an old-fashioned gateway into an unexplored city. The Viking's volume appeared new. Its perfectly aligned pages were as crisp and virgin as Nate's dollar bills, and a pen lay in the open crease, making the scene appear like a still-life, a tableau whose stylist had briefly stepped away to serve tea. She focused on the open pages that arched up off the table where they met the book's spine. The pages were turned, she saw, to the BEs. It was as if, while Emily had been laying Trevor down to sleep and counting out their cash, Nate, who'd lagged behind in this living room, had passed the time by looking up his own last name.

PART II

Saturday

CHAPTER 5

The Drive from Chicago

THE ONLY THING THAT lay ahead of George Bedecker was time. Not building plans or competitions or commissions. All that remained was the simple act of endurance, a steady plod until his allotment of days was up. George took comfort in the fact that he could see his own end in sight. He would watch himself suffer in solitude until his body and mind finally gave out. He would not be taken by surprise.

He sat hunched on the edge of the bed, its quilt rough to the touch. Through the motel room's venetian blinds, the early-morning sun glowed in harsh, parallel strips. George hated venetians. He cringed at the way today's homeowners rushed to buy houses with sweeping views and then installed blinds that sliced the panoramas to pieces. He designed his own structures with built-in, unobtrusive shade systems. It was the ultimate goal: to build a residence so airtight in its design that future inhabitants would in no way be able to mar it with their own attempts at furnishings, at hardware, at window dressing.

George stood and moved away from the bed. The sun was up

early today. Or, no, that wasn't possible. George was simply used
to rising earlier, well before daylight. It was almost 8:00 a.m. It
was time to get on the road. He had one more day and a half of
driving to go.

He wasn't a fast driver. Even as a young man he'd been
cautious. Even back then he preferred for someone else to sit
behind the wheel, an assistant or a contractor, whoever was in
the car. And driving fast wasn't necessary now. He didn't have
anyone on his tail. Architecture was a field covered not by inves-
tigative reporters but solely by critics. An architect, in the press,
was observed after the fact and from afar, judged from a distance
beyond human scale but still close enough to throw stones.

George had been in the business for more than forty years
and had a reputation, of sorts. He'd received international
accolades for both the Glasgow Conservatory and his residential works and had fended off his share of hurled rocks, but his
status as a master of the field remained in debate. He was no
Philip Johnson, certainly, and no Mies van der Rohe, but, to be
frank, Johnson hadn't been Johnson for most of his life. After his
peak, Johnson sank and devalued himself. He'd spent these later
years building monochromatic skyscrapers and juggling styles
the way croupiers shuffle cards. Was this something to aspire to?
Maybe. Johnson's obituaries would surely garner more ink than
most architects would earn over the course of an entire career.

Yet even at his peak, Johnson's daily movements were never
tracked by the media. Even the true icon, Frank Lloyd Wright,
had only been followed as a person when his life took tragicomic
twists worthy of Hollywood: when his homestead burned down
with his mistress inside, or when he was arrested for transporting
a woman across state lines with lewd intention. Considerably
less attention was paid to the movements of merely somewhat-
esteemed architects. So the chances were slim that anyone

would notice George Bedecker, *the* George Bedecker, as he drove slowly from Chicago straight past Cleveland and farther east. He had no reason to worry. He shouldn't be so anxious, yet he felt like a man on the lam.

He'd lied to Philippa, the one person who currently showed concern over his whereabouts, about his intended destination — but his and her relationship had never been entirely forthright. He had almost no clothing with him, only the suit he was wearing and a small leather satchel that held an extra shirt and underwear and toiletries. A full closet was waiting for him at his destination. He hadn't brought any current work papers, either. His office was still operating but purely in the literal sense. It had been some time since they'd won a prestigious commission. His assistants continued to clock in every day but were increasingly building their own projects on his dime, giving him a token slice of the minimal cash that they earned off these minor constructions.

The motel's bathroom was cold and clammy, and George balanced himself against the door molding as he brushed his teeth. He checked himself in the mirror, taking a close look at the shallow folds around his eyes. An inch above the thick plastic rims of his glasses, his temple was bare and slick where there had once been hair. He looked remarkably his age, a child of the first half of the last century. He and his buildings, aging into obsolescence in tandem. George was closing in on seventy, the age when most architects finally began to design their most indelible work.

He concentrated on keeping his hand steady, the brush moving mechanically up and down across his teeth, but as the bristles swept past his upper left incisor, the inevitable happened and his arm jerked from the shoulder, the brush cutting up into his gum and then, with another jerk, firmer this time, as if his elbow was being securely yanked by a marionette string from above, the brush, still gripped tightly in his hand, slipped out of his mouth. Not yet seventy and George Bedecker had designed his last building. He braced himself against the doorway and held his own near-impotent frame as motionless as he could, waiting for the tremor to pass. His doctors had been clear: His nervous system would go first, then his muscle control, and next, if he was lucky, perhaps his brain would slip away, too. George knew exactly what he was in for, but it would take some time, his slow descent, and right now he only needed to make it as far as Rhode Island, where he had a home waiting for him, and where he'd be able to lay his head down and rest.

CHAPTER 6

Wake-up Call

E MILY LIFTED THE bedside phone to her ear and listened. The clock's digital readout flashed 8:00 a.m. Next to her Nate didn't move. He didn't even appear to have heard the phone ring.

"Good morning, it's the front desk, wake-up call – "

"A what?" Emily interrupted the clerk. She sat up, noticed the damask upholstery. Yesterday hadn't been a dream. "I didn't ask for a wake-up call," Emily's voice croaked in a languid, low register. She hadn't arranged for a call, had she? Had Nate? They had nothing to wake up for.

"Bedecker, Primrose Suite, eight o'clock a.m. I have it on my list. I'm sure it was arranged," the woman answered.

What happened to 'the customer is always right'?

"I'm sorry for the misunderstanding," the woman said, like one run-on non sequitur to Emily's ear. And she hung up.

I'm sure it was arranged? Emily craned her neck and looked at Trevor, asleep, crashed out in the Viking's excuse for a crib. It was a portable Pack 'n Play, but Trevor slept soundly, confirming Emily's long-standing hunch that most of the specialized equipment new parents were conned into buying was unnecessary. A crib, a Pack 'n Play, a Moses basket, *and* a bassinet? For adults, technology was speeding ahead with the release of new, multi-use, all-in-one gadgets each season. For kids, corporations were draining parents of their hard-earned income by doing the opposite — separating out functionality, one device at a time.

"Em? Hon?" Nate said. Emily rolled over and looked at him. His eyes were shut. Seeing was customarily the last of his bodily functions to wake. "You awake?"

"It's early, go back to sleep," she said. His breath grew steady again.

Emily gathered the sheet around her as she reached to the floor for her corduroys. She rifled through the pants and found a quarter piece of nicotine gum in one of the back pockets. Tiny, the size of a birth control pill but with more immediate effects, she tucked it into her mouth. She'd barely ever smoked, only socially at parties. She'd always assumed she didn't have an addictive personality, but somehow the gum had gotten to her. She first tried it on a whim, two years ago, when it was making the rounds at the office. Someone (who? she couldn't remember) had brought a pack to a late-night brainstorming session. Emily wasn't addicted, she didn't *need* it. She'd given the gum up entirely when she was pregnant. It simply made her feel good, and there were worse vices. She slid into her pants, tossed her underwear aside — they had only the clothes that they'd worn yesterday and would have to do a hand-wash soon — and pulled her tank top over her head.

In the living room she went through the desk's narrow drawer and removed all of the city guides and stacked them on the desktop. The booklets made Newport look like a theme park, with its sugarcoated downtown lanes. The street where Nate and

Emily now owned a house wasn't on one of these picturesque thoroughfares. From what she remembered, it was on a slim cul-de-sac that was barely large enough for two cars to pass each other. Their house itself was purposefully middle-of-the-road. It was made to be lived in, with a small porch, an attic, and a basement. Nate's eyes had lit up over these mundane details, as if the entire house was an aluminum-roofed fuck-you to his father. Emily had seen the covetous look in Nate's eyes when they first walked up to the house, their babbling chipmunk of a real-estate agent leading the way, pointing out the slate walkway, the storm windows, the security system. *We'll take it!*

Emily hated feeling complicit in Nate's cold war against his dad, but she knew it was the right house for them. She'd joked to Jeanne about this, about its lack of pretension, about its authenticity. The house was "real," she'd told Jeanne. It was the kind of place where a family would live.

On most days, when Emily imagined their new existence inside this new house, she saw a contained and routine life, the kind of life they'd have if their old selves were put inside a dryer on high and came out a few sizes smaller. On other days, she let herself fantasize about the wildly exuberant life they might live here, an unlikely fantasy existence, liberal and hippy and unabashedly intellectual (with free-flowing cash and a formal dining room and vegetables growing in the yard) and without Manhattan's constraints. This glossy future was boldly unreal, but when she tried to conjure an in-between, she came up empty. Some days, recently, she worried that they might not have a future at all.

The day they'd found the house, they'd walked through the structure from room to room, opening all of the closets and cabinets, and Emily asked Nate what he thought their life would be like here. "Who knows?" he responded.

"But really?" she'd said.

"I don't know." He shrugged.

Nate had never been one to imagine the years to come. At night, in New York, after they'd moved in together but before Trevor was conceived, Emily spoke to him of their future. This was when she'd still imagined both of their careers soaring if they persevered long enough, though it turned out that perseverance had little to do with it. They'd talked about traveling, two weeks of hiking remote Patagonian trails in Argentina or Chile once their debts were paid off, and buying an actual Manhattan apartment, throwing their own parties. What Nate couldn't imagine, he said, was having kids. It was the sticking point. He could imagine marriage, he claimed to want that, but he always insisted that he couldn't picture raising children. Emily had hoped it was just a phase he was going through, and she was relieved when, after he found out she was pregnant and planning to have (and keep) their child, he stuck around. Now his love for their son was fierce. You'd think the boy was set to die in a week the way Nate maintained a watchful eye on him, his gaze following Trevor as if the child had a homing beacon lodged in his gut. The marriage question came up again after Trevor's birth (they'd unintentionally solved their stickiest issue, the baby thing), but by then, Emily was laughing it off. They'd missed the boat on marriage, hadn't they? She didn't want to wed just because they had a child. She wanted to wed because Nate was her soul mate. Most days she still thought he was. She looked at him and saw the Nate she'd met that first day in the cab from JFK: a man who seemed genuinely unable to take his eyes off her. But on other days, recently, he'd seemed aloof, unreachable. She still loved him, but she was no longer sure she understood him.

The future remained a moot topic for him even after Trevor's

birth. It was Emily who had to insist that they draw up wills —
not for financial reasons, they didn't have anything except debt
to leave behind, but to name a guardian for the boy in case
he found himself parentless. They'd chosen Emily's brother,
Bobby, and his wife, Dahlia, even though Bobby and Emily
hadn't spoken much in recent years. He was eight years older
and ever since he left for college, when Emily was still a child,
he'd returned only once or twice a year to the East Coast. But he
was a blood relation and lived in San Francisco, where his own
children ate primarily organic food and volunteered at an animal shelter on the weekends, and it was the kind of childhood
anyone, Emily thought, would want. Bobby was the one person Emily had considered calling yesterday and burdening with
their sudden carless straits. He wouldn't scorn Nate and her for
their inability to hold on to their vehicle and its contents — he
had a West Coaster's predisposition toward irrational generosity
of spirit. She could almost imagine telling him about her other
problems, too. But this version of Bobby, the sympathetic older
brother who'd help her get out of a jam, he was a fantasy, as well.
Her actual brother was a kind but distant figure to whom she'd
never truly opened up and whose generous spirit came tinged
with a self-righteous edge.

"I think I've got jet lag," Nate said now. "I can't sleep."

Emily looked up and saw him in the bedroom doorway, wearing one of the hotel's robes.

"I know. The little one outlasted both of us," Emily said.
Trevor usually awoke soon after eight, but hadn't yet stirred
and it was — Emily glanced at her watch again — almost eight
thirty. He'd spent two hours fussing in the middle of the night,
crying on and off, keeping Emily busy while Nate, oblivious or
exhausted, slept. Emily would have been awake all night anyway. The stress of the day, the idiocy of her week, the loss of the

car – on Emily, it had the cumulative effect of a strong liquid stimulant.

"No word on the Jeep?" Nate asked

Emily shook her head.

Nate walked over to her, lifted one of the city guides from the desk, and rifled through its pages. For a man with such a steady, calm exterior, Nate had a surprising proclivity for fidgeting.

"Good idea," he said, placing the guide back in front of her.

"What is?"

"Doing the tourist crap today. Anything we can walk to."

"Maybe they'll find our car," Emily said.

"You don't really believe that."

"No," she said. "Well, maybe."

"We can't sit around waiting for it to drive back to us. We'll hit up a landmark or two. We've got the time."

"Aren't we supposed to be locals?" Emily found that saying it aloud, professing that they were residents, made that fact feel almost real.

"As long as we're staying in a hotel, we might as well do all the shameless sightseeing. We'll never do it once we move in," Nate said. "Trust me." In New York, they made fun of tourists, even of friends who came to visit and insisted on seeing Broadway plays – well, not *plays* but musicals – though ever since *Cats* closed it had been harder to deride the out-of-towners. Manhattanites had lost their punch line.

"I haven't done touristy Newport since I was a kid," Nate said. He walked toward the window. The sun was starting to stream in around the edge of the drapes.

"You were here as a kid?" Emily said. He'd painted a picture of a glee-free childhood, and Emily had imagined his family dressed entirely in Puritan gray, eating Salisbury steak TV dinners. He rarely spoke about his family at all, in fact. When Emily first started dating Nate, she'd tried to draw him out with questions about his brother and his mother, both long dead already. In response to her inquests he merely shrugged and lamented that it all happened a long time ago.

If Emily were like Nate, a person who ordered his life by lists and numbers, this lingering family trauma, along with his financial poverty, would have made up the whole of her "cons" column about building a life with him. The pros were profligate, she reminded herself. The cons, she feared, were mostly on her side now.

"We, my family, vacationed in Newport once," Nate said.

"You told me you never went on family vacations."

"Barely. There was one short Newport trip when I was in grade school. I mean, during a summer when I was that age."

"You never mentioned it."

Emily had assumed that famous architects were rich, until she met Nate and he explained that even the biggies struggled. They sank into debt with each commission they lost and tended to set up their offices in the heartland, where space and talent were cheaper than in New York and L.A.

"I thought I had," said Nate.

A plaintive babbling — this one sounded like *dada*, Emily had to concede — came from Trevor's direction. Emily was struck by the capaciousness of their suite.

"I'm being called." Nate smiled and leaned in to kiss her, then abruptly pulled away. "Oh, honey, secondhand nicotine." He winced and made his way toward the bedroom and Trevor's cries. "You've got to give up the gum, honestly."

"You want me to smoke?" Emily said, following him and standing in the door to the bedroom.

"You hate smoking," Nate said. He was already at the side of the Pack 'n Play, leaning down to pick up Trevor. "It's an empty threat."

Emily glanced behind her and took one last look at the Newport area guide, which lay on the desk. Stupid sightseeing would be good for them, better than trekking to their new house and checking that the utilities were on and pacing the empty rooms, better than lamenting this life of hers and waiting for the future to hit. There'd be plenty of time for that later. Sightseeing would be a fine distraction, she thought, and mostly free of charge, too. They could walk the docks in the harbor and pretend to be legitimately married, utterly innocent Midwesterners seeing touristy Newport for the first time.

CHAPTER 7

Newport, 1974

NATE, AT AGE EIGHT, had been thrilled when his mother announced they'd be taking a family vacation to a place called Newport. He'd have been thrilled to go anywhere, seeing as he'd rarely been out of Ohio, other than one trip to Vienna when he was a toddler and a small slew of summer weekends on lakes in Wisconsin and Michigan in the years since. Travel was alluring, exotic, practically unheard of. And travel with his entire family? It seemed all but impossible. Whole-family vacations, up until that very moment, had been the kind of thing that other people did. Bart Oaken and his parents went to Europe every summer, and each fall Bart returned to school with a new French catchword and beret. Art Eberly spent Christmases in Dallas with both sets of his grandparents. Shawn Doohan, who couldn't make it the short distance from home to school without losing his permission slip — or even, once, his left shoe — went on lavish globetrotting family adventures while Nate, whose mother was *from* Europe, traveled almost nowhere. He couldn't even remember his one visit to

Austria, when he was an infant. Nate was told that he'd met his maternal grandmother during that trip. She died the following year and Nate's parents flew to her funeral alone while Nate and his newborn brother Charlie stayed home.

Nate's father traveled solo all the time for work. He spent months at a stretch in Copenhagen or Charlottesville or Bangladesh, coming home only for a night or two to repack his suitcase and check the mail. Those were early-to-bed evenings for Nate and Charlie. They'd huddle in their bunks, arranged one atop the other, and listen to a baseball game on the radio while their parents did whatever parents did in the grand open space that was the rest of the house.

Nate's father seemed to love living in a home of his own design, a home he'd built specifically for this family. According to the house's lore, George Bedecker had envisioned it as an update of Le Corbusier's apartment complex in Marseille, stacked concrete blocks with large wall-spanning windows set back into the structure. At age eight, Nate – whose father gave him monographs on Walter Gropius and Mies van der Rohe for Christmas when other kids got Matchbox cars – had seen all of the articles about their house. He'd laid eyes on actual newspaper stories featuring grainy photos of his own front yard. *Homage*, one article said of the Bedecker house. *Homage* was a word Nate didn't need to look up. He'd heard the term so often that it was part of his vernacular. *Homage* and *derivative* were the words most of the articles relied on to describe the spare square building where Nate lived. The cube lay nestled in the woods just outside Cleveland, a far cry from Marseille, from what Nate understood, though Nate's mother, Annemarie, tried to raise its standing by holding Sunday night "Culture Court" for her sons, introducing them to Wagner and Kandinsky and serving homemade dumplings and sauerkraut and torten layered with apricot. The one thing she hadn't managed to infuse into the home was warmth. No matter how much art she brought in, the Bedeckers' residential box was still constructed completely out of raw concrete and glass, a massive open square only divided to make room for the boys' beds, for their parents' bed, and for two utilitarian bathrooms. *Our house wasn't made for sleeping,* Nate heard Charlie tell one of his friends a year before the Newport trip, when Charlie was only five yet already viewed the world in a straightforward, nonjudgmental fashion. If there had been no Nate and no Charlie, Nate assumed the house would have been left entirely open, without walls whatsoever.

In Newport, the Bedeckers stayed in a hotel that surpassed Nate's expectations. He reveled in the small divided chambers, the satin drapes, and the bathroom tiled with tiny mosaic circles. Rather than concrete, the walls were wooden on the outside and wallpaper inside. On their first night, while Charlie unwrapped the shower cap in the bathroom, Nate opened and closed the drawers on the fragile wooden desk next to the window, taking out a toothpick-thin pencil and examining it in detail. The window itself was split into sixteen panes of wavy glass, speckled with age. The paint on the sash and the sill was a stark dove white.

The next morning, the family gathered for breakfast in the hotel's formal dining room and spoke in hushed voices as Nate's mother described the schedule for the week ahead. After breakfast each day, Nate and Charlie would have a swim lesson and then play with their mother on the beach. Later in the day, the boys would take a group sailing class. Nate nodded and reached across the table for a saucer filled with rosettes of butter. He carefully cut one of the petals off with his knife and spread it across his pancakes, the fat melting even before he had a chance to pour hot syrup on top.

The syrup, the sailing, the soft-serve window a block from the beach: Six-year-old Charlie was enchanted by the whole trip. He'd have been happy with the soft-serve only. The sailing and swimming were icing to him, but Nate, two years older, had been looking forward to an actual family getaway. He'd imagined his father ruffling his hair and letting them drink extra Cokes and watching from the beach as their sailing class debarked. As it turned out, Nate and his brother barely saw their father at all in Newport except at the breakfast and dinner tables — and dinner was so late (did everyone eat so long after dark on vacation? Charlie practically fell asleep at the table each night) that Nate was dazed through much of it. The only time they saw their father during the daylight hours was on their final afternoon.

The sailing lessons had turned out to be torture every day at 2:00 p.m. Aside from the Bedeckers, there were only two kids in the class: a set of brothers from Washington, DC. These other boys spoke a hidden code, making secret jokes about the people in rowboats and the yacht club's hot dogs. They'd been coming to Newport for their entire lives. Their swim trunks were brightly colored and the older one's featured a stretch of actual rope around the waistband. They knew everything. As the DC brothers yammered on, Nate and Charlie remained largely silent during the lessons. The other boys' noise was tough to compete with and the Bedeckers had more to learn anyway, having never sailed before. After each class was over and the other boys gone, Nate and Charlie came alive again, Nate summing up the events of the lesson.

"Hello, Cleveland! Rookie Charlie Bedecker outperformed

himself at the rudder today, slipping a fast one over the eyes of two bad trades from DC!" he'd say, mimicking Joe Tait, the voice of the Cleveland Indians on the radio. Nate and Charlie were like Tait and his partner, Herb Score. Score could go three full innings without saying a word. When he did speak, it was simple trustworthy narration, true to the facts. Strong and silent, that was Charlie. He was conscientious and thoughtful, his life taking place inside his own head. Nate, like Tait, could fill empty space – between batters or between sailing class and dinner – with off-center observations and a steady stream of electrifyingly empty words.

On the final afternoon their lesson was short, only a one-hour wrap-up where the boys were allowed to man the rudder and the sheet by themselves. Afterward they met up with their mother as they had every day, at the end of the dock, next to the sailing school's warped flagpole. She usually fetched them on foot, but today, since they were done so early, she'd arrived in the rental car, briefly leaving it idling while she ran up to the sidewalk and motioned to the boys to get in. This afternoon they'd be accompanying their mother on her daily trek to nearby Narragansett to pick up their father. Nate assumed it was a work project that had drawn George to Rhode Island and kept him tied up in Narragansett this week; Nate had grown to assume that this family vacation was, for George, merely another business trip. Nate imagined that while he and Charlie were at swim class each morning, their father was building a beach house for another boy's family.

Nate and Charlie slouched in the back of the rental car, their tan legs spread fat against the vinyl seats.

"I pulled on the halyard, Mom, it's really hard, all by myself – "

"He raised the sail, Mom, all by himself," Nate interrupted Charlie. The car reached the far side of the bridges and headed down the mainland coast.

"And no one else — "

"Those dopes in the other boat, they got their sail halfway up and practically capsized. Charlie didn't even need my help. He's a future sailor, Mom."

"Hey, Mom, do you know what capsize means?"

"You tell me, *lieben*." She briefly turned from the front seat to smile at Charlie, sitting in the middle of the backseat. As they drove parallel to the water, the road narrowed and the houses grew farther apart. Nate's mother appeared to be navigating by rote. She'd taken this road twice a day — to drop off George while the boys were swimming in the morning and to pick him up while they were sailing — since their arrival in Newport. "It will just take a minute," she'd told her sons about today's Narragansett drive. Tonight, back in Newport, they'd eat dinner together again, the last time they'd do so for a while, Nate figured. At the hotel, they always ate at the same table along the dining room's windowed wall. The hotel's linen napkins were embossed with tiny blue sailboats. The Bedeckers also used linen napkins for dinner at home, where small silver rings permanently resided next to their plates. After each meal at home, the boys twisted their napkins into the rings for safekeeping until the next day. George — Nate called his father by his first name, something that had started out as a joke when his dad wasn't around and later stuck when his father didn't seem to mind or notice — believed in minimalism and utilitarianism and made a frequent plea for paper napkins. Nate's mother insisted on cloth and wouldn't compromise. She insisted on keeping at least this small hold on tradition. Nate silently sided with his mother in the napkin debate. His mother was foreign and worldly even to her own sons, with her Austrian accent and relatives an ocean away. Their father's relatives were American, but the boys had barely met them. "It's okay," Nate told Charlie once, while discussing their lack of extended kin, "I'm your family."

"This is taking more than a minute," Nate said after they'd been on the road for twenty minutes, at least. Just as those words came out of his mouth, Annemarie turned the rental car up a driveway. They narrowly made their way through a tight opening in the tall, severe hedges that stood like ramparts in front of a deep lawn. The driveway led straight through that lawn to a house tucked into the far end of the land on a bluff above the beach. Nate could see waves in the background, breaking rough and white. The house itself was small. It was nothing grand at all.

"It's the old house," his mother said, as if in explanation.

It didn't look particularly old. Compared to much of Newport, where the homes had historic plaques out front that Nate's mother liked to read aloud ("Samuel Harford settled in this home, in the Federalist style, in 1812, after having lost all of his fortune when the tides turned, financially, at sea") this house looked new. By the front door it had a small spotlight, unlike the electric lanterns that dotted the porticos across the bridge.

From the side of the house, along a row of deep green rhododendrons as tall as elephants, George appeared and walked toward the front porch. He held another man by the elbow. The other man, older and stooped, walked with the loping gait of a novice hiker stepping from slippery boulder to slippery boulder in an erratically rushing stream. He began to fall and Nate held his breath as George caught him. There was a softness to George that Nate had never seen before, an instinctive empathy to his movements. He helped the man stand straight again, and after a steadying pause they continued their short trek to the porch.

"Too much to drink!" said Charlie, proudly, matter-of-factly, as if parroting something he'd heard on TV.

"Oh, *lieben*, no," their mother said.

But was Charlie right? He and Nate hadn't seen much drunkenness up close. Their father never drank alcohol, not even a sip. Their mother drank, though her drinks seemed to have no effect on her at all. Perhaps she didn't drink *enough*. A month ago, they'd heard Tait and Score narrate the Indians game against the Rangers. It was a losing season, already hopeless for Cleveland. In an effort to increase stadium attendance, the team's owners had instituted Ten-Cent Beer Night. Practically free beer if you came to the game! It worked. Even before the first pitch, Score was heralding the massive attendance, twenty-five thousand spectators or more, but by the time the eighth inning opened, one naked fan had rushed the field and the relief pitchers were being pelted with firecrackers. After a drunk attendee literally stole second base, the game was called. "It's unbelievable! Un*be*lievable," Tait reported. "Unbe*liev*able," Tait said again, and again, sounding sad and amazed at the same time.

"It's not drink," Nate's mother said now, watching George and the old man through the windshield. "It is okay."

Nate moved closer to his brother and put his arm around the boy as the two and their mother kept their gazes on the men. It was steamy in the car. Nate had thought that here, by the ocean, it would be chilly all day, but the sun beat down on them as they swam and sailed and walked along the old town beach, and while they watched their father stroll with a man who looked so strikingly like him that he could only be Nate's grandfather.

George had a dad.

The men continued their slow walk along the lawn until they reached the porch, where George awkwardly helped his companion up the steps and into a wicker chair. The older man, his face in a sour, stiff scowl, fell into the seat hard. Immediately afterward the screen door behind him opened and a white-clad nurse stepped out and adjusted the man's position, propping his shoulders against the back of the chair. George nodded at the nurse and then said something to the man, who snarled. Finally, with his head down, George walked quickly to the car and got in. "All right, time to go," he said, slamming the car's door and locking it. "Let's go."

Their mother backed down the driveway as Nate and Charlie continued to look out the window toward the house. The old man began to collapse over himself. The ocean in the background looked almost green from this angle, the same near-green as the lush, dusky rhododendron leaves. They drove past the hedgerow and onto the two-lane main street in silence. All that Nate knew about his paternal grandparents was that his grandmother was dead and that his grandfather wasn't much in touch with George. They had "never been close." Nate kept his eye on the disappearing hedgerow until the car turned a corner and it was out of view.

Charlie slid away from Nate and took his *Yes & Know* book out of the seat pocket in front of him. He uncapped the magic pen and concentrated on a word-find, locating nautical terms in the grid of letters. PORT was already circled, and MOORING. Nate put a hand on Charlie's shoulder and then looked away, out the window where real boats were coming into view.

"That was Grandpa," Nate said toward his father in the front seat. Nate had never used the word *grandpa* before. It was a term co-opted from other lives with a hint of hope.

George turned from the passenger seat and took a hard look

at Nate, sitting behind him. George's skin was red from the sun
and damp with sweat.

"That was your grandfather, Nate," George confirmed. Nate
was startled by his father's admission — after nearly nine years of
keeping the boy from his grandfather, George had conceded the
older man's identity with surprising readiness. Nate sat utterly
still in the backseat, afraid that if he moved, the moment would
pass. His father continued, "I'm so profoundly sorry. His mind is
not well."

"His mind looks okay," Nate said, because it was the man's
body that had appeared skewed. He looked dizzy, the way he
wavered when he walked. Perhaps George was embarrassed by
him, perhaps this is why he'd kept the man hidden from his
sons. George hated things (papers, paper clips, people) that were
messy and out of place. The air remained silent for a moment.
Nate wished he'd gotten out of the car and run up to the old
man, met him, touched his pale skin. "He looked fine," Nate
said, though that wasn't true.

Nate's father only shook his head.

"It's hunting, sons," Nate's mother finally added from behind
the wheel, as if an afterthought. In her sharp Austrian accent,
the words came out barbed. A boy could snag himself on her
honed consonants. "It's hunting, sons."

It almost made sense, his mother's words. In Ohio, there were
hunting accidents every season and Nate's mother frequently
lamented the senseless loss of life, or loss of a limb. Nate had
friends whose fathers had built gun cabinets in their garages
and hung deer antlers on their living-room walls. Nate's house
barely had closets or adornment at all. Nate didn't remark, as the
car drew closer to Newport, that his mother had never addressed
her children as "son" or "sons" before, or that a hunting accident seemed like an unlikely cause for the old man's afflictions.

He thought, instead, about how his father said the man's mind was not well, when, in truth, it appeared to be his arms and legs and face that were sick. Nate had seen his grandfather's arms swing. He'd watched his legs wobble as he tried to walk across the flat lawn to the porch. An ailment of the mind would be preferable, Nate thought, tougher to spot from a parked car, less embarrassing to George.

"Think about dinner," Nate's mother said as they crossed the bridge into Newport. Each night when the waiter appeared at their table, Nate and Charlie would still be debating whether to get the hamburger or the fried scallops or the spaghetti with shrimp. "It's your last night. Think about what you'd like to eat," their mother said.

But as they pulled up to the hotel and the evening's breeze began to slowly gather force, Nate didn't think about dinner. His mind wasn't on what he'd be eating or the pointers he'd learned about sailing today or the long-beaked gray birds he and Charlie had manically chased that morning across the beach's wet sand. The only thing on Nate's mind as their family vacation came to a close was the stooped old man living with a nurse in Narragansett.

And three decades later, when Nate found himself again in Rhode Island, with his own son this time and a whole life ostensibly ahead of him, the picture that he could not get out of his crowded, stressed, tired-to-the-core head was that very same image of his waning, distant grandfather and the old man's unmistakable, distinctive, sober, loping gait.

CHAPTER 8

Small City, Big Ideas

A T 10 A.M. ON SATURDAY, Newport's harborfront was crammed with pedestrians — the women wearing sweaters in off-primary tints that hadn't been popular since Emily was a teenager, the men sporting hair that was battened limp and listless under baseball caps and sun visors. These people looked as pitiful as Emily felt. Pitiful and distracted, in Emily's case: Her head had been drawn back to New York this morning when two more acquaintances who'd been at the Barbers' party left voice mails. According to Celeste Inge, the police had spent yesterday evening with the Barbers, in their apartment, asking questions. Emily could picture it, the cops' stiff uniforms stark against the Barbers' high-gloss white walls. Celeste said the cops had grilled the doormen who'd been on duty, too. "I heard they're going to question us guests next!" Celeste said in her exhilarated, rambling message. Celeste had a son just three months older than Trevor, and she and Emily had spent dozens of mornings together over the past year, wedging their two strollers into the corners of neighborhood coffee shops and downing steaming vats of latte. They were often the only actual mothers out in the neighborhood with their kids. Celeste had an afternoon nanny, but mornings she was on her own with the baby. She was one of the few people Emily missed.

Celeste was right about the cops, wasn't she? They would need to talk to the Barbers' party guests. It seemed so obvious and now Emily couldn't figure out why the guests hadn't been corralled for questioning already. Who would the police call in first? Not Emily, for sure – not all the way up in Newport. And yet, if the cops were smart, she'd be at the top of their list: hard as she'd been trying not to think about it, she had information they'd want. Still, they had no way of knowing that. Even the smartest detectives couldn't know what no one had told them yet. They couldn't possibly discern who, from the guest list, might point them in the right direction. They couldn't.

"We're now officially the have-nots," Nate said. He was pushing the stroller through Newport's narrow streets.

"Excuse me?" Emily said. By Emily's estimation, she and Nate had been the have-nots for as long as they'd been together.

"I mean, without the car." Nate looked hard at the oncoming traffic, as if contemplating making a swan dive into it. "Every time an SUV drives by I want to give it the finger."

"The cops could still find the Jeep." Emily hoisted the diaper bag higher on her shoulder. *Cops*, the word itself had a sinister ring, tough and explosive. "Once the thief realizes he's got a lemon, he might dump it by the side of the road. Anyway, look at everyone else here. They all look like have-nots. Newport's not what it used to be."

"Nothing's what it used to be," Nate responded as they walked toward the water. He turned his eyes to the ground and carefully steered Trevor and Ollie across a mismatched seam in the sidewalk. Emily used to joke (to Jeanne, the sole person in the world who would understand and not hold it against Nate) that Nate was the only guy on Wall Street hoping for a crash, or at least an extended recession, since it would even out the playing field for a while. Anything, she'd say, to stop the warp-speed widening of their own personal income gap. Things would be better in Newport, she knew, a place where everyone's ragged-edged seams were starting to show. Even Emily's mother, who'd always believed Emily belonged in New York, approved of the Newport move. She'd surprised Emily by telling her that it was time she and Nate shook up their life. Perhaps she sensed their financial despair — a situation that Emily had never overtly shared. Why worry her? Given Emily's mom's meager academic income and impending retirement, there wasn't a thing that she could do to help them.

It was time for a move, regardless. Yesterday, as they'd pulled out of Manhattan, Emily had glanced back at the city's staccato skyline, jammed with overlapping high-rises and thin streams of smoke. Along the East River, shadowy construction cranes leaned tall into the clouds. This was what their world had come to, developers building layer upon layer atop an already maxed-out landscape. Newport lay low to the ground and was comparatively sprawling. When Emily stepped away and looked at their life from a distance, she was unexpectedly charmed by the random chance of this move, the odd luck of landing in Rhode Island. The state was founded as a refuge for exiles and iconoclasts, originally settled by the first New World Jews, early Quakers, and devotees of Roger Williams — as well as the physically deformed and politically righteous colonists who'd been shunned farther north. And the legacy held. Providence remained honorably progressive and Newport was its smaller, old-money offshoot. In the abstract, Emily was growing to appreciate the idea of raising a child here. In the concrete, she wasn't so sure. Real life rarely lived up to her imagination of it.

"You're smiling," Nate said.

Emily nodded and started to walk again, pulling Nate and the stroller along with her. "This place might end up being okay," she said.

"Hey — " Nate got her attention as he steered the stroller through a clapboard doorway and into a shop. She ducked in after him and took a moment to adjust to the traditional whiff of the place, the reek of potpourri and mothballs, eau de antiques.

The large room was packed to capacity with nearly indistinguishable tchotchkes. Abutting the door, an ornate gold-trimmed chest housed a collection of glassy costume jewelry, each piece larger than Trevor's fist. A mahogany sideboard was haphazardly set with reproduction china, a skewed imitation of what a society matron's table might have looked like during the colonial era. Dainty, ancient Christmas ornaments, either left over from last year or early for the next, hung from every picture frame, coat hook, and window ledge in the place. Outside the far window Emily saw a sailing school preparing to take off for the day. High schoolers, it looked like. Maybe they were a team. Did high schools have sailing teams? In Newport they must. Emily could imagine it: a fourteen-year-old Trevor in Bermuda shorts and a worn T-shirt, complaining that he *doesn't want to go to practice*, that he has a stomach ache or sailor's knee or a *hangover*.

Emily shrank back from the clutter. If people were buying this crap, that meant that not everyone here was down-and-out. Some of them still had cash to burn. Emily no longer believed that someday she'd be one of those people herself. As a child in Cambridge, Emily had fantasized about growing up and owning a town house in Boston. In her dreams, the urban castle featured a game room, a screening room for movies, and a minifridge full of Grape Crush. She'd since given up that dream (she didn't *want it all* anymore, she merely wanted enough to remain consistently in the black) along with so many others. What she got, in return, was Nate.

He'd come as a surprise. Five years ago, she hadn't expected to have any man in her life at all, ever. She was in her early thirties back then and still deeply single and had assumed, with resignation, that a life partner wasn't in her cards. She ultimately convinced herself that she didn't need love, that a career in advertising, combined with expensive cocktails and girlfriends who could write prescriptions, would be enough. She grew numbly and nimbly accustomed to living solo, and fooled herself into believing she'd earn the urban castle on her own. Then Nate crawled into her cab and all of that changed. She discovered that being with Nate was like a sort of solitude. Not loneliness, at all, but like being completely within herself, at peace. This was love, she understood. This was love, the essential thing she had, during her decades of unfortunate dating, told herself she'd be happy without.

She'd cheated on Nate once, only one time with one person. It was right after she discovered she was pregnant with Trevor, almost three years into her relationship with Nate, when all of the facts of their lives were finally on the table. It felt, then, as if they knew each other inside and out. The finality scared her. Her life had changed at breakneck speed — what happened to the convincing arguments she'd spent so long crafting, her protofeminist rationalizations that life was better solo? What happened to that once-coveted town house with the elaborate screening room and wood-burning fireplaces? What happened to her larger-than-life dreams? She'd turned into a potato chip marketer, pregnant by the only pauper on Wall Street. With her anxiety in full swing, she'd called Henry Vartan, whom she used to sleep with frequently when she was single. She hadn't seen him since she met Nate, and calling him out of the blue after three years was like a dare to herself. She wasn't even sure that he still had the same phone number. He did. He answered on the first ring and invited Emily to come over. She was two months pregnant and not showing yet and took a cab to his apartment, where she trembled on the elevator ride up and then let him take her clothes off while she ran her hands down his taut, stocky body, nothing like Nate's. Afterward she felt completely alone, the lonely kind of alone. Sitting naked on the edge of Henry's bed, in his glass-walled apartment in the Financial District, watching as he pulled his boxers back up: This empty-hearted moment was the image that came to Emily's mind now each time she thought about being impoverished. That was her worst-case scenario, and she'd survived it. On the rare occasion that this image didn't stabilize her equilibrium (at least she wasn't sleeping with Henry Vartan!) she took an Inderal.

Did she feel guilty about Henry? She should, she knew that she should, but she was the one who'd suffered from the dalliance, and it had only made her want Nate more. She understood immediately that she shouldn't have risked Nate for one night with a nobody from her past. Who cared if Nate was financially undesirable, as economically impaired as she was? After the slip (a slip that only she and Henry and the nascent Trevor-fetus knew about), Emily never questioned her love for Nate again, not until recently. Not until, over this last month, he'd begun pulling away from her. It was just stress, she continued to tell herself. The other new mothers with whom Emily spent time — at the baby gym or music class, women with whom Emily had little in common except for the age of their children — frequently made jokes about their Wall Street husbands, men they rarely saw. "Either they're working really hard or they're all having affairs!" the women would say. They laughed hard about this, the assumption being that becoming fathers had rendered their men impotent.

Nate was neither impotent nor deceitful. He was a straightforward man, honest when it counted. If his distance wasn't due to stress, Emily worried that its roots were in the way his and her lives had diverged. He went to work every day and interacted with the outside intellectual world – a riveting proposition – while she stayed home, turned her brain off, and mixed baby formula. She cherished Trevor, she did, but as she spent her entire days with him at her side, she felt her interior life starting to wither and die, even more than it had during her career at the ad agency. As she sat across from Nate at dinner, she found that she had little to say that didn't involve rehashing the baby's bowel movements and eating habits, details that evoked slight smiles from Nate and polite silences. In her head she'd become a mother from the 1970s and began to fear she was proof that women had made no progress in the decades since. She wanted to rejoin Nate in his full life. She wanted to assert herself as an equal partner again. It's what she craved: her own intellectual existence outside the house. It was the one thing Emily's mother had that Emily herself, as an adult, coveted.

What would Emily's outside life be? She had no interest in returning to the soulless world of advertising and had spent countless hours since Trevor's birth coming up with new, down-home business schemes (artisanal cheese-making, nicotine-infused water, audio philosophy), dozens of ideas, looking for the one single brainstorm that would satisfy her intellect and, she hoped, bring in a paycheck, too. New mothers complained about how hard they worked! Yes, Emily was relentlessly tired during those first months with Trevor, when the days and nights bled together, but for so long she'd been subjected to the endless and arbitrary whims of irrational, ego-charged bosses. To suddenly find herself at the mercy of no one but a baby whose impetuous outbursts were age-appropriate? On most days this was a luxury. While Trevor was awake, he was an adorable time-suck, but the minute he went to sleep, or acquiesced to a half hour of *Baby Beethoven*, during those moments of respite Emily's beta-blockers allowed her to concentrate and devise and plan.

All of her ideas turned out to be insurmountably flawed. Nicotine water was an FDA-approval nightmare. Cheese-making happened to be more science than art — the humidity and temperature had to be monitored to the fraction of a degree. A philosophy audio library was already in the works out in L.A. She gave up on all of these as tenable plans. On a whim one night in bed, though, tired and limp after she and Nate had managed to find the time and desire to make love, she told him about her now-ditched idea to open her own dairy operation — something in soft goat cheeses, maybe, given that the soft cheeses were so much more forgiving than the hard varieties. When spoken aloud, she began to consider the scheme again. It sounded romantic and viable and appealingly hands-on. Still, she laughed as she described it. She let loose a self-deprecating guffaw, which apparently gave Nate the idea that her whole thing had been nothing but folly, and he laughed, too.

"Hilarious," he'd said. "You could also churn butter. We'd buy one of those colonial bonnets for you to wear. I could develop a bonnet fetish like *that*." He called her Bessie for the next two days. The name stung. Emily had stopped breast-feeding only a

month earlier and was finally beginning to feel less like a cow
and more like a woman again. She thought of her mother, a
feminist, yes, but one who'd always loved this kind of joke. It
was no surprise that Emily's mother and Nate had taken to each
other so easily.

Since then, Emily hadn't told Nate about any of her ideas.
They hadn't, honestly, had much time to talk. A few weeks ago,
while feeling especially disconnected, for the second night in a
row she'd woken up just after midnight to find that Nate wasn't
in bed with her. She could hear him on the other side of the
bedroom door, in the living room. She tried to slip back into
sleep, but the irregular tap of his fingers on their computer keyboard kept jarring her awake. He had a tendency to pound on
the keys with the kind of force most people reserved for slamming the return-change buttons on vending machines. After a
few minutes, she called out to him.

"Nate," she said in a whisper loud enough, she hoped, to be
heard in the living room.

"Shh," he said, walking quickly back to the bed. "You'll wake
Trev."

"Your typing is going to do that anyway. Can't you sleep?"

"I'm not tired. It's okay." It was pitch-black in their apartment
except for the faint blue glow from the computer screen. Their
windows looked out over an unlit courtyard, and after the sun
went down, unless the moon was full and bright, the only light
that came in was from the lamps of the strangers who lived in the
apartments across the way. At this hour, none of those neighbors
were still awake. The computer beeped from the living room, a
generic alert sound. "I was just surfing," Nate said. He rubbed
his eyes, pressing his palms firmly against them.

"Find anything good?" she asked.

After a pause, he said, "I thought it might be cool if I could locate the audio from the old baseball games I listened to when I was a kid, in Cleveland. I thought it might be fun to share those with Trevor someday."

"I guess."

"They must have recorded the games. You'd think the radio station would have an archive and put it online, but I can't find it. All that Internet bandwidth, and you can never find what you need."

"Unless you're looking for naked cheerleaders or driving directions," Emily said, her voice groggy.

"Naked cheerleaders, that's something I can share with Trevor someday." Nate said. "I should probably give up. I'll come back to sleep."

"Don't rush for me." Emily genuinely meant that. She felt spoiled, having the whole bed to herself. She stretched out her limbs and took advantage of the wide expanse of flat, cool sheets.

Nate returned to the computer and Emily lay awake thinking about Nate and his attachment to those baseball games. It was like a smack in the face, his constant pull toward nostalgia just as he and Emily were constructing their joint future. This time, though, he had a valid point. Those games had to be online somewhere.

Emily saw, then, how off-the-mark her life had become. Had she had any foresight, she'd have left the ad agency and used her experience to gain a foothold in the growing tech sector. Instead, she'd honed her skills in the old-economy model. By the time Trevor was grown, she'd be totally unemployable. And if she'd learned anything from watching so many tech start-ups flourish (and later die, as so many of them did) far beyond her reach, it was that the majority of these ventures were less about the intellectual idea and more about knowing how to raise the cash. Cash was the cog at the center of everything, especially as the country's brainpower was on the fast road to decay.

"We have eighty-five dollars to our name, and we're not spending them in here," Nate whispered into Emily's ear. She still stood inside the tchotchke shop's doorway; she hadn't made it any farther into the hushed, dusty museum of a store. He lay his arm loosely around her shoulder and pointed to the nearby wall, a Newport wall. Newport was safe. It was another, newer world, separate (even now, in the era of cell phones and wireless) from whatever was transpiring to the south, from the misguided, old-fashioned existence she'd left behind. She understood how physical distance might become a form of comfort.

"That framed map of Easton Bay? Twenty-two hundred bucks. It dates back to 1823," Nate said.

"And it doesn't offer point-to-point driving directions? A scam."

"A beautiful, antique, hand-painted scam," Nate agreed.

"I need some fresh air," Emily said. "You still have the cash?" Nate had taken charge of their money last night, after they finished counting it out on the bed.

"In my wallet."

Nate pushed the stroller out of the store and Trevor, deep in the seat, moved his head from side to side, his wide eyes the size of half-dollars. Like his ears, the boy's eyes were slightly too big for his face, giving him an unnaturally alert look whenever he was awake. Some of his alertness these days was real, though. There was an energy to the boy, simmering under his pale skin. He was on the verge of walking. Each time he pulled himself up on a coffee table or chair leg, he looked ready to let go and take off running.

"Hey." Emily motioned down the dock, past a yacht insurance office with a yellow life preserver painted on its sign. "Let's show Trevor the boats. He's going to have a future on boats if we stay here."

"I guess he will," Nate said, as if the idea hadn't yet occurred to him. "Did you bring sunscreen? I want to get his face covered."

Emily rifled through her tote. The bag was littered with old credit card receipts and appointment reminder slips from the pediatrician's office, the wayward pieces of paper mingling with her lipsticks and estranged pen caps and contraband that included the bottles of shampoo she'd stolen from the maid's cart at the hotel. She reached deep into the main pocket, gripped the tube of children's Coppertone, and pulled it out – along with two stray scraps that were stuck to the tube's slick plastic. The first was a coupon, two dollars off a six-pack of flavored Italian seltzer. The second paper was, unbelievably, a crumpled twenty-dollar bill.

"Nate?" She held it out away from her body as if it were otherworldly and dangerous. With the twenty added in, their cash would total more than $100. "Nate . . ." she tried again, but he was already halfway down the dock, unbuckling Trevor from the Bugaboo and directing the boy's attention to the water. He couldn't hear her. She stuffed the bill into her back pocket and strode quickly down the wooden walkway. The stiff creases of the crumpled twenty pressed against her skin through her pants, sharp yet light, like the feeling in her head, the guilt of pocketing the extra cash and the relief of now having an innocent secret, her own money, like an escape hatch. One forgotten bill that was hers to save or spend.

CHAPTER 9

The Drive through Pennsylvania

THE EXTERIOR OF THE Mooresburg, Pennsylvania, minimart appealed to George Bedecker. He was drawn to the square geometry of the flat-roofed store, the ordinary assemblage of gas pumps, the vernacular familiarity of the roadside way station. Inside the minimart, however, the precision gave way to Day-Glo lunacy. The stacked aluminum shelves were piled high with boxes and bags and wrapped pouches of artificially colored candy and salt nuggets and deep-fried nuts. Slim Jims, Tato Skins, Maxx bars, Casbah Crisps, Flav-R-Pacs. A mound of bagged charcoal and lighter fluid. The offerings stretched from floor to ceiling in no discernable order, nudging against refrigerated beverage cases and a heated glass cage in which withered hot dogs rotated in slow circles. A white light, an astral glow, kept the space so well illuminated that there were no shadows. It took George a moment to locate the ambient source: extended strips of fluorescent slimline tubing that hung on J-brackets from both the ceiling and the walls.

George had left the motel this morning without eating breakfast, but he wasn't hungry. George was never hungry. This wasn't a symptom of his illness, it was something that had been true of his life for as long as he could remember. Even during his marriage – to a woman who'd come from a large tradition of warm hearths and who served long-cooked European roasts that should have preyed on his sense of duty – even then he'd seen food as a means to an end, a necessary irritant.

Those roasts and stews, they were a lifetime ago, but he could still remember their heavy musks, odors that worked their way into his skin like ringworm and clung to the threads of his suit jackets long after his wife was gone. If he had a regret – a regret about his home life, not about his rapidly truncating career – that would be it, the way he'd remained cloistered in his own head until the end of his wife's life. He'd been present physically for her, beside her bedside, but in his head and heart he'd denied to himself that her end was so close. Out of fear he had looked away. The lesson he'd learned finally: Denial was a dangerous path.

He picked up two rectangular breakfast bars from the minimart's shelf. The brand name on their labels was familiar to him from the cereal boxes that lay tucked away in his small pantry in Chicago, at home. When he was there, cereal often stood in for dinner. Cereal, or soup and buttered rice. More often, he ate away from home. If he wasn't traveling, he remained at the office until well past dinnertime, eating whatever meal his junior associates ordered in for the evening. The office pantry was kept stocked with coffee, tea, and saltines. Occasionally he'd leave the office for an hour and take a taxi to Philippa's condominium, where she'd prepare him a small dinner of cheese and charcuterie, or noodles in sauce. Like George, Philippa saw food in a practical light, as a form of energy, a daily ration.

Today the breakfast bars would suffice. He approached the

store's cash register, where a boy in a shiny basketball uniform sat slumped over a tabloid. George lay the two foil packets on the counter, pulled out his credit card, and tapped it on the linoleum. The clerk, with a knee-jerk response to the sound of a charge card on the counter, snapped to attention.

"That's it?" the boy asked, picking up the foil packets and passing them under an electronic scanner. Next to the counter stood a shoulder-high copper rack hung with plastic Halloween costumes. The pirate suits were the right size for a six-year-old child, George figured. Or a maybe a nine-year-old. It had been a long time since he was able to tell the difference.

"I've also filled up the tank, gas," George motioned with his head toward his Audi outside. It was a relief that his neck and head were working today. On so many afternoons, his conscious physical impulses slipped out of reach, tumbling down the scale from control to mania. Today, everything was intact. The drive had been uneventful.

"That your Audi?" The boy asked, picking up the credit card from the counter and punching a code into the register. The Audi was the only car at the pumps.

"It is."

"Yeah?" The boy asked.

"Yes," George repeated. "It is." This was the first time George had used his voice all day, having been alone in his car for five hours. He'd have to get accustomed to silence; he was heading into self-imposed seclusion. Eventually he'd have a home nurse, if he remained in Narragansett, but not yet. For now, he was aching for solitude and airtight quiet. He was expecting that the seclusion would fall over him like a cool muslin drop cloth, but for all he knew it could end up crushing him like granite.

"Nice," the boy said.

George signed the credit card receipt. His small, fine movements, even on days like today, good days, were hampered. His signature emerged as a shaken scrawl.

George took the translucent yellow customer receipt and awkwardly folded it in half and then in half again, slipping it into his pocket. From his other pocket he retrieved and tightly grasped his car keys.

George walked the ten yards to the Audi, one foot in front of the other, a deliberate gait as he crunched over the loose black gravel. The air outside the store was slick with tar and engine fumes. Once he was safely in the driver's seat with the doors locked and his seat belt secured, he lay the two breakfast bars next to each other on the dashboard and started the ignition. The vehicle was free of distractions. No coffee in the cup holder, no road maps strewn on the floor, no sound coming from the radio. The only noise was the engine's subtle hum and a sudden voice command from the GPS, breaking the silence. The trip locator's voice was deep and demanding, the rasp of a middle-aged German Frau, most likely recorded directly at the central Audi plant in Ingolstadt. Each time the matron ordered him to take a turn or to veer left, it sounded as if she was scolding him for bad behavior. Yesterday he'd missed an exit and was forced to travel two hundred meters out of his way to get back on course. "You've strayed from the course! Please turn left to return to the highlighted route!" she taunted him. All he heard was *You've strayed. You've strayed. You've strayed.* He was a bad man. He'd never enjoyed driving, and now the art of it had changed for the worse. It had become interactive.

As he pulled onto the highway, George hunched close to the steering wheel and kept the car moving at a constant pace in the right-hand lane. He was used to sitting in the passenger seat or the back when he was in a car. As a passenger, he routinely let his eyes roam the landscape next to the road. Here, in the driver's seat, out of necessity he kept his eyes steadily on the pavement and the lane lines that marked his way. It was a narrow view, jolting in its lack of periphery, but it would get him where he was going. He'd survived brushing his teeth and navigating the first leg of today's trip, now his goal was to keep on course and forestall his deterioration for one more day, he and his Audi working in unison. An Audi, as if driving a German car might be all it took to be seen as the next Walter Gropius. As if all it took to conceive great buildings was an expensive European toy. *Le pauvre* George Bedecker. He was becoming transparent, even to himself.

CHAPTER 10

Nate Faces the Truth, the Half Truths, and the Possible Truths

NATE COULDN'T REMEMBER which pier he and Charlie had set off from for their childhood sailing lessons thirty years ago. What he remembered, instead, was Charlie's innocence, his unflappable enjoyment of the whole vacation. On their second day of lessons, Charlie stubbed his toe on the rough wood of the dock. His blood leached onto the boat's slick white deck. For a moment, Charlie had looked almost sick, devoid of color. Nate felt sick, too, when he saw Charlie go pale. He often wished Charlie would toughen up — yet when the boy was actually in pain, Nate softened and felt the urge to take the hurt on himself. Charlie's pain was only momentary this time. After the sailing instructor taped him up, he began to look proud. "I hurt myself *sailing*," he'd said with alert, nearly joyful eyes.

As for whether it was *this* pier that they'd sailed from in June 1974, Nate couldn't say. All of Newport's pristine, parallel docks looked the same. And anyway, memory loss was routine for the almost-forty-year-old male. What you had to take note of, he'd read, was a diminishment of short-range recollection, especially if accompanied by joltish mood swings.

For the past month, Nate had been monitoring his own behavior carefully but peripherally, without overtly admitting (or barely admitting, at least) that he was checking up on himself. He subconsciously quizzed his memory each night by reparsing the events of his day (what he'd had for lunch, which phone calls he hadn't yet returned, what color underwear Emily had worn), telling himself that he was creating a personal narrative simply for the sport of it. It wasn't a joke, though. With every twitch, every unexpected stumble, he was on the lookout.

On the Newport dock, his footing was steady and sure. His eyes were on Trevor, who gawked at the bright masts of the boats tied to the moorings. Trevor, who'd been dragged into this mess with no say of his own.

"He's going to have a future on boats!" Emily had said. It hadn't occurred to Nate that Trevor might grow up sailing. It seemed so obvious, but Nate hadn't let himself think about the future at all. And regardless, a life on the water was so contrary to Nate's past. After that one childhood trip, he had never sailed much again. He'd been a guest on friends' boats throughout the years, vessels considerably larger than those he and Charlie had maneuvered, but he'd never taken up sports, unless you counted weekend Wiffle Ball and the occasional halting squash game with the guys from work. As long ago as middle school gym class, it was clear that there'd be no career in athletics for Nate, unless tetherball went pro.

Today Nate simply wanted to live long enough to see his boy throw his first ball. He wanted Trevor to live long enough, too. Trevor was his son, the same way Nate was George's. Heredity was a terrifying concept.

"That's a sloop or something, a yacht, Trev," Emily said, approaching from down the dock.

"Hey," Nate reached out his hand.

"SPF forty," she passed him the sunscreen.

Nate took the tube while Emily undid the Bugaboo's protective straps and lifted the boy out of Ollie's bucket.

"Watch it — " Nate said. The buggy had started to roll and he grabbed it with his free hand, using his foot to readjust the brake.

"Thanks," Emily said. "Goddamn orphan."

The faulty brake was the most noticeable hazard of buying the stroller secondhand. They'd saved $400 by purchasing it from Ed Auberley and his wife after their youngest kid outgrew it. Ed had warned Nate about the brake — it worked, but it jammed open if you weren't careful. That was a small issue. The bigger one, which Nate hadn't anticipated, and he bet Ed hadn't, either, was the shame they'd shared after the transaction. Nate and Emily now knew that Ed and Marissa, who'd always seemed enviably flush, were so strapped that they'd sold their Bugaboo rather than recycling it or donating it to charity. And Ed and Marissa were aware that Nate and Emily didn't have the reserves to spring for their own firsthand stroller-of-the-moment. Just days after they completed the deal, Nate and Emily and the infant Trevor happened to run into the Auberleys on Lexington and Seventy-Seventh Street, where they'd all kept their eyes awkwardly averted from the Bugaboo's unmistakable red awning.

That's when Nate and Emily nicknamed the stroller Ollie, for Oliver Twist, the haggard little orphan boy. Since then, whenever Emily saw an industrial Stokke on the street — a Norwegian import far more technical than even a new Bugaboo — she'd glance pleadingly at Nate and joke, in her best cockney accent,

"Please, sir, may I have some more?" In Newport they hadn't seen a single Stokke. They hadn't even seen any Bugaboos other than their own.

"Hey, is it a sloop?" Emily asked, pointing to the boat on which Trevor's eyes, unblinking and singular in their focus, were fixated. It had a tall main mast and a small second sail. A jib, was that what they called it?

"Maybe?"

"We'll to have to learn the terminology," Emily laughed. "We won't want to embarrass the kid once he has school friends."

"Do you honestly think our kid is going to be in the sailing crowd?"

"Are there other crowds here? We'll see, I guess. I've sort of been picturing him at St. George's, once he gets old enough. I assume everyone at St. George's sails and plays lacrosse. But maybe he'll be in the theater crowd, all grunge and poetry. Whatever Trevor wants." She swept her palm across the boy's smooth cheek, and he smiled.

"St. George's," Nate said. "He'd be a day kid at the boarding school." Nate had boarded at the Hill School in Pennsylvania — it was there that he first met a number of the acquaintances he still saw in New York, at parties and banking-industry events and booze-fueled minireunions. In high school, Nate had cherished his day-student classmates and their insider knowledge, their split-level abodes. "I hadn't anticipated Trevor getting old enough for high school. I mean — " Fuck it, that's not a thought he was ready to have.

"Or us sticking around here that long?"

"Maybe," Nate said. He simply hadn't thought of Trevor as an adolescent or grown-up at all. The boy looked so much like Nate as a child, but with Emily's wry smile, that Nate found it easy to focus solely on Trevor *now*. He had Nate's dark hair and pasty skin, his oval face (already losing its baby roundness), long limbs and wiry-long toes. Finger toes, Emily called them.

The only other baby Nate had ever known, up close, was Charlie, born when Nate was two. All Nate remembered of those early years was Charlie's tendency to snag his diaper on their shared toys, his unexplainable blond hair (which turned dark by the time he was school-aged), and his cleft chin. After Trevor was born, Nate searched the baby's face for signs of Charlie, kept expecting to see a resemblance, but there was none. That fact made Nate sad, as if even more than before, it was possible to believe that Charlie had never existed. A reminder, any hint of him in Trevor, would have comforted Nate. He wanted to believe that his brother's life had meant something, but the younger Bedecker had died before graduating from high school, before having his chance, before — just two weeks before — playing his first trumpet solo. Nate liked to think that he himself would have been a different person if Charlie had never been born, that at least Charlie's presence had made Nate a better man (or at least his death had made Nate wiser about life), but perhaps Nate's path would have been exactly the same if Charlie had never lived. It was gut-wrenching to think this way.

As for Trevor, there wasn't much of Emily in the boy, either. Everyone — friends, work colleagues, the boy's pediatrician — commented that the boy looked exactly like his father. Still, Trevor's genes were only half Nate's. It was a fifty-fifty lottery, procreation. That's why he hadn't wanted a kid in the first place — or why he'd thought he hadn't wanted one — too much of a child's future was left up to chance, and risk terrified Nate. That was probably why he'd never truly succeeded on Wall Street. His new bosses, however, were looking for a conservative money manager. For once, Nate fit the bill.

"Do you smell that?" Emily held Trevor's butt up to her face.

"Oh, I guess not. He's still fresh." Trevor opened his mouth wide, the way he often did in the moments before launching a cry, but held silent. He twisted against Emily's arm hold and she readjusted her grasp and said, "It must just be the salt from the water. It smells a little rancid."

She stood Trevor on the ground and he clung to her leg.

"Em, seriously, we're on a dock." Trevor seemed to hear the edge in his father's voice and fell to the ground. "You need to keep your eye on him." Nate grabbed hold of the boy's arm and steadied him.

"Sorry," said Emily. "I'm just picturing our bright future."

Emily spoke incessantly about the future. As if it were something a person could bank on.

"This isn't Manhattan," he said. "Newport has good public schools. Trevor doesn't have to go to St. George's." Newport did have good publics, at least on the elementary level. This was supposed to be the appeal. Newport symbolized an escape from the rat race for both Nate and his son.

Newport's anti-allure (other than the disappearance of their Jeep with their detailed financial histories inside) was Nate's family history with the area. He'd never planned to move back to his father's ancestral homeland and, as a result, had almost turned down the Newport job, sight unseen. That would have been foolish, he understood now. There weren't any Bedeckers left in Rhode Island and their history here had been largely eradicated, given that, in public, George never spoke about growing up in Narragansett. He chose, instead, to portray himself as a self-made Midwesterner or a man rooted in old Europe. The only thing that remained of the Bedeckers in this part of the country was a boarded-up Narragansett homestead, empty and left to rot, for all Nate knew.

He watched a small motorboat, a whaler maybe, navigate

the narrow channel between docks. He touched Emily's arm as she lifted Trevor and held him high, helping the boy see past the boats to the open harbor. Nate hated keeping information from her. Until recently, he'd hadn't lied to Emily ever, never held back, but once he started he couldn't stop. And now there was a *New York Times* clip burning a hole in his wallet. The folded-up article had been there for more than a month, for forty-one days. It was nothing, probably, just a small mention of Nate's father. And yet the clip had awakened Nate's dormant health fears and put him on high alert. He'd told himself that he was justified in keeping it from Emily, that he would talk to her about it when the time felt right. Still, he was increasingly glad that he'd missed his chance to have that talk last night. There was no reason to scare her, not until he'd done the preliminary investigating himself. Not until he knew whether there was anything, honestly, to say.

"Here, I'll take him," Nate said, holding his arms out for the boy. Trevor was growing heavy, no longer an easy carry. Emily handed him off and then looked out over the water, which was choppy in the midday wind, and Nate did, too. He looked past the docks and beyond the boats. Across the harbor, south of Jamestown, Nate saw land. On that strip of coastline, he knew, lay Narragansett and the Bedecker house, the old Bedecker house, his father's childhood home.

CHAPTER 11

Where Do You Think We're Going?

T HEY'D ALREADY BEGUN spending the cash. First on necessities: a jumbo pack of Pampers, two cans of ready-to-drink formula, five two-packs of Gerber Organics, and a bunch of bananas. Then, as lunchtime approached, Emily insisted on splurging — and she didn't regret it — on two picnic sandwiches and an iced tea to split. They were down to $42.50, not even enough for dinner with wine, barely enough for a few hours of babysitting in New York. Emily knew that they could have saved the cash by eating at the hotel (they had to return to the Viking anyway, for Trevor's nap), but it meant the world to Emily, when in dire straits, to be able to eat a sandwich in the open air. Under the thin October sun, she'd fed Trevor a small tub of pureed sweet potatoes along with the pack of oyster crackers that the deli had thrown in for free.

Now Trevor was sound asleep in the Pack 'n Play. He'd caused a scene in the lobby when they got back to the hotel, kicking his legs against Ollie's footrest and emitting one chest-rattling cry, a single extended husky tone. Emily had smiled at the other guests in the foyer, hoping an awkward grin might substitute for an apology. By the time they reached their suite, the tired boy's neck had begun to go limp against the side of his stroller.

It was Emily's fault, hers and Nate's. They'd kept Trevor out for too long, almost an hour past his nap time. Children were ruled by bodily schedules, the triple demons of sleep and excrement and food that Emily, with her contrary internal timetable, battled against every day. When Trevor was a newborn, she and Nate had taken him out to eat almost every night. With Trevor strapped to Nate's chest, they'd dined at nearly all of the low-key cafés near their apartment (linoleum-countered joints that most of their friends walked by without a second glance), always arriving early to avoid the throngs of first-year analysts and lawyers who crowded their neighborhood as if they'd been seeded in the window boxes. These dinners out were slow and languorous, Nate and Emily so tired that they could barely lift their forks to their mouths, but at least they were outside the apartment! They'd fooled themselves into believing that they were still in charge of the household. They'd been the first in their crowd to Ferberize, as well, letting Trevor cry himself to sleep at five months.

Today, with Trevor out cold in the Viking's bedroom, Emily lay on the outer room's plush loveseat, letting her legs sink into the understuffed cushion. The chicken salad from her sandwich sat heavy in her stomach. She shouldn't have eaten it; stress and food were a dangerous mix. She watched Nate, who was hunting through the suite's minifridge. He squeezed a bag of salted almonds and flashed it toward her before stuffing it into his pants pocket.

"These will be good for later. Next time we're out, we won't have to shop," he said as he popped open a Diet Coke. He set the can on top of the TV and peeled off his button-down, smelling the underarms before hanging it in the closet. He stripped out of his T-shirt, too. He was still almost as slim as when Emily first met him four years ago. Even the small bulk that had accumulated around his waistline, the only bulge on his lithe frame, held its own well-defined shape.

"Later? Where do you think we're going?"

"We'll go as far as we can get with a Bugaboo and a boy. What's the record for that?" Nate picked up the soda and took a long swig.

"Not far," Emily said. "Unless you're planning to sneak into Doris Duke's mansion." She closed her eyes, giving her retinas a break from the room's overwhelmingly floral decor. The room could use fresher textiles, exposed hardwood, maybe some stolen art to perk it up.

"Doris Duke's *mansion?* They call them cottages, babe, not mansions," Nate said. "It's the local lingo. Cottages. How fucking cute."

"We can't afford them anyway. The admissions prices would eat up our whole stash." Emily had a feeling that they'd spend the rest of the weekend in this room, hoarding the cash they had left. As for the one daytime adventure that was free of charge, the Newport Cliff Walk, it wasn't ideal with a baby.

"Stretches of the path are jagged and au naturel," the concierge downstairs had said, smiling condescendingly. "They're in the process of renovating the final leg, smoothing out the largest of the boulders. It's not safe with a stroller."

Emily had a horrifying vision of Ollie tumbling off the Cliff Walk or into a bottomless crevasse, Trevor spread-eagled as he fell, his mouth open in a silent cry — finally he masters the silent cry! But it's too late! — à la Hitchcock. The horror! Emily had studied fear in college, from a philosophy standpoint. She'd focused on the ways traditional images of disaster snuck into eighteenth-century theories on existence. We're all haunted, it turned out, by our own idiosyncratic but also shockingly familiar doomsday prophesies: This was her lecturer's point of view. Even at the time, Emily had wondered if that was historically correct or simply the kind of thesis (fear! universal fear!) that the scholars at Michigan knew would get undergrads all worked up and keep them academically interested. It was a pedantic fireball. It was the kind of knowledge that was regurgitated at frat parties to impress the humanities-deficient econ majors. Econ majors: those guys would have turned into great cheese makers, all concerned with exactitude and numbers and toeing the line. Who knew back then?

She missed the innocent intellectualism of that time, entire years when she was expected to do nothing more than discuss Yeats and Rousseau, when she was surrounded by scholars who understood that these men's words mattered, that there was a larger world, that we were all cogs in the light of history. In the years since, Emily had drifted so far from this former self. Her life of the mind had morphed a life of the material — and the maternal — without her noticing it happen. That drift had hit her hard, smack-hard, at the Barbers' party. Standing in Anna and Randy's expensively spare living room, she couldn't deny who she'd become.

It was still early in the party (early for the Barbers, whose soirees tended to last well into the morning) when Emily found herself next to Sam Tully. He had propped himself against the buffet table (Edwardian, Emily thought) and was describing his new road bike to Nate. Sam said there was a shop on Fourteenth Street that would custom-design a machine to any rider's body measurements and cycling stance. All it cost was a slim month's rent. "A drop in the bucket" is how Sam described the price. Emily grinned when he said this and politely excused herself from the conversation.

Nate, who'd seemed to be having the time of his life, pulled her back toward him and whispered in her ear, "Should we go?" Yes! She loved this man! She nodded even though they had the babysitter booked for another two hours.

"Let me get my bag and swing by the bathroom," she'd answered. "I'll meet you at the elevator." Emily would have liked to own a bike tailored specifically to her stance. She'd have liked an antique buffet table, too, and a budget with enough wiggle room to hire caterers for weekday parties. What she'd have liked, in truth, was the bank account to support these things — she knew she'd never buy that bike, this buffet table, but for the price of either she could make a difference in the world. She was sure of it. She kept thinking about the economy's manic upswing. The pundits were claiming growth might hit record highs by the end of the year, growth that represented some sort of hope for a country rising in the new century, fighting back after a tragedy of epic magnitude. Though from what Emily could see, all the proceeds of that growth were being thrown toward the ridiculous — bespoke bicycles, personal airstrips, hand-massaged beef. None of it was coming her way (or the way of all of the children who were still starving, the middle class who were still fighting for health insurance). If the money were hers, she told herself, she'd build something to last. Whether in technology, in dairy, in philosophy, she didn't know. But she'd at least, with the cash, have a chance at mattering.

She grabbed her bag from the rack in the hallway and then tried the bathroom door — locked, a muffled "out in a minute" came from the other side. She continued walking west through the apartment, in the direction of Greenwich Street, as if these hallways were a part of the city's landscape itself. She turned and stepped into the study, toward a second bathroom, where all was quiet. The party wasn't large enough for people to be wandering this far into the abode. The study was solemn, unlike the living room and dining room, which were experiments in pop art, glossy white spaces punctuated with bursts of primary color and animal print. The study was dark and clubby, like a gentlemen's den from the Barbers' grandparents' era. Leather armchairs abutted bookcases filled with worn hardcover volumes. A brushed-steel desk appeared to be more for show than actual work. Along the wall next to the desk, a stack of framed artworks leaned at a thirty-degree angle.

Anna and Randy weren't art lovers by any means. At other people's parties, the guests joked about it, about how the Barbers had the most significant contemporary art collection of their crowd but didn't seem to care about aesthetics. The couple had a consultant who bought works on their behalf, works that were an honor to own, pieces by newly crowned up-and-comers whose names had cachet. Most important, the works tended to hold onto their value. "Insurance," Randy had said to Emily at a previous party, pointing to an oblong Byron LeRoi that hung in their entryway. "That's a whole kid's future, if they ever need it. Say my career tanks and Anna drinks her way through our reserves? We've always got backup in the art."

These people — Randy, Tristan, Sam Tully, and the rest — loved to talk about the dark side of their wealth, the looming truth that this economic upswing couldn't last forever. That fear lent a frantic energy to their unabashed extravagance, as if they needed to cram in all of the enjoyment they could today, before the world as they knew it died tomorrow. Rather than save to protect against hard times, they spent lavishly in anticipation of them. Regardless, when the crash came, Randy would still have his art. What would Nate and Emily have? Even less than they had now. The thought made Emily's heart crack. She imagined their future as a black hole.

In the hush of the study, Emily knelt toward the stack of canvases. These were small pieces; Randy probably didn't even know what was in this pile. The largest work was not much longer than two-feet across its long side. As she flipped through them, Emily didn't recognize most of the paintings. A few were representative and realistic, almost embarrassingly so. They resembled the kinds of still lifes (pears, daisies, mixing bowls) found on hotel walls in the 1950s. For all Emily knew, they were intended to look like hotel art. Ironic compositions weren't unheard of anymore. Even visual art had lost its ability to celebrate beauty for beauty's sake.

At the back of the stack Emily spotted a Matt Rufino. The canvas was covered with a thick layer of paint in a rich orange-rust hue, cut through by a few large swaths of slate gray. She'd made fun of Rufino in the past. He'd seemed such a fleeting fancy, with his broad brushstrokes that hinted at shadows but weren't clearly anything at all. His work didn't evoke emotion the way the best nonrepresentational art should, in Emily's estimation. Rufino had bragged openly about his most recent series: twenty-four paintings done in one twelve-hour workday, devoting only thirty minutes to each, from conception to completion. The Rufino in the Barbers' pile seemed to be an earlier work but equally hastily made. However quickly he'd painted it, it was worth a mint, and here it lay, hidden in a stack as if it didn't matter.

Even to Emily, who actually believed Rufino's work didn't matter in the grand scheme of things, this was an insult. This piece might be worth nothing in a hundred years, but today it could fund nearly anything. Paint slopped on a piece of stretched cotton by an imbecile, yet the person who owned it possessed a slice of power. Power: Emily had so little of it herself that she'd been essentially evicted from Manhattan, the epicenter of power. Here, though, was capital on a canvas. As Emily gazed at the Rufino — she'd slowly lifted it out of the stack for a closer look — more than anything, she simply wanted a piece of the power. She simply wanted a taste. She simply wanted a whiff of what fell in everyone else's lap. She simply wanted.

Emily, curled tight on the Viking's small sofa, felt a tug on her sleeve and opened her eyes. She found herself eye-to-eye with Trevor. The boy clung onto the sofa's upholstery, his fingers were white with tension as they gripped the damask, but the tug had come from above. She looked up. Nate.

"Hey, sleeping beauty," he said. "Trev's awake and clean and fed."

"You fed him?"

"You were asleep. I squeezed six ounces of formula and a tub of pears into him. That's enough, right? He acted like he'd had his fill." Nate had his shirt on again.

"A whole tub of pears? He never eats a whole tub." She'd only bought the pears because they were paired with the peas. "He's pear-resistant."

"He did. I opened up sweet potatoes, too, but he wouldn't touch them. His system must be out of whack." Nate reached down for Emily's arm and started to pull her to her feet.

"Come on, we should get some dinner," Nate said. "Let's get out of this room."

"Let's just order in, on our room tab," she said. "Please. We can't go out for dinner; we have a cash-flow problem."

"It's early, we can eat in the restaurant downstairs. If Trevor gets antsy we'll leave. I'm stir-crazy. Our neighbors were cranking their TV and my head is throbbing."

The shades in the room were open and Emily looked out at a straight shot of sky, gray twilight like a sheath of Irish tweed. She'd slept for hours.

"Okay," Emily said. Trevor let out a soft "bah" in affirmation, popping a hand over his mouth as soon as the sound was out. He was starting to look filthy in the wrinkled overalls and long-sleeve T-shirt she'd dressed him in yesterday morning. The small folds in his neck were red with sweat; she'd have to wash Trevor's outfit in the sink before they went to bed tonight. They should have bought detergent when they shelled out for the diapers. Should have, should have, should have: She could fill a composition book with all of her recent *should haves*. "Let's have a drink at the bar first, before we eat. We'll bring an extra bottle for Trevor and hope the formula makes him sleepy," she said. A drink would set her head right. Or maybe not, but it couldn't possibly make things worse.

"I've already packed the bag with a bottle and pacifier and that soft toy thing, the red-and-yellow dinosaur you keep in the stroller."

"It's supposed to be a lamb."

"Deadly, that little lamb." Nate growled, a raspy rumble, and Trevor smiled, the corners of his mouth pulling up deep into his high cheeks.

"I'll be ready in a sec. It'll be just like old times," Emily said as she stood, straightening her own wrinkled clothes and thinking about laundry detergent, about all of those little cafés they'd gone to with Trevor in the BabyBjörn, about their innocent past and about the days ahead, the years ahead, when Trevor would be long past his toddler stage and old enough to order food for

himself, to sit at the dinner table across from his parents, unwittingly bridging them like a genetic lariat. She imagined him
with his driver's license, behind the wheel of a junker coming to
visit her in whatever pit her life had landed. Or on the lam with
both of his parents, living in the wilds of rural Eastern Europe.
Or safe and successful in New York again, perhaps. Or right
here. She imagined there would be a day in the future, a day she
could almost fathom if she thought hard enough, when Trevor
would be an adult and Emily's dreams, and Nate's, would either
have come true already or faltered for good.

CHAPTER 12

Here Are the Things Nate Knows

B EING IN NEWPORT WAS starting to wig Nate out. The mere fact that he was thinking in terms like *wig out*, a phrase he would have used decades ago, had him suspicious that Emily knew something was up. It was inconceivable that she hadn't picked up on his recent evasiveness, his skittishness, his generalized angst (a condition more characteristic of her, in the past), the fact that he could barely match his own socks in the morning. She probably thought he was on drugs. Everyone was on something these days, though Nate had no clue what would make a man act as edgy as he'd been. Coke? Maybe. Possibly crystal meth, though Emily would know he'd never have the nerve to do meth (his fear of dentists would keep him off it, if nothing else). Maybe she simply thought he was drinking too much. They both liked to drink, but didn't everyone?

Across the Viking's lounge, Emily and Trevor were nestled into a small couch while Nate hovered at the bar, trying to flag the bartender. He wanted another Guinness, one last drink for the night. He thumbed a tower of cocktail napkins, the paper squares stacked tall like a silo beside a tray of garnishes (lemons, limes, olives, pickled green beans), and thought about his father, about that house just across the water, the old house, the house where Nate's grandparents had lived, where George had grown up. It was a house not built by George, but surely as much a part of him as the houses that he had created.

Nate had no clue how many structures his father had designed in total. Fifty? Two hundred? Most of them were either inconsequential (midsize office sprawls) or were prohibitively located in remote European industrial centers and small Asian travel hubs. In his entire life, Nate had been inside only five of his father's buildings.

The first, of course, was the Bedeckers' house, known as Bedecker House, where Nate had been sequestered for his entire childhood. Second was the Bedecker-designed Faculty and Married Students Housing Park at the University of Virginia. Nate had spent a night there back in 1992 – he'd slept on the floor of a friend's room while in Charlottesville for a wedding. The park dated from the mid-1970s, when George was already established and probably thought he should be building university libraries, not dorms. To Nate's untrained eye, these dorms were nothing special. Ditto for the Seacrest Tower in La Jolla.

Nate hadn't known the Seacrest was his father's building when he'd walked through its front door, in 1998, for a client meeting. He'd entered through the simple glass entryway, rung for an elevator (the elevators were in the front of the lobby, he'd run smack into them even before encountering the reception desk, an odd choice of placement), and risen to the ninth floor, where his meeting was held in a room with windows that spanned the entire top half of the wall. The bottom half of the wall was pockmarked, made of ruddy stone. The room, like the building, had a 1960s aura about it. "Nate Bedecker," his client said after the meeting was over, as if testing Nate's name for a sour taste. They were in the elevator, on their way back to the ground floor. "The building we're in was built by a Bedecker. Any relation?" Nate felt the air leach out of the elevator. The car seemed to plummet briefly and Nate reached for the wall, a slick stretch of metal with nothing to hold onto. "My dad," Nate nodded, pretending it was no big deal.

It wasn't until Nate attended a concert (the first of two: one Mahler, his mother would have been proud, and one Schoenberg, just a year ago) in the Houston Arts Center, again during a work trip, that he understood the scope of his father's work. The Arts Center was beautiful, glorious. Its acoustics were sharp. The ceiling lifted toward the horizon, its sweep giving the immense hall a feeling of airy lightness. Leaving the building after the Mahler concluded, reentering the outside world, Nate felt that he'd emerged from a warm cavern of sound into a society that was somehow better than he'd left it. The structure felt unintentionally elegant, and in this, it reminded Nate of his mother, Annemarie. The building, and the experience of hearing music in it, was thrilling.

Yet nothing compared to Nate's spontaneous visit to Copenhagen's Central Court. In 1999, after the rage in Eastern European tourism passed and all of Nate's friends had already swung through Prague (twice), Scandinavia was briefly hot as a destination and Nate found himself in Denmark. On the last day of his trip, he left his friends in a bar for the afternoon and, alone, walked the straight and narrow Copenhagen streets. Deep in the folds of his memory, he recalled that fifteen years earlier, his father had spent time in Denmark, building a courthouse. Municipal buildings were difficult, George used to say, yet he ate up the work (all work, even municipal commissions) without

discrimination, as if fearing imminent famine. When building
the court, he'd lived in Denmark on and off for almost two full
years. During those years Nate only got word of him sporadi-
cally through his mother (who herself seemed to be in tangen-
tial touch with her husband by then, just a few years before
her health declined) and, once, from a travel magazine article
that suggested tourists in Copenhagen steer clear of the court's
neighborhood due to excessive construction noise and dust.

A decade and a half later, in 1999, Nate wandered off the
street and found himself inside the court, in person. The lobby
in no way resembled the marble entryways familiar from government buildings in the rest of the world. There were no columns,
no neo-Roman facades. The ceiling was low, so rather than feeling as if it soared up – the sense Nate was accustomed to feeling
in lobbies – the expanse felt shallow yet wide, as if here, in this
space, time spread laterally instead of vertically, as if life had
become a parallel track where a man had to watch his head.
It should have been disturbing, the shortness of the walls, but
the space felt soothing and endless in its horizontal sprawl. If
there was something of Nate's mother in the Houston Arts Center, this down-to-earth space with a deceptively limitless span
evoked Nate's brother, as if the boy had been built into the walls.

Nate, the only man in the lobby not wearing a suit, was
so clearly a tourist that the woman behind the security desk
motioned him not through the security line but to a plaque
on the wall near the front door. George Bedecker's name and
the date, 1986, when the building was completed, were etched
onto the brass. Next to the plaque an audio headset hung on a
peg beside a row of buttons. A CD player was embedded in the
stone. Nate slid the headphones over his ears and pressed the
button marked *Englesk/English*, and, over the next fifteen minutes, he listened to his father's voice narrate the construction of

the building and the emotional toll it took on the crew involved. Nate had traveled across the Atlantic and heard, for the first time in his life, his father talking at length.

That's what Nate was hoping to discover across the water in the Narragansett house, when he finally got there: a taste of his father, the feeling he got in the Houston Arts Center and the Copenhagen courthouse, something bigger and better than the man himself. Plus some facts. Nate was looking for something that would give credence to his health worries (disease in the family? papers of some kind?) or to help him discount them once and for all.

He'd already been doing research of his own. Over the past month and a half, Nate had been searching the Internet at night while Emily was asleep, and had also been sneaking into chain bookstores after work but before coming home (but there was so little information in the stores). He hadn't spoken to anyone in person yet. He feared that actually talking about the disease with another human would be an overt acknowledgment of the danger he might be facing.

It all started last month, when Nate stumbled upon the small mention of George in the *New York Times* Metro section. The pertinent part of the clip was barely a sentence. "The great builder, flailing and staggering, unable to grip even a doorjamb, stumbled," the *New York Times* said in the midst of a small piece about an architecture gathering. The writer implied that George had been inebriated. Nate stumbled, too, when he read it. If he could be sure of one thing, it was that George hadn't been drunk. The man had spent his entire adulthood refusing alcohol, afraid to cede control. He would never take a drink at a party filled with reporters, as well as with so many of his competitors and colleagues. The article painted a George so unlike the quietly superior, reticent, physically unassuming man Nate knew. The George in the paper was a buffoon, a fumbler. When Nate read the clip, what he heard in his head was his mother's voice that day in Rhode Island, "It's hunting, sons."

For the first time, Nate could no longer let himself deny the phrase's real meaning, the message that his conscious self had shoved aside years ago. He'd convinced himself that denial was better than a deadly diagnosis. But now he was out of denial and his mother's words had reemerged in his head, whole. *It's Huntington's.*

All of this activity that the *Times* writer had mistaken for drunkenness could easily have been a sober symptom of Huntington's disease.

Nate's mother had tried to warn Nate again, not long before her death — more than ten years after that family trip to Newport. Annemarie was weak with leukemia and living in a hospice at the time, a Greek Revival palace set back behind a thick thatch of trees. Every night when Nate visited, while he was on winter break from college, she spoke to him incessantly in a strained whisper, a steady stream of warnings and life lessons that left Nate not with hope for the future but with a generalized fear of what the coming years might hold. "Watch your father, Nathan," she'd told her son on one of his last nights by her side, her Austrian accent growing stronger as she grew weaker. "It is inborn, *lieben*, if he gets sick, like his father, if you get sick, he will need to be watched, you will need to be watched."

It seemed impossible, back then, that George would ever falter — like his buildings, he was indestructible — so despite his mother's vague warnings, Nate distracted himself with the present. He didn't heed her at all. *It's nothing but deathbed talk*, is what Nate told himself. *It's nothing. She's on drugs.* After all, there was a chance that George hadn't inherited the disease from his father. Future be damned! Nate filled his time and his mind with school and then with work, with Emily, and finally with his son. *His son.* He'd been so alone until Emily and Trevor came along. He'd developed a hard exterior, a buffer against loss. But now he had Trevor. This was not a diseased family. That was a fact that he had let himself believe without wavering. Now, thinking about the risks he'd taken, he cowered inside.

According to every single website and medical manual that Nate had been able to track down, Huntington's early symptoms included the drunklike *ceaseless jerking and uncontrollable movements of the limbs, trunk, and face.* These were the same movements Nate had noticed in his grandfather the one time he saw him, in 1974. That year, Nate's grandfather would have been around the same age George was now. Despite Nate's usual facility for denial, this coincidence was too blatant to disregard. George might have Huntington's, and he might have passed it down to Nate.

Two weeks ago, en route from work to home, Nate hopped off the subway at Thirty-Fourth Street and walked west, toward Penn Station. There, nine floors atop a Duane Reade in a dated high-rise that leased space by the month, sat the offices of the Huntington's Disease Society of America. Nate had found the society after searching online, its name linked to that of Woody Guthrie, the only celebrity who, from what he could tell, had suffered from the disease. Nate figured he'd stop by their office and claim that his group at work was looking for a new cause or whatnot. Or he could pretend he was looking for a different office in the building and had come to the HDSA by mistake. He merely wanted to see the place, pick up some literature that he could be certain was accurate.

He took the elevator to the ninth floor, then followed the black-and-white signs to suite 902, where two men came out of the door, followed by a woman pushing a wheelchair. Nate hung back a bit and watched them. No, not *them*. He barely noticed the men and the woman. He was looking at the girl in the wheelchair. He couldn't place her age — somewhere between twenty and forty he assumed, but she was too disfigured to be sure. There was something childlike about her face, about the open, empty expression. Her bony lower body remained still, cramped in the chair, but her upper body was fluid, in constant movement — her angular left shoulder dipping suddenly down toward her hip and then up again, and repeat — the kind of movement that brought to mind a child's toy on an oval track, speeding up for the straightaways and then banking itself at each curve. This wasn't the stop-and-start jerkiness of the Parkinson's patients Nate had seen in late-night TV ads. This movement was steady, unending. Dip and then up and dip. And now, a hand shot toward her head and back down again. She'd lost control of her body. The odd near-grace of these movements immediately brought Nate back to his own early years. To the grandfather he'd seen in Narragansett.

Once the wheelchair was fully in the hallway, the woman pushing it turned around and locked the office door. Nate looked at his watch. It was 5:20 p.m. Of course they'd be closing up.

"Sorry," the man in front said to Nate, apologizing, it seemed, for blocking the hallway.

"No problem," Nate said, squeezing past them with the purposefulness of a guy on his way to an office down the hall.

When the group was barely behind him, Nate heard a grunt, a few deep, connected tones. He turned. The girl in the chair had made the noise. The woman looked down at her and said, "Maybe." It seemed the girl had asked a question, though to Nate it had been just noise. Then one of the men said, "I'll feed her when we get home."

Nate turned a corner in the hall and waited. Five minutes, ten, just to be sure that the four were gone. So that was what Huntington's looked like in someone his own age, Nate thought. That was the face of Huntington's. He tried not to see himself in that wheelchair. He tried to tell himself that maybe the disease would hit him late, as it had his father. He tried to convince himself that he didn't have the gene, anyway. That might be true, in fact. He told himself this. He tried to fill his head with thoughts of anything, afraid of what might come if he left any mental space unoccupied. And then he saw the face and body of that girl in his mind, and thought about Emily, who still knew nothing. He had to talk to her. He had to talk to her sometime. They needed to talk about Trevor.

Huntington's was genetic and dominant: The only way to get it was from a parent. If Nate's grandfather had the disease, there were even odds that he'd passed it down to Nate's father. And if Nate's father had it, that gave Nate a 50 percent chance of getting it himself: Either his father had passed down his Huntington's gene or he had spared Nate by giving him the healthy gene with which the tainted one was paired. Worst of all, there were no silent carriers of Huntington's — anyone who inherited the gene had a 100 percent chance of, sooner or later, developing the disease and all of its untreatable, escalating, fatal side effects. If George had the disease, he would die from it, horribly. If he'd passed it down to Nate, Nate would die in the same way.

For those who came down with the disease early in their lives — in their twenties, thirties, or forties — the first symptoms were cognitive and psychiatric. Depression, mood swings, irritability, extreme and unexplainable hostility, paranoia, psychosis. People were hesitant to acknowledge this disease, refusing to alert their younger generations that it ran in the family: Lunacy was nothing to be proud of. These brain-related symptoms often staked their claim when the patient was in his or her thirties or early forties, though sometimes later. Sometimes earlier. Next, the physical deterioration set in: the chorea shakes, clumsiness, loss of balance, inability to swallow, stumbling, incontinence. The patient could end up in diapers and with Huntington's characteristic grimace frozen on his face. He might have to be spoon-fed by a spouse. He might find himself abusing his caretakers and kids, spewing unconscious and angry expletives between bites of mashed peas as the disease progressed toward death, without remission, over the course of ten to twenty-five years. In the days that followed Nate's visit to the HSDA office, he thought, frequently, about how the wheelchair-bound woman seemed to have already lost her entire self.

The few Huntington's patients who came down with the disease later in their lives, in their sixties or so like George, were often spared the mental and cognitive symptoms and suffered only the devastating physical effects. Nate, if he had the gene, could come down with the symptoms any time. This year, perhaps. Or like George, older.

Once Nate understood these facts of the disease, he became consumed with the odds of it. George had had two children, and the odds of passing down the gene were fifty-fifty. So maybe Charlie was the kid who got the gene. If that was true, Nate imagined that his brother's death, hit by a car at age seventeen in 1985 while biking to his last swim meet of the summer, was merciful. Charlie had been slammed by a car driving in the wrong lane (a sober driver who'd blacked out from dehydration and the heat, they said, for only a second). Nate hadn't been there but he could picture it: Charlie hunched forward over the wide handlebars of his red Peugeot, a brand-new model that was half birthday gift from their mother, half paid for out of Charlie's allowance savings. He always rode it with the determination of a professional competing in a late leg of the Tour de France: his face intent, his legs circling at a rapid pace. When Nate tried to imagine the moment of Charlie's death, he saw him pedaling close to the side of the road, in the breakdown lane, exactly where he should have been. Charlie, who'd been wearing cutoff chino shorts and the ratty gray-striped T-shirt that he seemed to wear all of the time, didn't flout rules. The accident had been the fault of the car's driver, but that fact couldn't bring Charlie back. Perhaps it was a blessing for Charlie.

And then there was a possibility that neither Nate nor Charlie had inherited the gene, or perhaps both of them had. Genetics, like a coin toss: completely mathematical and a function of chance.

For now Nate seemed safe. He had shown no unusual shakes or memory loss. He was mentally acute enough to understand that it would be wise to finally speak to his father — to confirm whether George really had inherited the disease. He was also as aware as ever of his own weaknesses and limitations. He didn't yet have the strength to confront George for their first ever Bedecker heart-to-heart chat.

First, Nate wanted to see if he could confirm his hunches himself. There could be clues hidden like a treasure chest just across the harbor in Narragansett, in the house that Nate's grandfather had called home until George closed it up decades ago, turning it into his own private storage locker. It was the final resting place of their family history. It was also just a short drive away from the town that Nate, as of this weekend, was claiming as his own home.

Nate looked at Emily across the lounge. He caught her eye

and she quickly looked away again, down into her own lap and then at Trevor, whom she'd propped on the seat next to her. Nate watched as she dipped her finger into the tub of baby food they'd brought down with them, something green and indistinguishable, and then smeared a bit of it on the boy's nose. Trevor smiled, his cheeks taut and red, and slowly broke out into a high-pitched laugh.

PART III

Sunday

CHAPTER 13

The Drive to Narragansett

FOR WHAT WOULD GEORGE Bedecker be remembered? The more he considered this question – while biding time on the shoulder of Route 1, in the vicinity of Guilford, Connecticut – he was increasingly certain that if he was, in truth, remembered at all it would be for the wrong things. For dying a scandalous death – though he was trying to save himself from that possibility with this drive toward privacy. Or he would be memorialized for building the tired Biblioteca Rotunda in Mexico City. Or the Merchant Travelers Tower in Des Moines, a mixed commercial/residential complex with which he'd never been comfortable, but that, with its high construction costs and endless adaptations, had kept his office running for five years. Over the past century, architecture had proven itself a viable art form but a failure as a business model, and the tension between the two – between style and practicality – had been stretched tight, torqued. George wanted to be remembered for the pieces he'd conjured that were unwaveringly functional, aesthetically new, and affordable for their select uses. The Glasgow Con-

servatory obviously came to mind. And also the Faculty and
Married Students Housing Park at the University of Virginia, a
stretch of interconnected low-rises that reimagined group living
as a series of nestled bungalows in interlocking grids. The Cym-
balists Synagogue and Heritage Center in Tel Aviv would also
make George's personal favorites list, although the building, as
he conceived it, was never erected. The commission went to
Mario Botta in the end. Despite the fact that George's proposal
existed only as a model and computer rendering, the design
continued to inspire him.

And then there was Bedecker House, his own residence for
nearly two decades. Square and spare and utilitarian, it honored
Mies van der Rohe and Le Corbusier, envisioning International
Style as a launching pad for something inherently more inti-
mate. He'd seen the residence not only as a space where his own
family would live but also as a springboard for what he assumed
would be a movement to follow. When the house turned into
nothing more than a haven for his family's idiosyncratic life, and
then that family slowly left it, he sold the building to a young
couple who, too, could envision a future in the house. Unlike
Gropius's former home, Bedecker House would be no memorial open for public tours. It was designed to be lived in.

The mere act of mentally reconjuring these works calmed
George's shakes as he stood on the side of the Connecticut
highway, where seamless pavement met raw dirt. With each of
George's buildings he'd aimed to make people's lives better, to
provide consolation in the form of structure. This was what he
could offer. George leaned against the Audi, held his hands in
front of his face, stretching his squat fingers, and felt relief. His
hands had trembled and jerked on the steering wheel one mile
back, the car swerving slightly. George knew that even a small
aberration could be a matter of life and death on the road.

He stood within two hours of Narragansett. He could be there, inside the house, his feet planted on the floorboards of his ancestors, soon. Even if he continued driving cautiously and well under the speed limit, he'd be there by early afternoon. What did it mean that even as George sold Bedecker House, his own longtime residence, he'd held onto his father's home? That he'd kept possession of the modest ground where his father had lived his whole life, had raised George himself? George waited for a lull in the traffic stream and then cracked open the door to the car and slid himself inside, engaging the power locks and turning the key in the ignition. He would be remembered, he told himself. Of course he would.

CHAPTER 14

On Faith

NATE AND TREVOR SAT on an expanse of lawn around the corner from the Viking, across from a stone Unitarian chapel. Newport was a living, breathing slice of God circa 1750. Its cramped, old-town lanes were densely populated with clapboard churches and threatening gravesites and one staunch, domineering Quaker meeting house. Given this milieu, Nate tried to feel pious, but instead he felt only the grogginess of too many sleepless hours, of nearly four decades of living as a heathen.

Trevor had been up most of the night, refusing to be placated by Cheerios or formula, even resisting when Emily, at 3:00 a.m., brought him into the king-size bed where they'd drowsily sung reggae to him, making up nonsense lyrics and riffing on the classics ("No woman, *no cry*"), using their lips and tongues to mimic the Rasta beats of his lost CD. It didn't work. The boy kicked and punched at the air until, after he nailed Nate in the ribs with his tiny torpedo of a leg, they finally returned him to the Pack 'n Play. Eventually they all must have fallen asleep, because at 8:00 a.m. Nate woke to find himself on the floor, curled around a corner of that Pack 'n Play as if sheltering his child. If only he could. Emily was deep in slumber on the bed, her legs entwined in the sheet. And the phone was ringing. Nate reached up and grabbed the receiver before the harsh clang disturbed Emily. The phone call, it turned out, was a wake-up call. Emily must have requested it. With all of her nervous energy she probably wanted to get a jump on the day even though they had nowhere to go. He hung up the phone and let Emily continue to sleep.

Though Emily lay undisturbed, the call woke the baby. Nate changed and dressed the boy with little more than the usual struggle and grabbed Emily's overstuffed baby bag. He took her phone and wallet out of it and restocked it with supplies (a few diapers, a bottle that Nate filled with fresh formula, a sealed packet of wipes). Then he carried Trevor outside to this spread of grass. Together they watched as congregants lined up outside the chapel. The congregants climbed up the entryway's high steps, nodding their heads in silent greeting to one another. What were *their* sins? There must have been forty people waiting to enter and countless others already inside. One older man tripped and fell gently up the steps, rather than down. As the final churchgoers approached the entrance, they lightly crushed against one another in a delicate push to get through the door. Simple belief had to be a nice way to live.

"Oh, hey, buster!" Nate scrambled after Trevor, who had begun to crawl toward the deists. There was a morning chill to the ground and Nate plucked Trevor up and held the boy's hands in front of his mouth, warming them with his breath. Trevor poked a finger between Nate's teeth, and Nate gently nibbled on it. Trevor smiled, a genuine smile, but he was still looking at the church. He'd been making a beeline for religion, something he'd surely never get from his parents.

"You want a piece of the action, chief?" Nate smoothed his son's rangy hair. The boy smelled like hotel soap.

Before leaving the Viking, Nate had left Emily a hastily penned note: "Awake early, out for fresh air with T." Church was the opposite of what Emily and Nate usually considered fresh air. Religion, to them, fell somewhere between oppression and pollen, squarely in the realm of the rarely observed hindrance. Faith and fate, as Nate saw it, went hand in hand. And over this past month, he and fate had launched into an uncomfortable relationship. Here, though, standing with his son in the town where the boy would grow up — Nate fervently hoped that Trevor *would* actually grow up — eyeing a congregation of hopefuls, a crowd of religious dreamers praying for their hearts' desires, Nate felt, for a moment, appealingly small and abundantly blameless. He felt like just another cog. He felt improbably at home.

Nate had been brought up without religion, yet when he returned to Ohio for Christmas during his senior year of high school, he tripped over a small ivory Buddha. The diaper-clad demigod — sitting cross-legged in front of a woven prayer rug — had been installed in Bedecker House's glass-paned entryway while Nate was away. The kitchen windows, the smallest in the house (miniscule portals sandwiched between the industrial cabinets and metal counters), had been covered with ethereal white muslin shades. His mother, who'd shunned God for as long as Nate could remember, had suddenly fallen for Western Caodaism.

"Western *what?*" Nate asked.

"Western Caodaism," his mother said with an accent on *Cao-daism* that he couldn't place. She continued, "Existence is in accord, in every step."

Charlie, who'd been home for a few days longer than Nate, walked into the room as Annemarie said this. He smiled at Nate. Clearly this wasn't the first of these pronouncements from their mother.

"Existence in the accord?" Nate said.

"Come on, Nate! The great Western Caodaism, savior of the people!" Charlie smirked as he said this, though their mother showed no reaction. "Come on, Mom, I've done my research, and Austrians do not worship mass-produced ivory statues of naked Asians. Not even in the name of Caodaism."

"I don't worship the Buddha, *lieben*," she said, her voice gentle. She spoke with the slow cadence she'd used to placate her sons when they were children. "The statue is simply in homage to our Eastern brethren. We live in a greater world, never forget that."

Charlie tugged on the arm of Nate's sweater and led him out of the room.

"Don't we need to take action, intervene?" he asked Nate as they stood in the house's entryway. He wanted a directive from Nate. As the younger brother, Charlie had always deferred to Nate on family-related matters. He listened to Nate, took his perspective as Bedecker law even though, as Nate saw it, Charlie was the sharper observer, the quiet synthesizer. Nate was a pro when it came to the surface details, but Charlie understood what was going on at the heart of matters. Nate worried that once they became true adults, equals and no longer younger brother and older brother, Charlie would curse himself for having relied on Nate's skin-deep counsel for so many years.

"Nate, she's freaking out. We need to save her."

"How would we save her?" Nate said. "She's only trying to save herself."

"It's psychiatric, isn't it, what's going on? There must be doctors who could treat her, or clinics."

"What would she do at a clinic?" Nate said. "Clinics are for tennis lessons and heart patients."

They heard a body shifting in the doorway and both turned to look behind them. George stood staunch in the square space, openly listening to his sons. He turned to leave and then turned back. "Don't worry, boys, she'll snap out of it in a year or two," he said. "You'll have your mother back."

Two years later she'd withdrawn deeper into her own consciousness and Charlie was dead. He'd gone from *there* to *not* without warning, as if he'd never been alive at all. In the days after Charlie's death, Nate found himself reaching out his arms to feel the air in front of him, as if he might brush up against Charlie's chest. As if he weren't dead but simply invisible. As if his mass still existed and it were merely a matter of locating it. It was at Charlie's funeral that Nate, stoic in his disbelief, saw both of his parents cry for the first time. His mother's tears were like a wet veil over her face; his father's were softer and quiet in their unexpectedness. Nate understood, then, that these two strange adults truly shared something. After the funeral, they and Nate went their separate ways again, the bonds between them one person weaker. Two years after that, Annemarie was dead, too, the doctors promising that the speed of her leukemia had been a blessing and that she'd gotten the best care.

After Annemarie's graveside service, where Nate (a senior in college at the time) and his father stood with a foot of cold Cleveland air between them, Nate spent his final nights in the glass house. He boxed up his and Charlie's things for storage and signed a stack of papers: a contract with the storage facility, a form from the trust that Annemarie had set up and included just enough to cover the remainder of Nate's education costs.

"We're all that's left," Nate told his father on one of those nights as they sat across from each other in the kitchen. "What do we do?" He said it lightly, his voice tentative, and the *we* hit George and bounced back to Nate with the reflexive speed of a Super Ball. George had always been linked to his children through their mother and didn't seem to have the instincts, or interest, to be a father. Nate's questions were met with silence and headshakes. He could hear his father crying late at night, out in the living room, probably sitting in the Eames chair that was imprinted with the shape of his spine. Even through the heavy walls that separated Nate's room from this expanse, he could hear his father's choked sobs. George's grief was private but unbridled, as if the man, the man inside the man, had been set loose.

Nate finished his last semester of college and continued – then and in the years that followed – trying to reach out, with occasional phone calls, to George. He was the only other person on earth with whom Nate had shared Charlie and Annemarie. George handled Nate's calls (and the ensuing conversations about nothing, about Nate's New York digs or the greater implications of solar power or the weather) haltingly. Sometimes in the silences Nate felt his father's desire, perhaps, to make a connection. But before the silence could develop, before Nate or George could reach all the way across the line for some sort of tangible touch with the other, the call would be over. The calls finally dwindled to once or twice a year, and now the two Bedeckers came into contact on only rare occasions – once, in a call put through by George's longtime assistant, Danielle, to tell Nate that the trust, effectively empty, was being closed out. And once, over a decade ago, to announce another death, that of Nate's grandfather, George's dad. After Nate answered that call, Danielle put George on the line.

"The old man in Rhode Island," Nate said into the phone. "That's who's dead?"

He didn't understand precisely why his father was making a point to call with the news. Nate had never known the old man, though he'd thought of him often, of that one glimpse of him.

"He made it to old age," George said. "Confounding. He should have given up years ago."

"I never knew him. I'm sorry for your loss." These were the same platitudes people offered Nate when they heard he had a dead mother, a dead brother (two tragedies that had been numbed, in Nate, by time rather than platitudes). They were the only words he had in his possession when it came to talking about grief.

"If he'd been well, if he'd been accessible and in mental health, physically able, I'd have introduced you. You'd have known him. It wasn't a possibility by the time you came along."

There was a silence on the phone, like the arid, aural spaces that had filled the Cleveland house on so many empty Saturdays.

"I'll be going to Rhode Island to settle his things. That's why I've called. Before closing up his house, I'm planning to have my goods shipped from storage in Cleveland. I'll keep them there, now. It's an empty house, with a surplus of unused space," George said. After Annemarie's death, he'd relocated his office and residence to Chicago, seeing no reason to remain in Ohio, apparently, a place with either too many memories or too few. George had sold the glass-and-stone cube that served as the family's home in Cleveland, boxed up its contents and moved them into storage. "If you'd like me to have your boxes shipped at the same time, I can have that done. No one is living in the Rhode Island house anymore. The space is free."

Nate remembered the home in Narragansett, with its old-fashioned front porch and views over the water and creepily degenerated inhabitant.

"Why don't you just sell the damn house in Rhode Island?" Nate said. After all, George had found it remarkably easy to unload the Cleveland home, the house in which Nate grew up, a home that George himself built. The new owners had probably torn the place down by now. "You sold our home."

"Our house was mine to sell," George said. "The Rhode Island house has history." And after a pause, matter-of-factly, as if his words were rationed, "I loved the Cleveland house. I loved your brother, too. I loved Annemarie." And then, it seemed, there was nothing else to say. Nate would leave his boxes in storage in Ohio, cleaving his things from his father's, a decision that made their physical rift final.

Nate wanted to be as close to Trevor as George had been distant with his own sons. That was the thought he had on the lawn in Newport — that perhaps he could be the negative image of his own father. That, ideally, Trevor could love him back. When the last parishioners had entered the church across the way, Nate looked back down at his son. A steady stream of drool dripped straight from Trevor's lips to his now-damp T-shirt.

"Oh, kiddo," Nate said touching the shirt's wet spot, which stretched from Trevor's neck down his chest. The boy's diaper was wet, too. Nate could feel the familiar ooze as he wrapped his arms around Trevor's back and bottom, adjusting the boy's weight in his grasp.

He lay Trevor on the grass and reached into the bag for the diapers and wipes. What Trevor really needed was a dry shirt. Nate knew that finding one was a long shot, given their lack of clean laundry, but he rifled through the bag anyway. Emily usually kept a spare set of Trevor's clothes in the diaper tote. The kid was constantly in need of changing.

"Bah!" The boy said, reaching an arm into the air and smiling at nothing. The kid was happy this morning. Oblivious and happy. Nate held him down with one arm and continued looking through the sack, the unrecognizable detritus of Emily's life. Lipstick tubes and vitamins and coupons gobbed together with old lotion of some sort. He felt something soft and pliable in the inside zipper pocket. That was another thing women had over men: secret pockets. Zipper pockets in their purses, button pockets inside their coat linings, lockets around their necks that held the keys to their pasts.

Nate reached into the pocket and pulled out a tube of rolled fabric, held tight by a nylon hair band. Not a T-shirt, for sure. More like a diaper-changing pad. Emily had kept a diaper pad stashed in the bag for Trevor when he was a newborn, Nate remembered, but by three months the tot had grown too large to lie on it. Nate took the band off the tube and unrolled it, slowly, taking his spare hand off Trevor's stomach to lay the fabric flat on the ground.

The swatch was covered in slick colors, like vinyl, like a placemat. Frayed white threads fuzzed at its edges. Its colors, a deep copper-orange and industrial gray, were unexplainably appealing. Trevor rolled onto his stomach and took a look, as well.

Nate's eyes drifted over the piece the way he read a newspaper, from the top corners to the bottom, and that's where, in the lower right, in barely legible print, his eyes locked on a name.

Rufino.

He drew away from the cloth quickly, as if from a flame, and then leaned closer in. Rufino. It said, Rufino. He was looking at the Barbers' Rufino.

Naked, stripped from its frame, it resembled nothing more than an attractive shard of upholstery fabric. Nate, breathless and dazed, was stunned by how different a thing could look when shorn of its context.

CHAPTER 15

Breakfast at the Viking

MILY WOKE WITH A start: light in her eyes, silence in the air. It was 9:30 a.m. and the only trace of Nate and Trevor in the room was a note on the pillow. They were out for a walk, giving her a break. From the sound of it, they'd be gone for a while. She lay back down but couldn't sleep. As with yesterday morning, in new daylight the shock of their situation hit her with a fresh smack. They had no car, no home, no money, nothing but a useless work of art. In their escape from Manhattan, they'd already sunk several rungs below where they started out. She hadn't meant to steal the Rufino.

The entire seriousness of her action hadn't hit her until the theft was a fait accompli. And even then, none of it seemed real. She'd pushed it out of her thoughts over the past couple of days. It felt like someone else's misstep (because, truthfully, how could Emily Latham commit an actual crime? She wasn't competent enough to pull off a felony!) until Celeste mentioned, with such surety, that the cops would be questioning the Barbers' guests. It hadn't seemed real until that moment. At the time of the theft, four days ago, she'd been in a stupor.

She'd been alone in the Barbers' study, at the far end of their apartment, barely able to hear the party. The only noise that reached her was the occasional shrill laugh and the knock of platters against one another in the kitchen. As she held the Rufino, she looked back toward the study's door, which had shut behind her. She gazed up at the books arranged not by author or year but by color of the spines, and she ran her fingers along the flat wool of the carpet, and before she understood what she was doing, she reached into her bag and took out a pair of nail scissors. She lay the Rufino flat on the floor (yes, she'd made fun of his work in the past, but she could understand that there might be a bit of beauty in this piece, in its effortlessness and simplicity – effortlessness and simplicity being qualities that Emily was learning to deeply appreciate) and, as if slicing tape with a box cutter, she used one of the scissors' sharp tines to cut the canvas from its heavy frame. She replaced the empty frame to the back of the stack and then rolled the liberated canvas into a baton with the painted side in. She secured it with a hair band that had been at the bottom of her purse. Instinctively she wiped down the edge of the frame with the hem of her sweater. Finally she stuffed the canvas, now a ten-inch-long roll the width of a banana, into the inside pocket of her purse.

And now, in Newport, the Rufino was still in her bag, zipped inside a practically hidden pocket that she never used. She wasn't sure if it was a stroke of luck or a curse that the painting hadn't been taken with the car. It was luck. It had to be. Much as she'd like to be rid of the piece (in the light of day, she understood that there was no power in possessing an easily identifiable, and identifiably stolen, work of art), at least she could keep an eye on it. It wouldn't turn up at a pawnshop as incriminating evidence, linked to their vehicle.

The horror that she wouldn't allow herself to acknowledge, the detail that had helped her push the entire theft to the deep reaches of her brain, was this: If she were caught with the Rufino and jailed (she tried to convince herself that Anna and Randy would never press charges — that they'd tell the cops it was just a misunderstanding — but that was a stretch, she knew) Trevor would be motherless. She couldn't let herself get caught. She couldn't get caught. She was fine, she told herself. There were no clues, that's what everyone had said. There was no evidence. Emily simply had to maintain her composure.

In the moment when she'd first laid eyes on the Rufino, just before cutting it from the frame, she'd thought that perhaps the painting could buy her an intellectual life again, bringing her back in line with Nate. At minimum, it could give Emily a small bit of the financial security she'd always craved. Of course she'd been deluded about this. In Emily's hands, the painting lost its worth. She had no idea how to unload the thing and turn it into cash. She didn't have those kinds of connections. Or those kinds of guts. More than a criminal, she'd been a fool.

It was too much to acknowledge, so for the past three days, she'd willfully avoided the situation, told herself no one would ever know. She was beginning to understand, though, that moving to Newport hadn't nullified the theft. It hadn't negated the crime but had amplified it.

She should have dumped the Rufino in a rest-stop bathroom. She should have thought about her son before yanking a Rufino from its frame.

Wired on her own idiocy, Emily got out of bed, pulled on her crusty clothing, and settled into breakfast at the café downstairs, just off the hotel's lobby. Barely ten minutes after her coffee arrived, she spotted her two men standing beyond the check-in desk. Nate was on the in-house phone and Trevor, the tired trooper, was perched once again on a marble hotel counter.

She hadn't mentioned her crime to Nate. Well, she'd tried to say something several times, but it – her spontaneous proclivity to steal and the ensuing legal jeopardy in which she'd placed herself – was too humiliating to acknowledge even to her so-called life partner. How could she explain herself? Every time she attempted to bring it up, she stammered and went silent, and Nate, all caught up in his own head, hadn't seemed to notice.

The lobby where Nate and Trevor stood now was bright with the morning sun, but the restaurant where Emily sat, some thirty yards away, was dark as a cave, illuminated solely by the large-screen TV behind the bar. Nate's back was turned. Emily's eye fell on the diaper bag slung over his shoulder – he had her bag. He had the Rufino! Emily caught her breath and felt a wince stick in her throat. Then she understood that he wouldn't, couldn't possibly, stumble upon the artwork. It was in the bag's interior zip pocket, a pocket that a person would need a flashlight and foreknowledge to find. Nate, in all of his ten months of helping carry the bag, had never had to use that pocket. The diapers, cream, everything he would need was in the main pouch. He was a man, he wasn't curious enough to explore a woman's purse further. He wasn't.

He wasn't even curious enough to have glanced around the Viking and noticed her in the café. Trevor hadn't noticed her, either. Trevor's eyes were fixed on the miniature bulbs that circled the chandelier above, probably as beautiful as fireflies to him. He loved lights, sparkles, staring.

She knew she should rise up and run into the lobby, tap Nate on the shoulder, alert him to her presence, but she hesitated. He and Trevor looked so fine as a twosome. They rarely spent

time together without Emily hovering nearby. And she rarely
got a chance to spend time by herself. In the weeks leading up to
Trevor's birth, late last fall, she'd imagined her postpartum world
turning more internal. She'd thought that the loneliness would
eat away at her and so, from the start, she insisted to herself (and
to her mother up in Cambridge, and to Nate, to Jeanne, to the
cashier at the chain coffee shop on their corner in New York)
that she'd return to the workforce as soon as her son was a few
months old.

Confounding her expectations, life with a baby was as bus-
tling as office life had been, if significantly more mind-numb-
ing. Her schedule was packed with playgroups and dates at the
baby gym (kill me *now!* Emily thought every time she entered
the place) and swim lessons starting at six months. At night, too,
she and Nate fielded nonstop invitations from friends – friends
who also had kids. There were cocktail parties and dinners and
overpopulated fund-raisers for the Himalayan museum whose
name she could never remember and the Lower East Side com-
munity garden. Everyone, or everyone else at least, had help at
home, women who took the subway in from Queens in order
to watch other people's children, both day and night. When
Emily needed help, she relied on a roster of college students
and friends of the intern at Nate's office who happily babysat
for twelve dollars an hour. That's what freedom cost. Most of
the time, Emily thought it was worth it, but when she and Nate
stayed out too long, past the eleven o'clock news and into *The
Tonight Show*, she felt guilty. She worried that she was trying
to negate her child's existence (at a whopping twelve dollars an
hour) by returning to the era before he entered her life, before
he announced himself out of the blue with a missed period and
Emily's swollen breasts.

This morning, though, she didn't feel that particular guilt as she lingered over her breakfast while Nate handled their child. Father and son looked so unexpectedly natural together. From this distance they appeared whole, secure, of a piece. They were better people than she was.

She kept an eye on Nate and Trevor in the lobby, but she didn't stand up from the breakfast table. She did nothing to announce her presence. She peeled the crisp outer layer off the croissant in front of her and took a small bite. As she swallowed the pastry, a tiny nibble, barely more than a crumb, she watched as Nate and Trevor exited the hotel.

CHAPTER 16

Hitching

NATE HAD HITCHHIKED ONLY once before. That first
time, the prospect of crawling into a car with a stranger
had seemed less foolhardy — probably because Nate
was barely fifteen then, and because in his family's contained
Cleveland suburb there was little risk of being picked up by anyone he didn't already know. And because that time he didn't
have an infant Trevor on his hip and a paint-slopped stolen mas-
terpiece in his bag.

That time, on the side of the Ohio road, Nate had only Charlie
with him. Both boys were out of school on Thanksgiving break
and had spent the afternoon swimming laps in the chemically
fried waters of the town's indoor pool. The exercise was dim and
monotonous, back and forth from one side of the pool to the
other, crawl stroke and butterfly and the embarrassingly named
breaststroke, so much bodily exertion that got a boy nowhere
except back where he started. After an hour in the water, Nate
and Charlie dried off and waited outside the Y's front entrance,

a few minutes early for their pickup. "Towel dry your hair after you swim," their mother had told them when she dropped them off. "I'll retrieve you at three."

She wasn't there at three and still hadn't arrived half an hour later, when Nate reentered the Y and called home to see what was wrong. No one answered. It wasn't like their mother to forget them completely, and the boys walked back outside to look for her again. Once it was clear that she wasn't coming, they wandered down to the road fifty yards from the Y's entrance and thrust their arms out toward traffic, their thumbs extended. "Like this, *chico*," Nate said to his brother. "Stop looking so dangerous."

"I'm a threat, *my man*," Charlie said, shifting his weight to his right hip in imitation of a TV-movie pimp. Charlie was anything but intimidating.

"Fuck," Nate said under his breath only five minutes into the experiment. He dropped his hand to his side and slapped Charlie's down, too. Betty Heirly was approaching in her electric-blue pickup. Betty was the landscaper who came to their square home three times each summer to monitor the impatiens and trim the shrubs. She was an unfailingly earnest woman, a Beatrix Potter bunny come to life, and Nate had no doubt that she'd report the Bedeckers to their mother if she saw them hitching. Their mother's punishment would be strict. "Act cool," Nate told Charlie. The boys made fake conversation with each other (Charlie reciting the last ten presidents in order backward, Nate listing the Indians' starting lineup, complete with each player's earned run average) until the Toyota was out of sight.

The next driver who passed was recognizable as well: Craig Simon's father. He drove a Mustang, a '67 convertible, sand-colored and perfectly rust-free and achingly coveted by Nate and the rest of Craig's friends. Mr. Simon was a sleazebag, undeserving of the car and not the guy you wanted to bum a ride off. Nate withdrew his arm again, and again Charlie followed suit.

A dozen more cars passed and didn't stop, didn't even glance at the young teens who must have looked lost and harmless in their corduroys and unfortunately matching fisherman's sweaters. Their hair dripped onto their backs; their shoes lay fashionably untied. Nate's book bag hung heavily on his shoulder as the minutes dragged. The surplus canvas tote was filled with soaked swim clothes and towels, and just as he dropped it to the pavement, a Buick wagon eased over to the breakdown lane.

From the driver's seat, a boy leaned toward them. He was an eleventh grader, a popular-around-town guy with blond hair that swung in front of his eyes like a curtain. He would have been two school years ahead of Nate, if Nate had stayed local for his education instead of going away. Nate recognized him, though he didn't know his name.

"Hey," the boy said to Nate. "You live on Wainscott, in the see-through house?"

"Yeah," Nate said. Looked at from the right angle, the Bedecker home was invisible.

"It's on my way." The kid motioned for the boys to get in. Charlie looked frightened and excited by the adventure and didn't speak a word. He bounced almost imperceptibly on the balls of his feet.

"This is my brother, Charlie, the family mute," Nate said while crawling into the front seat. Charlie, still quiet, sat in the back. "You should see him mime, he's brilliant," Nate said. Charlie smiled, always happy to play along.

"No problem, talk is cheap," the driver responded. After ten minutes of silence the boys were home and out of the car.

In his head, during the car ride, Nate had worked up the story they'd give their mother, the explanation of how they'd gotten back from the pool. She'd crucify them for hitching, and the Y was too far away for them to have walked. Nate settled on the fib (a fabrication he relayed to Charlie as they entered the house) that they'd caught a ride from someone else's mom, someone their mother didn't know. Nate could make up a name, she'd never check. There was a time, a few years ago, when his mother wouldn't have believed that her son had local friends she'd never met. Over the past semester, though, while Nate was away at school, he'd grown more independent. Charlie lived at home and was still a child, but Nate, far away in Pennsylvania, bunking in a dorm for the second year in a row, believed that he'd finally grown into himself and out of his mother at the same time. He'd told himself that this distance was appropriate. Mature. Nate's roommate still spoke to his own parents every evening, just before making the trek across the soccer field to dinner in the Hill School's cavernous, wood-beamed dining hall. He shared every precalculus grade and each unrequited crush with his folks. It was juvenile and excessive.

"Hello?" Nate called out as he and Charlie entered the Bedecker house. A full hour had passed since they finished swimming. "Hello?" he said louder the second time, heaving the home's heavy side door all the way open, peering through the entryway and then into the kitchen before heading for the open expanse of the living room. The space was empty. His father's Eames chair had been cleared of the stack of magazines that usually lay piled on its cracked leather seat. The house even smelled uninhabited. It was the scent of something wrong, of catastrophe, maybe their mother had been gassed and was lying lifeless in the basement, maybe there'd been a nuclear war that affected only neo-Bauhaus structures made of glass and concrete. When Nate called home from the Y, he'd let the phone ring ten times before accepting that no one was there to pick up the extension.

"I bet she's sitting outside the Y wondering where we are," Charlie said as Nate walked a square around the living room's perimeter. "She probably got there right after we left. She's going to go loco when she gets back and sees our wet hair." Except, Nate noticed, they'd been out of the pool for so long that their hair was bone-dry.

Charlie went to his and Nate's bedroom and turned on the radio.

Nate was still standing in the living room twenty minutes later — too scared to go down to the basement, straining to hear Charlie's Top 40 broadcast through the wall, wondering what kind of fate had befallen Annemarie Bedecker, a woman who seemed able to withstand the strongest of disasters, or used to seem able — when he heard the low moan of the outside door opening. He turned around to face his mother, but there, in the entryway to the living room, was his father. The man cut a dark, stooped figure in his customary gray suit. He moved toward Nate, who had grown in the three months while away at school this fall. At five feet ten inches, Nate now stood two inches taller than his economically sized father.

George glanced at his son and then sat in the Eames chair and closed his eyes. The late-day light streamed in through the room's glass walls and fell directly on the man, deep into the creases of his face and the folds of his suit jacket. George reached up and pointed one finger behind him into the house. "She's in the kitchen," was all he said.

"Where were you?" Nate asked his mother, just a minute later. She was unloading carrots from a grocery bag and piling them in the stainless steel bin next to the sink.

She looked at the boy as if unsure of his question. "Your father has chosen to come home for the holiday." George hadn't been expected, but he frequently returned to Cleveland with little warning. "I retrieved him at the station. He's tired, Nate, he's here for a rest. We'll have veal for dinner."

Nate nodded and raised his hand to his hair, buffed soft from the chlorine, proving to himself that he really had been swimming with Charlie and really had been expecting his mother to pick them up. Three months away at school, and already the house was a different place.

It would be another two years before Annemarie installed the Buddha in the foyer, two years before her distancing act was complete. But that one incident — her small neglect of her children over a chilly November break — that was the minor moment that Nate returned to when looking for early signs of his mother's derailment. Lately the same moment had come to serve, in Nate's mind, as confirmation that even the best of parents slipped up on occasion. He'd long feared that rearing kids was one massive nerve-racking opportunity to fuck up someone else's life. That was even before he knew about his potentially toxic genes — an even better reason to have forgone fatherhood. It was also before he fully understood how just when you thought you knew a woman, it could turn out that she was in possession of a piece of steaming-hot artwork.

Maybe Emily didn't know the Rufino was in her bag. Nate hadn't known (it wasn't his bag, *after all*). Maybe she, like Nate, had been duped. Because, he thought, she couldn't have taken it herself. Could she? On Wednesday night, she'd drank the Barbers' booze and pretty well cleaned them out of cheese. She wouldn't betray the people who'd filled her glass, would she? Someone could have snuck the art into the bag when she wasn't looking. Sam Tully, in a true act against character, might have

ripped the Rufino from its frame and, in a panic, slipped it into
Emily's purse. That would be a perfect scheme for smuggling
it out of the state, come to think of it, in the bag of an unsus-
pecting woman about to drive to Rhode Island. But then, how
would the painting get so far into the purse, so surreptitiously
zipped into the pocket? And how would Sam reclaim it once it
was across the border? And what the hell would Sam Tully want
with a Rufino? He had Hockneys in his family, at least one actual
David Hockney piece (personally Nate would prefer a Rufino to
a Hockney, and he didn't think much of Rufino). Tully wasn't
the Rufino type. He hadn't put the Rufino in Emily's bag. The
simplest explanation was that Emily had put it there herself. She
had to have put it there herself. Nate tried to make sense of
this, to find a way into understanding it. Emily had taken the
Barbers' ridiculously overpriced trinket and, over the past three
days, had said nothing to him about it.

She hadn't told him.

Nate, for his part, hadn't suspected a thing. He'd been so
agonizingly mesmerized by his own Huntington's bullshit that
Emily had stolen a work of art by one of the most in-demand
contemporary artists in the world, and he hadn't even noticed.
No, actually, his Huntington's fears weren't bullshit. Art theft,
that was bullshit.

If Emily could hide the Rufino, what else was she conceal-
ing? Maybe she had an accomplice in the theft, Nate thought,
but he couldn't imagine who. If Emily were going to conspire
with anyone, wouldn't it be Nate? Shouldn't it be? They had
a child together, for fuck's sake. And he'd thought *he* was the
potentially damaging parent? Screw her. *Screw her*: This was his
initial thought, like the knee-jerk riposte of a spurned adolescent
(though, in fact, he had the sense that he was the one being
screwed).

Screw her, he thought from the side of the Newport road, where he was attempting to hitchhike with Trevor. Let her lie and steal, he was going to investigate his own secrets. Who needed to be dragged down by hers? He lifted Trevor, who lay slumped in his aching arms, higher onto his shoulder. Yes, he knew it was an objectively stupid idea to hitch with a kid. This whole plan to thumb it to Narragansett and back was absurd. Of course, absurd was starting to seem like Nate's norm. Two days without money and he'd lost his mind. As had Emily, clearly. She'd fucking stolen a work by one of the most renowned artists under age fifty. Nate understood nothing about contemporary visual art, yet even he knew Rufino's name.

A compact yellow Hyundai pulled over to the side of America's Cup Avenue. A waiflike girl in a cardigan sweater and braids leaned from the driver's side, across the passenger seat. *Innocent* was the word that crossed Nate's mind.

"Car trouble?" she said to Nate, through the open passenger side window. She looked and sounded as if she were in high school, at most.

"I guess so," Nate said with a lack of confidence. He felt bereft when he thought about the loss of the Jeep. Everything he'd taken for granted was now gone. Even if he got the Jeep back, it would be tainted with the knowledge of how easily it had been taken from him, by the fact that ever since it had been stolen, Nate's life had gone to pot. The car that had hit Charlie two decades ago had been brand-new, two weeks off the lot. A Honda. Nate remembered obsessing over that fact for years after Charlie's death, using these petty details as a distraction from his searing grief. He'd asked himself what it meant, that his brother had been hit by a car so new, a car so affordable and reliable. He'd wondered if the driver of the car (a man Nate could imagine only as an everyman) had immediately sold the Honda, or perhaps returned it to the lot, unable to get back behind the wheel of a vehicle that had so casually thumped down a teen-aged boy. He wondered if that man grieved for Charlie, too, or if he grieved only for himself, for the way the accident had stripped him of his own courage. For years after Charlie's death, Nate couldn't keep himself from staring down every navy-blue Honda he saw in Ohio, trying to avert his eyes but being unable. Once, in upstate New York during his senior year in college, he'd been driving with a girlfriend when they'd passed an acci-dent on the side of the highway, a blue Honda (a steel blue, but blue still) that had rear-ended a Mercedes. The damage looked minimal, but Nate gasped and stifled a sob. His grief – so well suppressed most of the time – could surge with no warning, like a knife plunged in his side from behind. The pain was acute and physical. Charlie, as his only sibling, had been a part of him. Their lives, in so many ways, had been one and the same. When the girlfriend asked what was wrong, Nate only shook his head. A week later he broke up with her.

"Are you looking for a ride or something?" the girl in the Hyundai asked now.

Nate nodded. He'd had his thumb out and was walking back-ward down the breakdown lane. It certainly seemed that he was looking for a ride. Or something. "We're going across the bridges. Hoping to, at least."

"I can't believe my eyes, a hitchhiking dad. Outrageous." She unlocked the doors and made a welcome motion with her hand. Her wrist looked barely thicker than Trevor's. "Over the bridges is where I'm headed. Just tell me how far to take you."

Nate hesitated, but the girl and her car looked safe. She'd been driving slowly and carefully as she approached, and she was pointed in the right direction. Nate wouldn't be hitchhiking at all if there were any other way (besides a taxi, a financially ridiculous idea given his current situation) to get across the harbor without a car of his own.

"We're heading to Narragansett," Nate said, leaning down toward her. A pink plastic gnome hung from the Hyundai's rearview mirror. Its naked form beckoned.

"Oh, posh. I can bring you door to door. I'm going to Kingston, but it's not like I have to get there immediately."

"I – I mean we – we don't want to put you out," Nate said, taking a step back toward the curb. The curb was a safe place to be. "Forget about it."

Forget about it. Because even if he made it to the old house, he wasn't sure that he'd be able to get inside. Even if he could, what did he expect to find? A medical chart? A diagnosis? He needed to keep a level head. He should see a specialist about Huntington's and wait to go to Narragansett until he had his own car. That was the sane way to go about things, yet here on a dangerously fast stretch of America's Cup Avenue, without his own wheels and with a kid on his hip, Nate was itching to do *something*.

"Narragansett is like, a minute out of my way, which is nothing," the girl behind the wheel, the malnourished cheerleader, was saying. "There's like fourteen thousand minutes in a day. I've got extras. Just tell me that you're not one of those rapists who uses kids as a decoy to get into girls' cars."

"No rapists here," Nate said. He still considered running from the car. Trevor looked happy to stay, though. Didn't he? The boy was watching the toy gnome sway in front of the girl's windshield. *Why not?* The gnome beckoned with each arc of its swing. *Why not!* Trevor reached out toward its pink tuft of hair. "If it's no problem, we could use the ride," Nate said. His left arm, which was wrapped around and under Trevor, was going numb. "Thanks."

He began to get into the Hyundai's front seat with Trevor, and then, with one foot in the car and one foot out, he stopped. It was like asking for an accident, sitting with his kid — and no baby seat — in the front. He withdrew and got in back, on the passenger side, moving an American history textbook and a Yoohoo bottle out of the way to make room for his feet. He pulled the seat belt tight across his and Trevor's bodies. The seat's new vinyl strained beneath their weight.

"I know that town like the back of my hand, my dad's practically mayor of Narragansett, thinks he's king of Rhode Island even though, literally, he's a tax accountant," the girl said, craning her neck around to look at Nate. She faced forward again and drove the car away from the curb. "Nonliterally, he's an egotist."

"All dads are," Nate said. The car emitted a circular hum, like a cocktail blender on low. "Dads of their generation, the old guys. Your generation's luckier. Women have power now." He looked at Trevor, the kid Emily had given him.

"Dude, when's the last time you were in a high school?"

As they pulled onto the Newport Bridge, Nate tried to ignore the fact that to get to the bridge they'd driven directly through the center of a cemetery, tried not to see this as an omen. He gazed intently at the road ahead as they navigated away from the harbor and into Jamestown with its sparsely settled coast. *Jamestown*, as if it were a colony waiting to happen instead of an overpriced resort town on the rise.

"Where in the Gansett should I bring you?" the girl asked, the car listing slightly to the right. Nate held onto Trevor tightly, shielding the small body with his own.

Nate gave her an address, the only Bedecker he'd found when he'd looked up the name in the Viking suite's phone book on the night he and Emily arrived at the hotel.

The girl took one hand off the wheel to fiddle with the air vents. "How long have you had your license?" he said.

"Fourteen months. I'm a pro. How long have you been a father?"

The neophyte driver, Nicole ("Not Nic, not Nicky, nothing cute, *gracias*"), drove at exactly the speed limit and took twenty-two minutes to get to Narragansett. After a few stops to examine misleading street signs, she turned onto the road Nate was looking for and then slowed to a crawl, checking for house numbers.

"That's — "

"That's it," Nate said, surprised, as they pulled through a hedge and into a driveway. Seeing the house again was like déjà vu but without the supernatural element. He was taken aback that he recognized the place, that the picture in his head hadn't been merely a figment. His brain remained healthy, he reminded himself. He *should* recognize places he'd been before.

The wood-sided home was still painted white with yellow accents, a broad front porch, sweeping lawn, and off-center front door. The rhododendrons framing the porch were mangy and overgrown but the lawn was mowed. Erected at least a few years before George himself was born, the house was strikingly more classic than Bedecker's own designs. Nicole brought the car to a stop halfway up the drive.

"The paint's definitely been retouched, but the place is standing. Holy shit," Nate said. *Shit.* At this rate, Trevor's first word would probably be *motherfucker*. Nate looked down at his son, who appeared to be all ears.

"What? You were looking for a place you thought burned down?"

Nate shrugged.

"Dude, in this part of the world, homes last forever," Nicole said. She put the car in park. "My folks' house was built in the old days, when people rode in buggies and didn't shave their legs. My parents haven't changed a thing. It's like they wish they were colonial people, Betsy Ross or something."

Nate unbuckled the seat belt and opened the door to get out, to take a closer look. The driveway's gravel was freshly raked. Someone was keeping the place up. Maybe it wasn't even in the Bedecker family anymore. Nate had previously dismissed that thought based on the fact that the address was still tied to the name "Bedecker" in the white pages — and Nate had never met a Bedecker to whom he wasn't related. Nate had barely met any Bedeckers to whom he *was* related. They were a small, and dying, clan.

"No one's here," Nicole said, outside the car herself now, standing next to the driver's side door. "I think you've been stood up. Want me to drop you somewhere else? I can take you to town or whatever." Though the landscaping was fresh, the shades were all tightly drawn and the driveway was devoid of cars. Nate didn't see any security company stickers on the front of the house or propped in the lawn.

Nate continued studying the outside of the house and didn't respond to Nicole's question.

"Dude," Nicole said, "you're a nice guy, but I'm not carting you all the way back to Newport."

"No, of course," said Nate. "I wasn't going to ask you to do that. You can leave us, we'll be fine." Getting back to Newport would be a challenge, sure — and they'd have to head back soon or Emily would wonder about them — but if they couldn't hitch a ride here on the street outside the house, they could go the expensive route and call a cab. A taxi back would blow through almost all of Nate's cash (his and Emily's cash), but at least they had the option as a safety net, one they probably wouldn't need.

It was a holiday weekend. This road was primarily residential, but plenty of cars were driving by. He'd come this far.

"You sure?" Nicole said.

"You bet," Nate answered, and within seconds Nicole was back in the Hyundai, door slammed, pulling away and waving good-bye to Trevor. The boy pushed against Nate and groaned, paused for breath, and groaned again. He wanted to get down and crawl. Or maybe sleep. His squirms tended to mean he wanted either movement or rest, polar opposites, from what Nate could tell.

The Narragansett house's front door was wrapped by a traditional sweeping porch, with wide wooden planks and bright white rails. The last time Nate had seen this porch, he'd been with his brother and mother. They'd been an intact family back then, in an era when Nate, the childhood Nate, had assumed they'd all live to be ancient. He'd stared long and hard at the house that time. Now, Nate didn't allow himself that languor. He carried Trevor up the front steps and gave the door a cursory push, but wasn't surprised to find it locked tight. He then searched underneath the doormat for a key, and beneath the two small tables (nothing there) and inside the seams of the rocking chair that sat next to the door. Trevor's moans had turned to whimpers and Nate pressed his lips against the top of the boy's head, feeling the fine, soft wisps of his baby hair.

After coming up keyless at the front door, Nate carried Trevor to the back of the house. It was just after 11:00 a.m. Was this when Trevor napped? Emily was the one who arranged the tot's rigid schedule. Trevor's eyes were closing now, a slow descent into sleep that seemed alarming only because the boy usually screamed when he was tired, but now even his groans had stopped. Perhaps the fresh air and Nate's gentle breath on the top of his head had lulled the boy into complacency. The back lawn was lush and quiet and Nate spread his jacket on the grass beside the tiny back porch, then lay Trevor on top of it.

Nate climbed the three short steps to the back entrance. The doorway here, the one that day-to-day inhabitants would use, was constructed of wood so old that paint lay piled up on the frame in consecutive layers like the rings of a tree. Nate flattened his hand over the latex as if channeling the structure's history. Between this frame and the door itself was a gap, the width of a nickel standing on its edge. Nate could maybe knock the door in if he took a running start, except that he'd never forced a door in his life and the whole point was to sneak in and out undetected. He searched under this doormat and around the edges of the porch. No key.

He could bust through a pane of the glass and reach inside to the door handle probably, if necessary, but if George still owned the place (and Nate continued to believe that was the case) there had to be a key. In Cleveland, Nate's mother had always left one hidden beneath a loose slate next to the door. She and Nate and Charlie all had their own keys, but George hadn't wanted one. He preferred to carry as little as possible with him every day. His blueprints and designs fit flat into his leather carrier. His heavy glasses resided permanently on the bridge of his nose. His pens and pencils were stored in a felt pouch that slipped smoothly inside his suit jacket. His wallet, Italian, was kept paper-thin, filled only with two credit cards and one single hundred-dollar bill for emergencies. He couldn't be bothered to carry *stuff* around. He rarely drove himself anywhere, so he had no car key. And he insisted that his minions work around the clock, so he never needed an office key. Someone was always at work to open the door for him.

So where was the key to this house? Next to the door sat a classic terra-cotta flowerpot, filled with a mound of dry dirt. Nate lifted the pot, hopeful, but the key wasn't underneath. He then gently dug through the mulch, with no luck. The tiny porch was largely unadorned. Three steps and a small landing with nothing on it except for the doormat and the flowerpot. The back of the house was remarkably serene. Off-white shades were pulled over all of the windows, and the neatly mowed grass was only marred by one patch of dirt, exactly large enough to have once held a picnic table and benches. The grass ended some thirty yards out, where the land sloped down to rocks and the sea. Nate looked over to Trevor, who was safely asleep and still.

Nate backed down the steps and took a wide-angle look at the residence. There was nowhere left to search for the key. The adventure was over. He took his phone out of his pocket and checked for messages, but he had none. It seemed odd that Emily hadn't called, concerned and looking for them, but he supposed that his message to her at the hotel had been competent and soothing. She sometimes said she could use a day off from Trevor, and it seemed she was taking it. There was no way, at 11:00 a.m., that she was still asleep. They'd all gone to bed well before midnight.

Nate could search for a ride or call a cab, take Trevor back to Newport, hang out at the dock, and pretend they'd been there all morning. Emily would never know and it wasn't as if Trevor could tell her. So this morning's trip had been fruitless. So what? Life was full of disappointments. He tallied his own recent misfortunes in his head, the list taking shape like an Excel spreadsheet of noteworthy inadequacies. Around him, the morning was silent except for the whirr of the occasional car passing the front of the house.

Nate had set himself up for failure; he'd acknowledged this even before he and Trevor strapped themselves into Nicole's car. They'd taken a ride twenty miles, across the bridges and down the coast, to find a house that he hadn't seen since he was a kid and to investigate his primeval and ongoing family history, trying to solve the depressing and probably damning secrets of his own inevitable genetic future, a future he was terrified of and aching to see all at the same time. He had nothing and everything to lose. Nate looked over at his child, a safe distance away and completely innocent of the future (of any future) that awaited him, and then walked back up the steps, leaned down, grabbed the flowerpot, and swung it at the window in the door. The glass shattered and the pot crumbled, and Trevor awoke with a scream and Nate tenderly reached through the broken panes (careful not to let the jagged edges scrape his skin), when suddenly, as if willed into existence by the commotion, a single key fell from its perch atop the doorframe. Nate withdrew his arm, picked up the key, and unlocked the house.

CHAPTER 17

Where Emily Goes When She's Alone

S O THIS WAS WHAT Bob Daugherty meant about the holiday crowds. It wasn't yet noon and the streets were teeming. Retired couples and middle-aged tourists lined up outside kiosks (kiosk after kiosk after kiosk) advertising harbor tours and private boat trips. The pedestrians on Newport's central drag waddled toward the large white tent erected on the harbor. *Oktoberfest!* a banner heralded in gothic letters, bright purple and a morbid red. Old men in lederhosen wove their way through the horde, accompanied by women wearing dirndls and fake braids and speaking in harsh Boston accents. A breeze came off the water; despite the warm sun it was certainly autumn. Emily held her canvas jacket close around her and drank from a paper cup of French roast. She'd paid for it out of her twenty dollars at a small chain shop off the main strip, leaving barely more than eighteen bucks in her secret stash. Nate would be back soon, though. As she walked along the water, Emily kept her eye out for him. This time, if she saw him and their son, she'd flag them down. Still, she delayed going back to the Viking. It was getting harder to face Nate – her lie seemed to have grown overnight and now coated her tongue like oil. She took her phone out of her jacket pocket and called Jeanne on speed dial.

It went straight through to voice mail.

"It's me," Emily said after the beep. "Calling from Newport. Newport!" she forced a laugh. Jeanne had left her five phone messages since Friday, when Emily had quickly spoken with her from the police station. Emily hadn't called back until now. Nate had a point, though. If they avoided calling New York, they'd only end up looking like fugitives. And Emily could use a friend. "I got your messages. Sorry I've been AWOL. The Jeep got stolen. We're living in a hotel, the Hotel Viking. I have no shoes." And with that, she'd run out of news. "No need to call back, I'm sure you're busy at yoga camp. Sorry for the Zenless message."

As she stuffed the phone back in her pocket, she felt a tap on her shoulder. She turned and found herself facing a stranger. He looked like a local, not one of the tourists, and he smiled at her expectantly. He was age forty or so, burly and firm.

"Ma'am? Hi? Mrs. Bedecker?" he said. She flinched and looked harder at the guy, searching.

"Officer Sebastian," he prompted Emily, pointing at his chest. "Eric. I took your statement, your stolen car?" He waited for her to catch on.

"Oh!" Of course! "Thank you. Yes!" How offensive that she hadn't even registered that he looked familiar. She'd been a wreck in the precinct. "I was pretty beat on Friday, I guess. I've never had a car stolen from me before," Emily said. She'd never had anything stolen from her, unless you counted her youth. "Emily. Emily Latham," she pointed to herself. The officer appeared awkward in his civilian clothes. "Nate's last name is Bedecker, but not mine."

"Emily," he said. "You found somewhere to stay?" He wasn't the officer who had driven them into town. That duty had fallen to a young rookie who'd remained official and zipped-up during their ride.

"The Viking took us in. Nate — " she'd almost said *my boyfriend*, but she had a hunch that people here didn't give birth to children out of wedlock, "Nate's stayed there for business, so they trust that we're not the kind of people who'd run out on a hotel bill. He's there now, napping with our son." She assumed that, by now, they'd had enough father-son time around town and made their way back to the hotel. Emily felt conspicuously alone. She felt conspicuously like a felon, too, now that she had a cop standing in front of her. She needed not to be conspicuous, as if it were so easy.

"The Viking?" the officer smiled. He seemed impressed. "You two looked shell-shocked when you came in on Friday. You three."

"The third always looks that way. He's ten months, just being in the world is a jolt to him."

The rest of Officer Sebastian's crowd — two women and one man who looked enough like the officer that Emily wondered if they were brothers — had now caught up, and the officer, Eric, made the introductions, explaining Emily's stolen car situation, adding, "They're new in town, bought a house up by you, Winnie." He nodded to the older woman in the group, probably only forty-five but weathered, as if she'd been tanning with a reflector in her lap for the past three decades. Emily tried to embed these people's names in her memory, making a point to repeat Winnie's name silently in her head, cementing it in the gray matter.

These were the first real people she'd met in town. She could easily run into them again, especially since one seemed to be a neighbor.

"*Willkommen.*" Winnie grinned and extended a hand weighed down by a cocktail ring with a walnut-size emerald. Emily tallied the carats in her head (trying to recall what Jeanne's old roommate, who worked in the gem department at Tiffany, had taught them about appraising). The stone could be worth close to half of what Nate and Emily had surrendered as a down payment on their house. It was probably worth a quarter of a Rufino. Emily shook the woman's hand. She missed her stolen Tod's.

"Thanks," Emily said. "We're looking forward to settling in."

"Which house?"

Emily didn't know her new address by heart and clumsily tried explaining where the place was situated, adding, "It's got a new-growth maple out front? The old owners put it in to replace a birch that rotted out last year?"

"The Schermerhorns'," Winnie said. "It's in decent shape, at least. I'd redo the roof, but that's just me."

Emily smiled.

"You have kids?" the second woman asked. "The Schermerhorns left the jungle gym up in back, I noticed."

"One son, ten months," Emily said. "You?"

"Two boys, already in school. Track me down if you need sitters. I'm a valuable resource. Eric has my number."

"And you?" Emily asked Winnie, filling the silence.

"Kids?" Winnie said. "Christ, no. But it's nice of you to ask."

Emily grinned and stepped slightly away, hoping that her clothes (two days into their luggageless weekend) didn't reek. Over Eric's shoulder, she watched a crowd begin to disembark

from a colossal cruise ship, a monstrously large vessel for this
harbor. The passengers streamed single file straight from the
boat to the Oktoberfest tent, merging with the men in tights. A
cruise ship would make a great getaway vehicle, Emily thought.
Women who played shuffleboard and ate at fruit buffets were
above suspicion.

Officer Eric and his friends continued to talk as the sounds
around them — the bellowing of the harbor-cruise hawkers;
the bells from the cyclists who sped by on the road, navigating the small slip of pavement between the cars and the curb —
encroached on their space.

"We're headed into Oktoberfest if you want to join. I get a free
pass," Eric said.

The cruise's passengers were still filing down the ship's slanted
ramp.

"I should get back to Nate. He's not really an Oktoberfest
kind of guy," Emily said. She didn't want to get dragged into
the festival, but she also didn't want to sound pretentious — like
a New Yorker who thought she was above corny local tradi-
tions — or suspiciously rushed. Historically, Emily had a habit of
making terrible first impressions. "Not that it doesn't sound fun,
Oktoberfest, you know? We're all about being tourists, checking
out attractions until Tuesday when we can move into our house.
But Nate's mother was Austrian, so Oktoberfest, you know, it's
too close to home." This sounded like a lie, she was sure of it.
She should keep her mouth shut.

"It's a good weekend to do the cottages, if you'd rather do that
sort of thing," Winnie said. Emily noticed how the term *cottages*
rolled off her tongue, matter-of-fact and without irony. "I hear
the Elms added extra tours for Columbus Day."

"The Elms?" Emily said. She almost added, *Nate and I aren't mansion people,* but she held back. Nate wasn't a mansion person. Emily, on the other hand, was embarrassingly eager to visit the town's historic residences.

Sure, given the state of the world, she knew she should hate mansion tours (so much excess!), should hate even the idea of a mansion tour, but she loved walking through grand houses where she knew that not only would the owners approve of her snooping, but they'd also moved out a generation ago, leaving the homes to museums and nonprofits that had now roped off the valuables for safe viewing from a distance. (If only the Barbers had roped off their valuables!) She craved stepping into a home that had history, that had been honestly lived in. She craved stepping into someone else's life, if only for an hour.

"The Elms is right on Bellevue," Winnie said. "Up two blocks and a half-mile to the south. Can't miss it."

"I've probably got time to do a quick tour right now," Emily said half to herself, half to Winnie, her new best friend and tour guide. Nate and Trevor would call if they needed her, wouldn't they? She had her cell phone, and she didn't want to sit inside all day, changing diapers, eating her way through the minibar, worrying about their life to come. Emily still had eighteen dollars burning a hole in her pocket. A tour couldn't possibly cost more than that.

The group started walking in the direction of Oktoberfest, and Emily followed. As they approached the edge of the tent, she could hear the metallic hum of accordion music and an airy wheezing, like ailing bagpipes.

"Last chance for Oktoberfest," the other woman, the one who wasn't Winnie, said. Emily should have caught her name, this woman who wasn't Winnie. She was sure Eric had introduced her by name, but now it was too late.

"Oh, no, thanks," Emily said. "I'll pass." And then, because it seemed they were waiting for her to say something more, she added, "This way?" She pointed up the road that continued beyond the tent and uphill. The street was jammed with traffic. "Is that the way to the Elms?"

"Winnie and I can walk you," Eric said. "Right? It's so close it's stupid for us to send you wandering. I still feel bad about your car. In Newport for less than an hour and you're robbed. Must not give you faith in the local law enforcement."

"We'll walk you," Winnie said to Emily. "We can drop you off and be back here in time for the Bavarian singers. As long as we don't linger." And then, to the other two, she said, "If you pick up our beer badges, we'll meet you at the grandstand?"

The limestone Elms was hulking, square and symmetrical and staunch, its bulk splayed heavily on the land. Laminated signs (PARKING THIS WAY and WELCOME TO A PRESERVATION SOCIETY SITE) were impaled in the wet dirt beside the pathway to the front entrance.

"Thanks," Emily said to Winnie and Eric. The walk had taken no time.

"Don't thank us. It's our duty to accompany a newcomer," said Winnie, who'd been talking nonstop since the walk began. "Eric has an in at all the tourist destinations. He's a VIP."

"I don't have an in," Eric said. "You make it sound like I'm on the take."

Inside the mansion's foyer, a woman sat at a desk with a small cashbox and a stack of brochures.

"Hello, Sergeant," she groaned to Eric. Emily turned to face the woman, whose skin sagged on her face, her cheeks weighted down by leaden makeup. "Nice to see you, *again.*"

"Back at you, Margaret," Eric said. "A pleasure."

"A sergeant?" Emily said. "I had no idea you were a sergeant." Emily could never remember the hierarchy of rank. Was sergeant higher than lieutenant? The only thing she knew for sure was that the captain was in charge. At least Eric wasn't the captain. Emily thrilled, her blood pulsing at her temples, to be standing so close to an actual police sergeant. She'd never been one of those people who believed it was smart to keep your enemies closer.

"I've been a practicing policeman for some time," Eric blushed.

"Oh, give it up, everyone's a sergeant," Winnie said. When Eric started to argue, she amended her comment. "*Practically* everyone. Everyone who sticks around long enough."

According to the placard next to the ticket seller, the guided tour cost fifteen dollars. Emily took out her money and approached the table.

"Lady, don't be ridiculous. You don't need a ticket," the ticket seller, Margaret, said. "It's on the house." And then, her tone flat and dour, a defeated sing-song, "Any friend of the law is a friend of the Elms. We'd like to treat you to a tour, on the house."

"Thank you, Margaret," Eric said. "Again."

"I'm happy to pay," Emily turned to face Eric. She had the crumpled eighteen dollars in her outstretched hand. "It's really nice of you to come along, to walk me up here, but I can afford my own ticket." It was nearly all she could afford, but she had the money. "I'd prefer to pay, to tell you the truth. I'd like to pay." She held the money out farther away from her body, as if waiting for someone to snatch it. "I'd like to support the mansion," she said. She wanted to be rid of her surreptitious cash. The minute it left her possession, she wouldn't be holding it back from Nate anymore. She'd no longer be hiding anything from him. Well, anything except a Rufino.

"You could use a treat, after what happened to you Friday. Don't worry about it."

"But — "

"Don't worry about it," Eric said firmly. "Take the free ticket. Take it."

"Take it," Winnie said, and then, just before walking out the door with Eric, "let the sergeant abuse his power. He won't accept no for an answer."

Emily dug her toe into the dirt on the Elms' front lawn. She hated her secret money and she hated the fact that she'd let the diaper bag out of her sight, but it would work out okay. The bag was with Nate, it was fine, the Rufino was safely stashed, she was sure of it.

"Please! Remain on the pedestrian walkway!" Kiara, the tour guide, yelped. Emily had drifted onto the grass. There were nine other people in the group, not counting Emily and Kiara, and they stood clustered in front of the mansion, shoulder to shoulder as if drawn together by tour-induced magnetism. So far they'd learned little about the Elms but quite a bit about Kiara: she was in her junior year at Salve Regina, led tours two days a week, and had a passion for the long-gone grand styles of Newport living. "Stay close," she cautioned, apparently unaware the small crew was already glued together. "I don't want to have to yell!" She screamed.

As for the mansion, Emily had expected Newport's estates to be set aside in their own sprawling district amongst rolling hills. But the Elms and the other nearby cottages sat on compact, intricately manicured grounds nestled right up against the neighboring suburban houses. Behind the Elms, on Spring Street, a row of side-by-side federalist shacks abutted the mansion's lawn.

"This is how the servants would have come and gone," Kiara said, leading the tour to a covered doorway at the side of the house. She gathered her faded prairie skirt in a tight fist as she descended the shallow flight of stone stairs toward the door. "The foliage canopy hid the servants' activities from the family and their guests on the floors above." Emily followed Kiara down the steps.

"We're touring colleges this week," the woman next to Emily said, motioning to her daughter. She spoke half in the direction of Emily, half to Kiara, who either cared or was good at feigning it.

Kiara nodded and smiled as she held open the door, motioning the rest of the crowd into the basement. "I love Salve Regina," Kiara said. "The endowment's huge, seriously, no one can figure out why tuition is so high, it's like, there's no middle class at Salve. But it's worth it. Seriously, I get to go to school *here*." She let the door to the servants' quarters close behind the tour and stepped back in front of the crowd. "Well not exactly *here*. But in Newport."

"We're in Rhode Island to tour Brown. Not Salve Regina," the mother said, with an impatient edge. Her daughter seemed patently disinterested in the college conversation, and in this tour, and probably in Brown, as well. She was looking down at her own waist, knotting and reknotting the drawstring of her cargo pants. Emily again felt a yearning for her own college years. She had *been someone* in college, she'd had a future. And now? If she was convicted of larceny? The thought terrified her. Even if she eventually got out of jail, she'd never get a job again. She'd be whispered about every time anyone from their old crowd bought a work of art, or stole supplies from their office, or snuck out of a party dubiously early. Her entire past would be nullified. The success she'd been as an undergrad? No one would care. Her potential would evaporate like a shallow puddle on hot tar. Trevor might be taken away from her as well. Trevor! She needed to remain calm. She could beat this. She could beat it for Trevor.

"This is the servants' domain," Kiara said. She walked backward as she talked, stopping briefly by the hot and cold kitchens to open the door to a small lift. "This is the dumbwaiter they used to haul the laundry up and down the flights. It's the only elevator in the house!"

"Check it out," one of the tour's two twentysomething women nudged the other and nodded toward a stone corner of the cold kitchen. "A pastry station."

"It's the pastry *deck*," Kiara said to them before leading the group over to the countertop. "It's far enough away from the hot kitchen that the stone could be kept ice cold, day in and out."

"And to think we just spent a fortune on marble," the second twentysomething said to the first. Then, noticing Emily eavesdropping, she said, "We own a bakery, small scale, in Providence. Near *Brown*," she rolled her eyes toward the college-tour mom.

"I almost went into the food industry," Emily said. "Cheesemaking." It sounded so real when she said it out loud, like a dream that had come *this close* to fruition.

"You're based where?" the first twentysomething asked Emily. "New England cheeses are having a renaissance, but you must know that."

"I'm in New York," Emily said, and almost corrected herself, almost told them she was a Newport resident, but what she felt, more than anything, was that that wasn't true. She couldn't possibly feel less like a Newport resident.

"Upstate?" The second girl asked. Unlike in Manhattan, there were cows and goats and dairy farms upstate.

Emily nodded. It was a small nod, a minor neck twitch, a half lie. Then she walked quickly into the next room, catching up with Kiara and the rest of the group. Her chest began to tighten, her head to float. She had just lied without premeditation, without even noticing it until the fabrications were out of her mouth. When had this started? Lying was a form of thievery, stealing facts and inserting them into her own life story. This tour was only supposed to last forty-five minutes, yet already Emily felt as if she'd been on it for days. She hadn't taken a pill since before dinner last night, and now her remaining meds were in the bottom of the diaper bag, with Nate and the Rufino. Crap.

She should sneak out of the Elms. She should go back to the Viking to find Nate. She should at least call him. She was rarely away from Trevor for this long.

"Follow me, this is a treat just for the underground tour!" Kiara motioned the group through a doorway, past a small throng of other tourists wearing headsets, who were taking the eight-dollar self-guided route. "Seriously, we're going to go all the way up to the roof next, eighty steps up! But first, even though you thought we were in the basement, there's one more level down!" There was always one more level down, Emily knew. Even when you were at absolute zero.

She lowered herself slowly onto the stairs, shallow and slick, a lawsuit waiting to happen. (Easy money! Emily thought before coming to her senses.) With her left hand she clung to the metal railing, cold in her grasp. At the bottom of the flight, the other tourers stood uneasily with their eyes to the ground. There was nothing else to do. This room was an empty expanse, a completely underground dungeon the size of a backyard swimming pool. Emily's eyes locked on the basement's brick walls, marred by soot and dust. It wouldn't surprise her to hear that the original owners had kept their prisoners here. She imagined the early WASP settlers had bound and gagged the Jews and Catholics who mistakenly wandered onto their property – but then she remembered that despite this town's appearance of privilege, Newport was founded as a bastion of acceptance. If Nate's partners were to be believed, to this day the year-rounders were devoted to diversity and rampant self-expression. And yachts.

"Welcome to the utilities rooms," Kiara said. She pointed up at the large pipes overhead. "If you turn to the cabinet on your left, this way," and she motioned to the crowd's left, "can any of you tell me what this contraption was used for?"

As if in answer, Emily's phone rang. She edged away from the tour, toward the back wall of the basement, and flipped open her cell. "Nate, thank God," she whispered into it.

"Emily Latham?" a voice said. Not Nate. She hadn't looked at the caller ID.

"Who's calling?" Emily kept both her voice and her eyes low.

"Ma'am, I'm Lieutenant Anthony Ogden, New York Police Department. Anna Barber gave me your name and number. We're taking statements from the guests who attended her party last Wednesday. There was a theft from the Barbers' home that fits the time frame of the party."

"Oh," Emily said, afraid to breathe. A lieutenant this time. "Yes, I had heard." The lieutenant didn't respond, apparently waiting for more from Emily. Her hand shook as she clutched the phone. "I didn't see any theft, if that's what you're asking."

"If you could recount your own activities during the party, it would help. When you arrived, where in the apartment you spent time, and when you left."

Emily suddenly felt like a suspect. The air in the basement was damp. "This cabinet was a lightbulb tester!" Kiara said, her voice slicing through Emily's interior tintamar. Being kept in this room as a prisoner wouldn't be so bad. It would beat being paraded in public, being locked in stocks. Being humiliated in Manhattan district court. "The house's spare bulbs were stored here, on the subbasement level," Kiara said, "and who would want to climb all of the way up to the main floors to replace a light, only to discover it was faulty?"

"That whole thing is a lightbulb tester? A lightbulb *tester?*" asked the prospective Brown student. "That whole cabinet? Whatever."

"This isn't really a good time," Emily said into the phone. "I'm on a historic tour, it's a holiday weekend."

"Of course," the officer said. "I can schedule a time to come up and talk with you in person."

"In person?" Emily felt a wheeze rising to the top of her lungs. "I didn't see anything. And I live in Newport now, you can't come up to Newport." She was trying to sound polite, but all that seemed to be coming out was anxiety. She wished Nate were here, and not just because he had her pills on him. "I wouldn't want you to waste your time," she said.

"We're covering our bases, Ms. Latham. One of the Barbers' other guests mentioned that she'd seen you walk to the back of the apartment, and that's where the theft occurred. That makes you a person we'd like to talk to, in our fact-gathering."

Fuck.

She inhaled deeply and held the air in her lungs, trying to bring on the cotton-like calm (a calm that even Jeanne admitted might be mostly placebo effect) that came with an Inderal, tried to visualize those pills migrating from the bottom of the bag that was with Nate to the base of her tongue that was here in the basement of the Elms. She feigned a swallow. Feel the peace, she instructed herself. She felt, instead, an escalating buzz. The subbasement's air grew heavy and solid. Who? Who saw her go into the Barbers' study? Who!

"I went to the back of the apartment, sure," she said, measuring out her words, trying to keep the pace slow and natural. "There's a bathroom there."

"Sure," the lieutenant said.

"Plenty of people went back there during the party."

"Yours is the only name that's come up so far."

"I wasn't the only one." She sounded angry. She needed to breathe.

Across the room, the tour group seemed to be planning an insurgency. "You call that a lightbulb tester? Did they even have incandescent lights when this house was built?" a father on the tour with two teens said, defiant. "Edison didn't get going with electricity until, what, the 1880s?"

"The Elms was completed well *after* Edison and his invention," Kiara shot back. Emily looked up. "This house is only a century old. It's new," Kiara said. Emily tried to focus on Kiara's words, on the fact that while the cops were wasting their time tracking down a useless piece of art, the rest of the world was continuing, in mundane fashion, to tour mansions.

"Who?" said the lieutenant on the phone.

"Who what?"

"Who else went to the back of the apartment during the party?"

"Who else?" Emily hadn't actually seen anyone else go to the back of the apartment, but surely someone must have, at some point? She couldn't be the only person who'd needed to pee while the powder room was occupied. But she blanked: She couldn't remember the name of anyone who was at the party at all, other than herself and Nate and Anna and Randy. She couldn't remember a single other person. "Anna," she said. "Anna Barber wandered back there. I saw her." Technically, Emily hadn't seen Anna leave the kitchen the entire night, but at some point, to go to bed at least, she had to have gone back toward the study.

"She lives in the apartment, ma'am. There's nothing questionable about her wandering back there."

"Are you kidding?" Emily said. She'd spoken more loudly than intended, and the tourers briefly glanced her way. They'd paid fifteen dollars apiece for this walk-and-talk. Emily lowered her voice. "Of course it's suspicious. I can't remember ever seeing a hostess — a hostess from this crowd — leave the kitchen area during her own party. Especially Anna. She's usually camped out at the doorway that separates the kitchen from the living room. First of all, because she likes to lord over the whole affair, anyone will tell you she's a control freak." Anna was a control freak. That was true, at least. "Plus, she's scared shitless that the caterers are going to walk off with pieces of her silver. So yes, it certainly is suspicious that she'd go to the back of her own apartment, out of eyeshot from what's going on. Trust me." Emily stopped, listened to her own heart. She was almost proud of her quick save, a sure sign that all of those years in marketing and advertising had paid off.

"Okay, so Ms. Barber was back there. Anyone else?"

"Like I said, there's a bathroom back there. I'm sure other people had to pee, but I didn't take down names." She tried to picture the party, exactly who was standing at the bar when she grabbed her first drink, when she went in for a refill, but all she could picture was the Rufino with its glaring swatches of gray and orange, like torn shards of police hazard tape. "You really want me to try to think back to who peed at a party I attended half a week ago? Are you serious? I mean, if Anna was back there, others were, too."

"Right." He paused. "Obviously, as you said, this isn't a good time to talk. How about I call you tomorrow? We can set up a time for me to see you in Newport on Tuesday."

"I'll look forward to it," Emily said, hanging up the phone. She remained against the far wall, reluctant to rejoin the tour, which seemed to have stalled in this room.

"This house obviously postdates Edison, you'd know that if you'd been listening," one of the Providence bakers said to the teens' father. "The house is practically new."

"New isn't a century old. A century old is just that. It's *old*," said the father, squaring his shoulders. "A century ago people weren't even driving cars."

"A century ago we were already in the modern age, buster," said the second baker.

The world was being overrun by idiots, and it was Emily who was being hunted by the police? She opened her mouth to talk — the modern age started more than four hundred years ago, with Machiavelli's push toward progress! — but then Kiara gestured to the crowd and began to lead them back up and out of the room. The modern age is long over, Emily nearly hollered at the departing tour.

Emily stayed where she was. Why talk, anyway? Who would trust the words that came out of her mouth? Everything she touched turned to crap. After nearly forty years of barely skating by, she was done. No money, no job, no brain cells firing, and the cops on the way. She had to tell Nate about the painting. She clenched her jaw and felt the courage drain out of her.

She slid to the ground, her body like dead weight, heavy on the floor. She'd stay here until tomorrow. She'd stay here forever. If the NYPD wanted to take her statement, let them come to the basement of the Elms. Let them arrest her on this soot-stained concrete floor, at rock bottom. It was over. *It was over.* Like the era of grand mansion living in Newport, Emily's life as she knew it was over.

CHAPTER 18

Trespass

THE NARRAGANSETT HOUSE WAS BEAUTIFUL. Not George Bedecker beautiful – austerely, intellectually, architecturally impressive – but classic, historic, kick-off-your-shoes-and-smell-the-sea warm. The wide plank floors and oak door frame of the back mudroom showed signs of everyday wear, divots and cracks and damp spots of raw wood where the paint's seal had cracked. Deeper inside, the home was decked out with the kind of furnishings Nate figured might come from a 1950s department store sale. The living room was filled with conservative, upholstered set pieces, all soft lines and matte finishes – with a few nineteenth-century antiques thrown in.

After changing Trevor's diaper, Nate put the boy down for his nap, laying him flat on the living room's fluffed, floral sofa. He pushed a console table against the front of the couch, caging his child into a makeshift crib. With the sleeping boy securely boxed in, Nate took himself on a full house tour, as calm as if he'd been invited in as a guest.

The place was noticeably clean and airy, smelling of floor wax and detergent, acerbic and citrus. The rooms were so spotless and dust free that, for a moment, Nate worried someone was currently living here, that he'd actually broken and entered into a stranger's full-time residence. No, he told himself, the house was vacant and had been for some time. The shades were all shut tight and the refrigerator had been emptied and wiped clean. The kitchen cabinets were stocked but only with canned goods and nonperishables. As if appraising the home's contents for auction, Nate looked in every drawer and cabinet as he canvassed the space. A tall chest stretched along the edge of a hall that connected the kitchen to the front vestibule. The cabinet's top-left drawer was practically empty, like George's buildings. Only a thin, spindly silver pen, barely tarnished, was nestled against the drawer's side, next to a small blank notepad, white with a barely discernible gray grid. In the right-hand drawer, Nate found merely a square, unmarked gray box containing standard silver paper clips. The house where Nate grew up had been similarly devoid of extraneous matter (of piles of change, skiffs of torn notepaper, clipped coupons), not just to the naked eye but below the surface as well. Even the closets at Bedecker House had been expertly organized and pared down to the basics, except for the armoire in Nate and Charlie's room. The boys had used that closed-door space as the repository for everything they owned, shoving their baseball cards and sweatshirts haphazardly inside, keeping the mayhem out of their father's sight.

Each time George left that spare, square house to go on a business trip, though, the place slowly settled into disarray. The situation was only temporary: Nate's mother could get the abode back up to Bedecker standards in less than a day, which was usually as much warning as George gave before his return.

When Nate asked his mother why she didn't simply leave the place in livable disorder all of the time (the house was only half George's, the other half was hers), she said, of the hyperorganized abode, "It's better this way." When Nate looked unconvinced, she continued, with a patient severity to her voice, as if doling out advice that might save him someday: "To appreciate this house it should be inhabited with a certain aesthetic. It is a joy to live here. Remember, the house breathes life into us, not the other way around."

Yet *this* house, George's father's house, was a comfortable New England homestead that seemed to breathe *because* of its past inhabitants, because of the patterns of daily living. This house, so far on the pendulum swing from the home George had built for his own family in the 1960s, was where George himself had grown up. And he'd clearly returned since Nate last saw him here, thirty years ago, tending to his own father, the elder, elderly Bedecker. If Nate needed proof that his father had been back (proof beyond the barely lined notepad in the hall cabinet's drawer, identical to the notepads George had kept in the hallway drawers at Bedecker House when Nate was a child, identical to the pads George had had on his drafting table at work), his eye caught on an envelope. It was propped against a riser halfway up the steps from the first floor to the second. Peeking out of the business-size envelope's clear cellophane window was an address, the address of this house, and above it, in a computer generated font: TO: MR. GEORGE BEDECKER.

As Nate opened the sealed envelope, two words came to mind: *mail tampering*. He feared he was adding mail tampering to his list of offenses for the day. He and Emily could end up inhabiting neighboring jail cells, she for art theft (but really, there had to be an explanation for the Rufino in her bag — he'd ask her about it, he would, as soon as he saw her) and he for the triple whammy of breaking, entering, and mail fraud. Then again, since this particular envelope hadn't been sent through the post office (it was stamp-free and had been hand-delivered to this step, apparently), it didn't legally qualify as mail, did it? Nate tore through the flap and removed the paper that was inside. As he unfolded it, he kept one ear toward the living room where Trevor remained quiet.

The letter wasn't a letter at all. It was a cleaning and landscaping bill. George's house had been scrubbed and his yard tended to three days earlier. The document didn't say if this was routine upkeep or a special service to prepare for the homeowner's arrival. It could easily be routine upkeep. George was fastidious enough to want his place carefully maintained even when he was gone — that had largely been Nate's mother's role when she was alive. Now, instead of Annemarie, George had Norman Carlson of West Warwick (as the letterhead announced) picking up the slack for $165 a visit.

Of course George would have a caretaker: this wasn't his main residence. He probably came here only once a year. Once every five years. Maybe every ten, for all Nate knew. George didn't take vacations, after all, and he was headquartered in Chicago now. Nate received yearly assessments from his father's office, summarizing family transactions, the moving around of the tiny bit of cash that was left from his mother's estate — not even enough for two months' rent on Nate and Emily's New York apartment. The typed-up annual assessment, with no personal note attached, was the only word that Nate had received from his father in the past five years. Five years since they'd spoken. Even longer since they'd been in the same room.

Nate left the bill on the steps and continued climbing to the second floor, which felt uncannily small, each of the three rooms just big enough for a full-size bed and dresser set. Solid white quilts lay over the beds, straw mats across the floor, roller shades shut tight over the windows. The dressers were empty except for the bureau in the slightly larger master bedroom. That bureau was filled with spare blankets, extra pillowcases, two pairs of pajamas, and, in the closet, a few pairs of pants, shirts, and jackets that Nate recognized as his father's. The man never varied his wardrobe, dressing in shades of black and white and chalkboard gray — city tones, the hues of stone buildings and slate facades — even, it appeared, while here, in the country and on the sea. Nate rifled through the medicine cabinet, looking for odd vitamins or prescriptions, even as he knew that there was no treatment for Huntington's. Still, wasn't lack of any clues a sign in itself? Wasn't no evidence of a positive diagnosis enough to assume the negative? Nate couldn't remember. Someone famous once said that you can't prove a negative, but Nate didn't know who. Emily was the quotation expert, the walking *Bartlett's*, still citing the B-list philosophers from her college seminars.

Nate felt an unidentifiable gloom, a sense of displacement as he crept through a house that wasn't his, in a town he didn't know, looking for clues to something that he'd probably made up. Trespassing. Add trespass to his rap sheet. He thought back to the front porch, where he'd searched for the house key fifteen minutes ago. He'd put everything back in its place, hadn't he? He didn't want the caretaker driving by and noticing something *off*, stopping in to check things out. He didn't want George dropping in, either, but it was Sunday already, if the old man (who didn't take holidays, Nate reminded himself) was coming for the long weekend, he'd be here already. Regardless, Nate's heart beat hard as he quickly and quietly ran down the stairs to check on Trevor (still sleeping soundly, still secure in his makeshift crib) and then ran back up again.

Finally he headed up another flight to the attic, measuring out his steps on the narrow stairs. His legs were still firm, firmer than they'd been in the Jeep two days ago, as firm as any healthy, appropriately aging guy. His mind was healthy, too, he'd definitely remembered to put everything back in place on the porch.

He'd also remembered to lock the damn Cherokee on Friday, surely he'd remembered that, and look where it had gotten him.

The rough-hewn stairs sagged under Nate's weight. When he reached the top, he was shocked by the light. The attic was bright. He blinked and waited for his tired eyes to adjust. While the shades had been drawn in the rooms downstairs, the windows here, eaves cut deep into the roof, were open to the glare rising up off the water below. The place was teeming with stuff, like the trunk of that stolen Jeep, boxes and garment bags and stacked rickety furniture. Nate slowly navigated around the clutter. On the left side of the room, nudged up against an old dresser, were boxes of clothing. Nate opened the one closest to him and found a pile of wool pants, two waist sizes larger than his own and much larger than the pants that George wore. The architect was always too thin, and Nate remembered his mother gently joking (not to George's face, of course) that the man practiced the same minimalism with his diet that he adhered to in his designs. Draped next to that box was a frayed overcoat in a deep brown. Nate dug into the pockets, but they were empty. Nate worked his way past a crate of *Scientific Americans*. Nate's grandfather hadn't been in the science world but was a dilettante in everything, Nate's mother had told him. The man Nate had glimpsed long ago outside this very house hadn't been much of anything for long, except a dabbler in business and a compulsive drinker, living mostly off his family money until he depleted it, long before his death, and then off Social Security and Medicaid. Everything of value except for this house was gone by the time George was grown and his school tuitions had been paid. Bitter and angry, it seemed, Nate's father had left this place to make his own way in the world and never looked back.

But George had, finally, come back. Nate had seen him here that one time in 1974, and that likely wasn't the sole visit he had made to check in on his father. Perhaps he'd returned again and again, without his wife and children. During Nate's childhood, George was gone so often that Nate, as a teenager, stopped asking where he went. And from the neat and stacked look of the packing job in the attic, these boxes had been gathered and stored up here by George himself, probably after his father's death. George had specifically told Nate, after he sold the Cleveland house, that he was moving his own things here.

Nate walked toward the windows and stumbled over a metal crate of old train ticket stubs, photographs of George as a kid, ancient postcards to the Bedeckers from people whose names Nate didn't know. While George had barely given his own sons the time of day, George's parents had documented their child's comings and goings in mundane detail. Next to the crate sat a carefully preserved file of papers, clippings, and notes. Nate lifted a heavy bound volume that was wedged into the side of the file – George's high school yearbook. George's portrait, smack in the middle of the B section of the senior photos, looked identical to the others on the page. The men all shared the same close-cropped haircut (as if a putting green had lodged atop each of boys' scalps), the same sports jackets, similar club-striped ties. Diversity had yet to spread to New England. In the casual candids that littered the yearbook pages, the scattering of identical tall, white teenagers looked like an optical illusion. Nate didn't see his father in any of these candids, and wasn't sure if it was because the teenaged Bedecker wasn't in the pictures, or because he was indistinguishable to the naked eye. Or because

Nate had wandered so far from his own past that he wouldn't even recognize it in a still photo.

The file's stack of magazine and newspaper clips documented George's early commissions, the more traditional structures he'd created long before the boxy Cleveland house, a decade prior to Nate's and Charlie's arrivals. Nate had seen these pictures only in libraries, in architecture books. At Bedecker House, George had kept no evidence of his early career. Here, though, that career was carefully preserved, most likely by George's father. George's mom, Nate knew, died young, just like Annemarie. George would have been in high school at the time, though from the look of him in his senior yearbook picture, where he was smiling and at ease in front of the camera, you'd never know that he'd dealt with death already. You'd never have known it, either, twenty years later when Nate was in college and his own mother died. After Annemarie's death, George offered Nate no words of wisdom, no sense that he'd been there himself.

Nate worked his way through the clips from the bottom up until he reached the final newspaper story, the most recent of them, published nearly four decades ago, a few months after Nate was born. It was a *Boston Globe* feature about Bedecker's commission to design Worcester's Human Rights Museum, a building that was never erected – though whether its failure stemmed from George's design (impossible to build on any level of civic budget, the article pointed out) or the city's inability to secure support was never determined. Stapled to the top of the *Globe* story was a faded photograph of Nate himself, a picture Nate had never seen but which wasn't so different from the blown-up images Nate's mother had propped in the one bookshelf along Bedecker House's front hallway. The baby in the picture, two months old or so, lay on a bedsheet in the small clearing beside the glass-and-stone house – the same clearing where Nate would later camp out with his brother. In the picture, Nate was on his stomach, eyes to the camera, one ear to the ground. On the white border beneath the image, in George's unmistakable, crisp writing (the photo had seemingly come from George; he'd thought to send his father a photo), it said only, "Here is Nate."

It could almost be Trevor in the picture. Nate thought back to Trevor eight months ago, lying on their living room floor in the city.

A screech came from down below, from the first floor – Trevor. Shit. Nate had been in the attic at least half an hour. The boy could easily be awake. Or hurt. Or *scared*. The screech came again and Nate ran quickly toward the stairs and was halfway down to the second floor when he realized it wasn't Trevor. It wasn't the boy at all. It was the old-fashioned three-note clang of a manual-chime doorbell. Nate scrambled down the rest of the flight, taking the steps two at a time, from the attic to the second floor where he froze on the landing.

Images of that caretaker came to him. Pictures of a nosy neighbor. A full-on feature film of his own deceit. He had nothing to gain by answering the door. No one except the teenaged Nicole knew he was here. He'd sit tight and quiet until whoever it was drove away. As long as the person outside – Norman Carlson or that neighbor or a knee-socked Girl Scout – didn't go around the house and see the window carnage by the back door, there'd be no sign that Nate had broken inside. He would sit still and wait out this episode, everything would be fine, he was sure of this – and his plan would have worked, he was certain, except that right then, with the third clang of the doorbell, Trevor broke into a screaming wail from the living room. His cover blown, Nate bolted from the second floor to the first, where he scooped the boy into his arms and then walked as innocently as he could toward the front vestibule. Through the door's frosted window, he saw the shadow of a man: pencil-thin, stooped, and dark. The stooped and dark posture, Nate realized as he reached for the door handle (time suddenly slowing down as he wished he could make it stop entirely), of George Bedecker.

On the other side of the door stood a uniformed cop, lanky and leaning over. His badge sat high on his shoulder, more name tag than chest decoration.

"I'm sorry," Nate said, standing on the threshold, taking a deep breath of the outside air. The man at the door wasn't George Bedecker. It took a moment for this realization to set in. This was either the first stroke of luck Nate had had in a month, or a catastrophe waiting to happen.

He opened the door wider to allow the policeman a better look at the immaculate domestic scene inside. This officer's hunched posture was painfully dour, like a willow tree. His lanky frame appeared brittle and ready to crack. Why was the cop here? Not about the Rufino, Nate told himself. They'd have no reason to search Nate out for the Rufino; Nate himself hadn't known until three hours ago that it was in his possession. The painting couldn't have a location-transmitting microchip embedded in it, could it? Did art collectors do that? No. No. If it did have a chip, the authorities would have found the piece before now. It wasn't the Rufino. The cop hadn't come for the Rufino. It must be the front porch; Nate had left something conspicuously out of place.

"My father — " Nate started to say, since, in most families, it wouldn't be a crime, really, to let yourself into your parent's house. Most people, as Nate had seen on TV and the movies and in everyone else on Earth's real life, actually welcomed their relatives into their homes. "My dad, George Bedeck – "

"There's been an accident," the cop interrupted, nodding his head as if in agreement.

Nate nodded back. Trevor breathed heavily in his arms, his breath leaving a wet spot on Nate's shoulder. The boy looked confused. He had the diffuse gaze of an infant roused midnap, unsure of whether it was day or night.

"A car accident," the cop continued. "You can follow me to the hospital. Or I can give you a ride. We tried to call, but your phone here is disconnected."

"A what? The Jeep?" Nate said. He needed to put Trevor down, he needed to think, he needed to get out of this house and away from its history. Someone had had an accident in the Jeep? "Holy shit, is Emily all right?" He'd screamed. He hadn't meant to scream. He leaned on the doorframe for support and looked at his watch. It was 1:00 p.m. He hadn't seen Emily since he and Trevor left her at the Viking more than four hours ago. He hadn't even heard from her. Emily was fine, though, she had to be. If there was a car accident, she was definitely fine, she wasn't the one with their car, it was the thief, the car thief. The thief had had an accident. Good, Nate thought. He continued to hear the doorbell clang in his head even though the room, the entryway, was completely quiet now. Emily had to be fine. "Where the hell is Emily?" he spoke loudly over his inner gong – the Pachelbel's Canon of his head. "What happened to the car? What's going on?" Trevor started to cry, scared. Or maybe it was Nate who was scared.

"Your father is George Bedecker, the George Bedecker who lives here?"

Nate nodded. Yes, it was his father's house. Yes, he was sorry he'd broken in. Yes, he nodded.

"He's been in an accident," the man repeated. "Your father has had an accident."

The wind rustled the cop's blond hair, exposing his receding hairline, the redness of his scalp. Other than in shape and posture, he looked nothing like George Bedecker. He was nothing but a messenger of news.

CHAPTER 19

The Drive: Prelude, Two Days Ago

BEFORE MAKING THE drive east, George had carefully packed up his things: papers, mostly, architectural plans, contracts. He layered them in boxes and filing crates, carefully smoothing each page as if putting a life to rest. He wasn't a sentimental man, he told himself. One only had to look at his work to understand this fact.

His life had been built in the greater world, in the physical structures that bore his name. There were certainly people who'd achieved less with their lives, he understood this. There were also people who had achieved far more. George had long lived in fear of death. He saw now, too, how much he'd feared old age, if he was fortunate enough to achieve it. With age came reckoning, even to those who strove to avoid it.

The first time George saw a computer rendering of his own work in progress was nearly fifteen years ago. He'd been stunned by the animation. In the rendering, of a plan for a San Diego office tower, the building's exterior was depicted as a dimensionless spread of bronze cut through by shadows cast from an imagined sun. The windows appeared as uniform rectangles of flat aureolin, as if lit from within by a paint roller. This was how George had lived his life: in blurred vision, sidestepping the details. His buildings, however, were intended to reflect reality.

The boxing-up of George's things (actual hand-drawn building plans, as well as printouts of those renderings) moved slowly — at a steady pace interrupted only by the occasional twitch, or slightly longer periods during which he sat down to wait for his tremors to pass — until, sandwiched flat between two folders of financial papers, George found a CD. Its surface was solid silver, bare of explanatory text. Yet George recognized the disc. He was surprised that he hadn't stumbled upon it sooner in recent years. All of his other relics were visual. It was a thrill, of sorts, to happen upon one so totally aural.

Since his apartment was nearly all packed, he no longer had a CD player hooked up, and he had no computer on hand. He slipped the disc into the pocket of his suit jacket and took the elevator down to the parking garage. He got into his Audi — the same one he'd drive east the next day, from this garage in Chicago to Narragansett. He started the ignition and slid the disc into the car's stereo. The voice that came out of the speakers was both his and not his.

"My plans for the courthouse? From the start they were fine, *fine*. The hold-up in the spring of 1984 was due entirely to the appropriation committee's dispute over the court's exterior. They had envisioned something in a pale gray, evocative of the dove, I suppose." George's tone was firm but round at the edges. He'd been younger when he'd taped this interview for the Copenhagen Central Court. He'd been younger, too, when he'd conceived the design for that courthouse. In the front seat of the Audi, his chest kicked — as if a Huntington's tremor had bumped up against his heart — as he listened to his other self, the one he used to be, the one who spoke on the CD. "I insisted on the glazed tawny sandstone that you see today. The tawny colors of the earth are an imperative symbol of justice. What does a courthouse honor if not justice?

"Justice is of the ground, a matter of the soil. In the end, this is where we all return, to the ground, good or bad, joining those who've come before. Justice is not a matter of treating the good with deference, but of treating all who are in the system with égalité, to quote the French. And nowhere are we as equal as in death. In death, the missteps that have marked our lives are irrelevant. Each of us is reduced to our essential biology." He'd imagined himself fierce, back then.

"To the contrary – " The interviewer interrupted. George remembered the man, a boy, really, probably the Danish equivalent of an intern at the time. They'd sat across from each other in the office that George's firm rented for the duration of the project, empty white rooms outfitted with drafting tables, desks, phones with cords and dials.

"Yes," George said before the interviewer could finish his thought, "this is a godless vision, burial in the earth as a last and final resting place. It is contradictory to logic, I suppose, that I have built a heathen-inspired design for a government building here. *Here*, in the capital of a Lutheran country. To you, as a Dane and a Lutheran, justice and belief are intertwined. To you, justice is godly. To me, it is of the earth. Life is hard, incomprehensible, guided solely by our individual abilities to control our impulses."

George – the George in the Audi, the George of the new millennium – leaned back against the car's headrest and closed his eyes. He'd left his family at home to build that courthouse twenty years ago. He'd left them at home for so many buildings. It seemed to be the right thing at the time, and now as well. His work had always been about people, about creating spaces to elevate the lives of other people. If that left him often alone, so be it. The courthouse hadn't existed before George Bedecker arrived in Copenhagen to construct it. Today, it defined that city's landscape. "The people and the earth on which they live, this is the highest plane. *This* is what deserves our utmost attention. Not the unknowable, an unprovable great beyond," his voice continued from the speakers, steady, strong, historic.

"When your life ends, *you* expect to be transported to some vision of heaven or hell. When my life ends, I expect to be returned without fanfare to that earth, to the tawny earth and its inherent implication of justice, where my trespasses will be of no consequence and my talents of no use. It's the place to where my ancestors have returned, both the good and the bad. And in that idea I find peace." The interview ended. George removed the CD from the player. He rode the elevator up to his apartment for the last time. He would sleep soundly through the night. He would pack the car in the morning. Wherever his life ended, whatever earth he returned to, it wouldn't be here. He would make the drive east.

CHAPTER 20

Head Trauma

FROM THE HOSPITAL'S EMERGENCY wing, Nate called
Emily's cell phone.

"Hello?" Emily's voice sounded far away when she
finally answered, as if she was at the bottom of a canyon.

"Are you okay? It's me."

"Oh God, I'm – are you at the hotel? I'm on my way, really,
I'll be there in ten minutes. I don't know what I'm doing here,
I don't know – " her voice caught, the edge of a cry breaking
through. She was breathing hard. It was the first time Nate had
heard her voice since he'd discovered the Rufino in her bag.
He was surprised that she still sounded like the Emily he knew.
"Sorry, I lost my feet for a minute," she said. "I lost my head,
Nate."

Nate was slouched down in a cold, plastic chair in the Kent
Hospital's waiting room. He held the phone to his ear and stared
at a loose heating vent in the wall across from him. Trevor was
out of sight, safely in the care of an overly enthusiastic nurse
who'd offered to show him around the children's playroom.

Over the intercom, from a speaker directly above Nate's head, a doctor was paged, his name a jumble of syncopated pauses and consonants and static. Nate was the only person in the waiting room. It seemed that in Rhode Island, Land of the Free, people didn't have emergencies.

"Em, listen, Em, I'm at the hospital. But I'm fine, Trevor's fine. We're fine."

After a deadly pause, Emily let loose a full, belated cry. Nate could hear tears. "Trevor?" she said.

"Believe me, he's fine, I'm fine." Nate's voice came out fast, like a mantra. "Em, it's not the little guy. He's great."

"He's fine."

"Trevor's fine, Em. It's George, my father. He's in intensive care."

Emily took some time to answer. Where the hell was she that her voice sounded so remote? Nate had considered not calling Emily. Given the Rufino situation, things would be complicated between them now, but until Nate heard her explanation, he was working hard to not wholly condemn her.

"Here? Your father's here?" she said.

"He crashed his car into a ditch on Route 1, outside Charles-town. I don't even know why he was behind the wheel; he hates to drive. The cops don't know what happened." When Nate's brother was hit by a car, on a day nothing like today, the cops knew exactly what had happened. There were witnesses to the scene who'd watched the out-of-control Honda slam straight into Charlie and his bike. Charlie died before making it to the emergency room. That time, Nate hadn't gone to the hospital. He'd waited at home by himself until Annemarie returned from the medical center, leaving Charlie in the morgue. During those hours alone, Nate had taken Charlie's baseball cards down from their perch in a shoe box on the armoire's top shelf and alphabetized them by team and sorted them by year, something Charlie always talked about doing but had never found the time. Nate, alone in the square house and scared, told himself that when his mother had said Charlie "passed," maybe she was wrong. Maybe he was still alive, and he'd come home tomorrow and would be grateful when he saw what Nate had done for him, organizing his cards. Nate's hands trembled as he flipped through the cardboard tiles; the air in the house began to feel thin and diffuse. Small, almost indecipherable tears slid down his cheeks as he moved a Hank Aaron card, a Topps from Hank's Atlanta Braves era, to the front of the stack. Nate didn't think, at that moment, he could live in this family without his brother.

That night, George flew in from Seattle. Over and over, in the years since Charlie's death, Nate had tried to imagine his father actually receiving the bad news, a truth over which he had no control. Nate tried to picture him answering the phone call out on the West Coast, and soon afterward standing alone at an airport gate waiting for the plane that would deliver him to his son's body. Trying to picture these unfathomable moments was easier than rehashing the known details of Charlie's death.

"Your father is in Rhode Island? Right now?" Emily asked.

"Right now. In the hospital." Nate had just spent ten minutes standing next to the inert, unconscious old man's bedside. It had felt like a dream.

"Is he okay?"

"Okay?" There had never been anything okay about the guy. "He looks terrible. I mean, not because of the accident. His injuries are internal, so there's barely a mark on him, but he looks like he's aged a century since I last saw him. Fuck, he's old." A decade put a lot of age on a guy, it turned out (it had been nearly ten years, Nate reasoned, since he'd actually stood next to his father, the years having accumulated like newspapers set aside for recycling). Nate did the math in his head: his father would be into his late sixties, the age when most architects reached their prime, yet George, flat on his hospital bed, looked like a mildewed retirement-home prospect. At least Nate's mother had died before she lost any of it — her looks, her mind, her grace. Charlie, too, dead before life could chew him up and turn him into an adult, before he realized what hell growing up could be. "George is in a coma," Nate said.

"A coma? Tell me where you are. I'll walk there. How far are you?"

"Don't come. We're in Warwick, and wherever that is, it's too far to walk." He wasn't ready to see her yet, anyway. He could only cope with one trauma at a time. "We'll find a way back to the Viking, there's nothing I can do here. I didn't want you to worry." The young nurse was walking toward Nate, pushing Trevor ahead of her in a yellow toy wagon. Trevor sang in non-sense words (*ba, ba, bop bop, ba*) to the smooth creak of the wagon's wheels over the linoleum. His face was marked with fierce red splotches. He'd been crying. Or screaming, most likely screaming. The nurse must have had him in a soundproof room, because Nate hadn't heard a thing. "I mean, the best that could happen, medically, is that he wakes up. And then? Who knows. I don't know why I'm even here."

"He's your father." Emily paused, he heard a door shut on her end of the line. "He got hurt *today*? And they called you?"

This accident: What were the chances that Nate would be so close to the scene, that the police would find him so easily, that he should have been at the Narragansett house at the exact moment when the officer showed up? It was unreal. A sign. Nate tried to see it as a gift. If his father woke up, Nate would have him at a disadvantage, stripped of his street clothes and strapped to machines. It seemed that a hospital, with his father weak and under supervision, was the best place to confront him. It was the kind of setting where people had reconciliations and came to terms with the truth.

"Em, I don't even know if he'd want me here. He could be out for days, for a month, forever. Go back to the hotel. Trev and I will find a way there and I'll keep my phone on."

"Okay." Emily sounded unsure.

Nate hung up, put his phone back in his pocket, and lifted Trevor out of the wagon. The boy wound his arms tight around Nate's neck. Where other babies' arms were like Michelin Man stubs, Trevor's body was already taking on sophistication, getting ready for complicated maneuvers. It was as if he had shorn his baby fat early in anticipation of a future as a major-league pitcher.

"Thanks," Nate said to the nurse, "I needed that break."

"I'd have kept him longer — it's nice to see a healthy kid, usually — but he got a little wild. Boy, he's a yeller," the nurse said with an uncomfortable laugh. "I changed his diaper, hope you don't mind. He was wet." She waved her hand, excusing any further gratitude. "See you later, alligator," she twiddled her fingers at Trevor as she walked away. Her steps were fast and staccato, as if relieved.

Nate couldn't imagine Trevor, someday, coming to a place like this to visit him, old and feeble. Or young and feeble, felled by Huntington's. Nate didn't want Trevor to ever see him the way they were seeing George right now. Was it better to cut your son off?

"Mr. Bedecker?" The doctor assigned to George's case stood in front of Nate.

"Call me Nate." He began to get up with Trevor in his arms.

"Please, sit," the doctor said. "Your father's suffered a serious head injury. His body was thrown toward the steering wheel and his head hit hardest. As for his brain function, we'll have to wait and watch for the swelling to go down in hopes that he'll become more responsive."

"Which means?"

"It's impossible to determine if and when he'll come out of this coma. If he does come out of it, I can't predict what his level of function will be." The doctor shrugged. "This kind of head injury, in my experience as well as wider experience, can have a good prognosis and recovery, but it is impossible to know at this point."

"You've seen this before."

"I specialize in head trauma," the doctor said. "Yes." He wore a cheap but sturdy suit under his white jacket, a respectable forest-green tie with a gold check-mark pattern. He actually started to smile, and Nate wanted to hug the doctor, take him home with him. A walking and talking fount of knowledge.

"So you're a neurologist? Can I ask you a question?"

"As I said, there's little I can tell you so far."

"It's just one question," Nate said, not sure if he wanted the answer — and not sure if this was the man to ask. The man Nate should be talking to was his father. After all of these years, it was time he talked to George. "My father, when you were examining him, his brain function, did you notice anything else wrong? I mean, I haven't seen him in almost a decade, and to be honest, it's a fluke that I was summoned after his crash because we're not really in touch, we haven't talked in years, even to say hello, he doesn't even know who I am, as a person. I just happened to be at his house at the wrong time. But I think he may be sick." Nate paused. It was the first time he'd voiced this sentiment. He expected that when spoken aloud, he would see how foolish he was — presuming that his father had a fatal genetic disease. Instead, the potential truth of Nate's fears coagulated and felt alarmingly present. Trevor reached up with his lithe left arm and started pulling on the neck of Nate's sweater. "If I sound crazy, I'm sorry."

"Sick has myriad definitions," said the doctor.

"I'm thinking Huntington's. I think he has Huntington's disease, chorea, Huntington's chorea. I think he has Huntington's."

The neurologist thrust his hands into the deep square pockets of his lab coat and stood still for a moment. His eyes were focused on the sterile air behind Nate. When he spoke again, his voice had lost its softness and was serious, intent. "Is he at risk for Huntington's?" When Nate didn't answer, the doctor asked, "Is your family gene-positive? Huntington's is not something that would show up in our standard tests, nor is it related to the injuries he sustained today. To answer your question, we'd have to do a gene test, or look at his symptoms once he's awake. It's rare, it's — " the doctor paused, "it's not something we see often. It's a rough prognosis."

Nate nodded, and after another moment of strained silence, of Trevor trying to chew on Nate's shirt, of the doctor shifting his weight from one foot to the other, Nate told the neurologist the story of his grandfather (the ostensible proof that the gene was in the family) and he recalled his hunches about his father (the gut feeling that the gene had been passed down to George, the article in the *Times*). The doctor sat beside Nate and took it all in. Nate imagined how he looked to the man, so healthy, with his own healthy son, their polished exteriors acting as deceptive cover for the potential deaths their bodies were harboring. In the world of Huntington's, good hair and the lack of a beer gut didn't mean anything. As Nate finished, an orderly approached, summoning the doctor to another case.

"There's no way to know without doing a test, and your father needs to be conscious in order to give consent for that test," the doctor said. Then, standing, looking down with a wince of a smile, a sympathy grimace (so much softer than the grimace that Nate had seen, in pictures, frozen on the faces of late-stage Huntington's sufferers), the doctor glanced from Nate to Trevor and back to Nate again. "You could get tested, too, you know." Then with one more pained look at Trevor, he added, "That's a loaded issue. It's not a process to be taken lightly. Even," he said, "if you didn't already have a child."

"If you're telling me I'm too late, I know that," Nate said, holding Trevor tightly. The doctor nodded, briefly placed a hand on Nate's shoulder, and then walked away, across the linoleum, toward his next patient, another life on the brink. Nate cupped his son's cheek in his palm and the boy's name (*Trevor, Trevor, Trevor*), thudded inside his chest like a heartbeat.

CHAPTER 21

The Things Nate Knows, Reprise

A BEAT-UP AUDI PULLED into the Viking's circular
drive. As the car moved out of the sun and into the
hotel's shadow, Emily saw that Nate was at the wheel.
She could make out Trevor's shape, too, strapped into a baby
seat in the back. Where had they gotten an Audi? The car's front
fender was crushed in and the right headlight smashed to near
nonexistence. The car was winking, making Emily feel left out
of a private joke.

Emily had been sitting on the Viking's steps for almost an
hour, ever since she'd fled her tour of the Elms. She had two
days to figure out how to deal with the NYPD. They had no
proof, she reminded herself. It was totally normal to go to the
bathroom at a party. It was basic physiology: Alcohol makes a
person pee. She'd had, what? Two glasses of wine and a vodka-
soda? Three glasses of wine and the vodka? Enough to have to
use the restroom. Who, though, had turned her in to the cops?
Who would have cared enough to notice that she'd wandered
toward the study? That information was innocuous. What she

feared was that the snitch might have seen more, might have
told the cops more. Get a grip!

Nate waved at her from the side of the Audi before leaning
into the backseat and unhooking the boy. She needed to tell
Nate about the painting. He'd been carrying it around all day!
But he hadn't mentioned it. If he'd stumbled on the canvas,
he'd have said something. She'd tell him. She'd tell him before
Tuesday, before she lied to the cops. She'd tell him after they
dealt with George and whatever it was that had happened to
him today. Her head was clouded by the Rufino, but she understood that George was top priority at this moment. She could
barely grasp the fact that George Bedecker was here, in Rhode
Island (she could barely grasp the fact that *she* was here in Rhode
Island), let alone that George Bedecker was ailing and that Nate
had seen him. And that somehow Nate had been beckoned after
George's crash. The hospital had found him. Or the cops? She
and Nate seemed to be cop magnets. Emily couldn't remember what Nate had told her. Someone had tracked Nate down,
and Nate had rushed to his father's side. For the past four years
Emily had been begging Nate to reconnect with his dad. Until
today, he hadn't seemed interested.

"What the hell, Nate?" Emily said as she approached, motioning to the beat-up car. Other than the whopping dents, it looked
new and impeccably detailed.

"Yeah, it's a little trashed." He looked defeated and tired.
"And the car seat is on loan from the cops, so we need to bring
it back. But at least the gas tank is mostly full."

"But where did you get it?" Emily asked.

Trevor, in Nate's arms, blinked at Emily and grinned. Without taking his eyes off his mother, the boy began to fervently
suck on the fingers of his right hand.

"It's the car George crashed," Nate said, as if this should be obvious. He tapped his fingers against the metal of the driver's side door, edgy. He'd just seen his father for the first time in eight years or something, nine years, Emily figured. "As long as we don't drive it after dark" – he motioned to the busted head-light – "we'll be okay. Em, you look like shit."

Her eyes were red and puffy, she was sure. She looked no bet-ter than he did. She'd cried at the Elms, after her tour left the basement and she was alone.

Nate gave the car keys to the valet and walked past Emily, straight up the front steps, toward the hotel lobby. At the top, he turned and looked at her.

"We need to talk," he said. She nodded, and Nate turned again and continued his walk into the hotel.

While Nate sat on the suite's couch, Emily lay Trevor in the Pack 'n Play, washed her hands, fetched Nate a glass of water from the bathroom (where she popped an Inderal for herself), and took out the room-service menu. She spread the menu on the surface of the small desk. Nate looked as if his head was about to combust. Food would be good – food and drink weren't a cure-all, but they helped. The important thing was to keep her body moving. These small motions accumulated power until they were as soothing as any beta-blocker. She needed to find steady ground, to give her thoughts room to breathe. She picked up the phone to dial for room service, but put it down when she noticed Nate staring at her.

"What?" she said. She stood still for the first time and returned Nate's glare. He hadn't said anything about his father's condi-tion since he'd gotten back to the hotel. George Bedecker was unconscious, maybe dying. Maybe the cops would go easy on Emily now that her father-in-law was in a coma. She didn't actu-ally believe this. "What is it?"

When he didn't answer, she said, "We can go back to the hospital if you want. We can spend the night with George. Is that what you want? You tell me, and we'll make it happen. If you never want to see him again, we can do that, too." Seeing his father in a coma had to be shocking to Nate, no matter how out of touch the two were. "We can do whatever you want. Just tell me." Emily needed to hear his voice.

"It's been a bad day," he said.

"For me, too," she said, then quickly qualified the statement. "Sorry. My dad didn't fall into a coma. My day's been fine." Her day had been a disaster.

She opened the minifridge in search of a shot of gin, but they'd finished the final little bottles last night and the maid hadn't restocked them today. All that remained were two cans of Heineken. "We need to call down for drinks," she said. The Inderal had taken her down a notch, but she felt a circumspect angst clawing at the edges of her peripheral vision. "We're practically dry. Some holiday, this Columbus Day. Welcome to the New World."

"Emily, sit down."

"Nate," she said. She glanced over to the ice bucket, empty. "Just one drink. You'll feel better afterward, I promise." Or two drinks, two drinks would be adequate. They both needed to feel better.

"Sit down," he said again, and hearing the insistence in his voice, she turned to face him. There was a hesitancy to him now. His eyes were wet, glossy. Nate looked like a child suddenly, like a blown-up Trevor come to life. He looked scared.

The Nate who'd driven up in the Audi fifteen minutes ago was a man with a father. This was a new Nate, not the Nate Emily knew and had known for four years. That man had been tethered to no one but herself and Trevor. And this guy? Emily felt woozy. It wasn't clear where any of them stood. Like a china table-setting after the magician swiped the cloth out from under it, everything was in its place again, but an inch or two off-center.

"You're making me dizzy with all your running around," Nate said. "Sit down. Sit the fuck down. That'll make me feel better."

Emily nodded and sat next to him, his serious tone startling her. They should go back to the hospital. Whatever their relationship, Nate should be by his father's side. Emily could bundle Trevor up and they could bring him along. It would throw the boy off schedule, but who cared? If nothing else, maybe this weekend would finally train the boy to be adaptable. And then tomorrow, or Tuesday, she'd find a lawyer. She'd actually prepare for her interrogation by the cops.

Nate reached out and grabbed Emily's hand and she felt his fingers touch hers, lightly, as if testing them for flexibility. Or testing his own.

"My father, it's not just the accident," he said.

She nodded. The couch was soft and deep and, when it came down to it, she didn't want to go to the hospital, she didn't want to bundle Trevor up and drag him away, and Nate didn't seem to want that, either.

"Talk to me," she said.

Nate nodded and then, in a tone so even that it sounded rehearsed, he said, "In 1974 I came to Newport with my father. I saw his father, who was sick. I think it was Huntington's disease. I think my father has it now. I think I may have it. I think I could have passed it on to Trevor."

"Your father, George?" Emily didn't understand. "You said George had a car accident, not Huntington's disease." Nate had never mentioned any disease in his family other than his mother's leukemia. Huntington's couldn't be a major disease, Emily told herself. It couldn't be that harmful if she'd never heard of it. "You found out your father has Huntington's? At the hospital?"

"Oh God, I'm sorry." Nate paused, looked away from Emily. "My mother tried to warn me, before she died, but I didn't listen. I didn't want to know, and it was just me then, it didn't matter. But now with Trevor — "

"But he's okay. He's healthy," Emily said. He'd passed every genetic test in utero, and aced all of his doctor's appointments since then. He was perfect! Oh, he had his idiosyncrasies. There were his ears of course, which stood out like nautilus shells from his head. And that unwavering gaze, staring at strangers with the rudeness of a social neophyte. But he was in perfect health! He was perfect to Emily. "The doctors say he's fine, Nate. He's okay."

"Looking fine doesn't mean anything," Nate said. And then he laid out for Emily the facts of the disease, its ability to hide for decades, for most of a lifetime. And then, the way it emerged and slowly killed its carrier. "I convinced myself I didn't have it, that it wasn't in the family at all, until a month ago. My dad was in the *Times* and they said he was drunk, but he doesn't drink. He hates to drink. The staggering, it's a Huntington's symptom."

Emily thought about the last month, week after week of Nate wandering through their life in a haze. All of the conversations they'd had about the move, about restaurants to hit before they left the city, about his new job. She thought about his surprising joy (surprising, it seemed, even to himself) when she told him, eighteen months ago, that she was pregnant with Trevor. Of his ridiculous reluctance to talk about his parents and acknowledge that he had any kind of past.

"You and your fucking avoidance," she said. "You can't will away a disease by not thinking about it."

Nate took the newspaper clip out of his wallet and handed it over to Emily. She glanced at it. "It doesn't matter, does it, if your father was actually drunk or not? Your mother blatantly told you the disease is in his family — what, you thought she'd lied?"

"I'm an imbecile."

"Is there a chance your mother was wrong? That you misunderstood? That I'm misunderstanding?" Emily said. "Are you saying this disease is in our family now? Or are you just bouncing the idea off me? Because I need facts. You can't come at me with this hazy theory and expect me to be okay with it."

"I don't know," Nate said. "All I have so far are theories. I'm sorry, I'm just sorry."

The night had grown dark outside and they hadn't switched on any lights and in the pale doom Emily listened and asked questions and gradually she realized how deep the gulf had become between Nate and her, how many secrets they'd kept. Nate was the closest person in the world to her, and she was (she believed, truly believed) the closest to him. Yet still they'd been occupying spaces secluded from each other. Nate was telling her that he might be dying, and that he'd known this for some time.

After he finished explaining in detail Huntington's disease and his fears, Nate got off the couch and strode to the window, turning his back as if to give Emily an out, a moment to flee for her life. Slowly, she rose up from her seat. She held her breath and walked the short distance to the bedroom, to the side of the Pack 'n Play. Trevor looked intact and at peace. His breath was sleepy and even, while Emily's was speeding up. Her head grew light and her eyes moved up and down the boy's body. He was lying on his back with his limbs splayed flat and long across the thin mattress beneath him, intertwined with the sheet's brightly silk-screened ducks and swans. "Trevor," she said, testing his name in the air. She leaned down and spread a hand flat across his chest. "Trevor," she said reminding herself that the boy had special powers. He was superhuman. He would be okay. He could beat DNA. He had to beat the DNA. In his short life, he'd hurt no one. She raised her hand off his body and sat down on the ground where she was eye level with her son. Through the mesh wall between them, she watched Trevor sleep. She heard footsteps behind her. Nate.

"You should have told me," she said, not taking her eyes off the boy. She clenched her muscles, holding her body as firm and still as possible, in hopes of keeping her anger contained. Unleashed, it would be uncontrollable. This, she understood as her insides froze, was what real fear felt like.

"I should have told you," Nate said from behind her. Emily nodded.

If he'd told her a month ago, though, when his own suspicions reached their full height, what could she have done? According to Nate's sequence of events, by the time he discovered that newspaper clip, that iota of ostensible proof, not only had Trevor been conceived, but he'd already been born and was more than eight months old. It was already too late. So what would Emily have done if she'd known this news a month ago? Two months ago? She'd have hoped. She'd have spent the past two months pinning her hopes on Trevor and his future and the health of her family instead of wallowing in her own petty dramas, convincing herself that her own dreams — her shoe purchases and her passion for the pills — were the most important thing in the world. She wouldn't have stolen the Rufino in a momentary delusion that it could help her achieve some sort of greatness. Who cared? *Who cared* about Emily's dreams? Trevor had to beat the odds. All this time that Emily had been telling Nate that children were nearly indestructible? It turned out she was talking about other people's children, not her own.

Emily, the Rufino, their fiscal distress. None of it mattered any more.

"While we're making revelations," she said still looking at Trevor, pausing to reconsider what she was about to say, "I stole the Barbers' painting. I stole the Rufino. It's in the diaper bag."

She expected Nate to laugh, to say, "good one, Em" or "very funny" or "this isn't a time for jokes." When he didn't say anything, she continued, "The painting, the one that Jeanne and Trish and Sam Tully can't stop talking about. I have it. I have it, Nate. You were walking around with it all day today. I stole the Barbers' precious Rufino and it's here in Newport with us. It's in the diaper bag." She looked up. Nate was standing next to her. "I stole a Rufino."

"I know," he said. "I saw it."

PART IV

Monday

CHAPTER 22

Morning in the ICU

G EORGE LOOKED EXACTLY as he had the day before, connected to tubes, withered, lifeless, and wrapped in a hospital gown. Nate couldn't remember ever having seen his father's bare arms before. The thin skin, bunched at the elbows, was pale and pockmarked. Nate felt wrong and voyeuristic as he hovered at George's bedside, yet Emily, who had met Nate's father only five minutes ago — the meeting being one-way, given that George was still in a coma — was already taking him in with no apparent unease. Emily (an actual art thief, Nate had confirmed last night, upending everything he thought he knew about her) stood at the head of George's bed, her arms folded lightly across her chest.

"He's real," she said.

"You thought — ?"

"I don't know, that he was a figment of your imagination? You've done a pretty good job, historically, of portraying yourself as an orphan."

"He's real."

"Should I leave? I'm not sure he'd want me here," Emily said, making no motion to exit. "Your father is pretty much naked. It's weird. Isn't it weird?" She rested her hand on a monitor next to the bed, then quickly removed it, as if afraid she might break something. "I haven't been in a hospital since Trevor was born."

The air in the room smelled like toothpaste, disinfectant. Emily, too, seemed sanitized this morning, watching her words and softening her edges, reining herself in, the aftereffect of last night's conversation. She'd lashed out at Nate last night. He'd deserved it. They were both in the wrong, that's how things shook down. So while he wanted to hate her (not for stealing the painting, but for spending days face-to-face with him, hours in the car talking nonstop, and never mentioning the thing, not even when the topic came up), he couldn't. She'd seemed as shocked by her own thievery as he was. Emily had walked straight out of a packed party in front of dozens of friends, acquaintances, and rich fucks, and done so with a world-class work of art under her arm. First the beauty of that action struck Nate, then the obliterating disaster of it.

"What the hell did you do?" he asked her last night after she confessed to the theft and told Nate that the cops had called her.

"I didn't mean to take it," she'd said. "It happened."

"It happened?"

"Something inside me had to have it. I didn't mean to take it."

"You did take it. You *took* it." Impulses were the bane of the human race, that's the motto Nate had lived by for as long as he could remember. "Holy shit, Em. Why? Why the fuck couldn't you have just left it there?" Trevor was in the suite with them, playing with his own toes in the Pack 'n Play.

"You've got to give the painting back. I'll go with you. The minute we have credit cards, we'll rent a car. You stole the fucking Rufino?" he said. Until the moment she'd confessed, some small part of Nate still believed that there was another explanation, that she hadn't taken the art, that she hadn't even known it was in her purse. He'd wanted to believe that, he'd been willing to suspend his disbelief. "You've been holding on to it all this time? You didn't think I deserved to know?"

She started wheezing, quietly, like an asthmatic in denial. "We can't return it now," she said softly. As he looked again at the painting, he understood: Returning the piece was impossible. She'd killed its value when she cut the canvas and rolled it. Even from a few feet away, the buckling of the paint and fraying at the edges, right along the border of the paint itself, was discernable.

"Your fingerprints must be all over that empty frame, and the Barbers' study," Nate said. "I cannot believe you didn't feel the need to tell me that you had the Rufino." He wondered if Sam Tully suspected anything, and if that was why he'd called Nate and left a message about the theft. No, Tully would have told Nate if he had any hunches. Tully, unlike Emily, wouldn't try to pull one over on him.

"I wiped down the frames with the hem of my sweater," Emily said, sounding like someone who'd premeditated her crime. "It was instinct. I'm sure I was sloppy. I can't believe I was so stupid." *I can't believe you didn't say anything to me*, is what Nate thought.

"Why didn't you tell me?" he said. He couldn't imagine that she – and now he – could possibly get away with this. "Why didn't you tell me?" He couldn't talk any further until he had an answer to that question.

"I don't know."

"You don't *know*?" He'd thought he was the dishonest one of the two of them, yet his subterfuge had a pure motivation. He hadn't wanted to hurt her unless he was sure of his hunch. She, on the other hand, had no excuse at all.

"I wasn't thinking. I was ashamed."

"There's no way you wiped off all of your fingerprints with your sweater. A sweater?"

"Would they know the prints are mine, anyway?" Emily said. "I mean, I don't think my prints are on file anywhere, are they?" she said.

Of course not. For the police to get Emily's prints, they'd have to come up to Newport to see her in person — which is exactly what they were planning to do on Tuesday. Couldn't she see that? He and Emily would have to devise an out before then. George's comatose state was starting to look like an appealing way to live. If it weren't for Trevor, that is. Nate and Emily had to get their lives together for the sake of the boy.

Today they were free of Trevor. Before falling asleep last night — exhausted, mentally worn, all cried out (Nate hadn't expected tears, but they'd come — his first and then Emily's small dry sobs) — Nate had called the front desk and asked about the babysitting service they'd seen mentioned on the room-service menu. Within a minute they were signed up for a full day of sitting, charged to their room, and at seven thirty this morning an off-duty maid showed up at their door. She was stout, in her fifties, bilingual, and trained in CPR. She possessed all of the attributes most coveted in Manhattan nannies, Emily noted once they were in the elevator and out of the babysitter's earshot. Emily had tried to give instructions ("He takes a nap at eleven; he'll eat anything, but I like him to stick to oatmeal before noon") but the babysitter merely nodded and said "okay" and "I sit many, many times" and confidently picked up the boy and easily soothed his cries, remarkably easily, while Nate and Emily slunk away.

It was starting to seem like a waste of good babysitting money. There was nothing Nate or Emily could do, or wanted to do, for George. He showed no signs of regaining consciousness. Emily put her arm around Nate's waist, and he turned his attention to her, to the genuine sympathy on her face.

"I'm okay," he said. "He's like a stranger to me." Looking at George's inert frame, Nate thought back to his elementary school, where the playground had bordered on a thick patch of woods filled with scurrying beetles and garter snakes. *You touch it*, Nate and his friends would taunt one another each time a wounded squirrel or sparrow fell at the forest's edge. *No, you touch it first!* The only motion coming from George's body was the shallow rise and fall of his chest.

Neither Nate nor Emily had said much this morning about their conversation from last night. Nate knew that the Huntington's thing was somehow bigger than Emily's art caper. They might find a way out of the art thing if they schemed together. There was nothing, however, they could do about the Huntington's. And Huntington's, unlike art theft, was deadly. "I don't know what else to tell you," Nate had said to Emily this morning. She countered with, "I need to let my head settle." Finally they ended up in this hospital room after Emily asked, seeming to honestly want an answer, "What do we do now?"

"He looks at peace," Emily said, her eyes on George. She was studying the old man's face. "All of that stuff" – she paused and Nate could feel her tense up – "that Huntington's stuff. He doesn't look like a guy who's been wracked with shakes."

"You can't tell. They always look peaceful in their sleep. The articles say that the tremors, the chorea, it subsides in sleep. It's like a return to babyhood, so much unexplained craziness during the day and then a solid crash at night."

According to the doctors, there had been no change to

George's prognosis. He was still in a coma, still suffering from brain trauma, still no word on when or whether he'd come out of it. It was fascinating to watch: a completely unconscious body, continuing, at minimum function. All men were simply carbon-based machines when it came down to it. Brain function was purely a bonus.

The door to the room opened and Nate stepped out of the way, separating from Emily.

"Good morning!" chirped a male nurse, carrying a tray. His starched uniform was leaning closer to gray than to white. "Breakfast, if the patient feels up to it." The nurse set the plastic tray on the table by George's bedside and Emily started laughing. Her guffaws came out choked, as if she was trying to stop them.

"Oh, come on," she said to the nurse. She let her laugh grow unbridled for a moment. "Does the patient *look* like he feels up to it?" The nurse glared at her and left the room.

Beneath the tray's steam-dotted transparent cover, Nate could make out scrambled eggs, dry wheat toast, and a sectioned orange.

"It's a bummer," Nate said. "When I was a kid, my father used to request dry toast for breakfast from my mother all the time. Dry and tasteless, it fit his personality." The word *lifeless* also came to Nate's mind. The word described his father even before the accident, but it felt tactless today, here.

"You know, I used to imagine what it would be like when I met your dad for the first time," Emily said, stepping away from the bed. "The great George Bedecker. I imagined him in his gray suit like in all the pictures, but what would I say? 'I love your work' or 'I was astounded by the Prague Art League building' or 'I'm the woman who loves your son'? It all felt so loaded, even in my head."

Nate and she had barely talked about George after their early months of dating, when Nate made clear that he and his father hadn't much spoken in years. George Bedecker was someone Nate read about in newspapers. *Doesn't that make you sad?* she'd asked. *I have a full life, a lot of people have less,* he'd told her. It was true, it was a fact that had helped him get through plenty of rough times and financial setbacks. It seemed a small consolation now, though. His father, lying here unconscious (his coma starting to seem sinister and escapist), held all of the secrets to Nate's past, and maybe his future. If Nate spent any longer in this room he'd lose his mind. Prematurely. Pre-prematurely.

"He's totally unaware. It wouldn't be a bad way to go," Emily said.

"He's a young guy, Em. He's not even seventy," Nate's voice was hard, chastising. He wanted her to understand. He wanted her to already know all there was to know and to have already synthesized everything she'd heard last night. He was being unfair. He turned away from the bed. "I don't *think* he's seventy. Walter Gropius was seventy-five when he started the Pan Am Building," Nate recited straight from one of his childhood monographs, information he hadn't known he'd retained. "George can't die. An architect's career starts at age seventy," Nate said.

He can't die, Nate thought. For so long Nate had assumed that he might never lay eyes on George, in person, again. Now the man was here, in the flesh, and Nate began to see that perhaps what he wanted from his father, what he was owed, was not simply hard answers but amends and restitution as well.

The eggs from George's hospital tray were cold. Frigid, hard, overcooked, and tasting like cement — even after Emily dressed them up with a shake of pepper and a splash of hot water. Nate didn't have an appetite anyway, but apparently Emily did. Sitting next to him in the waiting room, she nibbled on the eggs and the toast, her teeth making half moons in the wheat bread. They'd stolen the tray from George's room, though it hadn't felt like theft. George wouldn't be waking up in time for breakfast, or lunch or dinner, most likely, and the grub would go to waste. And did it really count as theft when the loot was so undesirable? That was probably the Jeep thief's rationale, Nate thought. *It's not stealing; this truck is a wreck.* Perhaps the same spin could be applied to the Rufino: it's not stealing; this art is shit.

The car was of little concern to Nate this morning. What he couldn't get out of his head were Emily's words: the old man was real. For years George had been someone Nate saw only in TV documentaries and in books, someone who lived through his buildings. It had been more than a decade since he'd been a real blood-and-guts human to his son, the way he was today. He was real. He was still alive, he was breathing (he wasn't in need of a ventilator, and the resident on duty this morning assured Nate that this was a good sign), he still had a brain in there, he still had time to mend his fences. He was still Nate's father. Or, he still had a chance to be Nate's father. Annemarie and Charlie had lost their futures, but it wasn't too late for George.

George still had a chance to *apologize*, though Nate hated that word. It had become so vapid, all of the *sorry*s that he and Emily loaded onto Trevor and exchanged with each other every day: sorry I'm late, sorry I didn't make the dinner reservation, sorry I'm not on the partner track, sorry the best job I could get was in Rhode Island, sorry I'm me, sorry you're stuck with me, sorry, sorry, sorry, sorry I'm an art thief, sorry. It was all so empty. Yet in this situation, an apology would be welcome, Nate thought. He pictured George coming out of his coma, slowly opening his eyes, registering the IVs attached to his arm, the strange sterile surroundings, the diffuse light coming in the high hospital-room window. He'd fret over the design of the place, the colors and textiles which mimicked nothing in the natural world. As he was trying to make sense of it all, he would turn his gaze toward the side of his bed and he'd see his son, his one surviving son. What would George say to his child? Would he even recognize him? How would he phrase his amends? Nate hadn't thought that far ahead. There were so many apologies for George to make: for his absent fathering, for completely taking off after Nate's mother's death, for possibly passing down his tainted genes, and for not alerting Nate to this possibility before he had his own son.

Emily put down the food and rubbed Nate's back. He'd expected her to wake up and be distraught, but he'd forgotten that she pulled together when faced with acute trauma – trauma not of her own devising. She could barely function when she misplaced her apartment keys or found herself in possession of stolen art (last night she'd told Nate about the low-level tremors she'd been feeling in her heart ever since grabbing the piece, of her futile attempts to put it out of her mind, not unlike his more successful attempts to deny the Huntington's), but when she'd discovered that she was unexpectedly pregnant, for example, she'd grown strong and taken control.

"Nate, it's ten thirty," Emily still had her hand on his back. "We should go see if the specialist is in."

Three hours had passed since they'd left Trevor, and Nate missed him already.

They ditched the tray of food on top of the waiting room's trash can, walked down the hall, took an elevator up to the second floor and, Emily first with Nate close behind, entered a small office. Inside, they faced the doctor with whom Nate had dealt the day before.

"I'm sorry I wasn't here when you got in," he said to Nate. "I do rounds in Westerly in the mornings."

"No, that's fine," Nate said.

"Sit." The doctor shut the office door and motioned to a small couch. He extended a hand to Emily and introduced himself. "I hear you have questions," the doctor said. There was barely room for the three of them in the office.

"It's about his father and Huntington's," said Emily.

"About having a test done, for Huntington's, and what that entails. I know there are tests, I don't know if he's had them," Nate said. If there was something to be done, knowledge to be found, he was finally ready for it. He was in a hospital, his father was sick, it was the time for action.

"There is a test, that's right," the doctor said. "I don't know if your father has had it, either, but it's not something you can request for him. You can't request it for anyone but yourself."

"He's unconscious. He can't request it himself," Nate said, though that information seemed obvious. He'd thought it would be easy to have his father tested. Surely the hospital had already drawn plenty of his blood.

"And as long as he remains unconscious" — the doctor again motioned to his couch, and finally both Emily and Nate sat — "his Huntington's status is of no consequence. To him, at least. Not everyone at risk for the disease wants to know his status. Plenty of people don't have the capacity to process that kind of news. And you need to be aware that a positive diagnosis can trigger insurance problems. Mundane as that sounds, it is a consideration. As such, it's your father's right to deny the test for himself." The doctor scooted back a few inches in his padded desk chair, as if making room for his words. "And he might not even need a test. From what you've told me, you haven't confirmed that he's at risk."

"That's what I'm trying to do. I don't – "

"You don't want to get tested yourself?"

Nate didn't know. He only knew that if George were tested, and it turned out he didn't have the gene, it would mean that Nate had nothing to worry about. If George was tested and he *did* have the gene, it meant there was still a 50 percent chance that Nate was negative. If Nate was tested himself, though, the results would be definitive. There would be no going back.

"Oh, seriously, can't you just test the man? He's in a coma. Nate's his next of kin. Just let Nate request the test," Emily said.

"Emily," Nate said, to quiet her down.

"My priority is in treating Mr. Bedecker's head injury and internal wounds. I'm going to write down the name of a counselor in our hereditary disease department" – he looked at Nate – "and you should speak with her as soon as possible, though there's a better HD clinic in Providence. It might be worth the trip. If you do decide to get tested, you can't do it today regardless. We have a counseling protocol. Once you've been through the counseling, you'll decide whether to have the test." He leaned over his desk and scribbled a name and phone number onto a page from his prescription pad, then handed the paper over to Nate. The doctor's cursive was precise and unexpectedly neat. "There aren't many conditions I can think of that are worse than Huntington's. And there's no treatment, as of yet, even if you test positive. There's promising research being done, but it'll be years before they're testing on humans, and that's only if the inhibiting drug proves out its promise. There's no way for me to sugarcoat this disease."

Nate understood. The diagnosis wasn't just a death sentence. It was a sentence to suffer, for a decade or more, prior to that death. To be rendered useless and *then*, after an excruciating wait, to die.

He shouldn't have had a child in the first place, that's what it boiled down to. He should have pressed Emily to have an abortion. He looked over to Emily, sitting next to him on the vinyl loveseat. She seemed to think his glance was a cue for her to speak.

"Isn't it better to know if you have the gene?" she asked. Emily was a firm believer in knowledge. "I think it's better to know." She sounded angry. At Nate, probably. He didn't blame her.

"There's no treatment," the doctor said again. He had the patience of a saint. Or of a pediatrician. "Of course, if you two plan to have more children, you'll want to know if there's a risk."

Nate saw Emily glance at him. Would they want more kids? They'd operated on the assumption, in New York, that they'd stop with Trevor. They'd both come from small families. Emily's only brother lived on the West Coast and was eight years her senior — it seemed like eighteen years, she liked to say. She often referred to herself as an only child. In Manhattan, when Emily and Nate had talked about having more kids, they'd agreed that it seemed financially reckless to try to raise two children when just one had put them in such economic straits. In Newport, they'd have enough space for a second child. Another kid: he couldn't believe he was even thinking about it. He might have already poisoned their first, and Emily didn't seem to be a moral exemplar for children these days. The phrase "Do as I say, not as I do" crossed Nate's mind.

"We should go," Nate nodded to the doctor. "I need to think."

"Call the counselor," the doctor said, opening the door to let them out. "We'll know in the next few days if your father is out of the deep end."

Outside the office, Nate leaned against the pale blue wall and looked at Emily. "You're not pregnant already, are you?" It was just a hunch, given the way she'd eyed him when the doctor mentioned more kids.

"What? I drank my way through our minifridge yesterday. I'm not pregnant. Come on, Nate."

"You'd let me know if you were?" After she'd found out she was pregnant with Trevor, she'd waited weeks to tell him. After she stole a Rufino, she'd waited three long days.

"Nate, I'd tell you." She shoved her hands in her pockets and moved slightly away from him. "I thought we only wanted one child."

Nate nodded. Though Charlie was gone, Nate couldn't imagine having grown up without him as a compatriot, as a witness to his own childhood and sharer of the family secrets. It was Charlie's steady, if dreamy, presence in the family that served as a reminder, when Nate was a child, that all of humanity wasn't crazy, that it might be possible to live in his household and still emerge a normal (because normal was the goal as an adolescent, nothing good came from sticking out) American kid. After Charlie was gone, Nate wondered whether his brother's good nature in the face of their father's stoicism and mother's dissolution had been due to some sort of innate optimism or simply a result of his youth. He had been younger than Nate, after all. The qualities Nate most admired about his brother: Perhaps Charlie would have grown out of them if he'd been allowed to age into adulthood.

"Let's get out of here," Nate said. "Let's just get out of here." He needed to be free of the hospital's confines, to be somewhere neutral where he'd be able to rethink things. His father was in a coma and unreachable at the very moment when he, Nate, had, for the first time in his life, found a real reason to reach out. It was the first time he could remember ever actually wanting to talk to the man. "Let's get in the car," Nate said. He started to walk toward the elevator. The hospital was making him feel lightheaded and sick.

"How about —" Emily said, stopping him. "How about you get the car, and I'll call the hotel. I'll meet you out front in a minute. I want to call to make sure Trevor is okay."

CHAPTER 23

Emily Calls Out

EMILY HELD THE CELL PHONE to her ear and counted her own heartbeats. Nineteen heartbeats, four rings of the phone (*answer damnit!*, she willed someone to pick up on the other end), and Emily was crying. She was bawling, fat wet tears worthy of Trevor's deepest tantrum. When out in public, she usually fought tears with a fierce strength. She hated pity, the instant sympathy people felt for a crier — but here, in a hospital, there was none of that. Half the visitors in the ICU were either in tears, on the brink of tears, or recovering from a crying fit. The ward was drowning in salt water and whimpers. Here, Emily was just another bawler. The gasps between her sobs echoed off the close walls of the bathroom stall.

"Hey, *chica*," Jeanne picked up her cell on the sixth ring.

Emily breathed out. "Jeanne, thank God." It was good to hear Jeanne's voice, a link to life before Friday, before Newport, before. Emily had been in the women's room crying for five minutes now, maybe ten. The only break had been when she'd pulled herself together for a few moments and called the baby-sitter, confirming that everything was fine at the Viking. In all of this time, no one else had come into the restroom. Emily kept expecting to be disturbed, but clearly everyone in this wing was using bedpans. "I can't believe you picked up," she said into the phone. "Aren't you supposed to be, like, ohm-ing and connect-ing with the spirit?"

Jeanne tended toward the trendy and had passed through a number of phases since Emily first met her in college. She'd dabbled in punk, the last wave; ardent socialism; the pork-only diet; Pilates; daily shots of wheatgrass. During her first year in med school, Jeanne took up speed-walking. The fads had all come and gone, except for yoga. As with the rest of America's masses, she seemed to be hooked on yoga for the long haul.

"Yeah, I thought I'd be ohm-ing, too. Honestly, though, I've never seen a crowd so taken with their technology. The women here send texts while in Warrior Three pose. And the food bites. I thought it was going to be macrobiotic, but it's minimum-calo-rie raw. I've been near fainting since I got here. My blood sugar, my electrolytes, everything's tanking. The only thing saving me is the guy who drives the van to town. He graduated from Vassar, and he's single and straight. And not bad in bed."

Jeanne had dated the same man for eight years when she was in her twenties, a corporate lawyer named Austin who prom-ised he'd marry her and then, every year, forgot to propose. She finally left him during the summer of her thirtieth birthday and had been making up for lost time ever since. Despite the set-backs in her own personal life, Jeanne knew how to have a good time. She was an optimist. She could be relied on when good news was needed. Plus, she was a medical resident, trained to understand head traumas and genetic abnormalities.

"I got your message," Jeanne said. "Sorry to hear about the Jeep. At least you didn't have a Rufino stolen from you."

"Who cares about the Barbers and their stupid art," Emily said.

Emily needed for the art theft to have never happened. If she wanted to sound credible to the cops when they came up to visit, she needed to believe, in her heart, that she had not done it. She wished, fervently, that she'd told Nate about it sooner. It would have been easy to tell him about it the night it happened, while she was still mid-freak-out, while she still hadn't hidden it from him.

"Yeah, they're nut jobs. But really, I'm so sorry about the Jeep," Jeanne said. Jeanne knew Emily as well as anyone, and knew Nate equally as well by simple transference. "Are you crying? Emily, it's going to be okay. I've had three bikes stolen since I moved to New York, plus that stereo, though the stereo was my fault, and look, I'm still standing. I did a perfect neckstand today. It was only a car, it'll be okay."

It would be okay. Emily nodded. She wished Jeanne were here with her, to see the nod. Talking was so hard. She and Nate had used up all their words last night and now Emily's brain was a vacuum. She summoned a thought and then felt it shift from her empty head to her vocal cords, coming out sad and flat, wet with her tears. Like a truism.

"It's not the car. Or the Barbers' stupid art." Though it was the art, partly. "It's Nate, and his dad. His dad is sick."

"George Bedecker? *The* George Bedecker?" Jeanne said. "Emily, I'm so sorry. I know Nate isn't close to his dad, but a sick parent, it's a brush with mortality. George Bedecker? Oh, Emily, sick with what?"

"I don't know. He was in a car accident. He's in a coma, head injuries, all the stuff that seems so run-of-the-mill on TV, all of that horrible wait-and-see stuff. He's here, in the hospital in Rhode Island. Nate's kind of tuned out to it all; I think he's in shock at seeing the guy. It's not the accident, though."

"So it's what? Head trauma falls all over the map. He could come out of the coma and be fine. Sometimes it's only a matter of waiting it out. The coma could be his body protecting itself. Humans have unbeatable survival instincts."

"No. No," Emily said. And then, before she could stop herself or reconsider her words she said, "He might have Huntington's. Do you know what that is? It's like, Korea, Huntington's, from Korea." Emily laughed. She actually laughed after she said this, a real, *can you believe it?* laugh. Life was funny, incredibly darkly humorous. She'd been out of New York for mere days, and already her world had turned more dangerous. "Why us, right? Nate thinks his dad has Huntington's." There. Emily had said it. She'd said *Huntington's* with the same finality that Nate had employed last night, as if words could act as a barrier between the speaker and the thing itself.

Emily lowered herself onto the toilet. The hospital stall was wide and deep (the proportions of a jail cell, she imagined), arranged to fit a wheelchair or a walker. Emily could live in here if she needed to; it was practically bigger than the bedroom that she and Nate had shared in New York. In Newport they'd have more space, but the trade-off seemed to be that they might have a fatal disease to deal with, too. "Jeanne?" Emily said, her sobs finished.

"It's *chorea*, with a c, not Korea," Jeanne said softly, "Huntington's *chorea*, it's from *chora*, the Latin word for dance. The Huntington tremors." She paused and then continued, her voice sad, "the tremors look like a dance." And then her words died out. It sounded as if she were going to pick up the crying, too, as if

Emily's tears were transferable. "Oh, Emily. Do you want me to come up there? I don't have to be back at work until Tuesday afternoon, tomorrow afternoon, and I have the rental car. I can be with you whenever, however quickly I can drive there. I'm already north of the city."

"No, God no, don't come up here. We don't have anywhere for you to stay. The three of us are crammed into a room at the Viking. We aren't in our house. I'm not looking for a hug anyway," Emily said. She was tired of people placating her without offering any tangible reward. "I don't need sympathy. I need some perspective."

She didn't need perspective. She needed a miracle, but she'd never believed in miracles. In lieu of a miracle, Emily would settle for hearing Jeanne say that Nate was overreacting. That he'd misunderstood all of that convoluted research, all of those Huntington facts that he'd laid out in his even-toned speech last night. It would be so easy for Jeanne to tell her that. It wouldn't be a miracle at all. It would be a fact, wouldn't it?

"Oh, Emily," Jeanne said again.

"Look, Huntington's," Emily said before Jeanne could again offer to drive up. "It's really that bad?" In the pause that followed, she thought of all the things that Jeanne could say, the answers that had prompted Emily to make the call: *It's not so bad, tons of people have it, what's a little chorea? I'll hook you up with a specialist. They're on the brink of a cure. Don't worry. Don't worry. Don't worry. It's just Huntington's, don't worry!* Emily thought back to when she was pregnant. Even before having the amnio (which came back fine, all of the prenatal tests came back fine!), she'd been shocked at how carefree she'd been, how certain she was that her baby would be born healthy. It wasn't like her to be so calm, but she'd gotten pregnant so easily, without trying, and her morning sickness had been mild and routine. Maybe she should have worried more. Or maybe, even now, there was no reason to fret. Jeanne was a good friend. Jeanne would tell her the truth. Jeanne wouldn't panic or overreact.

"I'm so sorry," Jeanne finally said. She waited a beat too long before continuing and Emily held her breath, tried to will herself back to yesterday, to last month, to the time before Nate started acting aloof. It was all starting to make sense: his withdrawal, his sudden quiet, his change in behavior that she'd dismissed as stress. The excuses she'd made! She could have questioned him instead of writing off his mood shift. She felt her tears welling up again. Her chest tightened as if under the force of an Elizabethan corset. "They could make progress, they really could," Jeanne said. "They didn't even have a test until twenty years ago, and there are advocacy groups pouring money into research. It could pay off. You never know, Emily. You never know."

You never know wasn't the prescription Emily was looking for. She couldn't lose Nate or Trevor. She couldn't lose Nate *and* Trevor.

"So you don't know, for certain, that George Bedecker has it?" Jeanne said.

"No. We don't *know*. But it's a solid hunch. I don't doubt my partner's hunches."

"You can't panic until you know for certain. You can't panic if he hasn't even been tested yet," Jeanne said, her voice awkwardly serious. "Even if he has it, like I said, they're doing research. They're always doing research."

They'd been doing research on cancer for fifty years. And where was that cure? *Research?* What did Jeanne actually know? She wasn't a neurologist, she was an ear, nose, and throat doctor. And a resident, at that. Jeanne hadn't even majored in the sciences in college. She'd studied American history.

"I'm sorry I asked," Emily said. "Forget it." The acerbic bathroom air was making her dizzy. She'd have to get used to it, wouldn't she? Used to the muted, tarnished colors of the hospital decor, to the fake-stone walls painted a creamy Mylanta blue, to the toilets that were so high they might as well be bar stools. She could easily be spending the bulk of her future in medical centers (assuming she wasn't in jail), pacing their waiting rooms and hiding out in their bathrooms.

"I can't believe that I fucking thought moving to Newport would rid us of our problems," she said. She looked at the sanitary napkin receptacle screwed to the wall of the stall and thought of stuffing the Rufino into it, no one would know. The hospital cleaning staff surely didn't dig through the bloody mess before tossing it in with the rest of the trash. "Our getting a leg up, that was a stupid fantasy. What the hell was I thinking?"

"Your move sounded good to me," Jeanne said. "What was your option? Staying in New York and continue trying to climb your way to the top? I mean, it's not getting any easier to make a million. Even my father finally left the city." A father. Jeanne had a father. She often complained about him and his propensity toward right-wing soapboxing in inappropriate situations — usually when he was bombed on manhattans. He'd moved from Park Avenue to somewhere dry and sunny in Arizona last year. But at least she had a father. That was something neither Emily nor Nate had ever honestly been able to claim, until now.

Jeanne had encouraged Emily to look at this move in a positive light. Jeanne had even given Emily a list of pediatricians in the area, so that Trevor would have a doctor as soon as they moved in. She'd helped Emily and Nate pack up in New York, actually acting jealous that they were going off on an anti–New York adventure. She'd told Emily that everything would be great up here, in Newport. Yet Jeanne herself was still happily calling Manhattan home.

"Emily, you'll either love Newport or you'll hate it, but it's too soon to tell, obviously, especially – shit, especially with this Huntington's stuff to figure out."

"You are like a fucking enabler, telling me not to fight Nate over this move, telling me it's the best thing that ever happened to me. It's already a disaster." Emily's voice ricocheted off the bathroom's slick, tiled walls and heavy metal door. An image of Trevor's face came into her head, the boy wailing, his too-big ears flaring and red. "Thanks, Jeanne. Trevor could die tomorrow and I spent the past three weeks virtually ignoring him so I could pack up for a move that you tell me, now, I might hate."

"Trevor is not going to die tomorrow," Jeanne said. Her tone was no longer sympathetic.

"You can't prove that. Anyone could die tomorrow."

"Right, that's an intelligent point, isn't it? You don't know for sure if George Bedecker has Huntington's. Are you sure it's not Parkinson's, anyway?"

"It's *Huntington's*," Emily said. It was a bad sign when a Parkinson's diagnosis would be good news. Emily almost cackled over the idea. "Oh, if only it were Parkinson's!" she spat the words out. "If only it were cancer! If only it were a field full of bunnies and rainbows! Bring on the rainbows!" How about some clowns, too? "I'm not a moron," she said. "I can tell diseases apart."

"Take a deep breath. Seriously, you need to get a hold of yourself. Huntington's is unbelievably rare," Jeanne said, a stony evenness to her voice.

Emily felt ashamed. Even in front of her closest confidantes, she wasn't accustomed to losing her cool. "Yes, Huntington's," Emily repeated firmly.

"If Nate's dad in fact has Huntington's, there's still a fifty percent chance Nate didn't get it. Did you know that? Look, I'll talk to people when I'm back at work," Jeanne said, overenunciating her words and speaking slowly, as if consoling a halfwit. "I'll corner one of the neuros. We have a decent department. You might want to find a way to chill in the meantime. Nate probably needs your support."

When Emily was first falling in love with Nate a few years ago, she'd briefly pitied Jeanne with all of her one-night stands and no one permanent to count on. Jeanne hadn't had a serious relationship since things fell apart with Austin. But look how achingly simple Jeanne's life had become! Here she was, griping about yoga, sleeping with the van guy, living in a studio apartment next to New York Presbyterian Hospital's east-side campus, saving just enough money to eat out every night, and spending her days researching other people's health problems. Today, Jeanne would hang up the phone and go to her midday Ashtanga session and then curl up with the strange young Vassar grad (who was inevitably hot and shaggy and painfully innocent). Maybe she'd even call her *father*, just to shoot the shit. And, eventually, tomorrow afternoon at the very earliest, she'd do what she could for Emily and Nate and George, which might amount to nothing. It would almost certainly amount to nothing.

"I can't believe you spent eight years with Austin," Emily said, the words coming out brittle and petty, shaming Emily even as she spoke them. "He was screwing Tania Osbourne, you know. They were going at it during the whole last two years you were dating him. He tried to sleep with me once. If you weren't so blind you'd have seen it." Emily didn't know if the Tania Osbourne bit was true, but there had been rumors, and it felt good to say it. Austin had hit on every one of Jeanne's friends — always when Jeanne was far beyond earshot — and no one ever told her. Not even Emily, who was supposed to be her closest confidante. "You'd have to be an idiot to have dated that shithead for so long."

The bathroom was still empty and Emily listened for voices outside the door or the sound of water running through the pipes, but what she heard, instead, was only the click of the phone as Jeanne hung up without a word. The electronic smack came across the airwaves like an admonition from another century, like Carlyle unable to reach the modern audience. Intelligence, wisdom, words to live by. Poor Carlyle, no one in the modern world gave a shit about what he had to say. Poor Emily. Poor Nate.

Emily hadn't planned to peek in on George again, but his room sat directly on her path from the bathroom to the elevator, and the door was open, and the situation — George languishing — seemed so much less loaded without Nate by her side. It began to seem, to Emily, remarkably straightforward. This man lying in Kent Hospital, this bundle of Bedecker genes, was the devil.

She stood for a moment at the door to room 207B. George Bedecker was still out cold. He was the evil one, not Emily. She was embarrassed about how she'd laid into Jeanne, but it wasn't her fault. It all came down to George. It was as if George were infecting her merely by his proximity. Oh God, that word, *infect*. George may have infected, down the family line, Trevor. Just the thought of that nearly killed Emily. She had the sense that everything bad — not just in the future, but in the past as well — was George's fault. Merely by existing as a cold bastard he'd damned them all.

She took one step inside the room, listened for a reaction, and then took a second step. The space appeared smaller without Nate in it. Even though the patient was unconscious, his room's overhead lights were on bright, illuminating the cracks in the floor and the nicks in the wall paint. The phone next to George's bed was heavy and square, from the era before cordless. The shades were pulled down over his windows. She took two more steps forward until she was standing directly next to the bed. Below her, George's body seemed to have sunk even further into his mattress since an hour ago. He was a small man, a fraction of Nate's size. She could probably crack him in half with her hands. She saw his chest rise, barely, with his breath. This was the man Emily had been encouraging Nate to reunite with, a man she'd never met and had truly known nothing about. This was a man she'd misjudged from the start. She'd thought that since he'd helped conceive Nate once, and since his buildings were so beautiful, he must have had a heart. She was wrong.

She gripped the bed's metal side rail and leaned closer over George Bedecker, but he didn't move, he didn't flinch. She knew that he was unconscious, technically, but shouldn't her presence, her face just a foot from his, stir him in some way? Didn't he feel anything? Didn't he feel? Or had that been his problem all along: a consummate lack of humanity, an absolute severance from the populated world?

Before she could stop herself she tightened her grip on the bed and screamed, "My name is Emily and I'm in love with your son – you have a son and his name is Nate Bedecker – and you're a coward, a sleeping selfish coward and an egomaniac asshole and a derelict, and all your big indestructible buildings, they're no excuse, fucker!"

Only after her voice stopped did she realize how loud she'd been. She'd gone at the man full force; it was a wonder she hadn't blown him out of his bed. For a moment, she stood stone still beside him, stunned. She heard a clock tick from somewhere on the other side of the bed. "Fuck you," she said under her breath.

Then she spun toward the door and ran out of the room and bolted down the hall, past a gaping orderly, not slowing until she was safely around the corner, out of view, where she abruptly came to a stop and began to walk purposefully, innocently, as if she had nothing to hide. The hallway was wide and empty and buzzing with fluorescent light. Someone had left a tray of empty coffee cups on the floor and she was tempted to take one, to smash it against the sterile cement wall. Instead, she pushed the down button for the elevator and, as she waited for it to come, she broke into a wide, unrestrained smile.

CHAPTER 24

The Route

N ATE IDLED IN THE AUDI outside the hospital's main
entrance. George's car was like his homes, clean and
nearly empty. The glove compartment contained nothing except the Audi's instruction booklet, the registration, and
a pamphlet to mark with the vehicle's regular checkups (there
hadn't been any yet, since the car was only two months old).
Apparently all that George Bedecker needed was GPS. Well,
GPS and comprehensive insurance, since it would cost a bundle to fix the damage he'd done to the front of the car. Nate
knew what it took to repair a Jeep, and a foreign car's repairs had
to be at least double.

Nate fiddled with the controls and glanced at the clock. What
time had it been, precisely, when he'd separated from Emily
outside the doctor's office? He had no idea. It had taken Nate
longer than expected to fetch the Audi. He'd had trouble with
that GPS. The minute he started the ignition, it began harping
at him. No, not *it*. She. Loud and husky like a middle school
gym teacher, telling him that he had *strayed from the set route*.

Every time he moved an inch she repeated her reprimand, so he stopped the car just a few spaces from where he'd started. GPS systems had off switches. Nate knew that, but couldn't find one on this machine. That's when he'd popped open the glove compartment, fished around the nearly empty little space for the user's manual, and silenced the audible command option. A car shouldn't be so difficult to control.

Now it was 11:05 a.m. The clock was accurately set, but the radio buttons weren't preprogrammed for favorites yet — Nate had fiddled with those, too. His father never used to listen to albums or the radio, if Nate remembered correctly. Occasionally, when his parents were both in Cleveland at the same time, they'd gone out to the symphony, but Nate thought it was just for special performances, an annual benefit and the like. Nate turned the radio on and then off again and then glanced up at the hospital's facade. Emily was inside phoning the babysitter, a smart idea. Usually it was Nate who worried when they left the kid at home and Emily who insisted that children were resilient. So what was taking her so long?

Nate shut off the ignition. He took the keys with him and carefully locked the car — something he'd never forget to do again, ever, for the rest of his life, however long that would be — and walked toward the doors of the hospital. The glass entryway automatically slid open as he approached and entered. The receptionist at the front desk looked at Nate blankly, apparently not recognizing him as the same guy who'd been in and out of this doorway three times over the past twenty-four hours. A huddle of old women, in their eighties or nineties from the looks of them and all wearing navy housedresses, congregated in a corner of the lobby. The floor of the entryway was carpeted, wall-to-wall lint. That couldn't possibly be sterile.

"Have you seen my girlfriend?" Nate said to the receptionist, "Five-foot-six, wearing tan corduroys and a white shirt?" She hadn't worn her jacket today. "Her hair's dark blond, or light brown — I don't know what you call it, it's in between, you know? — and shoulder-length?" He couldn't think of anything else to add. Emily was always Emily to Nate: corduroys, five-foot-six, sharp and eager to please, often nervous, a pro at problem solving, and beautifully unaware of her own allure. Today, she was going through emotional hell.

"Maybe?" the receptionist said. "Is she a patient or a visitor?"

"Don't worry about it."

Nate reached for his phone, but he'd left it in the car. No worry, Emily was probably right where he'd left her. Nate took the fire stairs up one flight to the ICU. He looked into his father's room. The old man was still out, the only sound a constant series of beeps from the machine that stood next to his bed. No Emily. Nate paced the hallway between George's room and the doctor's office. This was where he'd last seen Emily, but she was no longer on the scene.

He took the stairs back down to the cafeteria. She'd probably stopped in for a coffee. They hadn't had any caffeine this morning and she'd be craving a cup by now, but she wasn't there, either, and Nate realized that she didn't have any money. The thirty-five dollars that they hadn't yet spent was in his wallet. Unless she'd found a way to pawn off her stolen painting for cash, she had to be somewhere in this hospital. He walked quickly back to the lobby and, as he strode by, he caught the eye of the receptionist.

"Haven't seen her!" the woman said and smiled. Nate smiled back as if this were good news.

Nate half-convinced himself that Emily would be waiting for

him outside, by the car (illegally parked, but locked at least), but
as he walked out the hospital's front door again, he discovered
that she wasn't there, either.

Nate lingered in the parking lot — an expanse of chalky
asphalt bordered by a row of Dumpsters and what looked like a
defunct soccer field — and considered the possibility (the paranoid, deluded, yet not entirely illogical possibility) that Emily
really had actually left him. *I'm leaving!* It wasn't unthinkable.
He'd probably leave, too, if he were her. And she'd already
proven, with her felonious art activity, that she was acting on
impulse this week.

Her life would be better without him. Her life and Trevor's.
Nate assumed that if she left she'd take Trevor with her (and
probably leave the Rufino with Nate, implicating him if the
painting were found). That was probably why she was calling
the hotel, to arrange her getaway. It was the right decision. After
all, what had she gained from being with Nate? He'd failed as
a provider, and come up short in the emotional area as well.
She and the boy would set up a new life somewhere, maybe
even back in Manhattan if Emily could land a windfall or a
willing partner, and they wouldn't have to witness Nate's painful
decline. He'd read that it was common for Huntington's sufferers to leave their families, preferring to spare them the horror of
having to watch the painful onslaught of the disease, spare them
having to change the diapers of an angry, paranoid middle-aged
man for years upon years. It would make sense if Emily had chosen to leave. The worst part for Nate, really, would be not seeing
the little guy every day, not waking up to his cries, not trying to
silence the wails, not hearing him happily screech every time
the microwave's timer beeped. It would kill Nate not to see his
son. It would also kill him to see the boy — and in time become
a burden.

"You have strayed from the set route," the GPS said. Nate had unwittingly reactivated the gym teacher. *Fuck.* "Return to the set route."

A parade of vehicles — compacts and SUVs and two bicycles and one gaunt, attenuated sedan, a relic from the 1970s — began to file into the parking lot. Nate watched as the drivers (men and women wearing scrubs and lab coats and rubber-soled shoes) parked and locked their cars and bikes. The shifts were changing. It had been at least half an hour since Emily promised to meet Nate outside. She could already be in Newport, packing Trevor's things, dumping the Rufino in the harbor. In the end, Nate would ruin no one's life but his own. Emily would find happiness, for once. Trevor would grow up to be a sailor and a poet and a statesman and maybe even a healthy boy. A healthy man. It was all for the best, Nate reminded himself as he laid his head on the steering wheel and contemplated dialing Emily, on the off-chance she'd pick up his call. He'd be like George. He'd die alone, estranged from his loved ones. He'd be his father's son, after all.

The passenger side door clicked open.

Nate spun his head and saw Emily sliding into the car. Emily, with her tan corduroys and her white top and her nervous energy. She smiled wanly at him. Her eyes were red.

"I'm sorry I took so long," she said. "Trevor's fine. Marietta says he went down for his nap without a fuss. I think she was eating her way through our minifridge when I called, the little that we left in there." Emily stopped talking just long enough to buckle her seat belt and adjust her seat. "We should keep Marietta in mind, in case she does non-Viking babysitting. We're going to have to start over here. New babysitters, new dentists, the whole shebang." She didn't say *new doctors,* but it was implied.

Nate continued to stare at her, at her earnest concern, her

nervousness pouring off her sleeve, almost but not quite con-
cealed by her attempt at confidence, her dire need to project
confidence.

"I can't believe you're here," he said, reaching over and
touching her shoulder, rubbing the rough, real fabric of her shirt
between his fingers. She was here. He couldn't forgive himself
for thinking that she had run off. He couldn't, he saw now, go
through this alone.

"You have all my money, thirty-five dollars' worth," Emily
said. "And a brand-new Audi. You think I'd leave all that?" She
rubbed her eyes. "I never in my life thought I'd be so lucky."
Nate couldn't tell if she was serious. He put the car in drive and
the normally loquacious GPS kept its mouth quiet.

Fifteen minutes later, Nate and Emily were settled into a sprawling corner booth at the Gateway Diner clutching lukewarm
mugs of coffee.

"I thought he'd look bigger," Emily said. She was still thinking about George. She seemed obsessed with the daintiness of
George Bedecker. She motioned across the room at the waitress, miming a refill. Refills were good, they were free. Of the
thirty-five dollars Nate and Emily had left, they needed to hold
on to ten, to make sure the Audi didn't run out of gas, and at
least another ten or fifteen in case they had trouble getting their
accounts reactivated tomorrow.

"I thought your father would be more daunting, even when
unconscious," Emily said.

"You said that already."

"It's what I thought."

"No one looks big in a hospital bed." Nate's voice was quick.
He didn't have the brain space, at this moment, to focus on the

specific size of his father against the hospital's creased white sheets.

"That guy in Queens did. The man they had to cut out of his own home last year, he'd grown so large he didn't fit through the door? Even in the 'after' photos, when he was recovering from his stomach stapling, he looked huge."

"Emily." Nate said, simply to cut her off.

The waitress refilled Emily's coffee. Nate played with a stack of sugar packets, stacking them and then unstacking them, once, twice, three times.

"Emily, we've got some issues."

"A few," she said.

"The Huntington's. My dad complex. Your stolen artwork."

"When I stole the art, I didn't know that your father was sick," she said. "If I'd known, I wouldn't have done it. If I'd thought about it for even a split second, I wouldn't have done it. I didn't intend to complicate things. I don't think I'll go to jail, if that's what you're worried about. I doubt that the Barbers will press charges once they find out I'm the one who did it. We'd just have to pay them back, we'd find a way, and we could tell the cops it was a misunderstanding. I mean, don't the New York cops have more important crimes to deal with?" She breathed in, deep. "I cannot believe the city has enough money to send them up here to talk to me. We'll set something up so that ten percent of your paychecks, or something, go straight to the Barbers. We'll find a way. I'll find a job, someone will hire me. I am so sorry."

"Em, you can't get caught. It doesn't matter if the Barbers press charges — you committed a crime, the police can charge you even without Anna and Randy's consent." He paused. "They can't arrest you without proof. We have to make sure that there's no proof, and that you don't give them anything to go on when they question you. You can't slip up."

She nodded and spread her napkin on the table, flattening out the creases, pressing it into the surface. "The Huntington's, that's the real issue, right?" she said. "That, and the fact that you didn't tell me about it. And that I didn't know to ask." She looked down into her cup, as if to read the coffee grinds. "I miss talking, really talking," Emily said. "We used to talk, you know. Before."

Before having the baby, was what she meant.

"I was trying to protect you. And Trevor," Nate said.

"We don't need protection. We need to know what's going on. Don't you wish your father had told you what was going on? It's a cycle, Nate. You've been continuing his cycle, like an animal on one of those spinning wheels."

"I know that now, believe me." Nate knew it in an instinctive way. He couldn't relive his father's history, that fact was paramount. "I think we both need to talk more."

A customer entered the restaurant and the bells above the front door chimed. Nate thought of Trevor, who loved electronic buzzes and computer-generated alert sounds but often wailed at the tinny clang of old-fashioned bells. Come Christmastime, Nate figured that his son would be the only kid running away from department store Santas and their jingling, permanently grounded sleighs.

"Do you ever think Trevor would be better without us?" Nate said. The idea that Trevor would be better without him was something that Nate thought about every day.

"Oh, come on," Emily said. "Someone has to change those diapers, wipe the congealed drool off his chin."

"Right," Nate said. He and Emily were Trevor's parents, just as Annemarie and George had been Nate's. Despite George

Bedecker's detachment, he had fathered Nate, in his own way. "Do you think I have a complex?" he asked.

"From being overloved by your parents?" she laughed. "You're safe from that. You and the Europeans. All of those regimented European children, kept on strict schedules, sent to boarding school at age eight. To their credit, it's probably the last conti-- nent with complex-free kids."

"That's why you dated so many Euros before we met?"

"Just one," Emily shrugged. "And you fixed that pretty fast."

The morning when Nate and Emily first met, outside the Delta baggage claim exit at JFK, she was on her way home from Los Angeles. She'd spent the week with a French TV producer whom she'd been seeing for a couple of months. It wasn't until she started dating Nate that it hit her, hard, that she had no future with the Frenchman. "Marriage is *un-nec-ess-aire*," the Frenchman had told her the one time she tried to ask him where their relationship was heading. "Freedom is the essence of humanity." She'd told Nate about all of this later, when she was pregnant with Trevor and they were still unmarried and made the decision, for their own reasons, that they wouldn't wed. It seemed patently silly, the rush to marry because they were preg- nant, she'd said. They were together, a couple, with or without the vows. She'd laughed at the time, joking that the Frenchman, named Jonah, had turned out to be a prophet. Nate couldn't imagine being any more together, any more fatally linked, than he and Emily were now, today, here.

"No more secrets?" Nate said.

"No more secrets," Emily answered.

If they survived the Huntington's and the Barber crime, they'd owe each other their lives. They'd owe each other, but gladly.

"It's your phone," he said. A faint ringtone was coming from under the table. They'd given the babysitter Emily's number in case of emergency. They told her to call in case of nonemergency, too, if she felt like it. The NYPD also had Emily's number.

Emily reached under the table and yanked her bag onto her lap. She rustled through it and pulled out her phone, dark. "It's not me."

"It's not me," Nate said. His phone had a sharper ring, but from the look on Emily's face, he could tell he was wrong. He reached into his jacket pocket, and there was his phone, muffled by the layers of his clothing, one ring away from rolling over to voice mail.

As Nate flipped the cell open, Emily said, "We gave the hospital your number."

"The Newport cops, too," Nate said as he heard the officer on the other end of the line.

CHAPTER 25

Pilfering

"THE CAR?" EMILY ASKED. Nate said it was the New-port cops on the phone, not the NYPD. She prayed that the call was about the car, and not the art. Cops from different states surely worked together. The NYPD could easily have tipped off the Newport police that they had two fugitives in town. In this new light, the theft of their Jeep might even look suspicious, like a decoy crime she and Nate had arranged to throw the police off their scent, though Emily couldn't imagine how that kind of scheme would work. She leaned toward Nate and tried to hear the voice on the other end of his cell, a hint of the conversation he was having, but he kept the phone tight against his ear and she couldn't pick up a thing.

"The car," Nate mouthed to her and kept talking on the phone. The car! Thank God.

The waitress came and slid a plate of home fries, ordered by Nate a few minutes ago, onto the table. Emily spit the wad of Nicotine gum she was chewing into a napkin. The gum was a free sample, compliments of a nurse in the hospital's addiction center, which was conveniently located on the same hall as the bathroom where Emily had launched into her crying fit. She tucked the napkin-encased gum under her plate, picked up a fork, and started eating the potatoes. The stress of the cop calling had made her suddenly hungry.

"Find out what's left in it," Emily said through bites of fried starch. "Is it officer, what's his name, Eric?"

"All of our tax statements were in the car," Nate said into the phone. He was turned away from Emily, crouched against the restaurant's noise. "Right, but it would be great if no one rifled through the car until we got there, just so, you know, our papers aren't handled." He paused. "Sure, I know, but if there are any — "
He got up from the table and approached the cash register, where he grabbed a pen and started writing on a napkin.

"They have the Jeep?" Emily said when Nate sat back down, his phone call over. "I thought that eighty-five percent of the time, if they didn't find it in the first twenty-four hours, it wouldn't be found. Maybe it's a sign that we're lucky."

"I think the eighty-five percent is an abducted kid statistic, not stolen cars," said Nate. "And don't get too excited. The car's been stripped of its parts and there's almost nothing left inside."

The Jeep was being towed to a police lot in Middletown, but it wouldn't get there for another hour. The vehicle had apparently been bastardized. One of the few relics of their pre-Newport existence, and it had been trashed. They still had the stroller, Emily reminded herself, though perhaps they should trash that, too. A secondhand harbinger of a longed-for life, the Bugaboo was at the Viking with Trevor. Emily hoped the babysitter would think to take the boy outside.

According to the cops, almost none of their belongings were left in the car. Losing a few pairs of her favorite shoes seemed appropriate penance for Emily's way of life, if nothing else. "Glittering misery," Kant said of modern civilization. The phrase seemed hilariously arch to Emily when she was in college, but struck her as uncomfortably canny now.

Last night, unable to sleep and scared to look head-on at the tangled load of information taking root in her brain, Emily found herself thinking about the empty expanse of their new house. She and Nate had pored over the floor plan after making their offer, trying to determine how many pieces of furniture they'd have to buy to make the space look inhabited. Back then, weeks ago, Emily had joked about telling their new neighbors (or friends? wouldn't there be new friends, eventually?) that they were minimalists. Nate hadn't even smiled. Minimalism was a sore subject with him. Last night, though, awake and confused, she couldn't imagine furnishing the house at all.

Emily had been dreaming up her and Nate's future from the moment Trevor was born, auditioning scenarios inside her head — how would their future look if she never worked again? How would it look if she started her own company? How about if they had to file for personal bankruptcy? If they stayed in New York? If they moved to Paris? San Francisco? Baltimore? Newport? A minimum-security prison? How would they manage with a second child? With a dog? With a cheese factory in the garage? She'd been imagining her own future ever since she was a child, furnishing her nonexistent future town house and buying imaginary gifts for her imaginary Prince Charming. But now? The picture in her head was blank. She had no clue what the coming years would hold.

At two o'clock last night, buzzed and jittery, she'd gotten up from bed and taken an Inderal with a swig of a minibar Heineken. Would they have to move a hospital bed into their new house if Nate got sick? She didn't know how a person cared for a Huntington's patient. Would she be expected to look out for George while Nate was at work? No. No, Nate wouldn't do that to her. Nate wouldn't want George to be a hindrance to anyone, even to himself. As she'd slid back under the covers, Nate stirred from his sleep and said, with his eyes closed, "Do you hate me?" She'd shook her head, but he was already asleep again.

For a moment, she had hated him. She'd despised him for his history, for things that were beyond his control. For shutting her out, too. Now that they were talking, though, she found she couldn't hate him. The mass in her head was equally divided between relief that Nate and she were sharing their fears again (something they'd stopped doing months ago) and overwhelming terror about their unsure future. She wanted Nate to be healthy, Trevor to be healthy, more than she'd ever wanted anything.

"We're going to be okay," she said to Nate as they left the Gateway and strapped themselves into the Audi again, in the diner parking lot.

"I've created a mess," he said. "We both have." He started the car. "Where should we go?"

"I'm tired. We could go to the Viking, let Marietta leave early." They'd hired her for the full day, until 4:00 p.m. "Though last time we let a babysitter go early, that didn't end so well."

"The Barbers'," Nate said.

Emily nodded. "But lying down on a bed sounds really good right now."

"Beds are all we have left."

"Yeah, hotel beds. We don't even own them."

"No," Nate said. "It's what the officer told me. The carjacker left the AeroBeds, as well as a bunch of Trevor's toys that you'd put in boxes."

"In a crate. They were in a milk crate."

"Right, those toys. I guess they don't have much resale value."

While feeding and soothing Trevor, Emily had spent hours in their New York apartment looking at her and Nate's things, wondering which might go for a prime price on eBay or *Antiques Roadshow* if times got any tougher. It was a disappointing exercise. Their goods seemed so cheap when examined with the eye of an appraiser.

"No value at all," Emily confirmed.

It felt good to be sitting inside an unmoving car. A moment out of time, like being on a bridge but with a less inevitable destination. "Going back to the hotel, it's all lost its charm now," she said. "It's been a hell of a weekend."

"We don't have to stay at the Viking. We have beds again," Nate said.

Emily leaned forward in her seat. "Nate! We have beds," she smiled, for real. They hadn't lost everything. "Let's sleep at home. Let's bring Trevor to the place he'll remember as his childhood home — "

"His *first* childhood home."

"His first home. Just like we'd planned for our first days here, camping on the floor. We have electricity and water, and beds now, it's all we need. We can beg a couple of towels off the Viking and return them next week. They seem to trust us there, fools. And we could probably get takeout from the restaurant and charge it to our room before we leave, but damn, it'd be nice to stop charging things there, to have our own cash, legal tender, in our hands again."

"You really want to stay at the house?"

"Why not?" she said.

"We could make dinner," Nate said. "I mean, you could, if you want. Leaving Manhattan hasn't made me a better cook."

"We'd need food, Nate, ingredients. And pots and pans. These things cost money." She practically slobbered at the thought. The Viking's meals were all starting to taste the same, and the hospital toast and diner potatoes had left her wanting.

"If you're willing to make a feast out of mismatched canned goods, I know where we can get some," he said, starting the engine.

They were five miles up Route 1 before Emily got around to asking where they were heading. The sun was high in the sky, and they'd flipped the Audi's visors down, flush against the windshield. It was early afternoon and already felt as if a full week had passed since they'd left Trevor at the hotel this morning. He'd be waking up from his nap right about now, maybe heading out for that stroll. Maybe he'd be putting up a fuss for the sitter, but Emily doubted it. It's not that she had unusually high expectations for her kid, like those mothers who claimed to have reared angels even as their prodigies were smearing pudding on the wallpaper. It was that Trevor threw tantrums only when he was alone with his parents. Around strangers, he was eerily, naturally easygoing, a trait clearly inherited from Nate. A trait luckily inherited from Nate. Oh God, perhaps Trevor had gotten only Nate's good genes. She looked over at Nate and tried to see him as transient, as someone who might be gone soon. But he was a solid presence.

"Please tell me you're not taking me back to the hospital," Emily said as he slowed the car down to take a sharp curve. She sincerely hoped that Nate's food plan didn't involve cribbing another tray of George's intensive-care rations. She could make a feast out of nearly anything, but rehydrated eggs and Jell-O might not be worth the effort. She turned on the Audi's air-conditioning and it streamed out of the vent immediately, a clean white chill. The Jeep's A/C, on the other hand, usually took a full ten minutes to get up to speed, and even then it arrived as a slow fog, damp and clammy. She tilted the Audi's vents up toward the ceiling, away from her skin.

"We're heading over to Narragansett. It's only about fifteen minutes."

"They give away free food there? This really is the land of plenty."

"We're going to George's house, his family's old house." Nate's fingers trembled on the steering wheel. He lifted his right hand into the air, steadying it in front of his face for a moment before putting it back in position. He'd already noted that it was only the newness of the car that made driving it – this car that his long-remote father had crashed yesterday, had steered here from the Midwest – remarkably uncreepy. "No one's there."

Emily knew that Nate's father had grown up in Rhode Island, but she'd had no idea – until Nate spewed his truths last night – that there was still a local house in the family.

As if reading her mind, Nate said, "It's not like anyone's lived there for years. I don't know why I never said anything to you about my family having a house here." He paused and then said, "It seemed silly to mention the old place, it has nothing to do with me. But then once we were here, and we'd spent all this time talking about Rhode Island and plotting out the move, it felt as if I'd lied, by omission, not telling you that my father grew up here."

"Nate, I knew your father grew up in Rhode Island," Emily said. "I just didn't know that your father still owned a house here."

Nate's foot let up on the gas, the car started to slow down. "You knew my dad grew up here?"

"Nate, drive." It would really cap off this holiday if they crashed and left Trevor parentless. Their lives hadn't been worth so much, or much at all, Emily figured, until they had Trevor.

"I told you that my father grew up here? I usually tell people that he'd spent his whole life in Cleveland, since that's the way he portrayed it when he stooped to talk about his past. I know nothing about his time here."

"You never told me. You didn't have to. His history is pretty much in the public domain." Emily felt her words drop to the floor of the car like steel pellets. It was the great paradox of Nate's pain: He acted so encumbered by having a father whose famous structures towered every day over the American heartland, yet never seemed to realize that though George Bedecker had refused to open himself up to his children, he was a completely public figure to the outside world. Emily had known George Bedecker's name for as long as she could remember, the same way she'd always known of Georges Braque and Aaron Copland. It was only after her first date with Nate, however, when they'd known each other for two weeks, that she'd looked up the details of George's work. And his history.

"Bedecker believed that the Narragansett house influenced the tone of his earliest designs," Emily said now, paraphrasing from the hidden recess of her mind where she'd carefully and consciously stored that history. "Oh, not directly the house itself. It was a traditional house, repeating designs seen ad nauseam in the 1930s, but the way the house perched on the landscape and gave the surrounding environment the upper hand. 'Humans are only the inhabitants of a house, the land owns it,' he said. 'The house should thus form a dialogue with the earth on which it sits, not with the people who, on whim, will take up residence for a while.'"

"It sounds almost beautiful, when you say it," Nate said. The landscape outside the car was growing greener, more residential. "You knew we were moving to my father's home state and you didn't say anything."

"It was your place to say something. The last time I brought up your father's name you threw a boot at me."

"A shoe, not a boot."

"Well, it was a big shoe."

"I think this is where he was heading when he had his accident, to the house," Nate said. He inched over toward the shoulder to let a pickup truck pull past. Nate was driving uncharacteristically slow, as if afraid the maimed car might fall apart if he went over forty-five mph. "The place has been cleaned and prepped. Maybe he's working on a project in the area and that's why he was coming, but last time I checked, he wasn't building anything in Rhode Island. It's been a long time since I've seen evidence of anything he's working on. It's like he's thrown in the towel. Like running into a ditch on Route 1 was the inevitable conclusion to whatever is going on with him." Nate steered the car closer to the center of the road again, edging away from the narrow shoulder.

"You don't think — "

"That he was trying to kill himself? It's not his style, even in the face of Huntington's. He always believed in accepting life's hard knocks, on moving forward stoically and without complaint, without emotion at all," Nate said. "The good news is that his house is well stocked, with a pantry full of nonperishables."

The place was modest, not the kind of spread Emily expected, given that its design had ostensibly inspired George to build the Treehorn Retreat and the Armistice Library. The library was the only building of George's that Emily had been in since meeting Nate four years ago. It was a year into their relationship and she'd found herself in Baltimore for a commercial shoot. Between wrapping the final take and catching her train back to New York, she took a cab over to the library and spent ten minutes wandering the perimeter of its capacious central hall. The entryway was built to maximize the natural light. *Here is your father, Nate,* she thought as she lingered next to the buffed walls, nearly late for her train. She'd assumed that standing in George's building might help her understand the troubled son, her boyfriend who wouldn't talk about his family, but it hadn't helped at all. It had simply made her feel guilty, surreptitious. It had made her feel *wrong*: because as much as Nate despised his father, Emily, while standing inside of George Bedecker's building, couldn't deny the beauty in its design. It was breathtaking and awe-inspiring. It was merely a building, but the feeling of standing inside it transcended its dimensions and materials, it brought on a sense of the ethereal. Bedecker may have been no good at maintaining a family, but he'd mastered his work. This Narragansett house, however, was small and oddly traditional. It bore no resemblance to the library.

"I'll open a window. It's stuffy in here," Nate said.

"It's okay. It smells like fresh laundry."

"He had the place professionally cleaned. I found the bill." Nate opened the windows in the dining room and propped the front door open, letting air circulate through the house and back out again. The windowsills were covered in cracked white paint. The panes were framed by linen curtains that hung straight to the floor. Emily took herself on a tour of the first story. This house wasn't large, but it was bigger than her and Nate's new home. It had the kind of history, that sense of having been lived in, that their relatively new construction lacked. The oak floorboards in the hallway, leading from the dining room to the living room, sagged slightly as she walked.

"It looks like someone didn't appreciate the setup in the living room," she said, standing in the room's doorway. All of the furniture in the living room was upholstered in broad floral prints, like garden party dresses. In the center of the room, the couch and a console table and an end table had all been sandwiched together, evoking images of a massive furniture love-in. Nate came up behind her.

"Oh, yeah, I tried to make a crib for Trevor, when he was here with me," he said. "You'd think the son of George Bedecker could have constructed something with a little more style."

Right, Trevor had been here. Last night, Nate had explained their father-son investigation, the couple of hours he and Trevor had spent checking the place, snooping in the attic until the policeman arrived. The timing was odd, Nate being at his father's house exactly when police came looking for someone to claim the old man. Well, not *claim* him, like a body, but to claim him as kin, as a responsibility. Nate seemed to see it as an omen, a call to rise to the occasion. Emily felt drunk, woozy with emotional overload. She could only imagine how the hangover was going to feel once all of this sank in.

"Come on," Nate said. He left the room and Emily followed.

In the kitchen, they rifled through the cabinets — the refrigerator was empty, save for a box of baking soda and four unopened liters of sparkling water, the labels in Dutch. The tall maple cabinets, though, were packed with the kind of food that a paranoid gourmand might stockpile in anticipation of a nuclear winter. Dried beans, canned tomatoes, canned soup, jarred carrots and peas, boxes of rice, tins of sardines, instant oatmeal as well as rolled oats, dried apricots in a vacuum-packed bag, tea, honey, preserved lemons, and one box of graham crackers, which Nate had broken into and was eating his way through.

"Look at all the tuna!" Emily said. "When do you think

these cabinets were stocked?" There were eight tins of albacore packed in spring water. "It's a mercury overload waiting to happen." For the past couple of years, ever since the government issued its mercury warnings against tuna and swordfish, Emily had steered completely clear of the species. She'd replaced tuna with chicken salad in her diet, swordfish with swordfish abstinence.

"Some of these cans are recent," Nate said through a mouth full of graham crackers, looking at the expiration date on a container of processed pumpkin filling. "Though the graham crackers are a little soft."

"Leave me at least one sleeve of them," Emily said taking the pumpkin filling from his hand. In her haste she dropped it. It barely made a noise as it hit the floor's soft, dated linoleum tiles. She stooped and inspected the can, which had landed squarely on its side and wasn't dented. "We can make a graham crust and do a pumpkin pie, if there's a pie tin." She added the pumpkin to their stash on the counter (long-grain rice, canned tomatoes, raisins, honey, tea, Manhattan clam chowder, garbanzo beans, vegetable oil, soy sauce, garlic powder). In a cabinet under the stovetop, she found the pots and pans, worn but functional. She added two saucepans and a skillet to the pile of booty. She located a square cake pan that could substitute as a pie tin. Nate had already found the plates and silverware and was putting a small assemblage in one of the cardboard boxes he'd discovered just inside the back door.

"You're sure we have electricity and gas at the house?" Emily said, taking an unopened bottle of dish soap from next to the sink and adding it to the box.

"Sure." Nate said. "We have a phone line, too; the number was supposedly hooked up last week. The house is inhabitable. I mean, we were planning to be living there by now."

"A phone line? Should we grab one of the phones from here? I saw two in the living room, plugged into the wall." Simply having a phone listed in their names would give their residence a durable feel, Emily hoped. Setting up their house together would be one big step toward repairing, or consolidating, at least, their life together.

"That's stealing. This isn't our home." He put the graham crackers down and stepped away from the food, as if ashamed. Emily was the only instinctive thief in this couple, apparently. "We should replace all of this once we have money again, and let's put the living room furniture back in place before we leave today. This house should look untouched."

"Except for the hole you punched into the back door's window."

"Right."

"I'm kidding, Nate, I mean, assuming that the only owner of this house is your father, and you're the only kid he has, it's all coming to you someday, isn't it? Maybe soon. You have to face the fact that this might be it for your father," Emily said. She took a jar of cashew butter out of the cabinet and looked at its expiration date. "Look at the place. No one has lived here for ages. Sure, the floors have been mopped and the rugs vacuumed, but did you actually sit on any of the furniture? Dust rises out of it like powder from a Victorian wig."

Nate only nodded, but Emily was right, she knew she was right. This home, for all of its un-Bedeckerian nods toward comfort, hadn't had an actual inhabitant for a long, long time.

CHAPTER 26

History in the Family

Emily was outside bringing the first box — stuffed with plates, a can opener, and a silver gravy boat she'd found in the living room and insisted on taking — to the car, while Nate watched her through the kitchen window. His father's kitchen window. A man couldn't give birth to a son and not care about him whatsoever, could he? George had to care, at least instinctively. Especially given that he was critically injured and Nate was his next of kin, as Emily had pointed out. His only kin. They were the only Bedeckers left. It had taken them a near eternity, but they'd found each other. As Nate saw it, George would eventually get well enough to leave the hospital (the doctors were being conservative and cagey with their predictions, but Nate held out hope even if Emily didn't) and would be set up comfortably in the master bedroom upstairs, right on top of this kitchen. They'd have to hire some sort of home health aide to care for him — whatever George's health insurance covered — unless he made a miraculously quick recovery.

Nate missed Charlie with an immediacy he hadn't felt in

more than a decade. He flexed and straightened his knobby fingers. His fingers were fine, he was fine, and he picked up the second box, this one mostly pans and pockmarked sponges and a rusty corkscrew. He stepped out the back door (he and Emily had already swept up the barbed shards from the glass pane he'd shattered) and looked for Emily, who was behind the open car trunk, hidden from view. He heard her rifling through the car's contents. Of course. If his father was planning to stay for a while, he'd have packed his things in the trunk. They'd have to rearrange those things to make room for the boxes of food.

Nate carefully navigated the rough stone path between house and driveway, the haphazardly arranged slates rising and falling with the natural irregularities of the earth. When he stepped off the path, the ground, littered with slick, scrappy pebbles, crunched.

"Nate," Emily said. Her face appeared above the open trunk, strained. "Nate, it's a shrine in here." Her voice cracked. She sounded scared. "Did you look in this trunk?"

"What? No," he said. He hadn't thought to look in the trunk.

"Your father has constructed a shrine. Articles, pictures, I don't know what else."

"A shrine?"

Emily nodded and then stood quietly, waiting for him to respond. He imagined the trunk filled with boxes, each stuffed with his childhood report cards, with pictures he'd never seen of his mother and Charlie, with never-sent letters George had written to his oldest son. He stopped a few yards from the car. Maybe his hope for a past, the clues to his medical future, had never been in the old house after all. They were in the trunk of the Audi that Nate had been driving for the past twenty-four hours. He hadn't thought to open the trunk; this could be a sign that his mind was going. No. No. No. He'd always forgotten things.

He tried to remember all of the things he'd forgotten over the years, but of course, none of it came back to him. He was not the right person to judge whether his own mind was on the wane.

"You've got to see what's in here," Emily said, walking away from the car and toward Nate, briefly tripping over the box of plates she'd left on the ground and cursing herself under her breath. "Nate," Emily said. She was directly in front of him now and shook him (her hands on his shoulders, her face close to his) out of his thoughts. "Nate," she said, "your father amassed an entire shrine. To himself."

The trunk was as packed as their Jeep had been. It was less a shrine than the well-edited stash of a type-A hoarder. Nate and Emily lifted George's things, box by box, laying each on the ground next to the car. The boxes were mostly metal file containers, beautifully brushed steel holding carefully sorted documents and pictures. Two of the containers were jammed with business documents – ledgers from past projects, contracts, plans for buildings for which, in the end, George didn't get the contract. The drawings of these dead projects possessed a startling, ephemeral beauty. The plans were the only form in which these particular structures would ever exist. One entire crate was devoted to the never-constructed Bedecker bid for the Cymbalist Temple in Tel Aviv.

"There's a whole history of architecture in this trunk," Emily said. "I've been in some of these buildings." Even the ones that didn't exist, like the art museum George had designed for Cornell that never got built, Emily exclaimed that she had been in the one that *was* constructed, by I. M. Pei. "I didn't know your father was up for that job," Emily said, holding the plan close to the side of the car so that the Audi's shadow blocked the sun's glare from the page.

"I was a kid," Nate said. "I don't really remember it."

That wasn't true. Nate remembered the hours George spent working on the project (a four-month span when Nate hadn't seen his father at all), he recalled the names his father had slung at Pei after the place was built, and he remembered the acclaim that Pei received. But all of this had taken place off center stage, in the wings of Nate's life while he and Charlie hid out in their bedroom and listened to the Indians get pummeled by the White Sox. It was the only time Nate remembered his father swearing. The Cleveland *Plain Dealer* had run an AP piece lauding Pei as the quiet leader of twentieth-century design, and George, while Nate and Charlie lay in their bunks and pretended to sleep, spewed expletives that resonated off the glass walls of their house. "Horseshit!" he'd said, and Nate almost laughed, imagined using that word at school and the ridicule that would ensue. *Horseshit* didn't even sound like an insult. It sounded like an agricultural byproduct. "Pei's excuse for a museum is a cocktease!" George had spat. During this tirade, Nate didn't hear his mother speak, but he could picture her pacing between the kitchen and the living room, pretending to neaten up, working hard to stay out of George's way.

Nate looked over Emily's shoulder into a box of George's ledgers. Nate used to dream of finding a new picture of his brother. Charlie had died so long ago, twenty years last February, that Nate had lost access to his visceral memories of the boy. Instead, when he tried to conjure Charlie, the only images that rose into Nate's head were pictures from old photographs, from the small stack of photos that Nate had held on to. He ached to find a new memento, something to bring back a forgotten moment from his brother's life. Something that might evoke a posture his brother once held, a sweater he'd worn, a particular day on which he'd lived. Charlie had loved alpine cheeses and hard links of salami, Nate remembered this, but he could no longer picture his brother eating. Nate could picture his mother, who'd died only two years later, with acute specificity. She was his mother. He'd spent the bulk of his childhood studying her. That's what boys did: They studied their parents in detail, looking for signs of their own future. Younger brothers, on the other hand, were viewed only haphazardly and without scrutiny.

"This box is all work, too," Emily said, stacking another file on the ground and taking a tiny leather duffel from the back of the trunk. She opened it and after peering inside, said, "It's clothing, and not much of it. Do you want to go through it? It's an overnight bag."

"No," Nate said. He knew what his father's clothing looked like, each piece was a repeat of the others. He pulled out the final file crate, this one made of what appeared to be a light birch, and balanced it on the lid of the trunk. After flipping the top open, he lifted a paper from the crest of the stack and gave it a quick scan. He handed it to Emily when he was done, and he watched her face fall.

In the living room, after a period of silence, Nate spoke.

"He could have called me," Nate said. His gut ached, a sharp, searing ache as if he'd swallowed glass and it was working its way through his system. "If he didn't want to talk to me himself, he could have had his lawyers call, the guys who handled my mom's estate. They know how to reach me. Our number in New York was listed, for fuck's sake." Fuck it. He'd been so excited to discover, just over an hour ago, that the Jeep had been located and that he and Emily would be able to sleep at their house tonight. He'd actually been happy. He was a fool to have let his spirits rise.

Nate's father had probably known that Huntington's was in the family ever since his own father fell sick, ever since at least 1974. Fuck all of Annemarie's allusions to the disease. It had been George's responsibility to talk to his sons. If not in Rhode Island three decades ago, then later, when his own diagnosis came. Nate thought he would kill George if the old man weren't already in a coma. A coma. The man didn't deserve the balm of unconsciousness. Nate couldn't believe that just this afternoon he'd thought there was still a chance for reconciliation. "I come from a family of idiots," he said.

Emily didn't respond. She was on the couch, crouched in the ersatz crib that Nate had yet to dismantle, carefully analyzing the medical documents as if hoping for a mistake, something they'd overlooked, the April Fool's notation of a prankster medic. She wasn't going to find it. George didn't deal with the kind of people who played practical jokes. George Bedecker had Huntington's (he wasn't at risk for it, he wasn't waiting to see if he'd inherited the gene or if the symptoms would emerge – he *had* the disease, firmly diagnosed by experts) and hadn't bothered to call his son, his genetic son, to let him know.

"I don't think I believed you were actually right about Huntington's, about George having it," Emily said as she flipped through the file. "It's just, I know I'm the one with the doomsday prophesies all the time, but it seemed maybe you'd let your fears get the best of you." George was experiencing all of the early physical symptoms of the disease, but his head still seemed to be fine. So George's longtime misanthropic tendencies were his own, they weren't the illness. And George's head had been intact and he'd been thinking clearly eight months ago when, according to the medical records, he first went to a doctor complaining of shakes. George's tremors had become undeniable, it seems, and he'd finally faced up to the fact that his demise would mirror his father's. *History in the family,* the medical forms stated.

Nate held his head between his hands and squeezed, hard. He wanted to tear the insides out of his own body in one fast-action movement. In a favorite ghost story he'd told Charlie during their campouts on Bedecker House's lawn, the ghost of a butcher returned to his former neighbors' homes to rip out their intestines. The phantom thrust his specter of a hand into townspeople's abdomens while they slept, grasping their insides the way Dickens-era orphans grasped for pork sausage. That would be a relief right now, having his organs decimated instantaneously.

"I didn't think your father actually had Huntington's," Emily repeated. "Even if your grandfather had it, there was a fifty percent chance George didn't."

"You didn't think my father was real, either. Your track record's not so good today." The contents of this birch box, other than the folder that Emily held, were spread across Emily's lap and on the floor in front of Nate. He sat in a high back chair. "I'm sorry. I didn't mean that."

"I'm still trying to deal with our move to Newport, the implications — and sudden *fact,* you know? — of it. And up until yesterday, I thought my worst problem was that I'd transported stolen art across state lines." That was still a bad problem, Nate had to admit, despite the good face Emily was putting on it. As he'd told her, even if the Barbers didn't press charges, the authorities weren't going to drop the case. She and Nate needed to come up with a strategy before she talked to the cops again. "Do you get that? Everything else is like a dream right now, I have nothing to grasp on to."

"I know." Nate knew he should hold her, but there was room for only one in her crib. If Emily was numb, it only made sense that Nate would be, too. He physically ached, but his brain felt anesthetized. Sure Nate had expected this news, he'd been looking for exactly this proof. Bingo! He won. So where was the satisfaction? He hated his father. He'd always hated his father, but now having a firm reason for that hate made the revulsion absolute. There was nothing like a tainted gene to remind a man that he couldn't escape his past. Nate felt DNA skittering through his veins like water bugs, like rats darting beneath the subway tracks planning a siege.

"You might be okay," Emily said. "It's a fifty-fifty thing, right? We're due some odds. It's our chance to be lucky." She sniffled and stretched out on the couch, coming out of her crouch. "I feel as if I've been crying all day. So who is Philippa Antrim, anyway?"

"Who?"

"Here, on this envelope," Emily lifted a sealed manila envelope from her lap and handed it to Nate. On the front was a name, Philippa Antrim, in ballpoint pen, and a phone number written in George's neat print. The area code was in Chicago.

"I don't know, maybe his assistant? He used to have a woman named Danielle, but I haven't called his office in years, at least three or four. There was always someone at the firm in charge of George, keeping him in line, getting him to his appointments, reminding him to occasionally leave at night and lay eyes on his family." Nate turned the envelope over in his hands.

"Do you think we should – " Emily said as he pried open the tin clasp, " – open it?" she finished her sentence while Nate was already pulling the papers from the envelope's pocket. Everything would have to be put back in place again; they'd leave no trace. They'd take off for good and start their new life, bringing George's tainted genes and whatever else Nate had inherited along with them.

Inside the envelope was a will. Like Nate and Emily with the Jeep, George had put all of his important documents in his car. Like Nate and Emily, Nate realized, George was planning to settle here for the long haul. George was expecting to die his father's death, right down to the location. Nate felt a chill. Ice on his spine.

He called Emily off the couch and, it must have been something in his voice, she jumped up at once. She sat on his lap in the straight-backed chair, barely wide enough for one person, and together they read George's will.

"His office always seemed to be operating in the red," Nate said. "He's always been broke, so it's not like I'm surprised that he left me nothing." Nothing except the pittance that was left of Annemarie's estate, five thousand dollars at most. George's firm would be handed down to the two current senior associates. It was a bum deal for them. They'd inherit the debt. George didn't own his apartment in Chicago apparently. It wasn't in the will and Nate had a hunch that it was small and cheap and a rental. The man never spent time at home anyway. His entire estate consisted of the business and this house and the car that Nate had been driving. And when George passed away, these things — the house and the car — would go to Philippa Antrim of Chicago.

"I told you we shouldn't move any furniture, or take anything," Nate said. "It's not ours. It never will be."

"You're also the one who keeps telling me that your father isn't dead yet. This Philippa comes into her inheritance only after your dad's heart stops ticking." Emily was standing now, had left Nate's lap. "Maybe she's a relative on your father's side. You said you don't know much about the family tree."

Nate scanned the room, eyeing all of the possessions that would end up not in the Bedecker family, but with the Antrims. Nate shook his head.

"His will treats me like I'm my mom's son, not his at all," he said.

That statement hung in the air and neither Nate nor Emily moved, as if afraid to disturb this pronouncement.

"Could you be?" Emily finally asked, with too much enthusiasm. "People had affairs like mad in the sixties. How would your father have known? He was away so often, he was oblivious to you all, right? You've always said that your mother seemed like the kind of woman who should have led a greater life, who shouldn't have been confined to Cleveland, or whatever. Your mom could have easily had a lover. Your mother probably had a rich, private life that you never asked her about. I mean, you Bedeckers weren't bred to be big emotional talkers."

"What we were bred for, according to those medical records, is death," Nate said.

"You might not be George's son," Emily said, more firmly. "You might not have his genes. It's not impossible."

"I'm his son," Nate said. "Fuck, I'd be thrilled to discover I wasn't his blood relation, trust me." This wasn't simply because Nate wished for a clean-gene bill of health. He'd love to know that his mother had had some passion in her life before she checked out. And she might have, later on. After Charlie died and before Annemarie's leukemia set in, there was a one-year stretch when she'd seemed at peace, resigned to her fate in life. At the time, it seemed so outrageous to Nate, barbarous and inappropriate. Charlie had been in the ground for a short ten months, and there was his mother, letting her spiritual curiosity roam free, sending care packages to Nate, first-class mailers filled with meaningless aphorisms and bubble-wrapped bouquets of sage and oregano. *I might take a cruise,* she wrote in one brief letter. *I'm feeling the draw of the water.* Nate hadn't taken her seriously and could only imagine George's response to his wife taking off on the Atlantic Crown — the old man created houses specifically to give people a refuge from that world. She never went on the cruise. She fell sick a couple of months later and the old, sensibly European Annemarie returned.

"I wish I wasn't George's kid, really, give me any other gene pool to fish from. I'm his, though," Nate said. "We got tested when my mother was ill. She needed bone marrow. It was demented: neither George nor I matched to her, but we were a perfect match for each other. That only means we have the same marrow type, so I'm trying not to read into it. But it feels like an omen, or a curse." It felt like certain death.

Emily rubbed the back of her neck and tilted her face up to the ceiling, as if still trying to take it all in, trying to make sense, trying to call up an apt quotation from one of her favorite dead philosophers.

"Can we go get Trevor?" she said. Her voice was weak and barely audible. "I need to see you and Trevor and me, all in one place."

"Okay," Nate said, because he owed her, and he owed Trevor. For now, they were together and healthy. They had a car and their beds and a new home. For today at least (and maybe only for today, for this present moment), this fragile life of theirs was still in one piece.

CHAPTER 27

Contact with the Antrims

T HE JEEP DIDN'T LOOK so bad. "I think the Audi's in worse shape," said Emily. She didn't see a single new scratch on the Jeep's body. None of the windows were even broken, though when Nate mentioned to the mechanic who ran the car lot that the door had been locked when the car was stolen, the guy laughed. Apparently modern car thieves were overwhelmingly adept at prying open locked cars without damaging the goods.

"We're not going to find proof that it was locked. Let it go," Emily said.

The Audi, on the other hand, was a wreck. Looking at it head-on in the slanted 4:00 p.m. sun, Emily noticed how severely the passenger side had been smashed. With one headlight completely gone, the car looked sinister and bad-ass. Emily had never really liked German cars anyway. They were evocative of Schopenhauer and Nietzsche and men who believed that life was hell. Well, life was hell. "The Audi looks like crap in this light," she said.

"It drives," said the car lot guy, standing a few feet away. "The Jeep doesn't. You can leave the body here and take it as a tax write-off. I'll give you a receipt. It's better than nothing."

"Our insurance company will have to come take a look first," Nate said.

"You've got to be kidding me," the guy responded.

The Jeep had been stripped of its useful parts. All that remained were the two AeroBeds and Trevor's toys and his car seat, which Nate promptly moved to the Audi, strapping it in next to the seat they'd borrowed from the police and would return tomorrow. "Here, do you mind?" Nate handed Trevor to Emily and she rested him on her hip. The boy's drool-slicked chin brushed against her cheek and he laughed, a hiccup of a laugh.

On their way to the lot, they'd stopped at the Viking, where they'd reunited with Trevor (he looked so good, Emily noted, hale and healthy and happy to see his parents, bobbing his head up and down as if nodding in agreement, something he'd been doing since he was practically born every time he was happy) and checked out a day early, vowing to return to the hotel first thing in the morning with legitimate money to pay the bill. "The police have your info, so don't try to run!" joked the manager, the same one who'd dealt with them at their Friday check-in. Now the Audi's trunk was packed, not only with George's food and linens — they'd taken sheets and a bath towel from the Narragansett house as well — but with the Bugaboo, too. Tomorrow they would have cash finally, and normal life would return. A new kind of normal. A perverse version of normal. Normal until the NYPD came knocking. The lieutenant had promised to call Emily today to set up an interrogation, but so far her phone had stayed silent.

They'd left George's file boxes in the Narragansett living

room, stacked neatly beside an empty silverware hutch. They'd slipped all of his papers back into their crates, carefully sliding each leaf into place and then closing the lids tight. They left the house as clean and spare as they'd found it. Outside by the car after the house was closed up, Nate dialed his phone. He punched in the numbers affiliated with Philippa Antrim. As the phone rang through to Chicago, Nate handed his cell over to Emily. It seemed that he couldn't do it. He couldn't make the call. Emily accepted the phone and held it to her ear, hoping that it would ring over to voice mail so she could hang up, putting off whatever was waiting on the other side until another day. She and Nate had been dealt enough for one weekend (even a long holiday weekend). But someone did pick up, and Emily threw her shoulders back and straightened out her wrinkled pants and stood taller, as if the stranger on the other end had walked into her line of sight and was watching her.

"Hello?" It was a guttural man's voice, not Philippa, not Philippa Antrim.

"I'm sorry, I'm looking for Philippa Antrim?" Emily said, her voice taking on the upward inflection of a question. She sounded like a teenager or a telemarketer, she'd be lucky if this man didn't hang up. Or, she'd be lucky if he did. At the moment, that was a tough call. "I'm calling from Rhode Island, I'm sorry, really, I think it's a personal matter, but I don't know for sure," she said. There was a silence on the other end. "Are you there? Are you Mr. Antrim?" She longed for the days of the telegraph, when people had time to examine and edit their communications before sending them over the transom.

"I'm her son, Pete. She's not in. Who's calling?"

"My name's Emily Latham, my partner, boyfriend, found your mother's name in his father's papers, his dad is George Bedecker? He's — "

"I know George." He sounded upset about being disturbed, impatient. Emily looked at her watch. It was 1:00 p.m. in Chicago. "Is everything okay?"

"Not really," Emily said, and then, with Nate holding her hand, she told the junior Antrim, Pete Antrim, that George had had an accident, that he'd slammed into a guardrail on Route 1, had been in the hospital for a day and a half, that it was critical, that he was in a coma. She spoke quickly and awkwardly, repeating herself and doubling back until she got all of the details out.

For a long time, there was only silence on the other end of the line. Emily was proving to be a disaster when it came to phone calls today.

"My mother's in Atlanta for the weekend, but she can get a flight out in the next day or so, I'm sure. She'll want to be there," he finally said. "I guess I knew that George had a son somewhere, but he never explicitly spoke of family."

"Sure," Emily said, shifting her weight from one foot to the other. "Typical." Her heart was beating so hard she thought it might explode across the phone line. She continued talking, offering a quick stream of vague details, mentioning that George wasn't on a respirator, that he hadn't eaten his eggs this morning. She left out the Huntington's. It seemed private and not applicable. She also left out the will, since as Nate kept insisting, rightly, George was still alive.

"We found this number, and we're not much in touch with George," Emily said, "and he's not doing well, and we didn't know if Philippa was his assistant or a relative or what, but it seemed like the thing to do, to call." The right thing to do out of curiosity, out of need for Nate. On the phone with this stranger, who sounded as if he were Nate and Emily's age, living his own life in the middle of the country, Emily felt wrong: they'd called him for answers to their own questions, not because they felt any debt to Philippa Antrim, mother of Pete.

"His assistant? Is that what he tells people?" Pete said, caustic. What Emily had taken for impatience a moment ago was beginning to sound more like dejected weariness. "It's hard to believe that, really, after eight years together as a couple he'd be portraying her as an assistant. What a conjob."

"I'm sorry?" Emily said, again a question, again an apology. *Conjob*, that's one word she'd forgotten to call George Bedecker when she'd screamed at him this morning. Conjob. Shithead. It was all the same. She squeezed Nate's hand. His eyes were on the water behind the house. He seemed to be holding his breath. "It's hard for me to believe that after eight years George would barely have mentioned his only child," Emily said into the phone, her close breath condensing on the mouthpiece, "a son who grew up in his own house, who George lectured on the Bauhaus and Modernist movements from the time Nate was just six years old."

A taut silence took over the conversation. So Pete's mother and George were lovers. Or at least companions. Emily couldn't imagine the man she'd seen in the Warwick hospital bed having a love life.

"No harm meant," Pete said, breaking the tension. "He's in Rhode Island? My mother will want to be there. Let me get a pen, I'll need the hospital's number, and a way to reach you and George's kid — " Pete stumbled for a name.

"Nathan. His name is Nathan Bedecker."

"George is in Rhode Island?" Pete sounded more present, suddenly, as if the news was sinking in. "He said he was going to Brussels for a conference or what have you, a symposium, for a few weeks. He never calls while he's gone. My mother wasn't expecting to hear from him until November at the earliest. Not my idea of a romance."

"Love and delirium," Emily said, following Nate's gaze and looking out at the water, "have many points in common."

"Thomas Carlyle," Pete said.

"Badly paraphrased Thomas Carlyle."

"I didn't know anyone read him anymore."

Emily grinned, turning back toward the house to hide her small smile from Nate. "I guess they do," she said.

And then Pete fetched his pen and wrote down Nate's phone number and the contact info for the hospital in Warwick. Emily hung up the phone and just like that she and Nate had passed George off like a baton. He was largely out of their life again though, from the looks of it, the weight of these three days would never leave Nate.

At the car lot an hour later, Nate was, on the surface at least, managing to hold it together. He opened the Jeep's side door and ducked into the front seat, his legs hanging out of the car like magician's props. The Jeep's radio was gone, that was the first thing Nate and Emily were told when they got here, as if the sound system was their most coveted possession. The radio! The baby Rasta CD! How about the *engine?* That was gone, too, but seemed too obvious to mention. What about their tax forms, their clothing, Nate's laptop? All gone. As Nate slid out of the car, Emily smiled. It was so typical of him, doing a final, thorough search even after everything was confirmed gone. He hadn't changed, not completely.

"Come on," Nate said, taking Trevor from her arms and strapping him into the car seat — their car seat — in the Audi. "We should get to the house before dark, we're down a headlight, I don't want to be driving at night."

With all three of them seat-belted in, Nate started the motor and then laid his right hand on the seat between him and Emily. Slowly he opened his palm. A hundred-dollar bill, crisp, lay folded in it.

"For emergencies," Emily smiled. "It was still there?"

"And this, too." Nate reached into his shirt pocket and took out a small Ziploc of marijuana and rolling papers. Emily looked back to Trevor, oblivious, and then looked at Nate. "You told me you didn't smoke anymore."

"No more secrets," he said, starting the engine and driving toward downtown Newport. Trevor sneezed from the backseat, three rapid-fire rasps, and Emily turned to him and reached back to pull his hand out of his mouth. The boy had been trying to eat his own fist. His small O-shaped mouth dripping with saliva, he smiled. They all had their vices.

Nate effortlessly steered the Audi toward their new house. He seemed to already know his way around Newport, a city Emily feared she'd take years to master. She was so accustomed to Manhattan's grid. Here, amid the looping side streets and unmarked cul-de-sacs and narrow village lanes, she was oblivious again, a greenhorn.

After leaving the car lot, they made two stops. First they paused at a gas station to add a couple of gallons to the tank and then at a liquor store on Broadway ("Look, Trev! Broadway!" she'd said, spying a street name to which she could relate). When buying wine to drink at home, in Manhattan, they tended to grab a just-okay Cabernet or an embarrassingly cheap Pinot Grigio from the front racks at the shop where the bottles wore *Overstock* signs shackled to their necks. Nate and Emily liked to drink but never claimed to be oenophiles and could barely taste the difference between a twelve-dollar table wine and a grand cru, so what was the point of paying up? Tonight, though, Nate walked into the store and started immediately picking up bottles that cost fifty dollars and up.

"We have a hundred dollars to spend, on a bottle of red, something full-bodied and rich," he said to the proprietor, a woman in her sixties, tall and spindly and smartly dressed. "A red, right?" he said to Emily, who stood next to him, stunned. Rich wasn't exactly something they were accustomed to.

"You really want to do this?" Emily said. A hundred dollars could go a long way, given their current finances and the expenses she saw looming in their future.

"It's my hundred, I think I'm owed a good bottle of wine, at least."

Back in the car, Emily turned the bottle over in her hands. A Barbaresco (Italian, in the spirit of Columbus Day, explained the proprietor, who Emily thanked profusely for her help, explaining that this was an uncommon splurge), already aged and ready to drink, it would easily fetch $250 in a restaurant. Looked at in that light, it was a bargain. As she ran her hands over the bottle, Emily found herself disconcertingly eager to taste the wine, even as she was sure that it wouldn't give Nate any pleasure. He'd been understandably on edge ever since Emily got off the phone with Pete Antrim early this afternoon, ever since she'd explained, in one breathless swoop, that Philippa was George's longtime romantic partner and that Pete was Philippa's son, a man who had come to know George quite well.

"They're his family now," Nate had said. He'd looked back at the Narragansett house one last time. "That's it then. We'll bring back the car when we're done with it and say good-bye forever."

Even the Barbaresco's label was elegant. Emily had expected something fussy and foreign in an expensive wine label, but this one featured only a line-drawing of a woman's face in profile. Emily would hold onto this bottle after they drank the contents. She'd bring it out in a year or two, when they'd be able to look back on this weekend without fear. After enough time had passed, she and Nate would smile over their indulgence, maybe they'd spoil themselves with another expensive bottle then. Especially if they, all three of them, were all still alive and healthy and not yet incarcerated. And sane. They'd drink the wine tonight. Tomorrow she'd wake up at six and figure out what to say to the cops. She and Nate would lay out the options. Maybe she'd fess up. Maybe that was the only way forward.

"Shit," Nate brought the car to a sudden, hard stop two drive-ways away from their home. Emily instinctively looked at the windshield for a wounded bird.

"No, there. There." Nate said pointing to their house. A fig-ure was squatting on their stoop, bent over. Nate inched the car closer. Both of Nate and Emily's neighbors had their porch lights on bright, fighting off the falling darkness and casting a small glow on Nate and Emily's lawn. This squat plot of grass between their house and the sidewalk was narrow, only twelve feet deep. "We've attracted the only homeless person in Newport."

"No," Emily said, smiling, leaning closer to the windshield to get a good look. "We've attracted the last tourist of the holiday weekend, and she brought us a pizza." As Nate parked the Audi in their driveway (*their* driveway!), Emily unhooked her seat belt, opened the car door, and ran up the short walk to Jeanne, who grabbed her in a tight, tough embrace.

"You must hate me," Emily said. Emily hated herself for the way she'd treated her friend.

"Close," Jeanne said. She loosened her grip on Emily and kissed Nate, who'd arrived on the porch with a sleepy Trevor in his arms, on the cheek. Emily had tears in her eyes (again!), embarrassing tears that she quickly wiped away. "But I was get-ting really tired of all the yogis and yoginis."

Emily nodded and they all clustered around the front door while Nate fished the keys out from the envelope that Bob Daugherty had handed over exactly three days earlier. Nate shoved the door open and Jeanne turned to Emily and continued, "If you bring up my cheating ex's name again, even once, I'm out of here."

The pizza was lukewarm and its sauce tasted like grocery-store brand ketchup, yet still it was satisfying. "Fuck, this is good," Nate said, licking a drip of tomato off his finger. And the wine was outstanding. Nate had filled Jeanne's glass first, a copious pour. Seeing Jeanne, Emily felt moored.

"It's definitely rich," Emily said, after taking her first sip.

"I think it's supposed to be paired with a roast, not pepperoni," Nate said. "But it's good. It's really good."

Emily and Nate and Jeanne ate in a circle on the living room floor, sitting atop one of the pilfered bedsheets and passing Trevor from lap to lap. Emily's shirt — a T-shirt she'd borrowed from Jeanne, thrilled to be in new clothing after three days — was plastered with crumbs from the crust that Trevor was gnawing.

"You're only four hours from Rhinebeck, you know, if you ever get the urge to go away and spend a weekend ohm-ing," Jeanne said between bites. "And your house is perfect, by the way. I adore it."

"Liar," Emily said. Jeanne's intentions were good, but there was nothing to love about this house except for the fact that they owned it. "Look at that crown molding," she pointed toward the ceiling, and Nate and Jeanne looked up. Emily hadn't noticed, during their house tour, how shoddy the work was. The molding was coming loose from the ceiling at the corner of the living

room. The banister on the stairwell felt shaky, too. They'd have
to fix that before Trevor started walking, which could be any
day.

"What, you want to live in a museum, one of those show-
pieces on the Upper East Side with perfect moldings? Those
apartments are so lifeless."

"Like the Barbers' place," Emily said before she could edit
herself.

"The Barbers are ludicrous. That home is a mausoleum,"
Jeanne said. "The Rufino thing, it couldn't have turned out more
ridiculously, you know?" She arched her back and stretched her
sides, a cross between yoga and elementary school calisthenics.

Nate and Emily were silent and kept their eyes averted from
each other. Had Jeanne heard that the cops were coming up
to Newport? Emily hated how word spread in the city, how the
proximity of apartment living made everyone assume nothing
was private. Finally Emily said, her voice empty, as if she didn't
care about Jeanne's answer (but she did care, more than anything, she had to find out what Jeanne knew), "How did it turn
out?"

Jeanne looked at her. "No one called you?"

Emily gave an exaggerated shrug. "I got a call from someone
in the NYPD," she said, but she didn't know if that's what Jeanne
meant.

"They're calling all of the guests," Nate quickly added. "They
just want to talk to us."

"When did they call you?" Jeanne asked.

"Yesterday, in the morning?" Emily said.

"You haven't talked to anyone since?" Jeanne asked.

"No one," said Emily.

"Oh, right, you've been avoiding your phone now that you've

moved out of town. A clean break, and all. Well, the NYPD's investigation is over. What I hear is that — and I wasn't at the party, so you may know more than I do — Anna was hammered, completely tanked by the end of the night."

"We left early," Emily said. Nate, sitting across from her with his back leaning against a wall, looked as if he were holding his breath, playing a game of statue where the slightest movement might cause an intergalactic calamity.

"Well, she was tanked. Bess Van Rhyn says Anna was so gone she couldn't even tip the caterers, and Randy has no idea how all of that works, so Bess and Tyler had to pay the tip themselves and dismiss the help. Those kitchen assistants would have stayed until morning waiting for their cash if Bess hadn't intervened."

"So?" Emily said, unsure of where Jeanne was going. "What, you think the caterers took the art?" She wanted to vomit at the idea that the help would be blamed for her own felonious sin. She would confess to the cops. It wouldn't be so bad. Anna and Randy wouldn't press charges. They'd tell the cops it was simply a misunderstanding and plea to the court that Emily's sentence be light. They'd also never talk to Emily again, sure, but that was a minor loss, now that she and Nate weren't living in Manhattan anyway.

"Oh, God no, though I wouldn't put it past Randy, blaming those Barnard girls." Emily tried to catch Nate's eye, but he was staring unblinkingly at the pizza box. "No. They think Anna tore the painting out of its frame and threw it out. She has no memory of doing so, but she has no memory of most of the night, from what Bess says. Anna's actually accepted guilt. The police have an eyewitness who saw Anna go into the study in the middle of her own party. And Anna never uses that study. It's Randy's domain."

"You heard this from Bess yourself?" Emily said.

"She didn't call you? She left me like five messages yesterday while I was in my Brahma-Viharas seminar."

"I got messages from a bunch of people on Friday, but I haven't heard much since." Emily was starting to understand that with their move would come a sense of exile: out of sight, out of the Manhattanites' minds. Soon, Jeanne would be the only one calling to inform them of the gossip.

"No one can get enough of this Barber shit," Jeanne said. "It's like everyone's been waiting for Anna and Randy to slip up."

"Why – "

"Why," Nate interrupted Emily, finishing her sentence, "why the hell would Anna destroy her own painting?" And why, Emily thought, was everyone so eager to believe such an obviously untrue (as only she could prove) scenario?

"Because Randy is the art collector. And as of recently, apparently she detests him. He's been fucking the barista at Café Panino. Anna was getting her coffee there every morning, totally oblivious to the fact that the woman steaming her milk was Randy's special friend. Anna found out last week. Word has it that beneath her characteristically chilly facade, she's been seething. She spilled it all – Randy's cheating, her agony over the discovery of it, the way she wanted to crush his balls – to Lana Raines the night she found out about the affair. It seems Anna was under the misimpression that Lana was someone who'd keep her mouth shut."

"Holy crap," Nate said, as if waking from a dream to a reality far wilder than the one in which he'd fallen asleep. Emily might have plenty of reasons to resent Nate, but at least he wasn't sleeping with a coffee-bar clerk.

"I know," Jeanne said. "Sleeping with a barista. It's every I-banker's fantasy. His friends are probably slapping him on the back."

"No," Nate said. "Holy crap about Anna taking the blame for something she can't remember."

"She had the motive, and the drunkenness, to make it happen. I mean, she's given up everything for Randy," Jeanne said. "She could have had a decent career, but instead spends her days delivering his dry cleaning and planning parties for his friends. The very least she expected in return was exclusive sex from the guy."

"Emily gave up a lot for me," Nate said.

"No I didn't," Emily said in a voice that was nearly a whisper. "The cops —" Emily could barely speak, this turn of events felt so undeservedly fortuitous, "the cops believe this? I mean, do they have proof?"

"They have a witness placing her at the back of the apartment, which is sort of proof, but I don't think they care anymore. I mean, if Anna destroyed the Rufino — there was so much trash at that party, and it was all gone by the time anyone realized the painting had been taken. If Anna got rid of it, it's somewhere in the city's decaying mountains of refuse. And if she got rid of it, it's not a crime, right? You have every right to destroy your own property."

"Did they at least dust for fingerprints?" Nate asked.

"I don't know. Bess didn't say."

"I used that back bathroom during the party," Emily said with a sharp glance to Nate. "So they'd find my prints if they dusted, don't you think? I mean, everyone passed through that apartment."

"Anna confessed. It's all moot," Jeanne said. "And who cares? You're free of all that bullshit now that you've moved. You won't have to try to impress frauds like the Barbers anymore. Or like Bess Van Rhyn and her fellow vultures, for that matter."

"They're not all bad," Emily said.

"Whatever. You're going to be able to live high on the hog here. You'll be the big fish in this town." As Jeanne finished her sentence Trevor started to wail.

"He needs a bath," Emily said. She'd always liked Bess Van Rhyn. Anna and Randy, well, they were due for a fall, just not necessarily at the hands of Emily Latham. Serendipity was an unjust thing. "We need to get some real baby shampoo and soap."

Jeanne offered to do a shopping run, and after they finished eating, Nate and Emily drew up a list. Toilet paper, milk, instant coffee, the things they'd forgotten they'd need. Emily promised Jeanne that they'd pay her back after the fact, but it felt like a weak promise, heavy in her gut. Emily hated owing money. IOUs hung over her head like invisible highway signs pointing to her financial inadequacies.

"Don't worry about it, it's my housewarming gift," Jeanne said to Emily. To Nate, she added matter-of-factly, "Emily told me about the Huntington's. I'll do some investigating when I'm back at work tomorrow. Shit, I have to be back at work tomorrow, by one p.m.," she said. "How long's the drive to New York?"

Nate looked up, his face flat and expressionless. Emily turned her attention to Jeanne, to Jeanne's hands, which ran over the shopping list, the fingers as familiar as her own. It amazed Emily that Jeanne was here. Emily had screamed at her, bitter and vengeful screams, and instead of running away Jeanne had left Rhinebeck and driven to Newport and searched them out at the Viking, where the concierge told her that the Bedeckers had checked out. "Thank goodness your phone and address here are listed already," Jeanne said. She'd picked up a pizza and arrived at the house a mere half hour before the Audi drove up. "And you're lucky you showed up when you did. Another half hour and I was planning to head back to the Viking to see if the room you left was still open."

"You couldn't afford it," Emily said.

"No joke," Nate added. "I wonder if they'll end up charging us the full suite rate, or if they'll take pity and only bill us for a regular room. We'd have taken a standard room if one had been available."

"But we sure took advantage of having a suite," Emily said.

"After they forced it on us."

"Okay," Jeanne said, rising from the floor in one fluid movement, proving that yoga had given her flexibility and balance, if not inner peace. "I'll get on the shopping."

Emily walked Jeanne to the door. Trevor had crawled onto the empty pizza box, sinking his bare knees into a spot of congealed cheese. They'd give him a bath tonight, get him back into his routine. "Just make sure you pick up baby shampoo, if you see any? And laundry detergent, unscented?"

"Sure," Jeanne said, and was out the door. "I've got my phone, call if you think of anything else," she added on her way down the walk.

When Emily turned around, Trevor was still examining the pizza dregs and Nate was flat on his back, supine on the hardwood floor. His khaki pants blended into the polished bamboo as if he and the house were one already. The wine bottle next to him was empty, a one-time impulse purchase, gone. She could not believe that Anna had taken the blame for the theft. Emily wondered, briefly, if Jeanne might have the story wrong, but she had all of the details, they all fit. Bess Van Rhyn wasn't a gossip; she was a reliable source. And, in fact, the cops hadn't called Emily today for further questioning. As Nate would say, holy fuck.

"It's crazy, right, Anna taking the blame? Do you think we're off the hook? I feel like I should confess," Emily said, though she no longer felt that way. When Nate didn't respond, she continued, "Nobody's actually been hurt. Maybe we even helped Anna, if she was looking for a way to crush Randy. And the monetary loss, the cash that was in the painting, they didn't need it. So why do I feel so guilty?" She wanted Nate to absolve her of the guilt. Then, the only thing left to do would be to get rid of the evidence. They should have bought a house with a working fireplace.

Nate didn't move, and even Trevor took a timeout from examining the pizza grease to look at his father stretched along the floor in his grimy pants and a sweat-stained shirt, his hair sticking straight up and a pizza box next to his ear.

"You told Jeanne about the Huntington's," Nate said. He didn't sound mad, exactly. "I don't even know if I have it. I didn't think it was public knowledge."

Emily stood at the foot of the stairs, a few yards from him but not moving closer. "She's a doctor and a close friend. Trusting people isn't a crime."

Nate had bottled up so much inside himself that he — and Emily and Trevor to some degree, too — had become an island. The fact that there were so many boats in this town didn't help dispel that feeling. Since arriving on Friday, she and Nate hadn't seen a single face they actually knew, anyone they had genuinely known before they arrived in Newport — until Jeanne showed up.

"What if I'm dying?" Nate said.

"If you're dying, you're not going to tell Jeanne about it?" It would, in fact, be just like Nate to underplay his own death. That was exactly what George appeared to be doing. "We're all dying, Nate. It's just a matter of who gets there first."

In the silence that followed, a tree brushed against the house's side windows, scratching sharply against the glass. It was breezy out tonight. In New York, their apartment looked over the back of the building, into a courtyard. It was a real courtyard with trees and sky, not a New York City airshaft, and in the spring, when they slept with the bedroom window open, noises drifted up from their neighbors' perches below. A barely discernable voice, the slam of a door, a metal pot dropped onto the unyielding tiles of a kitchen floor. Emily and Nate were renters in the city, but most of their friends had bought apartments in coops, where the inhabitants didn't own their actual apartments, technically, but owned shares in the building itself. And thus *share* was the word that came to Emily's mind on those balmy evenings in New York when the sounds of her neighbors (from downstairs in her own building and from the co-op across the yard) rose up and mingled with her own life.

Here, though, they owned their actual house and the land on which it sat, as well as the small hedge that separated them from their neighbors. There was almost no traffic on their cul-de-sac street. At night in Newport, the only sounds Emily would hear would be Trevor's fussing and the occasional deep wheeze from Nate and the knock-knock-knock of branches on their windows. The life that they lived here would be their own.

CHAPTER 28

The Drive to Narragansett, the Final Leg

WHO WAS GEORGE BEDECKER? George considered this question as the sun beat down on Route 1 in southern Rhode Island. The highway loomed like his road to the finish line. Who was he? He had no innate pedigree. His parents had been middle-class Methodist drinkers with small goals that they'd accomplished by default. In Europe, this lack of lineage would have been a liability, but in America, in the lowdown trenches of architecture, all George had needed was an unremitting determination and a fail-proof work ethic. All it took was a lifetime of keeping his head down.

After George left home in the 1950s, and in the years that followed, his father seemed to be proud of him but often mystified, as well. From the start, Hank Bedecker followed George's architecture career with curiosity. He attempted to make sense of each accomplishment despite his lack of context in which to place it, a situation that caused Hank's praise of George's buildings to come across as muted and muddled. And then, Hank lost the brainpower to follow or praise anything at all.

George witnessed and monitored his father's decline. He visited Henry Charles Bedecker every six months during his decade of sickness. He watched as Hank lost his facial expression, then his stability, his muscle control, his capacity to feed himself, and eventually his power to swallow entirely. George's father screamed often, not in pain, but in offense. He seethed with imagined anger and misconstrued jealousy. One spring, he'd lambasted George for stealing and hawking the only thing of value in the Narragansett house, a sterling silver gravy boat. George tried to elucidate the situation, explaining that the gravy boat hadn't gone anywhere, it remained on the mantel where it had been displayed since the house's construction (*Look, Hank, the gravy boat is right here*). In response, Hank hurled a pineapple through the air. The fruit missed George's head by mere inches and shattered against the whitewashed wall at the back of the room.

A week later Hank slapped one of his nurses. These outbursts came as a surprise to George. His father had never been a violent man. Yet everything George had known about Hank turned untrue during that final decade. His father became someone else, not gradually but in a single moment. As Hank lost his physical strength and no longer had the power to throw fruit, let alone to stand and walk, his mien took on a fierceness. His face grew taut and angular, frozen at a cocked angle on his neck. In the mirror, George began to examine his own face for signs of gruesome change, but if the transformations were there, they were happening so slowly that he couldn't detect them. Would he wake up one day to discover that he, too, was someone new? And on whom would his slaps fall? He had done everything he

could to make sure that those punches would land far from his
own children, his own surviving son.

A small truck passed the Audi as George navigated the highway's subtle curves. Without realizing it, he had slowed to a
dangerously lethargic pace and now he softly increased the pressure of his foot on the gas pedal, easing up closer to the speed
limit. The road was beginning to look familiar. Unlike Chicago
and Cleveland, the other places that George had called home,
this part of the world had changed little since he lived here.
The trees still grew thick right up to the edge of the roadway
and the air had a blue tinge at mid-morning. It was the sense
of history, the ability right here to step out of modern life, that
made the place appealing. In Narragansett, no one would come
knocking at his door. The neighbors wouldn't wonder why he
wasn't trudging off to work every morning. Chances were, they
wouldn't recognize him. Eventually, when he hired an at-home
nurse, they wouldn't question it. People might stare, but they
wouldn't talk. He'd be seen as yet another deranged old man
who'd chosen to live out the end of his life by the sea.

His death would differ from his father's in only one respect:
George's sons would not be flying in to monitor his illness. One
son was long dead; the other, George hoped, would live for a
long time. Given the distance between them, this son would
never have to stand witness to his father's decline the way that
George had to Hank's.

Seeing his father's deterioration (seeing the emptiness in his
eyes and the manic insanity of his limbs) had unhinged George.
Ever since, he'd had nightmares in which he was his father,
nightmares that turned out to be premonitions. Knowing what
his future held only made it worse. His boy, Nathan, if he had
the disease, would at least be able to sleep in peace until the first

symptoms emerged. He wouldn't have the firsthand images –
like war photographs, like multicolor aneurisms – in his head.
By absenting himself from Nathan's life, George had saved his
son at least this anguish.

This was what George told himself, but what did he know?
He had lost his other son before bothering to know him. That
should have spared George the pain after the boy's death, but it
didn't. For years – and today, too – George's heart ached for that
son with the constancy of a pulse. If he could live his life over?
No matter, a man could not relive the past. A man was given
only one chance. George Bedecker's legacy would not be his
children. It would be his buildings, for however long they stood.

For most of his sons' childhoods, George had been away
from these children, absorbed with his work. More than once,
his mind turned to Longfellow: "The architect / Built his great
heart into these sculptured stones / And with him toiled his
children, and their lives / Were builded, with his own, into the
walls." What George had felt for his family – and, in those early
years, he felt strongly, if privately – those feelings were built into
the walls. The walls would stand staunch and strong and would
bring no harm. Perhaps someday George's surviving son might
look up at one of the structures and think, *This is me.*

This was what George was thinking as drove north on Route
1. He glanced down at the odometer again (miraculously he'd
inched above the speed limit) and then looked up to find a deer
leaping into the road. He slammed his foot on the brake and
yanked hard on the steering wheel and the last thing he saw
before hitting the ditch, before feeling the improbably slow glide
of his wheels from pavement to gravel and down to dirt, was the
deer bounding away, the animal's pliant body rising into the air
and off of the road and back into the thicket, unhurt. For a fraction of a second, George wondered if he could save himself,

too — if he rotated the wheel toward the road with a fast and firm jerk, could he bring the car back up to the highway? — but his split-second meditation over whether this was what he wanted, over whether a return to the living was worth it, was interrupted by the crunch of the Audi's fender as it accordioned against the rock-hard earth at the edge of the ditch. George felt his torso jettison fast forward, and the world went black in an instant.

CHAPTER 29

I'm Your Father

Nate considered not answering his cell phone when it rang. It was after 11:00 p.m., an hour when phone calls only brought bad news, and the number that popped up on his caller ID was from within Rhode Island. He couldn't think of anyone in Rhode Island to whom he wanted to speak other than Emily, and she was within shouting distance. And she had a New York phone number. Shit, Nate thought. If he and Emily were going to genuinely commit to their lives here, they'd need to get new cell phone numbers in the 401 area code. And he'd have to start acting like an adult and taking responsibility for his life.

"Hello?" he said, picking up the call. He ducked outside onto their front porch as he spoke. Emily was in the den, stretching sheets across their AeroBed.

"Mr. Bedecker?" said a woman on the other end of the line. "I'm calling from Kent Hospital." The hospital. Nate hadn't expected the hospital to call.

"I'm Nate Bedecker." He stared out into the front lawn, the grass an iridescent black in the dim of the night.

"Mr. Bedecker, I'm the floor nurse on your father's hall. He's conscious. He came out of his coma ten minutes ago."

"He's awake?" Nate said. He hadn't thought through the fact that his father might come out of his slumber and be okay *tonight*. The man had shown no signs, earlier, that he had any interest in rejoining the conscious world. He'd been so slack and acquiescent in his slumber. If he'd woken up back then, this morning (before Nate had uncovered the medical documents in the Audi's trunk) Nate would have had plenty to talk to him about. Now, Nate had no interest.

"Awake's a relative term. Your father is conscious, but not entirely coherent. He's heavily sedated. Both his body and his brain have gone through a shock. We have you listed as his next of kin."

"Which means?" Nate asked.

"The on-call neurologist is driving in and should be here within ten minutes." Nate heard someone talking in the background. "Fifteen. Fifteen minutes. You, or someone else from the family, should be here, too."

Nate raised his eyes and noticed an overhead light in the portico above him, a recessed central bulb in addition to the two electric lanterns that were propped on either side of the small porch. It was a nice touch. He'd left the front door cracked open and could hear Emily walking around the living room. Emily and Nate had practically cleaned out George Bedecker's pantry and linen closet this afternoon, and now the man was awake. Assuming he was still the same inveterate ass Nate had once known, George's first conscious request would probably be the prompt return of his chickpeas.

"There's no one else from the family. I'm it," Nate said. It was a stark truth. Nate was the only other Bedecker and his sole urge was to throttle George, to abuse him and return him to his sleep. And the nurse was inviting him to visit? He shouldn't, in truth, be allowed to go. He didn't, in fact, have any reason to. More than anything, Nate had the desire to ignore his father. That, Nate understood from experience, was the most stringent form of abuse. "I'm not coming in," he told the nurse.

"All right," the woman said. She sounded nonplussed by Nate's decision. He heard papers rustling. "As I said, your father has only been conscious for a moment and he's not coherent." Nate waited for her to try to convince him to drive in. His father was awake, after all, for the first time since his crash, and Nate was the man's only kin. "In your absence, if medical decisions need to be made for George Bedecker, do you authorize Ms. Antrim to make them?"

"Excuse me?" He pressed the phone closer against his ear, his fingers growing tired from clutching it so tightly. He tried to close the gap between himself, the nurse, the nurse's station, the hospital, and the whole insane situation.

"Ms. Antrim. She arrived a half-hour ago. She says she's his partner and his proxy. If you know otherwise, well, now is the time to speak up." Nate looked at the Audi and its busted headlight and, parked behind it, Jeanne's gleaming, completely operational rental car. "Mr. Bedecker, if you're not coming in, someone will need to speak for your father's needs."

Half an hour later Nate and Emily pulled into the hospital parking lot in Jeanne's rental car, with Jeanne at the steering wheel and Trevor in a car seat in the back. It was Nate who'd insisted that Jeanne come along. Jeanne was a doctor, and Nate was sure that he, with his longstanding biases, shouldn't be the one to make decisions for George. Neither should Philippa Antrim, a woman whose motives Nate had yet to suss out. Jeanne, however, would make fair and informed choices. There were plenty of instances in the past when Nate had questioned her — the way she tended to storm in and take over a room; the way she dressed, even when she went out for dinner, as if she were on her way to the gym — but she had been Emily's sounding board since college and, from what Nate had seen, she'd rarely steered her wrong.

As Jeanne turned the sedan into the hospital's parking lot, Nate gave directions, pointing her toward the only nonhandicapped spots that were within throwing distance of the building's front door. In the backseat Emily hummed to Trevor, who had been coming and going from sleep during the entire ride. His eyes, when he opened them, were wet and vacant. He'd been roused from a deep slumber in a strange home and then strapped into a car in the dark of the night.

"Do you want me to take him?" Nate said to Emily as they got out of the car. They didn't have Ollie with them. They'd have to carry the boy. In another month or two, he'd be too heavy to tote long distances. He'd be walking by then, though.

"Thanks," Emily said, stepping out of the way. The parking lot looked like a theater stage, all black except in the halo-like spots of light thrown down by the high-intensity streetlamps that dotted the pavement. Bugs darted around the bulbs giving the light a murky quality. "What do you think she's like?" Emily said.

"She?" Nate said. He knew who Emily was talking about.

"Antrim."

What do you think *he'll* be like, Nate wondered. Would George be babbling away in his delirious state? Or typically stoic? What would he say to his son after so much time, and with his life on the line? Nate slowed down his pace as he walked toward the hospital with Trevor. His feet moved with the deliberate weight of an army tank, choking off the progress of time, delaying the moments to come. George was inside the hospital and awake. In the sci-fi comics that Nate and Charlie had traded as kids, traveling in time was as easy as walking from one room of a house to another. Time was an easily manipulated dimension.

Jeanne and Emily walked ahead and were nearly at the hospital's front door. "Did you lock the car?" Nate said to Jeanne. She nodded.

"Are you okay?" Emily asked, coming back toward him. Nate wasn't moving at all now. He and Trevor stood in an empty parking space beside the hospital's front walkway. The blue handicapped sign painted on the asphalt circumscribed Nate and his son, like an accusation.

"I'm fine," he said, and started walking again, shifting Trevor in his arms and acting as if the boy's weight was what had hindered him.

Inside the hospital he nodded to the distracted night receptionist at the lobby desk. The woman, portly and strong and wearing a janitor's uniform, did nothing to halt this foursome even though it was well past visiting hours. Nate continued his glacial march in the direction of the stairs and then paused and backtracked to the elevator bank. It was only one floor up to his father's room, but the elevator would be slower. It was a hospital elevator, rigged to linger for a significant amount of time on each floor when it stopped. It was geared toward the pokey movers — the crutchers, the wheelchair-bound, the kids with IVs attached to their arms. The men who weren't quite coherent. What did *that* mean? The nurse had said George wasn't coherent. Nate couldn't fathom his father as anything but inexorably coherent. The elevator arrived on the first floor and the doors opened.

"Would you mind meeting me up there?" Nate said to Jeanne and Emily, who'd caught up with him.

"You sure?" Emily said.

"Yeah." Nate stepped inside the lift with Trevor and the doors finally closed on them. The space was cavernous. Two gurneys could fit inside, Nate figured. Or a partners' desk and two chairs. Or an entire kindergarten class, crammed together shoulder to toe like sardines. The car moved up so slowly that Nate couldn't detect the motion and was taken by surprise when the doors opened on the second floor.

Nate stepped out and listened. His father's room was just a few doors down the hall and around a corner; if George was raving like a lunatic, Nate would be able to hear it from here, but all was silent. A nurse walked by and the rubber soles of her shoes clung briefly to the floor with each step, a rhythmic squash against the linoleum. Nate and Trevor reached the corner and Nate peered around it. Two men and a woman in pink scrubs were gathered at the nurse's station at the far end of the corridor, but other than that the hallway was empty.

Nate picked up the pace and crossed the threshold into his father's room before he could lose his nerve. He wouldn't be the first to talk; he'd wait for his father to start, even if the wait was endless. Nate steeled his face and clenched his teeth, gritting through the uncomfortable, building pressure of enamel on enamel. If his head exploded right now, he thought, that wouldn't be the worst thing. He moved his numb, expectant gaze to the bed, worried and excited (not an optimistic excited, but excited in the old-fashioned sense, agitated and manic and likely to jump through a plate-glass window) about the prospect of meeting his father's eye. But George's eyes were closed. Nate breathed out and felt his chest loosen. George was asleep again. Or resting. He'd been through a shock, the nurse had said on the phone. Maybe George had fallen into another coma on his own, without Nate's help.

Nate was surprised not to see Philippa Antrim lurking in the room. An instinctive picture of her had taken shape in his head. She'd be lean and bony with her hair defiantly white and pulled into a knot at the nape of her neck. She'd be austere and would obviously have to be somewhat deranged, given how much time she'd spent with George. In the picture, she was standing over George's bed reciting endearments, love poems, the cable TV schedule, shopping lists of life complaints, or whatever it was that old, cold people said to each other.

Except that she wasn't there. The room was empty. Just three Bedeckers: George, Nate, Trevor. Nate turned so that his half-asleep son could see his grandfather. Trevor looked away, though, and nestled his tired head into the crook of Nate's neck. The boy smelled fresh, truly clean finally. Emily had bathed him back at their house, after Jeanne returned from her shopping trip a few hours ago.

"I'm your father, Trevor. And this guy, he's my father. You won't have to see him again after today," Nate said, and it felt good. He pried Trevor's arms and legs from around his body and sat him on the bed, next to George. With what looked like a Herculean effort, Trevor turned his head and peered at the patient, leaned toward him. He looked at George's face for only a second — just long enough to discern that it wasn't as alluring as *Baby Beethoven* or a stuffed lamb — before looking away.

After today, after all of the health decisions were decided, if George woke up again, Nate would say his good-byes. Maybe he'd tell the man off first, but it was too late for that, wasn't it?

An unexpected calm came over Nate. At least this once, Trevor
had met his grandfather. As much as Nate didn't want George
to have a role in the child's upbringing, he owed it to his ten-
month-old son to at least let him see where he'd come from. For
this single moment, Trevor and his grandfather shared the same
space. Trevor deserved that. The room counterintuitively felt
more tranquil than it had earlier today, when George was still in
his coma.

"I'm sorry," a voice came from behind Nate, and he turned. A
nurse he'd never seen before stood in the doorway. She looked
to be in her eighties, at least, as if she'd forgone retirement with
the intention of ministering to patients until she herself keeled
over. "I'm Dinetta Shelley. I'm the one who phoned you. We
had no warning. We had every indication that he was out of
danger."

It was only after the nurse spoke that Nate understood why
the room felt more tranquil. The hum of the monitors was gone.
The machines next to George's bed were dark.

A staccato croak escaped from Nate's throat. He held onto
the side of the bed for stability. George was gone. Nate was the
only member of his original family left. If he disappeared, too, it
would be as if the foursome who'd inhabited that glass and concrete cube so long ago had never existed. The only proof that
they'd walked on this earth would be the impersonal monoliths
built by George. And someday, perhaps generations from now,
those would tumble too.

Trevor pivoted in his seat and reached for Nate as if sensing
danger. He grabbed Nate's sleeve and tried to pull himself to his
feet. Trevor. Trevor was proof. Nate lifted the boy in his arms
again. Trevor would have to be a survivor, too.

"Dr. Nilchek arrived just before your father died and was with
him, as was Ms. Antrim," the nurse said. Nate looked at her and

nodded, stupidly and instinctively, and she continued, "It was his spleen. The doctor can explain it. He's in the waiting room whenever you're ready. Feel free to take your time."

"Thanks," Nate said. He felt a gaping nothingness in his heart. A deep and dark hole where he'd been full before. The threat of George — of him reappearing, disapproving, looming either as a flesh and blood figure or in his buildings — had perpetually, subconsciously been a part of Nate. In its place, he now felt nothing. In this room (between these chalky blue walls and the pockmarked and paneled ceiling, beneath fluorescent lights and the glow from a call button that hung precariously low beside the head of the bed) on a night when the last mosquitoes of the season were biting and the stars and the moon were hidden by a dense fog, at a moment when Nate's own life felt remarkably tenuous, this was where it all came to an end.

CHAPTER 30

Remember Him as He Was

E MILY LOOKED ON FROM the doorway to George's room. It was wrong, spying on Trevor and Nate, but she'd felt even more displaced biding her time down the hall. There, in that waiting room, the neurologist (not the no-nonsense doctor they'd met with this morning, but a younger colleague, one junior enough to still be saddled with overnight call on holiday weekends) was consoling Philippa Antrim. Emily had felt like an imposter. She wasn't a blood relative and she'd never met George while he was awake.

George was dead. That's what the doctor said. Emily's first reaction was guilt. She'd called George Bedecker an asshole. If anything could cause a notoriously reticent blowhard's heart to stop, that was it. He was an icon and she'd sworn at him in a high-pitched scream mere inches from his comatose face. She'd killed the man.

"I'm sorry," Emily said to the doctor, her voice timid and quiet, "but do you know exactly what caused his heart to stop?"

She tried to feign ignorance, sure that her culpability was obvious, trickling out of her pores and percolating under her words. She was a thief and a murderer! George deserved her strong reprimand, but she hadn't meant to shock him into death (into submission, yes, but not death). If Emily had been patient (Emily, who had never been patient) he'd have died on his own. Between the car crash and Huntington's, he can't have had many years left.

"His problem wasn't cardiac," the doctor said, and Jeanne translated (pausing to offer Emily a pill from her purse; Emily said no without even asking which particular sedative the capsule contained) explaining how it happened, how George had sustained abdominal trauma during the crash that hadn't been detected. He'd died from an undiagnosed ruptured spleen. The doctor continued to talk, apparently covering his tracks, trying to fend off a malpractice suit against the hospital. Emily was focused on the diagnosis. His spleen had ruptured yesterday, and hadn't bled out until today when he'd died. It wasn't Emily's fault.

Her second reaction was shameful: She felt relief. Not over the fact that she hadn't murdered the seminal American architect, but relief that he was dead. Nate would be free of the weight of his father. The thought wasn't just shameful. It was also incorrect, she saw now from her perch in the doorway of room 207B. Nate had been denied closure, and it could be a long time before he reckoned with the ghost of his father. And if Nate turned out to be carrying the Huntington's gene, it would be as if his father had never died at all. His father would be inside of Nate, a part of him.

Emily could already see the change in Nate. He looked older. His shoulders were rounded in the posture of a man well past middle age. His knees were bent as if shirking from the heft of

Trevor, who was in his arms. He looked down at the body in the bed and rocked back and forth, as if steadying himself against an ocean tide. Emily walked into the room.

"Nate," she said tentatively, putting a hand on the low of his back.

He passed Trevor to her and then laid his own hands on his father's arm. "He's still warm," Nate said. "I've never thought of my father as warm before."

"He looks exactly as he did this morning."

"I know."

"The doctor and Philippa both want to talk to you. They're in the waiting room."

Nate nodded and for the first time turned his attention from George's body. "You've met her?"

"I didn't talk to her, but I've seen her. She looks harmless. She's what I expected from a Philippa, I guess. She's like a Midwestern Oompa Loompa. Short and round with a shock of red hair."

"That's what you expected?"

"Minus the roundness." There was a boldness and brashness to Philippa, an unapologetic frankness to her look, which Emily respected. The woman was wearing a kimono-style silk dress that would have looked wrong on anyone else, especially anyone else her height — five feet flat, if Emily estimated right — but which gave her an appearance of fierce confidence even in this milieu, the monotonous environs of a hospital waiting room, a place that drained even the thickest skinned fighters of their strength.

"Let's go then, I want to get this over with." Nate took his hands off his father's arm and then lightly touched the man's forehead, as if feeling for a fever. He made no motion to leave the room.

"I'll be down the hall. It's the waiting room right past the nurse's desk," Emily said.

When Nate rejoined Emily a few minutes later, the hunch was gone from his shoulders. He caught her eye and she got up, leaving Trevor asleep on a bench next to Jeanne, who was leafing through a tattered copy of *Fit Pregnancy*.

The doctor had left to see another patient, but Philippa Antrim was still in the room. Her head was bent over an open book, a cheap mass market mystery with a scythe on its cover and fake blood dripping off the letters of the author's name. Emily had been watching her glare into the book, unmoving, not flipping the pages. Emily had been tempted to prod her, to toss a chlamydia prevention pamphlet in her lap just to get a reaction.

The woman didn't stir until Nate had fully entered the room. Then, she rose from her seat and carefully laid her book on the chair next to her.

"Fuck," Nate said when he saw her, the expletive slipping out just loud enough for Emily to hear as she came to his side. "My mother must be rolling over in her grave." Emily understood. Philippa couldn't be any less European if she was wearing an American flag. And she was the only clue left to who Nate's father had become over these past few years. As Philippa neared him, Nate opened his mouth to speak.

"Hi, I — " was all that Nate got out before Philippa interrupted.

"Nathan, yes?" she said. She barely came up to Nate's shoulder. When she reached out her hand to him she extended it up, instead of out. Emily was jarred by the motion. She'd thought perhaps the two would hug. Nate was George's only living progeny, the remnant from his old family; Philippa was the closest thing he had to kin today. Some form of affection must be called for. Emily focused her attention past Nate, down the hospital hallway. The doctor said he'd be right back, but he'd been gone for forever, it seemed, and the hallway was empty.

"I'm Philippa," the woman said and without warning she started to bawl, fat bulbs of water dribbling down her face, leaving track marks across her makeup like the cracks in a fossil. Oh God, Emily thought, this woman really loved George. She must have. Emily reached into her pockets for a tissue but had none. Nate looked dazed, as if he were having an out of body experience that had taken him to Morocco or Mumbai, somewhere far from here.

"Hold on," Emily said, and ran back to Trevor and the diaper bag. She returned with a moist wipe and handed it to the woman. Nate eyed Emily suspiciously. George had just died and Emily was offering a butt-wipe to the man's grieving lover. The woman took it and swiped her cheeks, removing a swath of her makeup along with her tears.

"Whoo!" Philippa said faking a smile, a wan smile. "Whooee!" Her voice was airy and drained. "I was hoping to save the crying until I got back to the hotel. I hadn't expected to be at George's deathbed today. No one prepared me for this." She shook her head and wiped her nose with the same wipe she'd used on her face. "I'm glad you called me, Nate. I need to thank you for that."

"We didn't know you'd make it out here so soon," he said. "Your son, he didn't say you'd be getting here tonight." Nate turned to Emily, "Did he?" Nate, after all, wasn't the one who had spoken to Pete Antrim. "We didn't tell him it was urgent. We didn't know. My father looked as if he could linger for a long time."

"Well, he's always been one for surprises. But what would you know?" she said. Nate only shrugged. Philippa's tears started up again. "Eight years with a man, and this is what it comes to."

Eight years. If George had been with Philippa for eight years, that meant the two were already dating, Emily figured, when Nate and George last spoke. Yet according to Nate, George had never mentioned her. Nate looked sad, but Emily was sure that he never mentioned *his* lovers in their father-son talks, either. Nate had conceived and born a child with Emily, and never even tried to tell his father about it. The wall had been built up and cemented from both sides.

"Eight years?" Nate said.

"Ever since he consulted on the annex."

"The annex?" Emily asked.

"At the library. At Loyola."

When Emily continued to look at her expectantly Philippa went on gently, as if reminding Emily of something she should already know, "I archive the rare books and academic papers? That's how we met? Great Lord, I'm glad I flew here in time to see him today." Philippa's tears, which had barely abated, were overpowering in the face of Nate and Emily's lack of them. Emily knew she would cry later, when they were home. Not over George, but for Nate.

"He'd told you he was going to a conference? That's what your son said," Nate said.

"Well," she finished with the wipe and handed it back to Emily, as if Emily were a bathroom attendant, "that's what he said. I don't ask questions. He lives — lived — his life. I led mine. And when we were lucky, they intersected. We were alike in that way. Habitual companionship is a shackle. Who needs it?"

"Me!" Emily burst out before she could stop herself. It came out more like *meep*, like a chirp, a call for attention. Nate might die young, but while he was here, she would shackle herself to him. There would be no part-time love in Emily's life. She wrapped her hands around Nate's arm while Philippa kept talking.

"The doctor is still here, somewhere. He's flighty, a rat, you wouldn't know that his VIP patient had just passed, but you should talk to him. And we have to make arrangements with the hospital, as you can imagine. I'm happy to make the arrangements, I can't go to my hotel, it's too sad. I've been here an hour and already I feel rooted in place. You have a son. Talk to the doctor and get that child home to sleep. Call me in the morning," she scribbled the name of her hotel on a small bit of paper she took out of her pocket. "We can talk tomorrow. We'll need to talk, and now, obviously, now is not the time. It's certainly been a long day for all of us. I'm just" — her tears started again — "bless me, I'm just glad I got here to see him one last time."

"He was awake when you got here?" Nate asked.

"He woke up when I was by his bedside," she said. "He was only alert for fifteen minutes before he died."

"Did he say anything?" Nate asked.

Emily saw the look in Nate's eyes, the hope that his father had explained the meaning of life — the meaning of Nate's life — before collapsing into the great unknown.

"He was disoriented."

"The nurse told me," Nate said.

"You should be thankful that you didn't see it. It's not the way to remember your father. Remember him as he was."

Was *when*? When he was an embryo? Emily wanted to ask. Because Nate hadn't told a single story involving his adult father in which he was a character worth memorializing.

"But he said something?" Nate asked again.

"He said something."

"What?" Nate said.

"It was barely a sentence. He wasn't himself. There was no *George* there. He was delirious and could only manage a few words."

"Just tell me what my father said."

"You know, no matter what, that he loved you, Nate."

"But what did he say?" Nate said.

"Please," Emily pled to Philippa, if only to end the agony. "What did he say?"

"Emily is a cocksucker," Philippa said. "He said, 'Emily is a cocksucker.'"

Nate laughed, hysterical hyena laughter, as he sat behind the wheel of the rental car. Trevor and Jeanne were both asleep in the back. Next to Nate, Emily assumed the classic subway strap-hanger position, gripping the handle above the passenger side door. She'd just finished explaining to Nate how she'd ranted at his father this morning. "My name is Emily!" she'd screamed before calling the guy an asshole. Apparently coma patients were like infants, you had to watch what you said in their presence. They took in more than you knew. Emily now clung to the car in case Nate tried to eject her.

The light had turned green but Nate didn't move the vehicle. He paused his laughs to catch his breath, and just as Emily thought he was done with the hysterics they started again.

"It's — " he said, and then the cackles rose in intensity, sounding like chokes as he tried to get a breath into his lungs. "Okay," he said, after the light turned red again. At nearly 2:00 a.m. on the back roads of Rhode Island at the tail end of a long week-end, the streets were empty. The air was dead, the atmosphere recouping for the day and the season ahead. "Okay, my father called you a cocksucker." He got one final laugh in. A small, tired guffaw to end the tirade. "It's true, Em. You are a cock-

sucker. I've seen you suck cock." He wiped a tear away from
his eye. He'd laughed so hard that he'd cried, more tears than
he'd shed over his father's body. "You know, George was always
a stickler for the truth. There was no small talk with George
Bedecker. And calling you a cocksucker, it's as honest as calling
Trevor a bastard. Even his insults were ultimately fact-check-
able." Nate wheezed, the last bit of laugh he had left, and then
inched the car forward as the light changed.

"Fuck you," Emily said, looking straight out the window at
the narrow band of road illuminated by their headlights.

"Lighten up. It's funny."

"It's not funny. I'm sorry that I ruined your father's last minutes on earth." If she'd known he was about to die from a crushed
spleen, she probably would have held her tongue. *Spleen*, on its
own, seemed like an appropriate way for George Bedecker to be
done in. In Machiavelli's era, after renowned misers died, their
spleens were burned by those they'd wronged. Emily looked
over at Nate, who had stopped laughing. His face was grave now.
"I destroyed his final day alive," she said.

"If you had known my father at all, you'd know that no one
but he himself had the capacity to ruin his day."

"Come on."

"Okay, maybe I. M. Pei. Pei could ruin George's day. But
you? He'd swat you like a mosquito. Or maybe he'd even give
you credit for your defiance. He was strong-willed himself, or
used to be, at least."

"I'm serious," Emily said.

"I'm serious, too." Nate slowed down the car and looked at
Emily. "And thank you."

"For what?"

"For calling him out. Someone had to. Even if he'd woken
up, even if he'd walked out of that hospital bed and continued

his life, padding around that empty family house until his genes nailed him, I don't know if I could have done it. I'm an emotional coward. And it would have killed me if he'd gone to his grave before anyone had a chance to give him flack for the lives he trashed. Cocksucker," Nate said, turning off the car's brights as they merged onto the Jamestown Bridge where, for the first time, they were joined by a smattering of other traffic, "Cocksucker, you have my sincerest gratitude."

CHAPTER 31

Home

NATE HADN'T SLEPT WELL since the moment he'd stumbled onto the clip about his father, more than forty days ago. He'd lain awake in bed each night, with his eyes closed, concentrating on keeping his breaths steady so that Emily would think he was out cold. He'd spent weeks like that, every night, breathing with the rhythm of a metronome as he parsed the details of his day until Emily was asleep, and then lightly thrashing and imagining his own doom for the next few hours — finally getting up to go online when the conjectured terrors became too real to handle.

Tonight, in their new home, he and Emily were both awake. She sat next to him on the AeroBed in their downstairs den, folding their tiny pile of laundry — the clothes they'd been wearing for four days straight. She was wearing nothing but Jeanne's T-shirt again, as if she and Nate had never left the house to go to the hospital. Nate was in his boxers. He took his wallet from the floor and removed the money from the billfold.

"Fourteen dollars left," he said.

"Seventeen," Emily said, adding three crumpled bills to his

stack. On leaving the Elms, she'd stuffed fifteen dollars into the donation box, her entry fee, leaving her with only these three singles. "I guess we don't have big needs, when it comes down to it."

"Huh. We could have afforded a second, cheap bottle of vino with this cash."

"Or something stronger."

"Like arsenic," Nate said and then forced a laugh, because he was joking, it was a joke, he wanted Emily to know he wasn't serious. "Or, you know, rum."

The night had started with Barbaresco and ended with a thud. Its reverberations rang in Nate's ears like the lingering echo of a struck gong. He and Emily both breathed softly, slowly, barely.

"If I ever turn into George, keep Trevor away from me," Nate said between measured breaths.

"Huntington's is not a scapegoat for the way he treated you," Emily said. "You're not going to turn into that. It's who he is as a man."

"Who he was."

"Who he was," Emily said. "There's a chance that you inherited his disease, okay, but you didn't inherit his character." She laid the last of the laundry — Trevor's sweater — atop the pile. "And you can lament that you never reconciled, but no car accident or genetic disease was going to make him a better person. So maybe you got the disease. Even so, you could have another thirty years left," at this Emily stopped, fought to regain her own strength. Thirty years, looked at in some lights, wasn't long at all. "Another fifty years, even. Don't go fucking those years up by planning your own death."

Nate nodded. "His buildings were beautiful," he said after a moment of quiet.

"Are beautiful," Emily said.

One of George's most prominent qualities had always been his steadfast refusal to change. Even his buildings catered only to his own whims, not the prevailing currents of their particular era. In architecture, over the long term, this was a strength. There was nothing faddish or facile about his work. The buildings were the best of him — as far as Nate knew. He was coming to understand that maybe the George of his childhood wasn't the only, or the best, George Bedecker. So what was the best part of Nate? Until last month, he'd always assumed that his greatest accomplishments, other than Trevor, were yet to come.

And now? He reminded himself (and tried to believe it) that there was a chance he was healthy. He could have a future, the kind of future he often caught Emily dreaming about: They'd move to a larger house after this one, somewhere with more land. They'd have two SUVs in the driveway, one that would be Trevor's eventually, and a slate roof and a side door falling off its hinges from overuse. They'd have neighbors who'd wander over for potlucks, and a crappy lawnmower that worked a quarter of the time if they were lucky. They'd forget about New York. They'd forget about the month before the move when he'd slowly come to doubt all that was good, when he and Emily had lost their sight. He'd tell Trevor about their Huntington's risk as soon as the boy was old enough to understand, and someday, if Trevor wanted to know for sure if he had the disease — and if Nate was still healthy at that time, still unaware of his own Huntington's status (and still untested, because tonight Nate couldn't predict how he'd feel tomorrow or next month about being tested, and that was fine) — they could get tested together. Trevor would not have to go through this alone. They would have one another, all three of them.

"What do you think Philippa will do with the old house?" Nate asked.

"She won't want it. She's not the old beach house kind of broad."

"She didn't seem like my father's kind of broad, either."

"I sort of liked her," Emily said.

"You can't be serious." From what Nate saw at the hospital, Philippa was bossy and outrageous, a tough woman for Nate to get his head around. "It's so incongruous, the whole idea of her. She seemed so harsh."

"Maybe hard people are the only ones to whom George could relate," Emily said. "If you could call what they had relating. Maybe she was right for him. It seems they needed each other, somehow."

"She said my father loved me."

Emily nodded.

"Do you think she'd lie about that?" Nate said.

"I don't think she's the type who lies to make nice."

Maybe there really had been another George, a parallel George to the one Nate had imagined for all of these years. That was a thought Nate could hold onto.

Emily moved closer to Nate, the inflated mattress shifting under her weight. "She doesn't know the house is hers yet, you know," Emily said. "We'll have to show her the will tomorrow. She'll see it eventually anyway." Nate didn't speak, and Emily continued, "We could buy the house from her probably, if you want to keep it in the family. We could put this place on the market and move the money over to that house. We could live there." Emily tucked her hair behind her ears and looked at Nate, intent, waiting.

"We couldn't live there," Nate said. "My grandfather died there. My father tried to die there, from what I can tell." He could feel the threat of his own death, in a primeval way, but even that, tonight, was a sign that Nate Bedecker was alive. Nate would live in his own, new house.

Now, that new house was silent, a fallow silence reminiscent of Bedecker House with its heavy walls and thick plates of glass, materials that all those years ago had kept the outside world at bay and deemed even the workings of the structure itself — the water, the heat — almost noiseless. Nate hadn't referred to an actual house as his home since then. He'd shuttled between dorm rooms and condo sublets and rental apartments, packing light and alone. He'd never refinished floors or skim-coated walls on his own dime. Here, they'd talked about doing a bit of work: built-in cabinets in Trevor's room, a new color, something earthy, in the master bedroom, and maybe, when they had the money (if they had the money), new tile and countertops for the kitchen and bathrooms. Feeling the sturdy silence of this home at night, he understood why people built their own residences from the ground up. An expression of self in a structure that would long outlive you: There was an appeal to this. He and Emily would do their small part. Someday, he hoped, Trevor would bring his own kids, his own healthy kids, back here and they'd see the cabinets that Trevor's parents had conceived and the tiles they'd laid. That was the best-case scenario. A house, a family history. This was Nate's future. A tentative future, certainly. But a possible future, for sure. Here.

No footsteps came from the guest bedroom, which sat directly on top of the den. Jeanne must have already fallen asleep up there, on the bed they'd inflated for her. Trevor was in the hallway, conked out in the Bugaboo, where they'd deposited him when they returned from the hospital. It wouldn't hurt him to sleep one night in his stroller, would it? He'd holler if he needed them, he always did. He always hollered. He always needed them.

Emily was thinking about Trevor, too. She bent over and lay her hand flat on the wood floor and felt its warmth. The last time she and Nate had slept on a floor was right after they bought their new mattress, less than two years ago. They'd thrown their old one out after it got wet and mildewed thanks to a leak from apartment 10J, above them. Together they hauled the rank bedding down to the trash room in their building's basement, and then, to replace it, ordered a Serta Aviator, a superfirm queen, at a discount directly from a North Carolina distributor. The catch was that it took three weeks to arrive. In the twenty-one days that they were bedless, Nate and Emily slept on the floor, atop the couch's rearranged cushions and their spare blankets.

On the day that their new bed was expected, Emily went to her annual doctor's appointment and fumbled when her gynecologist asked the standard question, "When was your last period?" Emily couldn't place it. "It was supposed to be last week, I think, but I missed it. I've been out of whack. We've been sleeping on the floor," she said. *Could you be pregnant,* her doctor wanted to know, and Emily laughed. She'd been on the pill for so long that she probably wasn't even fertile anymore. And she was so old! All of her friends who'd gotten pregnant at this age, well into their late thirties, had managed it only with the help of fertility drugs and, for so many of them, full-on in vitro. To get pregnant without trying, while on the pill? "I'm sure it's just the floor thing," Emily said. When her doctor gave her skeptical look, she agreed to a pregnancy test.

She'd waited another two and a half weeks to tell Nate the results — it was like divine intervention, the positive test at this age with no high-tech help, especially after she and Nate had spent so many nights talking about the idea of having a family and his insistence that he couldn't handle it. He hadn't wanted a child. He'd been vehemently skittish when it came to the subject of parenthood. So for more than a fortnight she kept the baby news to herself, questioning whether she would have this child at all. She didn't want to lose Nate. But as her breasts grew tender and she felt increasingly lightheaded every afternoon while sitting at her desk at work, she came to realize that she didn't want to lose the child, either. She wanted this child. When she finally presented Nate with the news after the fact, after she had already made peace with the truth of her unplanned motherhood, Nate, it turned out, wanted a child, too — he simply hadn't known it. She wouldn't have to live without either of them. She had felt so lucky.

She'd loved Nate entirely in that moment. She'd drifted since. She'd felt space between them — he and his Huntington's, she and her anxiety, her desperate grasp that turned literal when she took the Rufino — but she wouldn't let it happen again. She wouldn't let herself lose him.

If she'd known four years ago, during her initial moments with Nate atop the Third Avenue Bridge — before the pregnancy and their move to Newport and all that had happened in between — if she'd known back then that the man next to her was never going to earn enough money to keep them in Manhattan, that he had grave hesitations about becoming a parent, that he harbored deep-seated father issues and might die a disfiguring, early death (and could doom his own child to the same), Emily would never have agreed to go out with him. She'd turned down plenty of men for so much less. Nate was everything she hadn't been looking for, but tonight, she was okay with that — even as she felt the weight of the hard truths they would have to work through in the months and years to come.

A sliver of light from the slim moon came in through the den's windows. In the morning, the sun would wake them up first thing, long before Trevor's earliest cry. They would all be all right. He and she and Trevor. Emily breathed the house's air: two floors and a basement and an attic, no furniture, no belongings, not even a TV. Just a couple of AeroBeds and a stroller and two thousand square feet of possibility, waiting to be filled, and one small boy on the verge of taking his first steps. Everything would be okay, even if it wasn't. She monitored the soft, satisfying in and out of Nate's breath as he sat beside her. If she found herself, next week or next year or three decades from today, having to survive without him, having to suffer without their son — if Nate got sick or Trevor fell ill or she lost her mind or her wallet or her health — if everything went downhill from here, if the world ended in a bang tomorrow and took all of her dreams with it, at least, she thought, she will have had this.

"Em — " Nate stood. He grabbed her bag from the corner of the room and began digging through it.

"Hey," Emily said. "What do you need?"

He took the Rufino from the bag. "And the nail scissors. Do you still have them?"

"In the front pocket," she said, standing and holding out her hand. He brought the bag to her and she found the scissors immediately.

"You want to make the first cut?" he asked as he unfurled the canvas. It was so small, even when stretched out to its full length. The paint was laid on thick. The idea of completely destroying it made Emily's chest tense. And yet, the idea of the painting hanging around their new house made her even more uneasy. Tomorrow they'd make a fresh start, absent the traumatic evidence of their life before.

"It's all yours," Emily said, handing him the scissors. Her hands shook.

"Here goes." He slid the canvas between the two blades.

"Wait!" Emily said in a gasp, a burst of air. Nate paused at the sound of her voice and looked up. She wasn't ready. And then, she was. "Okay," she said. "Let's do it."

The scissors' small, sharp blades met little resistance as he cut through the thick paint, following the line of the gray brush-strokes as if trimming the wings of a paper airplane.

Nate handed the Rufino, now in two halves, to Emily. She took the pieces and the scissors from him and continued cutting, not along the painting's design, but in a straight path, creating neat, narrow strips less than an inch wide.

"I cannot believe I'm doing this," she said. "I cannot believe how effortless it is to destroy the thing." After the canvas had been reduced to strips, she cut the strips crosswise until, in the end, she was left with a pile of squares the size of postage stamps. She took the square with the bulk of Rufino's signature on it, and shred that into shards no larger than dots of confetti. Then, with a concentrated precision, she shred each of the other squares in the same way, rendering the artwork unrecognizable. It was no longer the thing it had been a minute ago.

She dropped the pieces into the plastic bag that had held the laundry detergent, and stood across from Nate, the two of them erect and wordless, the weekend hanging behind them like a disaster scene. They remained motionless, stunned, equally fear-ful and fearless, like survivors of a flood, the last singed escapees from a fire that had taken down their entire pasts. Emily looked into Nate's eyes, his face open and blank. The reverberations he'd heard earlier were no longer there. It was now as silent in his head as it was in the house itself. It was so soundless that he could, for the first time in a month, think. Emily moved closer to him, lifting her foot high, as if stepping over rubble.

"Now what?" Nate said.

Emily shrugged, shook her head, and almost started to smile, as if to say: Anything is possible.

Acknowledgments

In researching Huntington's I turned often to the smart and unflinching At Risk For Huntington's Disease blog (http://curehd.blogspot.com/), written by the pseudonymous Gene Veritas, and to Alice Wexler's excellent books on the subject, *Mapping Fate* and *The Woman Who Walked Into the Sea.* I'm also greatly indebted to Natalie Danford, Ruth Gallogly, Ellen Greenfield, Moira Trachtenberg-Thielking, Halli Melnitsky, Ellen Sussman, and Amanda Eyre Ward for reading versions of this novel. I owe continued thanks to the Creative Writing Department at Butler University for giving me a home while I write. There'd be no book at all without my tireless agent, Lane Zachary, and keen-eyed editor, Carmen Johnson — and the entire New Harvest/Amazon Publishing team (including Ed Park, who kindly sent me Carmen's way). Sincere gratitude goes to the Lynn and Dahlie clans — especially my parents, who provided the occasional emergency rations and on-the-house medical fact-checking. Finally, and always: to Mike and Evan, my rock-star storytellers and partners in crime.